CRASH AND BURN

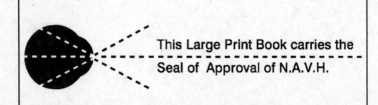

This Large Print Book carries the
Seal of Approval of N.A.V.H.

CRASH AND BURN

LISA GARDNER

THORNDIKE PRESS

A part of Gale, Cengage Learning

GALE
CENGAGE Learning·

Farmington Hills, Mich • San Francisco • New York • Waterville, Maine
Meriden, Conn • Mason, Ohio • Chicago

GALE
CENGAGE Learning®

Copyright © 2015 by Lisa Gardner, Inc.
Thorndike Press, a part of Gale, Cengage Learning.

Thorndike Press® Large Print Core.
The text of this Large Print edition is unabridged.
Other aspects of the book may vary from the original edition.
Set in 16 pt. Plantin.

LIBRARY OF CONGRESS CATALOGING-IN-PUBLICATION DATA

Gardner, Lisa.
  Crash and burn / Lisa Gardner. — Large print edition.
    pages cm — (Thorndike Press large print core)
    ISBN 978-1-4104-7502-2 (hardcover) — ISBN 1-4104-7502-6 (hardcover)
    1. Police—Massachusetts—Boston—Fiction. 2. Traffic accident victims—Fiction. 3. Boston (Mass.)—Fiction. 4. Large type books. 5. Psychological fiction. I. Title. II. Title: Crash and burn.
PS3557.A7132C73 2015b
813'.54—dc23   2014047242

Published in 2015 by arrangement with Dutton, a member of Penguin Group (USA) LLC, a Penguin Random House Company

Printed in the United States of America
1 2 3 4 5 6 7 19 18 17 16 15

CRASH AND BURN

CHAPTER 1

I died once.

I remember now, as much as I am capable of remembering anything, the sensation of pain, burning and sharp, followed by fatigue, crushing and deep. I'd wanted to lie down; I recall that clearly. I'd *needed* to be done with it. But I hadn't. I'd fought the pain, the fatigue, the fucking white light. I'd clawed my way back to the land of the living.

Because of Vero. She needed me.

What have you done?

I am weightless now. I understand, absently, this is not a good thing. Cars shouldn't be weightless. A luxury SUV was never intended to fly. And I smell something sharp and astringent. Alcohol. More specifically, whiskey. Glenlivet. Always prided myself on drinking the good stuff.

What have you done?

I want to cry out. As long as I'm sailing

through the air, about to die for the second time, I should at least be able to scream. But no sound comes from my throat.

Instead, I stare through the plunging windshield, out into the pitch-black night, and I notice, of all things, that it's raining.

Like that night. Before . . .

What have you done?

It is not so bad to fly. The feeling is pleasant, even exhilarating. The limits of gravity defied, the pressure of earthbound life left far behind. I should lift my arms, spread them wide and embrace the second death looming before me.

Vero.

Beautiful little Vero.

And then . . .

Gravity takes its revenge. My car is weightless no more as it reconnects savagely with the earth. A shuddering crash. An echoing boom. My body, once in flight, now tossed like a rag doll against steering wheel, dashboard, gear shift. The sound of glass cracking. My face shattering.

Pain, burning and sharp. Followed by fatigue, crushing and deep. I want to lie down. I *need* to be done with it.

Vero, I think.

And then: Oh my God, what have I done?

My face is wet. I lick my lips, tasting

water, salt, blood. Slowly, I lift my head, only for my temple to explode in agony. I wince, tucking my chin reflexively against my chest, then rest my aching forehead against hard plastic. The steering wheel of my car, I realize, is now crushed against my chest, while my leg is twisted at a nearly impossible angle, my knee wedged somewhere under the crumpled dash. I have fallen, I think, and I can't get up.

I hear a sound. Laughter. Or maybe it's keening. It's a strange sound. High-pitched, continuous and not entirely sane.

It's coming from me.

More wet. The rain has found its way inside my vehicle. Or I have found a way outside. I'm not sure. Whiskey. The stench of alcohol is so strong it makes me want to vomit. Soaked into my shirt, I realize. Then, my gaze still struggling to take in my surroundings, I spy glass fragments scattered around me; the remains of a bottle.

I should move. Get out. Call someone. Do something.

My head hurts so damn much, and instead of velvet black sky, I see bursting white lights exploding across my field of vision.

Vero.

One word. It rises to the front of my mind. Grounding me. Guiding me. Urging me

9

forward. Vero, Vero, Vero.

I move. Laboriously, the keening sound replaced by a soul-wrenching scream as I attempt to extricate myself from the driver's seat. My vehicle appears to have landed on its front end, the dash nearly crushed against me. I'm not upright, but tilted forward, as if my Audi, once it broke its nose, couldn't regain its balance. It means I have to work doubly hard to unpin myself from the accordionized space between my seat and the steering wheel and collapsed dash.

Airbag. The excess mass wraps around my arms, tangles up my hands, and I curse it. Back to screaming and fighting and ranting gibberish, but the senseless rage spikes my adrenaline until at least the crushing fatigue is gone, and now there is only pain, an endless, terrible pain I already understand I can't afford to contemplate, as I finally wiggle my way sideways from between the driver's seat and the dash. I collapse, panting heavily, onto the center console. Legs work. Arms, too.

Head's on fire.

Vero.

Smoke. Do I smell smoke? I suffer an immediate bolt of panic. Smoke, screams, fire. Smoke, screams, fire.

Vero, Vero, Vero.

Run!

No. I catch myself. No smoke. That was the first time. How many times can a woman die? I'm not sure. It's a blur in my head, from the smell of wet earth to the heat of flames. All separate and yet together. I am dying. I am dead. No, I am merely dying. No, wait, I am dead. The first time, the second time, the third?

I can't sort it out.

Only one thing matters, has ever mattered. Vero. I must save Vero.

Backseat. I twist myself around. I hit first my left knee, then my right, and scream again. Fuck it. Don't care. Backseat. I have to get to the backseat.

I fumble around in the dark, licking rain and mud from my lips as other impressions start to register. The windshield is shattered, but also the moonroof, hence the inside rain. My once gorgeous, relatively new and luxurious Audi Q5 crossover SUV has been shortened by at least a foot, if not two, the front end sustaining the worst of the impact and the front doors most likely too warped to open. But the back appears to be relatively intact.

"Vero, Vero, Vero."

I realize for the first time I am wearing

gloves. Or used to be wearing gloves. The glass has shredded them into large bloody flaps that hinder my movements. I wrestle the first one off, then the second, then jam them self-consciously in my pants pocket. Can't toss them on the floor. That would be littering and I treat my car better than that. Used to treat my car better than that?

My head hurts so damn much. I want to curl up in a ball and sleep and sleep and sleep.

But I don't. I can't. Vero.

Forcing myself to move once more, I rummage right, then left, fingers fumbling in the dark. But I find nothing. No one. I search and search, first the backseat, then, more shakily, the floor. But no small body magically appears.

What if . . . She could've been thrown, tossed from the airborne vehicle. The car had tried to fly, and maybe so had Vero.

Mommy, look at me. I'm an airplane.

What have I done, what have I done, what have I done?

I must get out of the vehicle. Nothing else matters. Out there, something in the dark, the rain, the mud. Vero. I must save her.

I drag myself by the elbows from the front of my crumpled car to the back. Then, a sharp turn for the rear passenger's door.

But it won't open. I yank the handle, smearing blood. I shove against the door. Cry, beg and plead, but nothing. It won't give. The damage, the child's safety lock. *Shit!*

One other exit. The way back, rear cargo hatch. Moving again, painfully slow as the pain in my head turns to nausea in my stomach, and I know I'm going to vomit, but I don't care. I have to get out of this car. I have to find Vero.

The puke, when it comes, is a thin liquid spew that smells of expensive single malt and a long night's regret.

I drag myself through the heinous puddle and keep going. First lucky break: The collision has jarred the rear hatch open.

I push it the rest of the way up. Then, when crawling proves too much for my bruised — broken? — ribs, I drag myself out with my arms and belly flop onto the ground. Mud, soft and oozing, eases my fall. I roll over, panting from the pain, the force of my exertions, the hopelessness of my situation.

Rain, rain, go away, please come back some other day.

Mommy, look at me, I'm an airplane.

I'm tired again. Fatigue, crushing and deep. I could just lie here. Help will come. Someone who saw the accident, heard the crash. Another motorist passing by. Or maybe someone will miss me. Someone who cares.

An image of a man's face pops into my mind but is gone before I can catch it.

"Vero," I whisper. To the falling rain, the oozing mud, the starless night.

The smell of smoke, I think idly. The heat of fire. No, that was the first time. Focus, dammit. Focus!

I roll back over and begin my journey.

The road appears to be high above me. There is mud, grass, scraggly bushes and sharp rocks between it and me. I hear distant sounds, cars whizzing above me, like exotic birds, and I realize, as I belly crawl forward inch by inch, that the vehicles are too far away. They are up; I am down. They will never see me. They will never stop and help me find Vero.

Another inch, two, three, four. Gasping as I hit a rock. Cursing as I tangle in a bush. My trembling fingers reaching forward, searching, searching, searching. While my head screams in agony and I pause, time after time, to retch pathetic little spits of bile.

Vero.

And then: *Oh, Nicky, what have you done?*

I hear that keening noise again, but I don't

stop. I don't want to realize that the distressed animal making all those sounds is actually me.

I don't know how long I wriggle myself up through the slipping, sliding mud. I know by the time I crest the hill, I'm covered head to toe in black ooze, and far from disturbing me, it amuses me. It's fitting, I think. I look as I ought to look.

Like a woman who's crawled from the grave.

Lights. Twin pinpricks, looming closer. I get up on my hands and knees now. Have to, if the passing motorist is to see me. And it's okay, because my ribs don't hurt anymore. My body has gone numb, the screaming in my head having overloaded all circuits and left everything else curiously blank.

Maybe I'm already dead. Maybe this is what the dead look like, as I get one foot beneath me and, slowly but surely, rise to standing.

A screech of brakes. The oncoming car, fishtailing briefly as the driver overapplies the brakes in the wet conditions. Then, miraculously, it stops, right before my raised hand and pale, rain-streaked face.

"Holy —" An elderly man, clearly shaken, is briefly illuminated by the interior light as he opens the driver's side door. He steps out uncertainly, rises to standing. "Ma'am, are you all right?"

I don't say a word.

"Is it an accident? Where's your car? Ma'am, you want me to dial nine-one-one?"

I don't say a word.

I just think: Vero.

And suddenly, I remember. I remember everything. An enormous explosion of light, terror and rage. A shooting pain not only through my head but through my heart. And in that instant, I recall exactly who I am. The monster from underneath the bed.

Across from me, as if sensing my thoughts, the old man recoils, takes a small step back.

"Um . . . just stay there, ma'am. Just . . . I'll, um, I'll phone for help."

The man disappears back inside the dimly lit interior of his car. I don't say anything. I stand in the rain, swaying on my feet.

I think, one last time: Vero.

Then the moment is gone, the memory passed.

And I am no one at all, just a woman twice returned from the dead.

CHAPTER 2

The call came in shortly after 5 A.M.: single MVA, off the road, unknown injuries. Given that the town in question didn't have a nighttime duty officer — welcome to the wilds of New Hampshire — county patrol was dispatched to handle the situation. That officer, Todd Reynes, arrived fifteen minutes later — again, welcome to the wilds of New Hampshire, or more accurately, long, windy back roads that never lead directly from here to there — just as the EMTs were struggling to strap a single muddy, bloody woman onto a backboard. The driver, he was told, had definitely suffered extensive injuries and reeked of enough alcohol to make standing next to her a risk for a contact high.

A second motorist lingered nearby, the old guy who'd found the woman and placed the initial call. He was keeping away from the action but acknowledged Officer Reynes with a short nod, clearly prepared to make a statement or sign on the dotted line or do whatever it was you did to officially end your part of something you never wanted to be involved with in the first place.

Officer Reynes returned the nod, already thinking this was pretty straightforward. One drunk driver, about to be hauled away by the EMTs. One smashed-up car, soon to be towed by the next available wrecker. That would be that.

At which point, the rain-soaked, mud-covered, blood-spattered woman got a hand on the first Velcro restraint, yanked it back with an ominous rasp, then sat bolt upright and declared wildly: "Vero! I can't find her. She's just a little girl. *Help.* Please, someone, God. *Help!*"

Which is how Sergeant Wyatt Foster of the North Country Sheriff's Criminal Investigations Division came to be standing roadside shortly after 7 A.M., pavement finally drying out, but now covered by every available law enforcement unit between Concord and Canada. Well, maybe that was an exaggeration, but not by much, he thought.

Wyatt exited his vehicle, wincing against the raw bite of a late fall morning only just now lightening up. It had been pouring solid for days, enough to spur flash-flood warnings while encouraging the random construction of arks. Good news was that the weather was finally drying out. Bad news was that the strong storm, which had continued through most of the night, had probably obliterated most of the useful evidence that might have helped them find a missing girl.

Dogs, he thought. This was a job beyond mere men; they needed canines.

He spotted one of his detectives, Kevin Santos, standing fifty feet ahead, peering over the edge of the road. Kevin had on his thickest field coat, even though it wasn't winter yet, with one hand jammed deep into a pocket, the other clutching a large white Dunkin' Donuts coffee. Wyatt walked on over.

"Any chance you have two of those?" He gestured to the coffee.

Kevin arched a brow. Younger than Wyatt by ten years, he possessed a nearly encyclopedic memory that had earned him the nickname the Brain. Now he once more proved his powers of greatness.

"Bought four. Situation like this, you can never have too much coffee."

He gestured to his vehicle, where, sure enough, a cardboard cup holder rested on the front hood, holding three remaining cups of java. Wyatt didn't ask twice.

"Catch me up?" he said, after the second sip had started warming his blood.

Kevin pointed ahead, or really down, as the edge of the road gave way to a fairly significant ravine. Not a lot of trees, but shrubs, downed logs, rocks and other general woodsiness that finally, one hundred, two hundred feet down, seemed to give way to what was usually a babbling brook, but this morning, by virtue of Mother Nature's bounty, was a rushing stream.

Right in front of the brook/stream, Wyatt could just make out the rear end of a dark SUV, hitched up at a funny angle, rear cargo door flung open.

"Audi Q5," Kevin supplied.

Wyatt arched a brow, suitably impressed. Luxury car, new to the market. Told him a lot of things right there, none of which he particularly cared for. In the old days, you could count on your DWIs to be drunk old men or stupid teenage kids. Now most under-the-influences seemed to be well-to-do soccer moms as high as kites on various prescription medications and deep in denial. In other words, not the kind to go down without a fight.

"Vehicle appears to have exited the road

right about here," Kevin said, gesturing to the ground with his coffee-cup hand.

Wyatt looked down. Sure enough, right where the pavement surrendered to muddy earth, tire tracks became clearly visible, battered by the rain but deep enough to hold their own.

"Seems like a pretty straight shot down," Wyatt murmured, eyeing the Q5's final resting place.

"Working theory is that she missed the curve."

This time, Kevin gestured down the road, where the pavement bent to the left, while the Audi had definitely gone right. "Must have already been drifting," Wyatt said, eyeing the angle of the roadway behind him, then once more checking ahead. "Otherwise, car should've made it farther along before going off."

"Might've already been asleep. Passed out. That sort of thing. Todd knows his DWIs."

Wyatt nodded. Officer Todd Reynes was an experienced patrolman who'd spent time on the DARE task force. He had a nose for drunks, could spot 'em driving from miles away, he liked to say. He was also a helluva hockey player. Two useful skills in the mountains of New Hampshire.

"Todd said he'd never smelled anyone in

such a state. She must've had an open container in the vehicle that shattered on impact, because her clothes were drenched in whiskey."

"Whiskey?"

"Actually, turned out to be scotch — Glenlivet. Eighteen-year-old single malt. The good stuff. But I'm cheating — already saw the remains of the bottle."

Wyatt rolled his eyes. "So our driver drinks a little scotch, pours on even more scotch and misses the corner. Maybe too drunk to see it. Maybe already passed out. Either way, goes sailing off into the night."

"Sounds about right." The Technical Accident Reconstruction team would sort it out, of course. They'd shoot the scene with a Total Station, which worked much like the surveyor's tool used by road crews, mapping angles, trajectories, point A and point B. Then the computer would spit out a complete guide to what, where, why and how. For example, an unconscious driver would've gone off the edge at low rpms, or even no rpms — foot off the accelerator. Whereas a woman driving erratically, fishtailing here, overbraking there, would leave other evidence behind. Both Wyatt and Kevin were qualified TAR team members. Had done it before. Would do it again.

But that was not this morning's task. This morning they, not to mention the dozens of other local, county and state uniformed officers, were swarming the cold, muddy scene with one goal in mind: find a missing girl.

"So," Wyatt spoke up briskly, "assuming the vehicle vacated the road here, and shot through the air to land on the ground there . . ."

"First patrol officers started searching within fifty feet of the vehicle. We're now backtracking all the way up the ravine to the road, obviously. Terrain is steep, but not too dense, and yet, as you can see . . ."

Their view from this vantage point was nearly bird's-eye. Granted, a few hours ago, in the middle of the night, in the midst of a storm, it would've been one dark mess. But now — Wyatt glanced at his watch — at 7:25 A.M., with dawn breaking and a damp gray daylight filling the muddy, shrubby space . . .

They could visually scan a significant part of the ravine without ever taking a step. And everywhere Wyatt looked . . . he saw nothing but mud.

"Dogs," he said.

Kevin smiled. "Already called them."

They stepped off the road and headed down into the muck.

"What do we know about the girl?" Wyatt asked as they trudged their way down to the wreck. Mud was still very soft, making footing difficult. He kept his eyes focused on the terrain, partly to keep from breaking his neck and partly to keep from destroying anything that might be useful. His coffee sloshed out of the small hole in the top of the cup and ran down the side of his hand. Sad waste of an essential beverage.

"Nothing."

"What do you mean nothing? How's that even possible?"

"Driver was out of her mind. Alcohol, injuries, God only knows. Todd says she went from stony-faced shock to near hysteria in a span of seconds. EMTs finally strapped her down and carted her away before she hurt anyone."

"But she mentioned a daughter?"

"Vero. She couldn't find her. She's just a little girl. Please help."

Wyatt frowned, not liking this. "Approximate age?"

"Didn't find a car seat or booster in the rear seat of the vehicle. Neither was the passenger side airbag deployed in the front. Put that together, and we're talking about a kid too old for safety seats, but too young to call shotgun."

"So probably between the ages of nine and thirteen. One of those so-called tweens."

"You'd know more about that than me, my friend."

Wyatt rolled his eyes, didn't take the bait. "Blood trail?" he asked.

"Please. Inside of the vehicle looks like a slaughterhouse. Female driver suffered a number of lacerations, before the accident, afterward, who knows. But by the time she untangled herself from the wreckage, then crawled through shattered glass to the rear of the vehicle . . . It's a miracle she had enough strength left to hike back up the ravine, let alone flag down a passing motorist —"

"Hike back up the ravine?" Wyatt stopped walking.

Kevin did as well. Both of them cast looks to the roadway, now very high above them. "How else would she have been found?" Kevin asked in a reasonable voice. "Nobody was going to notice a car smashed into a ravine in the middle of the night. Hell, you and I could barely see the vehicle in daylight, peering directly down at it."

"Shit," Wyatt said quietly, because . . . Well, because. He was an able-bodied man, reasonably physically fit, he liked to think, and not just due to being a cop, but because his other passion was carpentry and there was nothing like a few hours with a hammer every week to keep the bis and tris solid. But even with all that, he was finding *descending* the ravine, fighting his way through sucking mud while combating dense, prickling bushes, hard enough. He couldn't imagine coming *up* all that distance, let alone in the pouring rain, let alone after having just survived what was obviously a serious accident.

"She flagged down a man by the name of Daniel Ledo," Kevin said now. "Guy said she never spoke a word. He's a vet, spent some time in Korea. According to him, she looked shell-shocked, as in the literal definition of the word. Didn't really snap to it until the EMTs were loading her up. Then she spotted Todd, and boom, she's off and running about this girl, Vero, she couldn't find Vero, we gotta help Vero."

"She couldn't find Vero, seems to imply she'd been looking."

"Sure," Kevin said.

"Plowing her way through the mud and muck. It's why she tore herself out of the car. Why she made it up to the road. Because she was trying to find help for her missing child."

"Fair enough."

"And we . . . ?"

"Still got nothing. Two hours of solid searching later by over a dozen uniformed patrol officers, not to mention our even more qualified friends from Fish and Game. I got here thirty minutes before you, Wyatt. Guys were already on site, on task. Started with a search grid of fifty feet out from the wreckage. Are now working a five-mile radius. I have no issues with our search efforts thus far."

Wyatt understood what his detective was trying to say. A body thrown from the vehicle should've been easy to recover. A scared girl hunkered down for the night, waiting for help, should've responded to the coaxing calls. Which left them with . . .

Wyatt gazed around him at the tangle of underbrush an injured, disoriented kid could roam for hours. He looked ahead of him, to the former brook, now fast-flowing stream, that could carry away an unconscious form.

"Dogs," he said again.

They moved on to the car.

The Audi Q5 premium SUV should've been a thing of beauty. Charcoal-gray exterior paint with equal parts black and silver sheen. A two-tone interior, boasting silver-gray leather seats, jet-black inlays and chrome accents. One of those vehicles designed to haul groceries, half of a soccer team plus the family dog, and look damned good doing it.

Now it sat, ass cocked up, front end buried deep into the muddy earth, rear cargo door ajar. It looked like a sleek urban missile that had misfired into the woods of New Hampshire and was now stuck there.

"Twenty-inch titanium-finish wheels," Kevin muttered, voice half awe, half longing. "Sport steering wheel. Eight-speed tiptronic automatic transmission. This is the 3.0 edition; means it has the six-liter engine that can go from zero to sixty in under six seconds. All that power and you can bring along your golf clubs, too!"

Wyatt didn't share Kevin's love for automobiles or statistics. "But does it have all-wheel drive?" was all he wanted to know.

"Standard issue for all Audis."

"Stability control? Antilock brakes? Anything else that should've helped a driver navigate a rainy night?"

"Sure. Not to mention xenon headlights, LED taillight technology and about half a dozen airbags."

"Meaning the vehicle should've been able to handle the conditions? A dark and stormy night?"

"Unless there was some kind of unexpected mechanical or computer error . . . absolutely."

Wyatt grunted, not surprised. Cars these days were less a box for transport, more a computer on wheels. And a fancy-looking Audi like this . . .

Hell, the car had about a dozen different built-in controls designed for its own self-protection, let alone the safety of its driver. So, for it to have ended up in this condition . . .

Best way to work an accident was backward, as in, start with the end point — the wreck — and work in reverse to pinpoint the cause — the braking that never happened or the fishtail that led to swerving into the guardrail. In this case, the vehicle appeared to have landed at a forty-five-degree angle, taking it on the nose, so to speak, with resulting distributed front-end damage: crumpled hood, shattered front and side windows, and other damage consistent with a massive front-end impact.

He didn't see signs of paint chipping or scraping on the sides, implying the Audi had not rolled down the embankment through the tangle of bushes, but had rather sailed over them. Enough speed, then, for a nose dive off the proverbial cliff. Straight angle, at least by his dead reckoning; graphing it with the Total Station would certainly tell them more. But the vehicle appeared to have left the road at their coffee-drinking point above, then flew briefly through the air before it returned abruptly to earth, slamming nose first into the muck.

First question: Why had the vehicle left the road? Driver error, especially given the driver's apparent state of intoxication? Or something else? Second question: At what speed and what rpm? In other words, had she sailed over the edge, pedal to the metal, a woman on a mission, or had the vehicle drifted into the abyss, passed-out driver waking up only to attempt too little too late?

Good news for Wyatt. All these modern computers with wheels were equipped with electronic data recorders that captured a car's last moments much like an airplane's little black box. The county sheriff's department wasn't considered cool enough to have their own data retriever, but the state would download the car's data onto their computer and bada-bing, bada-boom, they'd have many of their questions answered.

For now, Wyatt kept himself focused on the matter at hand. A missing child, female, approximately nine to thirteen years of age.

Footprints currently surrounded the

wreckage, but given the quantity and size, Wyatt already guessed they came from the first responders, on the hunt for a child, rather than the occupants of the vehicle, exiting through the front passenger's side door. Just to be thorough, Wyatt pulled on a latex glove, stepped forward, and gave the passenger's door an experimental tug. Sure enough. Stuck tight. He tested the rear passenger's side door, found it compromised as well, the force of impact having warped the frame too much for the doors to function.

Which left him with the open rear hatch. He headed that way, inspecting the ground for more prints. Mostly, he just saw boot imprints, consistent with what most law enforcement officers wore.

"They inspect the ground first?" he asked Kevin. "Todd, any of the first responders? Check for footprints?"

"Todd said he swung his flashlight around. Couldn't see a thing, given the conditions. But even without footprints, he figured the driver must've exited the Audi out the back; it's the only working door."

"So assuming the child's conscious, she'd have to have gone out this way, too," Wyatt filled in. "I wonder . . . Mom the driver probably felt the crash had just happened, right? She regained consciousness, looked

31

for her kid, panicked when she couldn't find her, then began her heroic journey for help. But maybe, factoring in the alcohol, the force of front-end impact . . . Maybe Mom was knocked out for a bit. Maybe, in fact, she didn't regain consciousness until fifteen, twenty, thirty minutes *after* the wreck. During which time, her daughter tried to rouse her, panicked at not getting any response and set out on her own."

Kevin didn't have an answer. It was all hypothetical, after all, and the Brain preferred stats.

"Cell phone?" Wyatt asked.

That Kevin could handle: "Recovered one from beneath the dash, registered in the driver's name. That's it."

Wyatt considered the implications. "Do you know any kids who don't have cell phones?" he asked Kevin.

"Me? You're assuming I know kids."

"Your nieces, nephews . . ."

"Sure, they all have iPods, smartphones, whatever. Generally speaking, it's in our own best interest to keep some kind of electronic device in their hands. Otherwise they might talk to us."

"So assuming our kid is a nine- to thirteen-year-old girl, it's probable she also has a phone, in which case . . ." He tried to

think of how to best put it into words. "Why not use it? Why not simply stay inside the car, where at least it's relatively dry, and call for help, for herself, for her mom, instead of heading out into a storm? We have a cell signal?"

Kevin nodded. "Driver's phone shows the service provider to be Verizon. Same as me, and I have four bars."

"So it's not that she couldn't call. But maybe . . ."

He was trying to think it through, put himself in a scared girl's shoes. Kids could be resourceful, tougher than you thought. He knew that from both professional and personal experience.

"Poor girl's adrenal system had to have been screaming fight or flight," Kevin offered up. "Maybe she chose flight."

"Or maybe she's hurt, too. Hit her head, disoriented." Frankly the possibilities were endless. Which made him uncomfortable. He couldn't help but picture Sophie, nine years old, already been through hell and back, with her thousand-yard stare. In this situation, what would she have done? Given her reputation, probably retrieved her mom from the front seat and dragged her up the muddy ravine with her bare hands. She was that kind of kid.

And she didn't hate him. She just didn't smile at him. Or talk to him. Or acknowledge his existence in any meaningful manner. But that was okay. The battle was still early and he had many more tricks up his sleeve. Maybe.

"Let's follow up on a possible cell phone," Wyatt said. "Contact the driver's service provider, see if there's any other names attached to the calling plan, you know, like a family plan or something. Because if she has a phone . . ."

"We can track it," Kevin filled in.

"And where there's a cell phone . . ."

"There's a teenage kid attached to it."

"Exactly."

Happy to have finally offered up something useful, Wyatt continued with his cursory inspection of the wreck. He passed around to the driver's side door, where the spiderwebbed glass had shattered out, onto the ground. Maybe hit by the driver's elbow from the inside. Or pounded out by her fist as she desperately sought escape.

He peered inside. As was consistent with most front-end collisions, the dashboard had been compromised, the steering column shoved into the driver's seat. He could make out a tangle of unspooled seat belt, which would indicate the driver had been wearing

one at the time of impact, then removed it in order to make her escape. Must've been tricky for the driver to extricate herself from such a mess, he thought. Especially given her own likely injuries — foot or ankle fractures from stomping the brakes in a futile attempt not to go sailing into the abyss, knee damage from the collapsing front dash, or even bruising to the stomach, ribs, shoulders, from the seat belt. He'd seen drivers burn their hands on the deploying airbags, break their thumbs on the steering wheel, crush their sternums against the steering column.

And this crash had been a hard one. He could tell by one more distinct clue: blood. Lots of it. Staining the steering wheel, smeared across the dash, printing the back of the light-silver seat, the top of the door. The driver had been bleeding, probably lacerated in several areas given the large shards of broken clear glass — the scotch bottle — and smaller tinted pebbles from the shattered safety windows. He could make out entire bloody handprints where she'd obviously sought leverage, grabbing the dash, the edge of the seat, something, trying to haul herself out.

He wondered if she'd been unconscious for the bulk of the crash. Passed out driving one moment. Woke up wrecked the next. Or had it been worse than that? Had she regained consciousness just as her vehicle went airborne? Screamed? Tried frantically to apply her brakes? Or reached back reflexively for her daughter, as if at this late date, she could somehow undo the terrible mistake she'd obviously made?

Wyatt couldn't decide. Maybe he respected the driver's efforts to drag herself out of the wreckage and crawl back to the road in order to seek help for her child. But then again, wasn't that kind of like respecting the arsonist for escaping the burning building?

He frowned, his gaze falling on the gear shift, which sat in neutral, instead of drive as you'd expect. He glanced over his shoulder at Kevin.

"Anyone been inside the car?"

"No."

"Turn off the engine?"

"Nah, must've stalled out. I don't know. Todd was first one on the scene. Once he heard about the kid, that's been our focus."

Wyatt nodded; protecting life always took precedent. "Gear's in neutral," he commented.

Kevin's turn to think. "Shifter might've been bumped? Lots of things bang around during impact. Loose objects, purses, elbows. Or maybe the driver, while trying to wriggle herself free, knocked it into neutral."

"Maybe." Wyatt straightened, not completely satisfied, but now was not the time. Later, after the vehicle had been towed from the site, when entire doors and whole seats had been meticulously removed and sent to the state's lab for testing, then they'd get down to it. The position of the driver's seat. The mirrors. Imprint from right hand here; imprint from left hand there. Not to mention the Total Station analysis as well as the stats recovered from the electronic data recorder. An accident like this wasn't reconstructed in a matter of hours, but in a matter of days, if not weeks.

But they would do it. Thoroughly. Meticulously. So the whole world could know what a Glenlivet-swilling mother had done to herself and her child one dark and stormy night.

As if on cue, Wyatt heard barking from above. Canine unit had arrived.

He straightened, stepping away from the vehicle, glancing at his watch instead.

Eight twenty-two A.M. Approximately three hours and fifteen minutes after first callout, they had an accident still to investigate and, more important, a child yet to find.

In the end, he decided, all paths led in the same direction. Back up the muddy ravine, to the silver ribbon of road, where this tragedy had first started and where the search dog now waited.

He and Kevin started climbing.

CHAPTER 3

"Look at me, Mommy! Look! I can fly."

She runs away from me, arms stuck straight out from her sides, rosebud mouth supplying the appropriate airplane noises. I admire her long dark hair bouncing behind her, as her little legs chug around the tiny space.

I wonder if I'd been this energetic when I'd been her age. Or this brave as she leaps over one obstacle, weaves expertly around the next.

I think somewhere in the back of my mind, I already know the answer to this question and it's better off left alone.

Enjoy this moment. Four-year-old Vero, learning to fly.

She giggles, revving up now, gaining momentum. And the sound of her joy lifts the weight off my own chest. She turns a corner, around the ragged brown sofa — stuffing coming up through a tear, someone should fix that, should I have fixed that? — and I can see her face, chubby cheeks flushed pink, gray eyes bright beneath thick lashes, as she zeroes in on her target and heads straight for me.

"Mommy! I can fly, I can fly, I can fly."

I love you, I think. But I don't say it. The words don't come out. I stand there, bracing for impact as she barrels toward me.

Slow down. Take it easy. It's almost as if I know what's going to happen next.

At the last second, her tiny foot catches the leg of the coffee table, and for a moment, she is genuinely airborne, body stretched out, hands and feet grappling in empty space.

Vero's eyes, widening.

Her mouth, forming a perfect startled O.

"Mommy!" she yells.

Shhh, I try to whisper. Don't make a sound. Don't let him hear you.

She lands hard. Thump. Crack.

Then the screaming begins in earnest.

Shhh, I try to whisper again.

As those gray eyes well with tears, bear into mine.

A man's shout from the bedroom of the apartment. Followed by footsteps, heavy and ominous.

"Mommy, I can fly," Vero says, and she's no longer crying. She is providing a statement of fact.

I know, I want to tell her. I understand.

I wish I could reach out, touch her hair, stroke her cheek.

Instead, I close my eyes, because somewhere in the back of my mind, I know what's going to happen next.

I wake up to machines beeping. Bright lights, strong enough to hurt my eyes. I wince reflexively, turning my head away, then immediately wish that I hadn't, as fresh pain explodes in my forehead.

I'm in a hospital bed. Lying straight on my back, hands tucked to my sides by scratchy white sheets topped by a thin blue blanket. I examine the metal bed rails framing each side of the bed, then the wires sprouting from an attachment on my finger leading to all kinds of monitors. My mouth is dry, my throat parched. I would moan but don't feel like making the effort.

I hurt . . . everywhere. Head to toe, knees to elbows. My first thought is that I must've fallen from a twenty-story building and broken every bone on impact. My second thought is, why did they bother to put me back together again? If I finally got the courage up to jump, couldn't the rest of them leave well enough alone?

Then I see him, head slumped forward in the chair next to the foot of my bed.

My heart constricts. I think: I love you.

My head explodes. I think: Get the fuck away from me!

Then: What the hell is his name again?

The man's face is weathered, heavily lined with worry and stress even in sleep. But it gives him a lived-in look that is far from unattractive. Closer to early forties than late thirties, dark hair shot through with liberal streaks of gray, body still lean after all these years. I like that body; I know that with certainty.

And yet, I don't want him to wake up. Mostly, I wish he'd never found me here.

"Mommy, I can fly," Vero whispers in the back of my mind.

I think of that old pilots' joke: It's not the flying that's the hard part; it's the landing.

The man opens his eyes.

It comes as no surprise to me that they are brown and somber and deep.

"Nicky?" he whispers, arms already springing out, body on high alert.

"Vero?" I croak. "Please . . . Where is Vero?"

The man doesn't speak. His body collapses back, my first words having already taken the fight out of him. He places a hand over his eyes, maybe so I won't see the answers lurking there.

Then this man I love, this man I hate — what the *hell* is his name? — whispers heavily, "Oh, honey. Not again."

CHAPTER 4

"Her name's Annie. Good girl, too. Four years old, a little rambunctious, but has the drive. Won't find a better worker; that's for sure."

The handler, Don Frechette, reached down and scratched his dog affectionately behind the ears. In response, Annie, a high-spirited yellow Lab, waved her tail so hard she nearly whacked her own face.

Wyatt liked dogs. Last cold case he'd worked, the cadaver dog had found a fifty-year-old bone in a dry creek bed. The bone had looked like a desiccated twig and smelled like dirt. One of the younger officers had nearly cast it aside before the accompanying forensic anthropologist had caught his arm. *This old thing?* the officer had asked. *But it's just a stick.*

The forensic anthropologist had found it funny. Later, however, she'd confessed to Wyatt that she considered the whole thing amazing as well. The bone had long since lost all organic matter, she explained. What was left for the dog to scent? But the dogs always know, she mused. Forget the latest advancement in GPS tracking and forensic analysis; anytime she was out in the field, she just wanted a good dog's nose.

Tessa had expressed an interest in getting a dog. Maybe he could take her and Sophie puppy shopping this weekend. Visit the local animal shelter, bring home a new addition to the family. Surely that'd earn him some points with the kid.

Or would that be trying too hard? Tessa had made it very clear the worst thing he could do was try too hard.

It wasn't that Sophie hated him, he reminded himself. Maybe.

"Conditions?" he asked Frechette, gesturing to the man's light rain jacket, then the dog's thin coat, given the low-forties chill.

"Not a problem. We'll warm up soon enough. I don't mind the cold. Pools the scent, keeps it low, easier to track for the dog. And Annie fatigues faster in heat. Morning like this, clear skies, low temps, she'll be raring to get to work. Now, you said it's a car crash."

"Yes, sir."

"Glass?"

"Quite a bit around the vehicle."

"She'll need her boots, then. Other terrain?"

"Mostly mud, one briskly moving stream. There's some prickly shrubs, the usual mess of random rocks and broken branches. Getting down is a little tricky, given the grade. But once you're in the ravine . . . Decent hiking, actually. God knows the Fish and Game officers have probably already made it to Maine and back."

"Fish and Game? Who's working?"

"Barbara and Peter."

"Oh, I like them. Good people. And they came up with nothing?"

"We've all come up with nothing." Wyatt wasn't surprised the dog handler knew the Fish and Game officers. New Hampshire was big on woods and short on people. Sooner or later, felt like you knew everyone you met and had met everyone you knew.

"Need any more information on the child?" Kevin was asking. "We believe she's female, approximately nine to thirteen years of age."

Frechette gave Kevin a funny look, then peered down at Annie, who was nearly dancing with anticipation. "Hey, girl, you need a description? Plan on calling the kid's name? Or maybe use your color-blind eyes to find a pink coat?"

Kevin flushed.

"We don't need vitals, Detective. All we need is Annie's nose. Trust me, if there's a child out there, Annie'll bring her home."

After a bit of discussion, they settled on a search strategy. Having worked with several different dogs in different situations, Wyatt already knew most handlers had their own opinions on the best way to get the job done. Given that their search area was relatively small, and now scent contaminated by dozens of officers who'd already been swarming the scene, Frechette wanted to approach it like a tracking case. Start Annie in the back of the car, last suspected location of the child, and see if she could pick up a trail from there. A strategy better suited for a bloodhound than a Lab, Frechette confessed, but he remained sold on his girl's skills. His dog had the training, had the drive; she'd find their missing child.

A little yellow Lab puppy, Wyatt thought. Red bow around its neck. *Here, Sophie. Got this for you.*

Most likely Sophie would accept the puppy, while continuing to regard him with her thousand-yard stare.

Wyatt was in trouble. He'd figured it out six months ago. He hadn't just fallen in love with an amazing woman, Tessa Leoni; he'd fallen in love with her kid. And while dating in your twenties was all about hoping the parents liked you; dating in your forties was all about hoping her kids accepted you. In that regard, nine-year-old Sophie was proving a tough nut to crack.

Not that she hated him. Maybe.

They headed back down the ravine.

The other officers were dropping back, per the handler's request. Wyatt had issued the command by radio. It was a tough call to make, pulling back the human searchers in order to bring in a canine. But the rule of thumb was that one dog was worth 150 volunteers. Meaning Annie was the best hope they had, and for her to do her job, she needed all the searchers and their various scent profiles out of her way.

Some of the state and local officers were already passing them, heading up as they headed down. Now Barbara and Peter from Fish and Game paused on their return to scratch Annie's nose. Not having been issued her work command yet, Annie responded by preening happily.

The searchers all looked tired, Wyatt thought, but not dispirited. The search hadn't been going on long enough to be considered a failure but, at the four-hour mark, was becoming more concerning. How much ground could a young child have really covered in the early hours of the morning? And why wouldn't she backtrack at the sound of their voices?

They had passed from an easy search into the land of more troubling. These officers, especially Barbara and Peter, were experienced enough to know it.

They arrived at the crashed Audi. Frechette whistled low under his breath as he took it in.

"Damn. Talk about a nose dive. It's like the thing sailed over a cliff or something."

Wyatt didn't comment. Without any results from the Total Station, he wasn't sure about the "or something."

Annie took in the wreckage as well, whining low in her throat. She was no longer dashing about, but regarding her handler fiercely. She knew, Wyatt thought. With a dog's unerring sense, she understood it was time to work.

Frechette told the dog to stay. She whined again but did as she was told. The handler walked around the scene, taking in the broken glass, the bloodstains, the pieces of warped metal. He was looking out for his dog, Wyatt realized, as was his job.

The handler came around, peering in the

rear passenger's side window. "Think the kid sat back here?"

"That's our assumption," Kevin spoke up.

"Clean," Frechette commented.

Wyatt frowned. "What do you mean?"

"I mean, most of us carry a lot of shit in our cars. Extra jacket this time of year, snacks, bottles of water, I don't know. Mail we haven't taken into the house yet, dog leashes, random junk. At least, my vehicle has most of that stuff. Bet yours does, too."

Wyatt couldn't argue with that. He stepped closer. First time around, he'd been focused on the damage in the front. This time, he saw Frechette's point. The floor of the rear of the vehicle contained some shards of glass, most likely from the broken whiskey bottle or dragged from the front as the driver had crawled through. But, yeah, the normal detritus of everyday life — old coffee cups, bottles of water, snacks for the child, iPad for playing in the car . . . Nada. The rear seats, cargo area, held nothing at all.

Apparently, the only item the driver thought you needed for a road trip was a bottle of Glenlivet.

"That a problem?" Wyatt asked the handler.

"Not at all. Good news, really. I was worried the back might have more glass, be hard on Annie's paws. Way I see it, we can load her into the cargo area, have her jump into the rear seats and get to work. Hey, Annie!"

The yellow Lab, still obediently sitting next to Kevin, whined in response.

"Wanna work?"

A single enthusiastic bark.

"All right, honey. Let's go to work. Come, Annie. Come!"

The dog bolted to his side, a yellow bullet that paused only long enough to home in on her handler's face, awaiting the next command.

"Up!"

She leapt into the cargo area.

"Go!"

She was in the passenger's seat, not sniffing, not exploring, big brown eyes still riveted to Frechette's face.

"Okay, Annie," Frechette called through the open rear hatch. "Here's the deal. There's a missing girl and you're gonna track her. Track, do you understand?"

Wyatt thought this was a pretty colloquial approach to dog training, but what did he know? Annie certainly seemed to understand, ears pricked, body on high alert.

"Scent up!"

The dog dropped her head, began snuffling over the seat, the door handle, the window. Her lips were peeled back slightly, as if she was taking the scent not just into her nose but into her mouth and tasting it.

"Go find, Annie. Go find!"

The dog whined, now working the rear seats in her own grid pattern, back and forth, back and forth. She was on the hunt, no doubt about it, her attention no longer on her handler, but 100 percent focused on catching scent.

She backtracked. Moved from behind the passenger's front seat to behind the driver's seat. More anxious sniffing, another low whine. Exploring both rear car doors thoroughly, up and down, side to side. Then a first exploratory paw, stepping off the seat onto the glass-studded floor.

Thank God for dog boots, Wyatt thought. He couldn't have watched it otherwise.

More whining, anxious, distressed. Then Annie was back on the seats, side to side, back and forth. Then with a graceful hop she was over, in the rear cargo space, diligently working that space inch by inch.

Some dogs lie down to signal they are on scent. Others barked. Wyatt wasn't sure of the nuances, but best he could tell, Annie wasn't having any luck yet. And it was pissing her off.

She glanced at Frechette, whined again, clearly frustrated.

"Scent up!" he repeated.

The dog dropped her head, back to work. She leapt from the cargo area to the rear seats. Then, after another few minutes of careful exploration, backtracked to the middle of the bench seat. She snuffled, paused, snuffled.

Then, facing forward, she leaned forward toward the glass-strewn center console, her movements slow and careful. She understood glass, Wyatt realized. Or at least had enough experience with it to know to proceed with caution. More sniffing, above the glass. And then.

Woof.

She retreated to the center of the bench seats. Woofed again. Jumped over the seat backs to the cargo area. Another bark, tail up, eyes back on Frechette as she ran to the rear bumper, body on high alert.

Frechette got the message. "Track, Annie. Track!"

She sailed out of the car, a tad too enthusiastically, then had to backtrack to recover the trail. But within a matter of minutes, she was on scent, head down, sleek body moving effortlessly over the ground as she jogged from side to side, bush to bush. She began to ascend the ravine; they followed.

Moving in the dog's wake, Wyatt began to notice things he hadn't spotted before. The way this one bush had a broken branch. Another offered up a long strand of dark hair caught between two leaves. A person had come this way, and to judge by the freshness of the snapped twig, very recently.

Tracking was never completely linear. They stayed ten feet back, allowing Annie plenty of space to work as she jogged forward, eased back, raced right, then regrouped to the left. An older, wiser dog might have paced herself, whereas Annie had clearly thrown herself into the chase. Come hell or high water, she was gonna find her target.

They worked their way up the ravine in a slow zigzag pattern, as if the initial person hadn't known where she was going. Had been stumbling around in the dark.

More evidence: a dislodged rock, trampled grass, a scrap of torn fabric. Wyatt flagged each item for future collection. They'd have to map this trail, sketch it up, then retrieve all evidence for testing.

Two-thirds of the way up, they came upon a large boulder, streaked on one side with a reddish-brown substance. Blood, Wyatt realized. Heavy enough not even the rain had been able to wash it away. They paused as Annie worked the base of the boulder, whining anxiously. The girl had been injured, then. Maybe, as they'd discussed, she'd regained consciousness before the mother and gone in search of help.

A lone child, standing roadside in the middle of the night . . .

They didn't talk anymore. Annie moved forward. Wordlessly, the three men followed.

Cresting the hill, Annie began to bark. Now she dashed into the road, racing straight ahead, then right, then left, then around and around in a twenty-foot circle, nearly frantic. She crossed the road, darted back. Headed back down the ravine ten feet, came leaping back.

"Track!" Frechette commanded, frowning at his charge. "Told you she was young," he muttered under his breath, half excuse, half explanation.

Annie didn't look at him anymore. She continued running in circles with growing frustration.

Abruptly, the dog sat. She stared at Frechette, barked twice, then lowered her head and lay on the ground. She was no longer a friendly, eager canine. In fact, she wouldn't look at them at all.

"What does that mean?" Wyatt asked.

"She's done. Not only lost the trail, but she's worked herself into a state over it. She'll have to rest before we can try again. Give us thirty minutes."

Wyatt nodded at the handler, who stepped forward to tend his despondent charge.

"Dogs don't take failure well," Kevin commented.

"Neither do I." Wyatt headed back to the edge of the ravine, peering down at the meandering trail they'd just followed. So someone — the missing child? — had made it this far, and then . . .

"Sir."

Wyatt turned to see Officer Todd Reynes standing by him. "Todd," Wyatt greeted him. "Heard you were the first responder. Thanks for taking the lead in looking for the missing kid."

"Not a problem. Sir, that's the search dog, right?"

"Yep. Her name's Annie. Young, we're told, but did a good job tracking the trail this far. Now, however, you can tell she's a little frustrated."

"She's lost the scent?"

"Apparently."

"I think I might know why."

Wyatt arched a brow. "By all means, Officer," he said, indicating for the man to explain.

"See that sign there?"

Wyatt turned toward the roadside. Sure enough, fifteen feet down was a yellow caution sign warning of the sharp turn ahead.

"When I first arrived on scene, I noticed the caution sign because Daniel Ledo, the man who placed the initial call, was standing beside it. While right about there" — Reynes pointed to Annie, still lying on the ground, gazing up at her handler mutinously — "was the ambulance."

Wyatt straightened. "You're saying —"

"That's where the EMTs loaded the driver onto the stretcher."

Wyatt closed his eyes. He got it now. The scent the dog had picked up, the trail they had just followed up the ravine. Not the missing child's after all, but the driver's.

"Always the risk," he muttered. "I mean, you can tell the dog to track, but you can't tell her who to follow."

He crossed to Frechette to break the news. Frechette reiterated that his dog needed a break, but in twenty or thirty minutes, they could try again.

Which they did. Twice, with the same results.

According to Annie, one scent came out

of the vehicle. One scent trailed up to the road. They circled her around the wreck. They brought her to the fast-flowing stream.

Annie grew increasingly sullen and resentful. She'd done her job.

One scent. One trail. One person, who mysteriously disappeared in the middle of the paved road.

That was Annie's story, and she was sticking to it.

"Houston," Wyatt declared shortly after 10 A.M., "we have a problem."

CHAPTER 5

What did you dream of when you were little? Did you plan on growing up to be an astronaut or a ballerina or maybe even a superhero with a red cape and the ability to leap tall buildings in a single bound? Maybe you were going to be a lawyer like your mother or a fireman like your father. Or perhaps you couldn't identify with your family at all. You mostly dreamed about getting the hell out and never looking back.

But you dreamed.

Everyone dreams. Little boys, little girls, ghetto-born, white-picket raised. Everyone aspires to be someone, do something.

I should have dreams, I think, but for the life of me, I can't remember what they are.

The doctor is in the room. She stands near the door, talking to the man who claims to be my husband. Their heads are together and they speak in hushed tones, like lovers, I think, but don't know why.

"Before the accident, was she sleeping any better?" the doctor asks.

"No, few hours a night at best."

"How about her headaches?"

"Still bad. She doesn't say anything anymore. I just find her lying on the sofa, an ice pack across her forehead."

"Mood?"

The man gives a short bark of laughter. "On a good day, merely depressed. On a bad day, fit to kill."

The doctor nods. Her name tag reads DR. SARE CELIK. She is beautiful, with dark coloring and exotic features. I wonder once again about her relationship with my husband. "Emotional lability is a common side effect of post-concussive syndrome," she is explaining. "Often for loved ones, it's the most difficult. How about her memory? Short-term recollections better?"

"When she first regained consciousness, she claimed not to recognize me at all."

Dr. Celik arches a brow, finally appearing surprised. She flips through a chart in her hand. "Needless to say, I ordered a head CT, not to mention an emergency MRI upon admittance. Both came back clear, but given her past history of TBIs, I'll order follow-ups in the next twenty-four hours. How did she handle the situation? Agita-

60

tion? Rage? Tears?"

"Nothing. It was like . . . She claimed to not know I was her husband, yet the news didn't surprise her."

"She'd been drinking before the accident."

My husband flushes guiltily, as if somehow this is his fault. "I thought I got all the bottles out of the house," he mutters.

"Please remember what I told you before: Alcohol directly impedes the brain's ability to heal. Meaning for someone with her condition, any alcoholic drink at all is counterproductive to her recovery."

"I know."

"Is this the first incident?"

He hesitates and even I know that means it isn't.

Dr. Celik regards him sternly. "There is a strong corollary between brain injuries and alcohol misuse, particularly in patients with a history of alcohol dependency. And given not one, but three concussions in a matter of months, your wife is vulnerable. Even a single glass of wine will affect her more strongly in the short term, while putting her at long-term risk for substance abuse."

"I know."

"This latest accident will most certainly set her back. It's not uncommon to see an almost exponential effect from multiple

TBIs in a short time frame. I'm not surprised her amnesia has returned. Most likely, she'll also experience intense headaches, difficulty focusing, severe exhaustion. She may also report sensitivity to light or some other heightened sensation — smell, sound, sight. Conversely, she might describe feeling as if she's 'under water' — can't quite make the world come into focus. Of course, such episodes may spike her anxiety and lead to increased mood swings."

"Great." The man's voice is grim.

"I would keep the household quiet. Establish a daily routine, stick to it."

"Sure. Just because she doesn't remember me is no reason for her not to do as I say."

The doctor continues as if he hasn't spoken: "You should expect her to tire easily. I would limit screen time — no video games, iPad usage, even TV shows and movies. Let her brain rest. Oh, and no driving."

"So . . . quiet home life, in bed by ten."

The doctor gives him a stern frown. In response, the man/my husband runs his hand through his rumpled hair.

I feel a whisper of memory. Standing in another room at another time.

Please, Nicky, let's not fight. Not again.

I realize I must have loved this man once. It's the only way to explain how much his presence hurts me now.

Dr. Celik is still talking about my ongoing needs, follow-up care. She's obviously familiar with my case. Multiple TBIs, she'd said. I feel like I should know what that means, but the letters won't stay still in my head. They flip upside down, backward, a dizzying display of alphabet acrobatics. I give up. My head hurts, the familiar sensation of a migraine building behind my temples.

I think of Vero, learning to fly.

I did have a dream. I can almost remember it, like a word on the tip of my tongue. Once, a long time ago, in a tiny apartment that smelled of stale cigarettes, greasy food and general hopelessness, I fantasized of green grass. I pictured open fields and places to run. I wished for the sun upon my face.

I yearned. A giant aching need that took me years to identify.

I yearned for someone to love me.

Oh, Vero, I'm so sorry.

Dr. Celik leaves. The man who is my husband returns to my side. His face is serious again, deep lines creasing his dark features. But again, not unattractive.

He tries to smile when he sees that I'm awake; it doesn't reach his eyes. He's worried. About me? Something else?

His collared shirt is light blue, unbuttoned at his throat. My gaze focuses on the exposed patch of skin, sun-bronzed from years spent outside. For a fraction of an instant, I can picture myself kissing that spot, trailing my tongue along his collarbone. I don't just remember him. I can taste him. It makes me shiver.

"Hey there." He takes my hand, as if to reassure me. His thumb is calloused.

My head pounds again. I am suddenly, bone-numbingly tired.

He seems to know. "Headache?"

I can't talk. I just stare at him. His fingers release mine, rub my temples instead. I nearly sigh.

"Do you remember the accident?" he asks me.

I don't, but I can't speak yet, so I remain silent.

"According to the CT scan," he continues, "you've suffered another concussion, the third in six months. For that matter, you bruised your sternum, dislocated a few ribs, and earned enough stitches to rival a quilt. But the ER docs have already done a nice job of patching you up. It's the concussion, your *third* concussion, which has the neurologist concerned."

"Causes . . . migraines," I murmur.

"Yes. Not to mention varying degrees of confusion, anxiety, general exhaustion, light sensitivity and short-term amnesia. Plus, you know, other minor complications such as not recognizing your own husband." He tries to sound lighthearted; it doesn't work. "Your memory will come back," he says, more seriously. "The headaches will fade. You'll regain your ability to focus and function. But it's going to take time. You need to rest, give your scrambled brain cells a chance to recover."

"Alcohol is bad."

He stills, regards me carefully with his dark-brown eyes. "Alcohol is not recommended for people suffering from traumatic brain injuries."

"But I drink."

"You did."

"I'm a drunk." He doesn't say anything, but I can see the answer on his face. That once upon a time, he thought he would be enough for me. Obviously, he isn't.

"What did you dream about when you were little?" I ask.

He frowns. He gets crow's-feet around his eyes when he frowns. It should age him, make him less attractive. But again, it doesn't.

65

"I don't know. Why do you ask?"

"Why not?"

He smiles. His thumbs are still moving on my temples, massaging little circles. This close, I can catch a hint of spice wafting from his skin, a clean, soapy fragrance that is both familiar and slightly intoxicating. If I could move, I would lean into him, inhale deeper.

But I don't. Instead, I feel a darkness growing in the back of my head. A feeling of dread to counteract the allure of his scent.

Run.

But of course, I can't. I lie on a hospital bed, pinned by white sheets and a concussed brain as my husband rubs my temples, strokes my hair.

"I dreamed the first time I saw you," he murmurs, his voice low and husky. "I spotted you, across the proverbial crowded room. You weren't looking at me at all. But I saw you and I . . . I felt I'd waited my whole life just for that moment. To find you. You consumed me, Nicky. You still do."

His breath feathers across my cheek. Once again, I respond to the scent, would turn my head if I could.

Run.

Then I see it, a faded bruise along his jawline. I can't help myself. I pull my arm from

66

beneath the bedclothes. I touch the bruise, trace it with my fingertips, feel the rasp of morning whiskers he hasn't had a chance to shave. He doesn't retreat. But his fingers fall from my temples and I can tell he's holding his breath.

I inflicted that bruise. I know that without a shadow of a doubt. I hit this man. And I'd do it again, if given half the chance.

"You hate me," I whisper, not a question.

"Never," he says. An obvious lie.

"You hate me," he corrects, more quietly. "But you refuse to tell me why. Once, we were happy. And then . . . I still dream, Nicky. What about you?"

I've gone wrong, I think, taken a misstep. Because even if I don't remember who I am, I like to think I know what I once dreamed, and it wasn't this. It was never this.

Vero, I see her again, the image dark around the edges. Like the vision is fading from my tired mind, becoming impossible to focus. She turns, as if to walk away, and my first thought is to grab her hand. It's important to keep her. I can't let her go.

She looks at me. Her face is thinner, older, I realize with a start. She's not a toddler anymore, but a girl, maybe ten, eleven, twelve.

"Why me?" she asks, voice plaintive.

"Vero," I whisper.

"Shhh," my husband says.

"Why me, why me, why me?"

She's turning away again. Leaving me. I reach for her arm, but it slides free. I can't hold her. The world so dark. My head about to explode. Or maybe it already did.

"Vero!"

"Nicky, please!"

I'm thrashing. I'm fighting. I know that, but I don't know that. All that matters is that I get to Vero. He's going to keep me from her. I realize that now. And it's not the first time.

"Nurse, nurse!" Someone is yelling. The man who claims to be my husband is yelling.

Vero, Vero, Vero. She's walking away from me.

I run. In the hospital bed? In my mind's eye? Does it matter? I run; then I catch up to her. I snag her arm, hold on tight.

Vero turns.

As maggots burst from the empty sockets of her eyes and wriggle around her gleaming white skull.

"You should've told me that little girls were never meant to fly."

■ ■ ■ ■

One moment. One memory. Then it's gone.

And I'm no one at all, but a woman twice returned from the dead.

The nurse comes. I don't fight anymore. I lay perfectly still as she administers the sedative. I stare straight ahead. Past the nurse's bent form. Past my husband's haggard face. I stare at the open doorway and the two detectives waiting for me there.

CHAPTER 6

Wyatt and Kevin arrived at the hospital just in time for the show. Their person of interest was thrashing wildly in the bed, while a man yelled for help and attempted to pin her down. Next came the nurse hustling in to administer a massive dose of sedative, and there went Wyatt's best opportunity to get to the bottom of things.

Their female driver, Nicole Frank according to the vehicle's registration, passed out cold. Only the man remained, breathing heavily and looking ragged around the edges.

Husband, Wyatt would guess. Or boyfriend. Whatever. Wyatt needed answers, he needed them now and he was willing to be flexible. He'd already sent a detective to the courthouse to request a search warrant for Mrs. Frank's medical records, which would include the woman's blood alcohol levels. He also had deputies backtracking from the accident site to neighboring liquor stores to prove exactly where and when she had purchased her eighteen-year-old bottle of scotch. In the short term, they were pursuing charges of aggravated DWI.

Of course, there still remained the issue of the missing child.

The nurse exited the room, barely sparing them a glance. That left the man. Late thirties to early forties. Six feet, one-eighty. Rugged sort of handsome, Wyatt thought women called it. Not a desk jockey, but a guy who actually worked for a living.

"Mr. Frank?" Wyatt took a guess.

"Yes?" He was staring at his wife with concern. Now he shifted his attention enough to shoot them an annoyed glance. Which Wyatt found interesting. Assuming the man's daughter was the one missing, shouldn't he be grateful to see two detectives? Even desperate, the concerned father demanding immediate answers? Instead his primary concern appeared to be his wife. Meaning he didn't care about the girl at all? Or he already knew what had happened to Vero and why they couldn't find her?

Wyatt felt the first thrum of adrenaline rush. He shot a look at Kevin, who seemed to share his suspicions. Both men, rather than surge forward immediately, instinctively fell back. In domestic situations, aggression rarely worked. Far better to be on the parent's side. Be cool, be calm, be conversational. Then, bit by bit, spool out enough rope for the parent to hang him- or herself.

Wyatt started the process. Polite, nonconfrontational: "Can we speak to you a moment?"

"My wife," the man started.

"Appears to be resting. We have some questions."

"You're the police," the man stated. But he wasn't arguing. He was heading toward them. He was going to play nice. Perfect.

Wyatt made the introductions, himself, then Kevin, earning the name Thomas Frank in return. Thomas, can I call you Tom? No, Thomas it is.

Wyatt offered the man some coffee. Another friendly gesture. This time of late morning, the hospital was a busy place, so maybe they could find a quiet corner to chat. When the husband appeared undecided, Wyatt and Kevin simply started walking down the overlit hallway to the hospital cafeteria. Sure enough, the husband fell into step behind them, too tired to argue.

One coffee purchase later, they had Mr. Frank tucked behind a fake ficus tree and it was time to get down to business.

"How do you know Nicole Frank?" Wyatt asked, just to be sure about things.

"Nicky? She's my wife."

"Been together long?"

Thomas Frank smiled thinly. "I know it sounds corny, but for me, she's always been the one. First time I saw her, I just knew."

"How'd you meet?"

"Film set. We were both working for a production company down in New Orleans. I was with set design; she worked craft services, you know, doling out food. I spotted her day one of a thirty-day shoot. Meant I had exactly one month to ask her out."

"How long did it take you?" Wyatt asked curiously.

"Three days to say hi. Three weeks to get her to say hi back. She was shy even then."

"Been together ever since?"

"Yes."

"What brought you to New Hampshire?"

Thomas glanced up at them. His eyes were bloodshot, heavily shadowed. A man who hadn't been sleeping well at night, Wyatt would guess, and that was before this. Wife troubles, work troubles, kid troubles? Again, Wyatt felt buzzed by the possibilities.

But Thomas merely shrugged. "Why not? It's a good state. Mountains to hike, lakes to swim. Plus no sales or income tax. What's not to love?"

"And your current job?" Wyatt asked, keeping with the slow-and-easy approach.

"Still in set design, only now I'm self-employed. I design and manufacture specific props, set pieces that are harder to find. Nicky helps — she does the fine-tuning, painting, cosmetics, that sort of thing."

"Shouldn't you be in LA?" Kevin asked. "Or New York? Someplace like that?"

Thomas shook his head. "Not necessary. Films are shot most anyplace, especially if the state or town is offering tax incentives. New Orleans, Seattle, Nashville, even Boston, lots of production work around here. And I don't need to be on site. I have my contacts from the old days. Now the set guys come to me with what they need. I design it, build it, ship it. Done."

"And Nicky, too?" Wyatt repeated.

"Yeah. Like I said."

"Where was your wife last night, Mr. Frank?"

Thomas shifted uncomfortably, no longer meeting their gazes. "I thought at home," he said, voice already rough. "Last I saw, she was asleep on the sofa."

Kevin and Wyatt exchanged a glance. Time to start unspooling the rope, Wyatt thought.

"What time was that?" Wyatt asked, voice still perfectly polite.

"I don't know. Eight, nine P.M."

Wyatt regarded the man closely. "Little early to be down for the night," he commented, as Kevin joined the fray:

"Last you saw —"

Thomas slammed down his coffee cup. "It's not her fault!"

Neither detective said a word.

"I mean, we were fine. Everything was fine. Happy couple, happy life. Except then, six months ago, Nicky fell down the stairs. Was doing laundry, I don't know. I found her passed out cold on the basement floor. Took her to the emergency room, where she was diagnosed with a mild concussion. No big deal, you think. Rest and recuperate. Except she had difficulty sleeping after that. And would lash out, no good reason. Headaches, fatigue, difficulty focusing. I did a little reading. Symptoms were consistent with someone recovering from a concussion. Told myself — and her — to be patient. Just a little more time. Except then just a few months later, I found Nicky sprawled on the front porch. She'd been walking out the door, she thought. Except she must've tripped or something. Bad news, she hit her head again. Two concussions, three months."

The husband stared at them. Wyatt and Kevin returned his look, expressions stonier this time, allowing him to see their skepticism, feel the heat.

"Post-concussive syndrome," the man bit out. "My wife isn't a drunk. At least she didn't used to be. She's not violent either. At least she didn't used to be." He turned his head slightly, revealing the shadow of a bruise along the man's jaw. "But the falls, multiple brain traumas . . . The neurologist tells me each subsequent injury has an exponential effect. I don't really understand it. I just know my wife . . . She's not herself these days."

"So you left her unattended yesterday evening," Wyatt murmured.

"I went to my work shed! We have a separate building, on the rear of our property, that houses all my tools, equipment. That's where I work, and for the love of God . . . I've been tending Nicky, most days, all days. Now I'm behind. Because that's what happens when you have a sick spouse. You get behind on work while having even more bills to pay. She falls asleep, I bolt out the door. I'm not saying it's a good thing. I'm saying it's what I have to do to hold things together. Docs want her in a stable environment on a normal routine. Losing our house right now because I can't pay the mortgage doesn't accomplish either of those things."

"Where'd she get the scotch?" Kevin drawled.

Thomas Frank flushed. He picked his coffee cup back up, took a sip. "I don't know."

"Car keys?" Wyatt piled on.

"In the basket by the front door. It's not like she'd been banned from driving; the docs just don't recommend it."

"Probably don't recommend her drinking either." Kevin again.

Thin lips. "No. They don't."

"But she does." Wyatt, jerking the man's attention back to him. Because now was the time; he could feel it. Thomas Frank was agitated and angry. Fractured and unfocused.

And he'd just given him most of his and his wife's life story, without ever mentioning a little girl name Vero.

Wyatt leaned forward. He stared deep into Thomas's eyes, as if searching for the truth, or maybe just trying to figure out if the man really was as big an asshole as they suspected. From the other side, Kevin did the same.

Closing in. Dropping the hammer.

"Tell us about your daughter," Wyatt said. "Where was she last night?"

Thomas Frank didn't recoil. He didn't shudder reflexively or even jerk away. Instead, he regarded them blankly. "What?"

"Your daughter, Vero. The little girl who's missing."

Of all the reactions Wyatt had been expecting, this wasn't it. Thomas closed his eyes. He sighed heavily. "I don't have a daughter."

"Nicky's daughter, then —"

"Sergeant . . . We don't have kids. Any kids. Not mine, not hers, not ours. And I would know. We've been together twenty-two years."

"Look, ever since the first concussion, Nicky has had trouble sleeping. She has horrible nightmares, except the dreams, episodes, whatever, don't always happen at night. It's like her brain has been turned inside out and upside down. She can't remember people she knows — say, my name, but on the other hand she rants about people who don't exist. Best I can tell, the real has become imaginary, the imaginary, real. We've consulted with doctors, played with some meds. But the best advice the docs have for us is to practice our patience.

78

Traumatic brain injuries take time to heal."

"Vero doesn't exist." Wyatt had to test out the statement. Because of all the information he'd expected to learn from this conversation, that wasn't it.

"There is no Vero."

"But you know the name," Kevin pointed out, looking as perplexed as Wyatt felt.

"She's called it out before, mostly in her sleep. Plus there've been some . . . episodes. Look, in the beginning, I got confused myself, maybe there was something I didn't know. But here's the deal. If you really get her going about this . . . Vero . . . the story, who she is, constantly changes. Sometimes Vero is a little girl, maybe a baby that Nicky is caring for. But once I found Nicky hiding in a closet, because she and 'Vero' were playing hide-and-seek. Then there was the evening she burned dinner because 'Vero' had been yelling at her all evening. Teenagers, she told me. I think . . . Hell, I don't know what to think. But Vero isn't a real person. More like a massive mental misfire."

"When Officer Reynes was at the scene," Wyatt pressed, "he claimed your wife was pretty adamant. She'd lost Vero. She was just a little girl. She had to be found. Your wife sounded pretty convincing."

"Welcome to my world." Thomas Frank

79

sighed again. He didn't sound sarcastic; more like a man who was very tired. "I can give you the name of our neurologist, Dr. Sare Celik," he offered. "Maybe she can help you understand."

"Could the name come from a family member? A sister, past friend?"

"Nicky doesn't have any family. When I met her she was just a teenager and already on her own, had been for a couple of years. She doesn't like to talk about it. In the beginning, I pressed. But now, twenty-two years later . . . What does it matter? Everything" — Thomas Frank paused, eyed them meaningfully — "*everything* has been great since then. We've never had any problems; Nicky's never had any problems. You have to believe me on this. My wife is just . . . sick. Ask the doctors. Please, talk to them."

"Walk us through last night. What happened?"

"Nicky cooked chicken," Thomas replied immediately, "meaning it was a good night for her. Focus is tricky with TBIs. Sometimes she starts a project, say, cooking, and then . . . blanks out. Walks away or something. But yesterday, she started and finished baked chicken, with no fires in between."

"What were you doing while she cooked?"

"Returning some calls. In the house, in case I needed to jump up and turn off a burner, but trying to squeeze in some work."

"You ate dinner. Wine, beer?"

"Alcohol isn't recommended for people recovering from brain injuries," Thomas recited.

"That doesn't answer my question."

"No wine, no beer, no alcohol. We ate chicken, a garden salad, and garlic bread."

"And then?"

"We watched some TV. Home and garden channel, light stuff. It's important that my wife not get agitated."

Wyatt got the time, name of show, and wrote it down.

"So it's now eight P.M. . . . ."

"More like seven thirty. Nicky dozed off on the couch. I glanced at the clock, figured it was too early to call it a night, so again, I should get some work done. I placed a blanket on my wife, then crept out the back to the work shed."

"When did you return?"

"I don't know. Eleven P.M."

"And you discovered Nicky missing?"

"I noticed she wasn't on the sofa. But my first thought was that she must have gone upstairs to bed. I watched the evening news, then headed up myself. That's when I re-

81

alized my mistake."

"What'd you do?"

"Went around the house, calling her name. Then wised up and checked the driveway for her car. Noticed that was gone, too, not a good idea in my opinion, so I called her cell."

Wyatt nodded, encouraging the man to continue.

But Thomas Frank simply shrugged. "She never picked up. I honestly didn't know what my wife was doing till the hospital called and said my wife was in the emergency room. That's the first I knew of the accident."

"What do you think your wife was doing from eight P.M. to five A.M.?" Wyatt asked.

"I don't know. Driving," Thomas stuttered, "drinking" being the other obvious answer.

"Any person she might have met? Friend, confidante?" Lover?

"We're new to the area. Had barely unpacked when Nicky suffered her first fall. We've only met medical personnel since then. Not . . . friends."

Wyatt thought Mr. Frank sounded a tad resentful.

"Any reason she'd be on that stretch of road? Restaurant, shop, favorite haunt around there?"

"We haven't gotten out much."

"Your wife partial to a particular brand of scotch?"

Thomas thinned his lips, refused to answer. Wyatt wasn't surprised. In all the DWI interviews he'd done of family members, they were the last to volunteer information. There was a reason they were called enablers, after all.

Wyatt changed tack. "And Vero? Any reason to get the police involved on a wild-goose chase to find an imaginary child?"

"She doesn't mean it like that. You and I know Vero doesn't exist. But for Nicky . . . Vero, something about her, is very real."

"So what set her off before?" Wyatt asked. "When we first arrived."

"I have no idea. I often don't. Routine and redundancy; that's my wife's life for the next year."

"In between bottles of scotch?"

"Look." Thomas Frank leaned forward, rested his hands on his knees. "I don't know what happened last night, but you can check my wife's record. This is her first offense. Can't you just issue a ticket or something?"

"Issue a ticket? Mr. Frank, your wife is facing at least one count of aggravated DWI. It's a felony offense."

"But she didn't hurt anyone!"

"She hurt herself. According to the statutes, that's good enough."

Mr. Frank sat back. He honestly appeared appalled.

"But . . . but . . ."

"Not to mention," Wyatt continued, "she's tied up hours of county and state resources looking for a child who doesn't exist."

"It's not her fault!"

"And yet —"

"Please, you have to understand . . ." Thomas Frank appeared wild-eyed, nearly panicked. "My wife is not a bad person. She's just sick. I'll take care of her. Watch her more closely. It won't happen again."

"I thought you had to work. Behind on the bills and all that."

"I'll take a leave of absence. Or hire a companion or something. Please, Detectives. There's no need to pursue any charges. My wife is going to be all right. I promise you, I'll take care of everything."

Wyatt eyed the man carefully. Thomas Frank, he decided, was not lying. He honestly believed he could take care of anything and everything. And yet . . . there was something here that just didn't feel right to Wyatt. Detective's intuition, twenty years of experience that suggested when a wife was in the hospital, the husband was the most likely suspect. Wyatt didn't know anything about this post-concussive syndrome. He just knew families, all families, inevitably had something to hide. He took one last shot over the bow:

"What about Vero?" Wyatt asked. "Gonna take care of her, too?"

And had the satisfaction of finally seeing the man flinch.

CHAPTER 7

Vero and I are having a tea party. We are
sitting at a kid-size maple-wood table, Fat
Bear sitting across from her, Priscilla the
Princess sitting across from me. The room
is bright and sunny. Light-green walls
covered on one side in a mural of climbing
roses, set off by fresh white trim. Vero's
twin-size bed is pushed against the far wall,
hidden behind yards of pink gauze. It's a
beautiful room, perfect for a little girl, and I
feel a pang because I know already that
neither of us likes it here.

Vero passes the porcelain teapot. I delicately pour a stream of apple juice in my
dainty china cup. I repeat the process for
Fat Bear, with his overstuffed brown limbs
and happily rounded belly, who sits to my
left. I notice for the first time, Vero has
taped *X*s over both of his glass eyes. Same
for Priscilla the Princess.

I glance at Vero, a vision in pink chiffon

and yards of pearls.

"It's okay," she tells me. "They're not afraid of the dark."

I nod, as if this makes perfect sense, and set the teapot in the middle of the table. The hand-painted rosebush is moving on the wall. It appears as if some of the pink petals are falling from the flowers onto the ground. As well as something darker, more ominous. Blood dripping from the thorns.

"Have some tea," Vero says.

We sip in companionable silence, each munching a vanilla wafer. Between the apple juice and the sugary cookie, the meal is too sweet; I feel vaguely nauseous. But I don't stop. I need this moment, any moment, not nearly enough moments, with Vero.

"He's going to leave you," she says now. I understand she's referring to Thomas. "He thinks you're crazy."

I don't say anything, simply set down my thimble of tea. I wish I could reach across the table and take her into my arms. I want to comfort her, tell her everything will be all right. I want to tell her I'm sorry. I didn't know any better. These things happen.

But I don't want to lie.

I realize for the first time that the table, the room, is really too young for her. She's not a child of six, but closer to twelve, with mascara coating her steel-gray eyes, a harsh slash of overly bright lipstick smearing her lips.

She stares at me, takes another sip of apple juice. Or maybe it is scotch, eighteen-year-old Glenlivet, straight from the bottle.

"It's not your fault," I whisper.

"Liar."

"If I could go back, I would."

"Bigger liar."

"Vero —"

"Shhh . . ." She stands abruptly, and I hear it now: heavy footsteps coming from down the hall.

I can't help myself. I shudder, and across from me, Vero smiles, but it is not a nice look.

Now that she's standing, I realize her dress is cut nearly to her navel. Not at all appropriate for a twelve-year-old. And peeking from beneath the flounces of pink are green and purple smudges, bruises covering her arms and legs.

The footsteps, looming closer. As more petals fall from the climbing rose, fresh blood dripping from the thorns.

I want to touch this marble statue of a woman-child, who already holds herself too tight and defies me with her gaze to comment on the neckline of her dress, the state of her limbs.

"Be strong," I whisper, but we both know that is not the problem. Vero has always been tough. In this world, however, those who can't bend eventually break.

Footsteps. Louder. Heavier. Ominous.

"You shouldn't have come."

"I miss you —"

"You killed me."

My mouth opens. I have nothing else to say.

"Run," Vero states firmly, the child more in command than the adult. "Get the hell out and don't look back."

But I can't bring myself to leave her.

Again.

"He's here! Don't you understand? He's going to find you, and when he does . . ."

"It's not your fault," I hear myself say again, but Vero is already turning away from me.

"Stupid loser. Get out. Get away. Run, dammit! Run!"

I want to do all of those things. Instead, I do none of those things. I push away from the table. I approach this little girl who is not so little anymore. And even though I know what's going to happen next, I take her into my arms.

For one second, she is there. I can feel her. I can smell her. Vero. And in that moment, as always, I know exactly what I have done.

Then her flesh dissolves within my embrace. And I cradle nothing but a pile of bones, covered in hundreds of fat white maggots that wriggle against my skin.

In my arms, her skull slowly rotates, regards me with dark, empty sockets.

"Run," Vero's skeleton orders me.

But it's too late. He's already here.

My eyes bolt awake. Bright overhead lights. Sterile hospital room. I don't think anymore. I move.

Grabbing the first batch of wires and wrenching them from my body. Blood sprays from the back of my hand as the IV needle is ripped away. From the thorns of the roses, I think wildly, watching the red drops fan across the hospital bed. He's here. He's here.

I can't figure out the metal rails. They are up, trapping me on the bed. I shove at them desperately, trying to force them down. When that fails, I scramble to the end of the mattress and jump, bare feet hitting the cold floor, hospital gown flapping loosely as I bolt for the open door.

Gotta run. Where, where, where?

I make it out to the broad hallway. It's too vast, overexposed. Anyone can see me. As if on cue, a nurse down the hall shouts out a warning.

Run. He is coming. Or maybe he's already here.

I flee, mindless, oblivious, fueled by instinct. My feet hurt, my ribs, my chest. I don't care. Nothing is more important than my desire for flight. I want a closet. Someplace small and dark. Like an animal retreating to its den. A closet could save me.

I hear footsteps pounding behind me, then more voices, joined in alarm.

I skitter around the corner, and he's standing there.

"Nicky," Thomas says.

He spreads his arms, blocking my path. His face is expressionless. I can make out nothing but his dark eyes, boring into mine.

"He's here," I state wildly.

"Shhh," my husband replies.

"No, no, I have to run. I have to get away. Vero says so."

Something flickers in his gaze. For a second, it's almost as if he believes me. Then:

"Listen to the sound of my voice, Nicky. Just focus. My voice. Talking to you. My voice, calming you."

"I have to get out of here!"

"Focus. One thing. My voice. All that you hear. All that matters. One thing, Nicky. Focus on my voice. The rest will go away."

I don't want to focus. I'm upright, swaying on my feet, and my ribs are too tight and I can't catch my breath and there's a skeleton in my head and maggots on my arms and doesn't he know the rosebush is still bleeding and I failed her. So many times, so many ways. Over and over I go back to her. And over and over again, I fail.

I'm tired. Suddenly. Absolutely. I don't think I can stand anymore.

"Everything is all right," Thomas murmurs. "Come on, honey. You must be cold. Let's tuck you back in bed."

He takes a step closer.

"Why me?" Vero whispers in my head. But she is not whining anymore, just making conversation.

"Is your head all right?" Thomas continues. "Do you have a headache?"

On cue, my head explodes. I grab my temples, squeeze my eyes shut. In that moment, Thomas closes the gap between us. His arms snap like a steel trap around my shoulders. The hospital personnel fall back. Why not? The husband has arrived. Clearly, he's got this.

"The sound of my voice," he commands.

So I do. I listen to the sound of his voice. And with the weight of his hands upon my shoulders, I turn and fall in step meekly beside him.

In the hospital room, he effortlessly slides down the metal rails, then helps me onto the tall bed. He tucks my trembling legs beneath the sheet, smooths the blue coverlet high across my chest.

I stare at him resentfully, prepared for his expression of gloating. He has won, I have lost, even if I don't understand the rules of engagement. When he glances back, however, I'm startled to see that his eyes are overbright, his expression distraught. He catches himself, makes a visible effort to pull himself together. For my sake or his?

"Please, honey," he begins, "you can't keep doing this. You're calling unnecessary attention . . ." His voice breaks; he looks away. He's upset. I've upset him. I feel bad, like I should apologize. Those dark, dark eyes, I think. How I loved him once. Love him still?

He swallows heavily. "I know you don't believe me. I know; everything feels upside down, topsy-turvy. But I love you, Nicky. I have only ever wanted the best for you.

Whether you remember that or not."

"I want to go home," I whisper.

He smiles tiredly.

"I don't think the doctors will let you. You're very sick, Nicky. Three concussions and you've bruised your ribs."

"You'll take care of me."

"Based on the past six months, Dr. Celik would beg to differ."

"It's not your fault I drink," I say.

He doesn't answer.

"I won't touch any alcohol," I promise more rashly. "Just get me out of here. The lights are too bright. They hurt my eyes."

"The police want to question you," he says bluntly. "Here or at home, Nicky, you have to face them."

"But I don't remember anything!"

"Not even buying the Glenlivet?"

His question, spoken coolly, brings me up short. Do I remember buying the bottle of scotch? Maybe. Kind of. Is that even a real answer?

"I want to go home," I say again.

He opens his mouth. He closes his mouth. It's obvious he doesn't know what to do with me anymore. Will he leave me?

Will I miss him?

"Do you remember the promise I made to you, our first night together in New Orleans?" he asks abruptly.

I don't. It must show on my face.

"Once upon a time, you said your home was wherever I was," he says.

The words mean nothing to me.

"Once upon a time, you said my love made you strong."

I have no answer.

"And once upon a time, you said as long as we were together, it would be enough."

I don't know what to say; he's telling me stories from someone else's life.

He seems to know as much. His shoulders come down. He regards me expressionlessly. "We made a deal that night. Anytime you thought you smelled smoke, you'd reach for my hand. Do you smell smoke, Nicky?"

I frown at him. For the first time, his words sound familiar, as if I should know what he's talking about. Slowly, I shake my head.

"Did you smell smoke last night?"

I have to think about it. "After the crash," I murmur.

He doesn't say anything. Just a muscle flinches in his jaw. A sign that he's heard. A sign that he hurts.

"I died once before," I hear myself say.

My husband is not surprised by this news.

"There are only so many times a woman

can come back from the dead."

"We're going to get through this," Thomas says evenly.

My turn to smile. Because I might have forgotten his name, but I still know when he's lying to me.

Vero, I think.

Then I reach out and take my husband's hand.

CHAPTER 8

"How goes the battle?" Tessa asked.

On the other end of the phone, Wyatt contemplated his girlfriend's lighthearted question and promptly sighed heavily. "Long morning," he admitted. "Long, strange morning. But the good news is, I think we should get a puppy."

"What?"

He could already picture her, sitting up straighter, blue eyes blinking in bewilderment.

"A cute yellow Lab," Wyatt continued. "One that will wag its tail and cover you with kisses every time you come home. That would be perfect."

"Perfect for whom? Dogs have to be fed, you know. As well as taken outside, exercised regularly. And Sophie and I are never home."

"Mrs. Ennis would help."

"Mrs. Ennis is seventy years old —"

"And still the toughest broad I know. In fact, if things don't work out between us, I might just set my cap for her."

He could practically feel Tessa rolling her eyes. Which was exactly what he needed. A break from the pressure of a case that might not even be a case. And yet he was sure it was a case. At least a motor vehicle accident.

"So why a puppy?" Tessa was asking him.

"Because a puppy makes everything better. Just ask Sophie."

"Low blow."

"Of course, I reserve the right to present the puppy. We both know I need the brownie points."

"You've been giving this some thought," Tessa said.

"Spent the morning with a search dog," Wyatt volunteered. "Which might have gone better if we'd been searching for a real person, versus some brain-damaged woman's mental delusion." He couldn't help himself; he sighed again.

"Day going that well?"

"Yeah, which means, sadly, I'll never make dinner. Now that we've eliminated the ghosts, we have a real crime scene to analyze and auto accident to reconstruct."

"Catch me up; what do you know thus far?"

Over the phone, Wyatt could hear Tessa shifting her position, most likely getting more comfortable in her black leather desk chair. She wasn't just asking a question; she was interested in the answer. Which was one of the things Wyatt liked best about dating a fellow investigator. Tessa didn't just inquire about his day; she was more than happy to review it with him. And sometimes, as the saying went, two heads were better than one.

Sitting in his county cruiser, waiting for the state police to arrive with the electronic data retrieval box, Wyatt took her up on her offer.

"Single MVA, off road, possible aggravated DWI."

"Blood alcohol level?"

"Well, first complicating factor. Driver smelled like a distillery. According to hospital records, however, her blood alcohol level was only .06 —"

"That doesn't meet the threshold for DWI."

"Ah, but the patient suffers from something called post-concussive syndrome. Has taken one too many blows to the head over the past six months. According to the doctor, for a person suffering from a TBI, even a little alcohol can go a long way. So I'm not willing to dismiss it just yet. We could potentially make the argument that for a driver with this condition, .06 is sufficiently impaired."

Wyatt had given the matter a lot of thought, mostly because it was his thought to give. Given the unique laws of New Hampshire, county cops had the power to prosecute all misdemeanor cases. Meaning Wyatt didn't just build a case; he got to present it, too. Factoring in the driver's injuries, this crash could end up being a felony DWI, in which case the county attorney would take over, but Wyatt would still be responsible for the arraignment bail hearing and probable cause hearing. He liked to joke he was half cop, half lawyer. Though given the way the legal system worked these days, you had to be more like 90 percent lawyer just to survive.

"Interesting," Tessa was saying now. "So you have an unimpaired, impaired driver."

"It's possible. Now, booze in question came from an eighteen-year-old bottle of scotch —"

"Expensive."

"Please, you should see the car. Guys traced the purchase of the bottle to a liquor store ten miles from the accident scene,

100

purchased on a credit card. We're going through security footage now to see if we have actual film of her making the purchase. But so far, not bad for a morning's work."

"And yet you're bothered by . . . ," Tessa pushed.

"Liquor store closed at eleven. Accident happened around five A.M. So what was the driver doing between those hours? Because if she was sitting around drinking, her blood alcohol level should obliterate .06."

"Friend, associate, to help her out?"

"Possible."

"Husband?"

"Claims he was occupied in a work shed. Apparently hadn't even realized his concussed wife was missing."

"No card for him on Valentine's Day. Where'd the car go off? Busy area? Plenty of shops, restaurants, bars, to keep your driver entertained?"

"Nada. I've counted two gas stations between the liquor store and scene of the crash; that's it. So again, what was she up to for six hours?"

"Maybe . . ." He could hear Tessa thinking about it. "Maybe she wasn't doing anything. Maybe she was just . . . hanging out. Trying to collect her thoughts. When I was patrolling, you'd be amazed how many parked cars I came across in the middle of the night, occupied by lonely souls. If your driver is concussed, suffering from a TBI, maybe she's confused, too. Another lost soul looking for the light."

"So she buys a bottle of scotch. Drowns her sorrows . . ."

"Sips her sorrows. Only .06."

"Then hits the road. Searching for a little girl who doesn't exist."

"Little girl?" Tessa's voice picked up.

Wyatt winced. He hadn't intended to mention that part. "When the first officer arrived at the scene, the woman claimed she couldn't find her daughter, Vero. Only her husband of twenty-two years claims there are no kids. Not now, not ever."

"So she's delusional?"

"Apparently, her brain has been compromised by multiple TBIs. She fell down the stairs doing laundry, then another fall outside, then, of course, the car accident. Long story short, her memory is shot, and she has ongoing problems with headaches, light sensitivity, and extreme mood swings."

"With all due respect, forgetting things isn't the same as making things up."

"What do you mean?" Wyatt asked.

"Did you confirm with the doctors that this woman is indeed delusional?"

"Physicians don't talk. HIPAA and all that. What we know we got from the husband."

"Please. Wouldn't be the first time the husband was the last to know."

"But they obviously don't have a child —"

"And yet she's looking. I mean, even if she's delusional, why that delusion? Of all the short circuits running through her head, why this one? I'd check the odometer, too. Because maybe that's what she was doing for the six hours. Driving around searching for her lost girl."

"Who doesn't exist," Wyatt repeated.

"And yet is clearly important to her. First time she's done this?"

Wyatt hesitated. "Didn't think to ask that question."

"Friends, support system?"

"New to the area."

"Job?"

"Self-employed. Husband and wife work together making props for Hollywood."

"Meaning her only family, only contact, is her husband." Tessa's voice picked up. "The one telling you they don't have kids. The one reporting his wife has had three 'accidents' in six months."

Wyatt got her point. Same thought had crossed his mind, too. And in a cop's world, where there was paranoia, there was often probable cause.

"You suspect domestic violence. Which, I have to say, is what worries me, too." Wyatt thought again of the bruise that had discolored Thomas Frank's jaw. From an impaired wife, lashing out in agitation? Or from a terrified woman acting in self-defense?

"Fits the profile," Tessa was saying, "not to mention a man who beats his wife . . ."

"Might also beat his kids. Leading to what, the death of a girl who doesn't exist? Let's not get completely lost in the land of wild conjecture. I already spent the morning, not to mention significant county and state resources, on a wild-goose chase. At this point, my boss, the sheriff, would appreciate a lot more facts and a lot less fiction."

"Have you even talked to the woman —"

"All in good time."

"You haven't interviewed the driver?" Tessa sounded dumb-founded.

"She'd just been sedated! Woman's having medical issues, thought we covered that."

"So you haven't even questioned her directly —"

"First thing tomorrow. Doc says she needs more time to recover. Which gives us the rest of today to get our ducks in a row:

Single-car accident. Lone driver. Possible aggravated DWI."

He could feel Tessa rolling her eyes at him again. Crazy part was, her daughter rolled them exactly the same way.

"Fine. I'll play by your county-cop rules," she granted him. "So looking at just the accident . . . If your driver's blood alcohol level was only .06, why'd she crash?"

"Inclement weather. Impairment from her brain injury combined with said blood alcohol level. Either way, she went off the edge of a steep road; car flew down an embankment."

"Went off or drove off?"

"Waiting for the state police to help us with that one; we need the info from the vehicle's electronic data recorder."

"Suicide?"

"She had her seat belt on, which is one vote in the no column. Then again, open bottle of scotch could be taken as a vote in the yes department. However, and probably most interesting, after the accident, the driver clawed her way up a two-hundred-foot ravine in the pouring rain to flag down help."

"Certainly sounds like a woman with a will to live," Tessa commented.

"Except." Wyatt couldn't help himself. He

paused uncomfortably. "She didn't seem to think she needed help for herself. Instead, she begged for assistance to help find her missing girl. She pleaded for Vero."

"The little girl who doesn't exist?"

"Yeah. That one."

"Some delusion," Tessa said knowingly.

"Don't you have a lunch to attend?" Wyatt asked her irritably. "You know, with your favorite detective, D. D. Warren."

"The one and only."

"Good luck with that."

"Luck? Please, I need more like heavy armor."

Which made Wyatt roll his eyes at her, before ending the call.

The state police were good guys. In New Hampshire, all members of law enforcement attended the same training academy, from city to county to Fish and Game. Kept everyone on the same page and helped build bridges in an area long on mountains and short on people. Especially north of Concord, where law enforcement resources were particularly scarce, the various agencies relied upon one another for backup. And not just for manpower, but also for equipment. Contrary to those TV cop shows where crime labs looked like space stations and SWAT teams started out with a hundred grand in equipment per officer, real-world policing required more cooperation . . . and at times, sheer inventiveness. Wyatt had run undercover drug stings with surveillance equipment that had been pieced together from three different towns. Sometimes it felt less like policing and more like passing a collection plate.

Now Wyatt approached Jean Huntoon, who'd arrived with the state's data retrieval computer. The two had met twice before. They shook hands, made the obligatory comments on the weather, then hoofed it down to the crash site. Huntoon was a slender five six and cycled hundred-mile races in her free time. She also hadn't hiked in and out of the ravine half a dozen times, Wyatt thought resentfully, as the younger officer beat him to the vehicle.

"Sad ending for a beautiful car," Huntoon observed.

"Apparently even crossovers weren't meant to fly."

"Distributed front-end damage. Took it right on the nose." Huntoon looked back up the way they came. "Must have left the road up top, sailed right down. No other vehicles involved?"

"Don't think so."

"Brake marks?"

"Nope."

Huntoon arched a delicate brow. "Never a good sign. All right, you got questions. Let me get some answers."

Huntoon hefted her computer onto a relative flat spot near the frame of the shattered windshield, got out some cables, and went to work.

There were a couple of ways to conduct a vehicle autopsy. One was to dismantle the car in the field and ship away entire parts, doors, seats, the little black box, to the state's labs. As it was a county case, someone like Wyatt would follow his evidence to the labs, overseeing every step of analysis and data retrieval.

But Wyatt was feeling a pressure he couldn't completely explain with this one. Maybe because the case had gotten off to such a rough start, dozens of officers tied up in a wild-goose chase. Now he felt as if the investigation had gotten away from them and he needed to rein it back in, define the parameters of exactly who, what, when, where, why and how.

He needed the accident to present factually as just an accident. Run-of-the-mill. Nothing new to be seen here. Then he and his team could settle in, get it done.

Hence he'd called Jean Huntoon to meet him out in the field to retrieve the Audi's electronic data, rather than waiting another day to handle it in the lab.

Bad news about hooking up to the vehicle directly; Huntoon had to work around the shards of broken glass and bloodstained dash. An experienced officer, she whistled cheerfully as she rigged the cables from the car's electronic data recorder to her computer. She played with this, fiddled with that, then stood back to let her equipment do its thing.

An hour before, Kevin and a couple guys from the TAR team had wrapped up mapping the scene with the Total Station. Add that data to the info from the vehicle's EDR and Wyatt was hoping they'd have a nice, neat blueprint of single-car accident 101.

"Nice prints," Huntoon observed now, gesturing to a pair of bloody handprints on the front dash.

Wyatt nodded. It was true. Vehicles were notoriously tricky to fingerprint. Too much overlay and not enough viable surface. His personal favorite was to print the inside lid of the glove compartment box. Steering wheels, doors, gear shift, mostly yielded garbage. But the inside lid of the glove compartment . . . nice, smooth plastic.

Generally accessed only a few times by a few people. He'd scored some lovely incriminating prints from the glove box in his time. Things cops were proud of.

"Blood testing?" Huntoon was asking, indicating the gory mess smearing the driver's side door.

"Gonna let you guys do the honors. Whole door will ship out later tonight. Probably tear out big chunks of the dash as well. Less dilution that way."

Huntoon nodded in agreement. Taking a blood sample involved swabbing it with sterile water, which in turn diluted it. In this day and age of modern forensics, a good cop didn't just find evidence; he protected it.

"Female driver?" Huntoon asked.

"Yep."

Huntoon gestured through the shattered windshield to the driver's seat. "Seat setup looks similar to mine, about right for an average-size woman."

Wyatt crossed behind the vehicle so he was standing outside the driver's side door. Huntoon was right about the seat position, and now was as good a time as any to consider the rest of the driver-side setup.

"Seat belt is spooled, so I'm assuming it was on," he said. "Mirrors . . ."

Mirrors were hard to tell. Ideally you needed to sit in the driver's seat, but given the amount of broken glass, let alone that neither door would open, that was impossible. Wyatt eyeballed it now, would return to it later when they'd removed the doors.

He bent this way, crooked his head that way. "Appear to make sense."

Huntoon joined him in the juxtapositioning-the-mirrors game. "Nothing looks off to me."

Her machine beeped. She crossed back over to consult the screen.

Wyatt finished up his brief assessment. "So seat setup, mirror placement, all consistent with female driver five four to five six. Nothing yet to indicate anyone else in the vehicle. In fact, we have a search dog who would swear the driver was the lone occupant. And now you're going to tell me . . . ?"

"Stability control was deactivated."

"What?" Wyatt drew up short. Of all the things he'd thought Huntoon was going to read off her data collector, that wasn't it.

"This model has stability control. You know, to help the vehicle autocorrect if the driver goes into a skid, takes a corner too hot, that kind of thing. The vehicle's computer senses the potential threat and will

111

take over braking and/or deceleration on its own. Except in this vehicle, where the stability control had been shut off."

"Manual override button?" Wyatt asked, as that was his memory with these high-end cars. They gaveth, but the driver could taketh away. Again, according to his memory, because God knows he'd never get to experience such vehicles on his salary, some drivers preferred an edgier experience. They wanted to push the limits of the car's high-end capabilities without the computer's self-preservation instinct kicking in.

"Exactly." Huntoon looked at him. "Your female an adrenaline junkie?"

"I have no idea."

"Vehicle was traveling at approximately thirty to thirty-five miles an hour," Huntoon read off next. "But get this: no rpms."

Wyatt stared at the officer. "Engine was in idle."

"Gear shift's in neutral." Huntoon nodded her head toward the shifter, which they could both see in the front. Wyatt had observed its position earlier; he'd simply assumed the driver herself had knocked the vehicle out of gear.

"How does a car achieve thirty-five miles an hour while in neutral?" Wyatt asked in confusion.

"Gotta be some hill," Huntoon said, looking at the road above them.

"Yeah. Or some push."

Huntoon glanced up again, her dark eyes considering. "That would do it. Still thinking accident?"

Wyatt said simply. "Ah, shit."

CHAPTER 9

Investigator Tessa Leoni regarded her reflection critically in the mirror. She was not a woman prone to overanalyzing her wardrobe. In the beginning of her career, the state of Massachusetts had been kind enough to take care of the matter for her — each and every shift she'd turned out in state police blues. After the incident, when she and the state had agreed it was mutually beneficial to part ways, she'd become a corporate security specialist. Which, best she could tell, involved trading in her dark blue uniform for navy-blue Ann Taylor suits. Maybe once you wore blue, there was no going back.

Tessa grimaced, did her best not to think about the obvious comparison. Such as once a cop, always a cop. Except, of course, she wasn't.

All in all, she was doing well, she reminded herself. Her daughter was happy, at least as happy as a cautious, hard-eyed, constantly on-the-alert, recovering-from-trauma child could be. Mrs. Ennis, their former neighbor and now live-in font of all wisdom, was happy, not to mention cooking up a storm with a little help from cable TV.

And . . . And Wyatt.

Tessa hadn't expected to date again. Let alone discover a man she respected, found attractive, and actually trusted. He accepted her, all of her, including a history that included allegedly shooting her own husband. Not just any man could do that.

And it's not that Sophie truly hated him. At least, not any more than any other man.

Tessa sighed, returned her attention to her attire. Navy-blue suit. Sharply tailored jacket coupled with matching straight-legged slacks. She looked taller, leaner, tougher.

All good things when having lunch with Boston detective D. D. Warren.

Why was she doing this again?

Because it was her job and she was a professional and she could handle this.

Tessa's stomach clenched. She felt nervous and resented the sensation. She and the good detective had a history. For starters, D.D. was the one who'd investigated the shooting death of Tessa's husband. But the two women had managed to work together — kind of — to track a missing family a while back.

Whether D.D. appreciated it or not, Tessa had once worn the uniform. She remembered the isolation of being a female cop. And probably more than anyone, she could understand what D.D., with her recent injury, was going through now.

Hence, lunch.

Tessa finished fussing with the collar of her plain white shirt. She looked less like a corporate security consultant and more like a federal agent. But that was okay. She wore what she wore. She was who she was.

Tessa was not a woman who harbored illusions. There were good things in her life — Sophie, Mrs. Ennis, Wyatt and, hell, maybe one day a puppy. But there were also other things. Decisions made, actions taken, that could not be undone. She still bore the scars; she still suffered the nightmares.

And yes, she did wonder: Did a woman like her deserve to be happy?

She looked at her daughter, and she didn't know how to want anything less.

Which meant for now, she would be a grown-up and take a wounded detective to lunch.

■ ■ ■ ■

Tessa arrived at Legal Sea Foods in the Pru Center fifteen minutes early. She hoped to choose the table, preferably one in the corner, and set the stage.

Of course, she found D.D. already waiting. At a corner table. Back to the wall. She rose slightly when Tessa was led over by the hostess. The detective moved easily enough; Tessa had to look for the weakness to spot it, the way the detective held her left arm against her ribs a shade too tight.

They shook hands, professionals. D.D. was wearing her signature caramel-colored leather jacket, with wide-legged tan slacks and a deep teal-colored button-down shirt. Man's shirt; Tessa would bet money on it. Further evidence the good detective wasn't back to fully functional. But her short golden locks retained their usual level of wild curl. Woman still had some fight left in her, then.

Good, Tessa thought. She was looking forward to it.

"How's Jack?" Tessa asked, taking the seat across from D.D., with her back to the room. Jack was D.D.'s young son. Two, three years old? Where did the time go?

117

"He's going through a nursery rhyme stage. We read a lot of Mother Goose, sing lullabies. Sophie?" D.D. asked.

"Good. Into gymnastics, tae kwon do and target shooting."

D.D. was regarding her with a faint smile. "I hear other rumors as well. You and the New Hampshire sergeant Wyatt Foster? Thought there was some chemistry during the Denbe case."

"We've been dating six months."

"Nice. Introduced him to Sophie yet?"

Tessa hesitated; she couldn't help herself. D.D. arched an inquiring brow.

"We tried two outings," Tessa confessed. "Mostly . . . she stared at him. You know, the way you and I might regard a serial killer or registered sex offender. She was never sassy or disrespectful . . . but I wouldn't have blamed Wyatt for running for the hills. Sophie can be very intense."

"They should build something together," D.D. recommended. "Wyatt's a carpenter, right? Maybe he can teach her how to make something. Sophie will suffer his presence for the sake of the power tools, and in the meantime, maybe some of Wyatt's laid-back New Hampshire charm will work its magic. They'll bond."

"Pretty good for a woman with a little boy."

"As a detective you have to be prepared for all kinds of evil. Even nine-year-old girls."

D.D. picked up her menu. Tessa followed suit. The waitress came; they placed their orders. Shrimp for Tessa, clam chowder and baked cod for D.D. They both drank water. Then it was time to get down to business.

"Heard about your arm," Tessa said, gesturing to D.D.'s stiff posture. The detective had recently suffered an on-the-job injury to her left arm. Rumor mill was it was serious and ongoing. As in she might never again be fit for duty. The department had a heart about such things. Most likely, the detective would be offered a desk. Except D.D., like Tessa, wasn't a woman meant for sitting.

"Figured as much." D.D. eyed her sharply. "Here to talk to me about my future employment opportunities?"

"Never hurts to know," Tessa responded mildly. "And it must not hurt to listen, given that you agreed to lunch."

D.D. gave a single-shouldered shrug, maybe not totally convinced, but not arguing either. "Do you like what you do?" she asked, clearly curious.

"More than I thought I would. For example, working the Denbe case . . . an entire family gone missing, racing against all odds to find them. You and I, we do best in situations that provide a challenge, as well as a sense of purpose."

"Kind of an extreme case. Where you got a lot of help from the BPD, I might add."

"You'd be amazed how many extreme cases exist in corporate America. You have money, egos, and world domination at stake. People can get a little nuts."

"You like it."

"I do. Which, I'll be the first to say, surprised me. And to be honest, the hours are better. My daughter knows that nine times out of ten, I'm coming home for dinner. And watching her game on the weekend. And getting four weeks' paid vacation a year, while earning a salary that lets us spend that time someplace sunny."

"Now you're just being mean."

"It's true. My job is superior to yours in every way."

"Not every way."

"Highly challenging, incredibly lucrative, and family friendly. Tell me what working for a corporate security firm can't offer you."

"Phil," D.D. said simply. "And Neil. My

120

squad mates. You've always been a lone wolf, Tessa. Whereas I've always loved my team."

Their lunches arrived shortly. They made small talk, caught up on mutual acquaintances. Bobby Dodge, a state police detective, was doing well. Still married to Annabelle, now had three kids, just bought a fixer-upper out in the burbs. Big yard, D.D. reported. Kind of place perfect for a swimming pool, trampoline and summer barbecues. Oh, and they'd gotten a puppy, an Australian cattle dog. Most likely to herd the kids.

Around and around she and D.D. went, exchanged stories on people they knew, cases they'd worked. Until lunch was done, Tessa had charged it to her corporate card and they were back to the matter at hand.

"You'll think about it?" Tessa said at last. "Maybe come in for a sit-down interview? Never hurts to know what's out there."

D.D. nodded. Her love of her team aside, if she couldn't pass the fitness-for-duty test, she was done as a cop. Tessa was offering her a lifeline by even considering her for Northledge Investigations, and they both knew it.

"Speaking of dogs, state has a new development on an old case," D.D. said as they rose to standing.

"Oh yeah?"

"Guy was out playing with his dog," D.D. said, "tossing a stick for him in a nearby stream, when he happened to notice a small black handgun beneath the water. He turned it in to the police; the lab matched the pistol to the bullet used to kill John Stephen Purcell. You know, that hit man murdered three years ago."

Tessa didn't say anything.

"Just got me thinking," D.D. said casually. "There are still a lot of unanswered questions from that night —"

"My daughter's doing just fine," Tessa interjected curtly.

"I don't begrudge that. I don't." D.D. shook her head. "But, Tessa, you and I . . . You're right. We're meant to be doing things. Hell, we're meant to be wearing badges. And the kind of people who wear the shield are supposed to uphold the system, honor the law. There are lines that shouldn't be crossed. And you —"

D.D. broke off. What she suspected, she could never prove, and they both knew it. While Tessa remained silent, because what she had done she was never going to say, and they both knew it.

"I'm not trying to threaten you," D.D. said at last.

"Then what are you trying to do?"

"Give you a heads-up. Rumor is, lab geeks recovered a print. No statute of limitations on homicide, right? Meaning if new evidence is recovered . . ."

She didn't have to say the rest. Tessa understood.

D.D. stepped away from the table. "The Purcell case isn't the BPD's," she remarked, as they headed through the restaurant, toward the front doors. "State assigned it to a new guy, Detective Rick Stein. Word on the street is he's a supercop, the kind of guy who hates open cases and unanswered questions. I'm sure you'll be hearing from him soon enough."

"Fair enough," Tessa said.

"You could come forward, volunteer information now," the detective suggested.

Tessa merely shot her a look.

"You're still a lone wolf, Tessa," D.D. remarked softly, as they pushed through the doors.

"I never got to work with your squad mates," Tessa answered.

D.D. merely smiled. "Thanks for lunch. I'll think about it."

They went their separate ways.

CHAPTER 10

Thomas has returned. He had left, telling me I needed to rest, though we could both tell he was the one who was exhausted. Now he's back and I'm pleasantly surprised that I both remember his name and feel almost happy to see him. He has brought me a change of clothes. Black yoga pants, an oversize cable-knit sweater the color of cinnamon. The clothes don't appear instantly recognizable to me. And yet, when I hold them to my nose and inhale . . .

A flash of memory. I am curled up on a chocolate-brown leather sofa. A book is in my hands, a cup of tea on the glass coffee table near my feet. While across from me, Thomas sits in a matching chair, deeply engrossed in the morning crossword puzzle.

I'm suddenly hungry for oatmeal, but I don't know if that makes any sense.

Dr. Celik appears in the doorway, carrying a brown paper bag. She glances at me absently, then focuses her attention on Thomas. They resume their low-voiced huddle across the room. Like intimates, I think again. I wonder if I'm the jealous type. Or if Thomas has ever strayed. Did I know? Did I care?

I don't know if I'm a good wife. Apparently, I'm a high-maintenance one. And, given the bruise on Thomas's jaw, one capable of lashing out. But am I sweet, nurturing, tender? Or bossy, domineering, a real shrew?

Mixed-up memory or not, it feels like I should know that much about myself. Basic personality traits, dynamics of a marriage, emotional snapshots of a life.

Maybe I'm simply too tired, because I can't bring anything to mind. The feeling of sinking underwater, isn't that what the doctor had described to Thomas? Because that's how I feel. As if I'm partially submerged, just floating along, the world drifting farther and farther away.

Dr. Celik's voice rises sharply. I don't have to be a rocket scientist to understand she doesn't want me to go. Most likely I require observation, further tests, and a bunch more poking and prodding by the nurses who show up hourly to read my stats and otherwise terrorize me.

Under water or not, I haven't lost my resolve. I can't stay here. The machines are too loud, the lights too bright, the sound of footsteps too echoey down the linoleum hall. A hospital is no place to recover from a concussion. It's way too *everything* for a woman who requires significant R & R.

More debate, another sharp exchange.

"You understand you are signing her out AMA — against medical advice? That it's my expert opinion your wife should remain in the hospital at least another twenty-four hours. That she remains at risk for cerebral swelling, not to mention a brain bleed. As in, you take her home, and she could die there."

Will I recognize my house? I try to picture it. A gray-painted Colonial with black shutters comes immediately to mind. Maybe a vision from a magazine or maybe my actual home; I'll find out soon enough. I try to imagine a cat or dog but come up empty. Apparently, my husband and I are content with our own company. We work together; Thomas told me that. He designs props, set pieces, and I help finish them. Live together, work together, sleep together.

We must love each other very much, or it's no wonder I bruised his jaw.

Then . . . another memory: myself, sitting

in a brightly lit sunroom. Green tendrils of hanging plants softening the oversize bank of windows. Tile floor, eclectic colors on the wall. Myself, sitting in the middle, painting. And smiling. I can actually feel it on my face. I am happy.

Thomas's voice, booming from the doorway behind me: *Hey, honey, wanna grab lunch?*

My smile growing. Happier.

"Nicky."

My mind zooms back to the present. Stark hospital room. Me, lying on the bed, my husband now standing beside me. "Doctor Celik is willing to let you go," he tells me, which immediately strikes me as odd, because that's not how their exchange had sounded to me at all. "But you have to promise to rest, and we'll need to return in a few days for a follow-up."

I nod. It hurts my head, but not terribly. Then I promptly crinkle my nose. Thomas is now carrying the paper sack once held by the doctor. I smell blood, earthy and strong. But also . . . scotch. The good stuff. I don't know whether to roll away in disgust or lean forward in longing.

"Your clothes," Thomas says, holding up the bag, marked with the symbol for bio-hazard.

It takes me a moment; then I get it. From last night, he means. From the accident.

I can't help myself. "We can take them? I thought, the police . . . You said there would be questions."

"Your blood alcohol reading measured .06," my husband tells me. "Legal limit in New Hampshire is .08. At this time, they have no grounds to charge you, let alone seize personal property."

I nod. I wonder if I should be impressed my husband knows legal statutes so well. Or worried.

"But the items are bloody . . . destroyed." I'm still confused. Why does he have my shredded clothes? Why does he care?

He doesn't answer the question, but gestures to the fresh garments he'd stacked at the foot of my hospital bed.

"Think you can get dressed?"

"Yes."

"Good. I'm going to run down to the pharmacy to fill your prescriptions; then I'll be back. Give me twenty minutes."

"What time is it?"

"Five thirty."

"It's dark outside."

"Yes."

"Vero's not afraid of the dark," I inform him.

Thomas sighs and leaves the room.

Our house is a two-story Colonial. I can't tell the color given that it's night. But after driving forty minutes along quaint back roads and winding side streets, Thomas pulls into a driveway, kills the engine. Both of us sit there for a moment. Not talking. Just alone in the dark.

Then Thomas pops open his door, comes around and assists me.

My ribs still ache. My chest, if I try to inhale too deep. But I find if I keep my movements simple, my pacing slow, I can manage well enough. There are four steps up to a covered front patio. A lone porch light illuminates the door, which appears to be painted the color of wine. Or is it blood? Didn't we laugh about that once?

Thomas unlocks the door, gestures for me to enter.

My house has a vaulted foyer. Slate tile below, black wrought-iron chandelier above, switchback staircase straight ahead. I move to the cherrywood side table without even thinking. Two framed pictures. One appears to be us, younger, happier, laughing on a beach. The frame features broken pottery tiles and I immediately think of Mexico. Good trip. We'd breakfasted on tequila and spent the afternoons racing WaveRunners through crashing surf. We'd been dangerous and silly and madly, passionately in love.

I miss Mexico. Still do.

Next up, a black-and-white portrait. Not a couples shot at all. Just me, backlit by something, maybe a table lamp. You can't see my expression, only my profile, wisps of dark hair curling provocatively. There is something pensive about the photo, and I set it down reflexively.

"I always liked that picture of you," Thomas says. He throws his keys in a basket on the table, trying to watch me while not appearing to be watching me.

I know without asking that he took that photo and I'd been crying right beforehand. A raw, eyes-streaming, nose-running, throat-hiccupping jag that had concerned him so much he'd gotten out his camera in order to distract me.

Sometimes I cry for no reason.

See, I remember something about myself after all.

I follow Thomas deeper into the home, coming face-to-face with the chocolate leather sofa, the glass coffee table. The kitchen is off the family room. Lighter, maple-wood cabinets, because I didn't want the room to feel too dark. A backsplash of seafoam-green glass tiles because they reminded me of the ocean. A parlor table for two, wrought-iron base, butterfly mosaic inlay because I always yearned to fly.

This is my room. As well as the sunroom directly off of it, with its crazy alternating lime-green and pink-magenta walls. Thomas had groaned the second he saw the colors. Don't make me do it, he'd dramatized in mock horror. But it was my room, my space, and I could have it any way I wanted, so I'd gone with lime green and pink magenta.

Just as long as it didn't have a painted rosebush, climbing up the walls.

"Work shed is out the back," he says now, gesturing to the door off the sunroom. "Here is where you work. There is where I work."

"Not side by side?"

"Not too often. I build; you paint. And between the two of us, the work gets done."

He leads me upstairs. No pictures on the wall and for some reason this surprises me, as if I'd been expecting them. The second floor has three bedrooms, including a master with its own bath. That room has a tray ceiling and a truly massive four-poster cherry-wood bed.

My first thought is there is no way I picked out that formal monstrosity. Thomas must have done it, because I already hate it.

He doesn't say anything, just completes the short, guided tour.

"Why such a big house for just the two of us?" I ask. "Do we entertain often, host many guests?"

"We liked this house, even though it was bigger than we needed. And, given that we do work together, sometimes it's nice to have extra space."

I walk into the smaller of the two extra bedrooms. It features a lovely white-painted wrought-iron daybed, covered in a quilt of butter yellow.

"I like this room."

He doesn't say anything.

I touch one corner of the quilt, finger it in my hand. It is hand-stitched, handcrafted. But not by me, I think instantly. The skill demonstrated here is well beyond my pay grade. And yet . . .

I know who made this quilt. I miss her.

And just for a moment, I feel it again. That sense of hollowness deep inside my chest. Yearning.

"You can sleep here if you want," Thomas says quietly.

"Okay." I don't even look at him. This room is mine; the master is his. He can tell me whatever he wants. I know better.

Thomas wonders if I'm hungry. Actually, I am. We return downstairs, where he whips up two cheese omelets. I slice up a cantaloupe, admiring the fine edge on the knife's blade. If this kitchen is my domain, clearly I take my equipment seriously.

We sit at the parlor table and I realize I'm moving automatically, already following rhythms that must have developed over the past six months we've lived here. A party of two, banging around twenty-four hundred square feet, with cozy taste in furniture and surprisingly few pictures, knickknacks or personal decorations on the wall.

I wonder if we finished unpacking all the moving boxes. Or if we're simply people who prefer a very clean approach to home décor.

After dinner, Thomas suggests we watch a movie. But I can tell he's fading again, clearly dead on his feet. In contrast, I finally feel awake, curiously wired, as if the fog is lifting and if I just focus long enough, try hard enough, all the secrets of the universe will be mine.

I tell Thomas he should go to bed. He tries to protest. I shoo him away, and finally, with a frown, he takes the hint.

As he disappears upstairs, I pick up the remote and determine I have no problem running the system or finding all my favorite channels. As long as I don't think too much, just act, I have no problems at all.

I tune in to TV Land. Watch old episodes of *Gilligan's Island,* which seems a safe enough show for a woman with multiple head injuries. Not too exciting, no threat of violence. Well, other than the Skipper smacking Gilligan with his hat time and time again. I draw the line at *Golden Girls,* though. I'm not that desperate.

I turn off the TV, roam the family room. I discover a pile of books, mostly paperbacks. Apparently I like to read Nora Roberts, while Thomas favors Ken Follett. I reenter the kitchen, and then, because I simply have to know, I go through all the cabinets and then the pantry.

Sure enough, no alcohol. Not a single can of beer, not a single bottle of wine. Let alone a decent bottle of scotch.

For a moment, I'm disappointed. Terribly, dreadfully. Because wouldn't a nice glass of single malt be perfect right about now?

I leave the kitchen, head upstairs. My breath grows ragged in my chest, but I survive the hike. Back to the little room with the lovely butter-yellow quilt.

There, I lie down fully clothed, my legs straight, my hands folded on my chest. Like a girl in a coffin.

And then, I inhale.

Vero.

She is little again. Small and bubbly with chubby cheeks and fat fists. Airplane noises as she runs around the tiny room, leaping over pillows, willing her body into flight.

I love you, I love you, I love you.

Vero flies. Vero falls.

Ominous footsteps down the hall.

I'm dreaming, I tell myself.

I'm still dreaming, I remind myself.

As I watch Thomas burst into the room.

CHAPTER 11

The Franks lived in a relatively new gray-painted Colonial. Black shutters, covered farmer's porch, a winding brick walkway that curved through an attractive front flower bed. This late in the season, the bed still offered up some ragged pansies and those cabbage-looking things Wyatt never knew what to call. Meaning someone had taken the time and effort to update the plantings in the fall. Nicky Frank? Her husband, Thomas?

Many things to learn, which was why Kevin and Wyatt decided to start the morning with a personal house call.

Tessa's comments from yesterday were still weighing heavily on Wyatt. How much did they really know about Nicky Frank, having never talked to her directly? Including but not limited to, how much did she remember from her past three "accidents"? Because cars rarely went sailing off the road while in neutral. Coulda happened, he supposed. Driver falls asleep, knocks the car out of gear while coasting down a steep grade, but it didn't feel probable. Which made Wyatt wonder about the scotch as well. Had Nicky been drinking of her own accord? Or had someone been doing their best to make sure a woman with a known brain injury and doctor's orders not to imbibe didn't wake up at the wheel?

Sometimes when working a case you had a strong lead, and sometimes you mostly had a hunch. Good news about being the sergeant — Wyatt got to follow his hunches. Countywide search for a girl who still had no record of even existing notwithstanding. Yeah, the sheriff had had words with him on that one. But even the boss agreed, something about this couple, the wife's series of accidents, the enduring delusion of a missing girl, seemed off.

Wyatt did the honors of knocking. Front door was dark cranberry and appeared freshly painted. Looked to him like when the Franks bought the home six months ago, they'd spent some time and energy sprucing up the place. A sign they were finally settling down? Because Kevin had run the couple's background last night, and to say they moved a lot would be an understatement. Two years was the longest they'd stayed in one spot. Otherwise, their MO seemed to be here today, gone tomorrow.

Chasing business, a husband covering his tracks or a couple that was just restless? More questions to consider.

Wyatt liked a challenge.

Hence his relationship with Tessa.

He knocked again, louder this time, more insistent. Finally, the sound of footsteps moving through the house. A second later, the door opened and a rumpled-looking Thomas Frank stood there.

"Morning," Wyatt said brightly.

The man, barefoot and in sweats, stared back at him. "What time is it?"

"Eight A.M."

"Isn't that a little early for house calls?"

"We brought coffee."

Thomas scowled.

"Sir," Kevin spoke up, pressing the point. "We have some questions for your wife."

"She's asleep; she needs to rest —"

"It's okay." Behind Thomas, Nicky appeared on the staircase. She was also dressed casually — yoga pants, an oversize sweater — and her hair was wet, as if she'd recently showered.

Even from this distance, Wyatt could make out the harsh lines of stitches slashing across her forehead, left eye, right jawline, let alone the myriad of bruises and abrasions marring her skin. Yesterday, she'd looked bad. A day later, she appeared even worse; probably would until the bruises ran their course. But the woman was standing. Head up. Eyes clear.

Wyatt felt that thrum, big-game hunter on the prowl. This morning was looking good.

Thomas retreated, reluctantly allowing the two officers into his house. Wyatt and Kevin didn't hesitate but moved fully into the home, closing the door behind them. Wyatt's first impression was that the house was nice in a clean, modern sort of way, but curiously sterile. Less a home, more a set piece. Here is the Pottery Barn sofa; here is the appropriately scaled coffee table; here is the soft and comfy area rug. Not until they hit the kitchen, which led into a shockingly bright-painted sunroom, did he have any sense of personality. Then, to judge by the way Thomas avoided looking at the brightly painted walls, Wyatt would guess the room represented Nicky's sense of style and not her husband's.

Kevin set down the cardboard carrier bearing four coffees on the kitchen counter. Thomas sighed, accepted the bribe. But Nicky poured herself a glass of water.

"Do I drink coffee?" she asked her husband, her tone genuinely curious.

"You prefer tea," Thomas supplied.

"But I love the smell."

Thomas looked up at his wife. "You don't have to talk to them, you know. You didn't meet the legal threshold for impairment, remember?" He shot them a look, as if it was important for them to know that he knew. "Not to mention Dr. Celik said you need to rest. If you're feeling tired, you should go lie down. I can handle this."

Big, strong caretaker, Wyatt wondered, or just a husband who really didn't want his wife to talk to the cops?

What made it really interesting was that he could tell Nicky was wondering the same thing.

"We have only a few questions," Wyatt offered up. "Whether the driver is intoxicated or not, we're still duty bound to investigate all accidents. Routine inquiry and all. Won't take much time."

"I don't mind," Nicky said. "We can go into the sunroom. If I need anything, I'll let you know."

Thomas still didn't look happy, but he took his coffee and walked away.

According to the background info, Thomas did indeed own and operate his own company, Ambix Productions. Last year, he'd made a quarter million, which would explain the nice house, fancy cars. The Franks currently had forty thousand sitting in the bank, a decent nest egg if the wife continued being unable to work. So hardly a couple on the edge of financial ruin, as Thomas had seemed to imply at the hospital. Maybe he was a conscientious guy, or a workaholic. No doubt his wife's string of injuries had cut into his hours, and not just for a week or two, but apparently for the past six months.

Meaning he had good reason to be over-protective of his wife? Or again, more fun secrets and lies? Days like this, Wyatt honestly loved his job.

With Thomas gone, Nicky escorted Wyatt and Kevin into the bright sunroom. She moved gingerly, Wyatt noticed, still a woman with substantial aches and pains, but she seemed to be in good spirits.

"I like this room," she said now, as she took a seat in one of the cushioned patio chairs. Wyatt and Kevin made themselves comfortable in two more matching wicker chairs, situated across from her. "This is my room," she continued, curling a leg beneath her. "And the yellow bedroom upstairs; that's my room, too."

"You recognize your home?" Wyatt asked. "Feel comfortable here?"

"Yes. As long as I don't think too hard. If I just do things, you know, reach for a plate, I'll find it immediately. On the other hand, if I stop and try to remember where plates might be . . . That's when it gets more complicated."

"You're working off muscle memory," Kevin spoke up.

Nicky shrugged. Her dark hair was starting to dry, curl around her face. She was an attractive woman, Wyatt noted, or would be once the bruises and lacerations healed.

"Whatever works," she said. "I think, given the state of my head, beggars can't be choosers."

"Any headaches today?"

"No. I'm just . . . sore. Everywhere. Like my whole body went through the spin cycle or something. The doctor provided some pain pills, but I think in the short term, Advil will be my friend."

"How is Vero?" Wyatt tried out. "She feeling better, too?"

Across from him, Nicky stilled, regarded him frankly. "Do you think I'm crazy, Sergeant?"

"Don't know yet."

"I don't have a daughter."

"And yet yesterday —"

"I'd just been in a major accident, whacked my head. Yet again. Clearly I was dazed and confused."

"Have you ever had a child?"

"No. I'm infertile. Children have never been an option for us." She smiled thinly. "Funny, I can barely remember my husband's name. But my own barrenness — that's a memory I can't escape."

Wyatt paused, not sure what to make of this confession. She couldn't have children, but maybe secretly still wanted one, so under duress, her subconscious made one up? Possible, he supposed. But getting well beyond the bounds of policing.

"Why the name Vero?" Kevin asked.

"I don't know."

"Family name? Your mom, sister, great-aunt, somebody's?"

"I don't have a family."

"No one at all?" Wyatt interjected.

She gazed at him clear-eyed. "No. No one at all. It's just Thomas and me. Trust me, it's enough."

Okay. Wyatt made another note. Tessa's concerns from yesterday were making more and more sense to him. Because clearly, Nicky Frank lived a very isolated life. Just her and her husband. Except her husband wasn't the one who kept having "accidents."

"What do you remember from Wednesday night?" Wyatt asked.

"The night of the wreck."

"Yes."

"I don't."

"You don't?"

"I don't. Nothing at all. I try to picture it . . . My mind is blank."

Wyatt glanced at Kevin, who responded with a nod.

"Mrs. Frank," Kevin spoke up. "Mind trying something with me? It's a guided memory exercise. Might help jog something for you."

"What does it involve?"

"Just relax and sit there. I'm going to try to walk you through the evening in more detail, focusing on your senses. You know, what you smelled, heard, that sort of thing. It's like coming at the memory sideways versus head-on. Sometimes, that makes a difference."

"It's not hypnosis, is it?"

"Not at all."

"Because I have enough issues with my brain. I don't need anyone tampering with it."

"No tampering, no suggestions. I'm just going to ask you a series of questions, and

144

you answer with what first comes to mind."

Nicky pursed her lips, continued to regard them uncertainly. But then, a short, faint nod. She was going for it.

"All right. Just close your eyes. Breathe deep. It's Wednesday night. Five o'clock. Where are you?"

"I'm at home."

"What are you wearing?"

"Jeans. Black turtleneck. Gray fleece."

"How do the clothes feel?"

"Soft. Comfortable. It's one of my favorite outfits."

"What are you doing in the house?"

"I'm . . . starting dinner. Chicken breasts. I marinated them this morning in Italian dressing. Now I need to cook them. I think I will sear the outside, then finish them in the oven. I should make rice, too. Maybe steam some broccoli." She pauses. "I have a headache."

"Do you take something for it?"

"I already did. Four Advil. But it's not enough. The smell of the chicken . . . it's making me nauseous."

"What do you do?"

"I need to lie down. Sometimes, I wrap a towel around an ice pack and place it over my eyes. It helps."

"Now?"

145

"I get the chicken in the oven. I set a timer so it doesn't burn. I give up on the broccoli, but the rice is safe in the cooker. I don't need to worry about that. I get my ice pack, head for the sofa."

"Where is your husband?"

"I don't know."

"Is he in the house?"

"I don't know."

"Maybe in the work shed?"

"I don't know."

"Okay. You lie down with your ice pack."

"I think I fall asleep. It's dark and cold and comforting. I close my eyes. I like to sleep. When I sleep, Vero comes to me. She's happy, wearing her favorite flowered dress. She wants to dance, so I take her arms and we swing round and round. Except we are in the small room now, with the ratty blue rug and the tightly shuttered windows and the twin beds pressed so close together they might as well be one. The end is coming. This is our good-bye room. I know every time I look at the carpet. I should stop. It's so hard to keep seeing her like this. But I love her. I've always loved her. And I'm sorry. I never knew just how sorry a person could be, until it's like a weight and it's sinking you, and oh my God, the footsteps again. Down the hall. We both need to escape. Except only one of us ever makes it. Always me, never Vero."

"Nicky . . ." Wyatt studied the woman intently. Her eyes were still closed. She wasn't looking at them, but lost in her memory of a memory. And she was crying. Whether she was aware of it or not, tears were streaming down her face.

"You wake up?" Kevin asked softly.

"The timer goes off. Chicken. All done."

"What do you do?"

"Thomas. He's standing in the living room. He's staring at me. Maybe I called out; maybe I said her name. I shouldn't have done that. I get the chicken out of the oven. I put it on plates. I dish up rice. I set the table. Thomas watches me. He tells me I did good. One of my first successful dinners. We eat in silence. We didn't used to eat like that, you know. We used to talk and talk and talk. We used to love each other."

Wyatt and Kevin exchanged a glance.

"What do you do after dinner?" Kevin asked.

"I wash the dishes."

"What about Thomas?"

"He has to work. His job is very important. He works. I clean the kitchen. But I drop one of the plates. It breaks on the floor. My hands are shaking. I'm tired.

147

Weak. I used to be better than this, but now I'm tired all the time. Thomas is very patient with me. He has so much work to do, let alone the burden of babysitting his wife. I clean up the plate carefully, put the pieces in the outside trash, where hopefully he won't notice them. I don't want him to be upset."

"What happens when Thomas is upset?" Kevin pushed.

"I don't want Thomas upset," Nicky repeated.

"After you clean up the plate, what do you do?"

Nicky fell silent. Her eyes were still closed, the tears now drying on her cheeks. "I shouldn't do it," she whispered. "It's bad. I shouldn't do it. He'll be angry. I shouldn't do it."

"Do what, Nicky?"

"Shhh," she whispered. "I'm leaving him."

"But I don't," she picked up, thirty seconds later. "I can't. I need him. He's all that keeps me safe."

"Keeps you safe from what?" Kevin asked.

"You have no idea."

"Do you and your husband have enemies? Has someone threatened you?"

"Blood drips from the thorns. Those awful roses, climbing up the wall."

"Nicky —"

"You don't understand just how bad I am."

She spoke clearly, but once again Wyatt felt a twinge. She sounded more and more like an abused wife to him, a woman conditioned to think of herself badly, to feel as if she was constantly failing her husband.

"I'm tired now," she said quietly. "My head hurts."

"Just one minute more," Wyatt pushed. "Does your head hurt now, like it did that night?"

"Yes. I should get ice. Lie down."

"What were you wearing again?" Kevin backtracked, a strategy to ground her in the interview once more.

"Jeans. Black turtleneck. My favorite gray fleece."

"You're comfortable?"

"Yes."

"Lying on the sofa. But your head hurts."

"Yes."

"When do you get your coat?"

A pause. Eyes closed, Nicky frowns. "Coat?"

"Or did you grab your car keys first?" Wyatt prodded. He made a mental note to check with the hospital. The staff had bagged the clothing Nicky had been wearing that night. Just because they didn't have grounds to seize the clothes didn't mean they couldn't ask the nurses or EMTs about them. Had Nicky come in wearing a coat? Because there hadn't been one in the car.

But Nicky was shaking her head. "I'm resting on the sofa."

"When do you get up again?"

"Vero," she whispers.

"Vero?"

"I tried to fly. Just like Vero. But little girls were never meant to fly, you know. She crashed. I crashed. And now I have to find her. It's the whole reason I came back from the dead."

"You got in the car to find her?" Kevin asked.

"No, I got out of the car to find her."

"Where were you driving to, Nicky?"

"Driving?"

"You're in the car, you're heading out into the night."

But Nicky shook her head. She opened her eyes, stared at them directly. "I'm not driving," she said. "I'm resting on the sofa."

Wyatt studied her intently as the first piece of the puzzle clicked into place. "So who brought you the scotch?"

But Nicky wouldn't answer.

CHAPTER 12

"I thought they only had a few questions for you."

I study my husband. The detectives have left, Thomas reemerging in their wake. I think of what the detectives didn't tell me; for example, approaching a memory sideways is like brushing against sinister shapes in a darkened corridor. My memories feel cold even to me. As if they don't want to be disturbed.

"Do we have friends?"

Thomas regards me curiously. He has showered while I was talking to the police. His hair is damp against his neck. It makes me want to touch it with my fingertips.

"Not yet," he says.

"What do you mean?"

"We just moved here; then you fell down the stairs, and . . . Feels like we've been meeting with specialists ever since."

"I don't remember falling down the stairs."

"Doc said that was common with concussions."

"I don't remember doing the laundry."

He shrugs. "It's your chore. You didn't like me doing it, said I ruined your delicates."

The words strike a chord in my mind. Yes, I said that. And yes, laundry is my job. Yet I can't picture the washer and dryer. Maybe it's like the plates in the kitchen. I can't try to remember where they are; I have to simply reach for one.

"Am I allowed in your workshop?"

Thomas's lips curve into a crooked smile. He leans close, whispers in my ear: "Why? Worried I keep the bodies of my dead wives in there?"

I tell him seriously, "Yes."

"Come on, then. I'll take you to the work shed. You can behold the brilliance for yourself."

He's already dressed in jeans and a button-up blue flannel shirt. Now he throws a tan vest over the top and walks to the back door off the sunroom. For the first time, I notice the work boots placed neatly beside the door. He slides them on, while gesturing to my own bare feet. Belatedly, I retreat to the entryway, where I open up the hall closet and pull out a pair of rubber-soled L.L. Bean slippers without thinking about it. Another muscle memory, from six months of living in this house, setting these patterns.

It's cold outside. I shiver from the damp as we both step through the door. The sky is gray, the ground still wet from days of rain. Late fall in New England is not beautiful. The trees are skeletal, the grass brown. November isn't a season as much as it's a transition; from the fiery reds of October to the soft white of December.

We should spend November in Arizona, I think, and almost immediately know that we talked about it. I had brought it up, after one of my crying jags, when the short days and gray skies felt like more than I could bear.

But clearly we hadn't gone. Maybe because of my concussions. I was high maintenance even then.

The work shed is bigger than I pictured. Certainly larger than a garden shed, closer to a single-car garage. It has aluminum-gray sides, like a prefab building plopped down on the back of the property. We don't have any visible neighbors to be horrified by the unattractive sight, just us, and I guess we didn't mind, because we're the ones who put it here. Thomas poured the slab himself; he's handy that way. Then men came with the panels, and in a matter of days it was done. Basic but insulated, with a gas heater and full electricity. No plumbing; Thomas comes into the house for that.

In the spring, I wanted to plant shrubs or build a berm covered in bushes and flowers to soften the view of the ugly shed from the house. Another project Thomas and I had talked about. Another project that now, given my series of "accidents," we'll probably never get done.

Sergeant Wyatt had implied that I was isolated, maybe even at risk from my husband. How many concussions could one wife have, and six months later why didn't we have friends? Even the beginnings of a relationship with our neighbors?

But we don't. I knew that even before I asked Thomas; it's just him and me and has been for a very long time. We tell each other we are happy but I think we're lying. And maybe not even to each other, but to ourselves, because that's the easiest lie to tell, and the most difficult to unravel later.

The door of the workshop has a deadbolt lock. Thomas pulls the key out of his pocket, does the honors. I think the deadbolt is overkill, until I see all the materials inside.

Don't think where the plate is; just reach for the plate, I tell myself. But the logic doesn't work here. There is no muscle memory to call upon; I step inside the musty depths and immediately lose all sense of bearing. This is Thomas's domain, not my own, and already I feel confused and faintly anxious.

Thomas snaps on the overhead lights. I wince, putting up a hand reflexively to block the intensity. Thomas catches the gesture and flips another switch, eliminating half of the lights. Only then can I lower my hand, take it all in.

The space feels surprisingly large, the rafters exposed, roof vaulted. Straight ahead is a row of folding tables, placed end to end. Workspace, like a countertop for production designers.

The walls are lined with pegboard and metal shelving units, the pegboard dripping with various tools, the shelving units weighed down with pieces of wood, plastic pipes, other raw materials. The perimeter of the shed is too much for me. Too jumbled, too busy. Instead I find myself focused on a single piece of machinery, new, about the size of an extremely large printer and set in a place of honor on its own table. When I approach the machine, I smell plastic and feel a curious sense of dread.

We fought about this. He wanted it; I didn't. Apparently I lost, because here it is and I'm still resentful.

"What is it?" I ask.

Thomas is regarding me closely. Does he wonder if I remember the machine's history? Is he debating how much to tell me even now? After all, if the wife can't remember the argument, who's he to refresh her rage?

"It's a three-D printer," he says at last.

I nod, and several more pieces of memory click into place. "You create a digital design of the custom object, any object, then feed it to the printer and it builds a three-dimensional replica in plastic."

"That's right."

"Like a fake knife for a movie set?"

"I could, but there are already companies that specialize in weapons. Common items such as those most prop guys just order out of catalogues. I might design a custom trophy, say, for a scene where the underdog finally wins. Mold the top out of plastic, mount it on a custom wooden base; then you would apply gold leaf as the finishing touch. Then later, as part of the movie promotion, we might create dozens of tiny replicas to give out to studio heads, critics, whomever."

I nod. What he says makes perfect sense. So why am I sure he's lying to me?

I hear myself say: "Three-D printers can be used to build plastic guns."

"True."

"Do you do that for movies?"

"Again, common set pieces such as fake guns are cheaper to get out of catalogues."

I look at him. "Do you make real guns?"

"Why? Just like Hollywood props, real guns are cheaper when ordered out of catalogues . . . or purchased on a street corner."

"But a plastic gun would be untraceable."

"I believe street dealers are pretty good at filing down serial numbers or removing them with acid."

"You researched this."

"Because these were the arguments you brought up when I first suggested buying the machine. Three-D printing is changing the world, from manufacturing to medical science to, yes, movie props. I'm trying to keep us cutting-edge. But you see danger everywhere."

He's right; I do. Which makes me wonder what happened to trigger such an acute sense of paranoia.

"Do you like your job?" I ask him now.

I'm curious for his answer.

"Yes. It's creative, tangible, flexible. We can live anywhere, work any hours we want. We are very lucky to be able to do this."

"Do I like our job?"

He shrugs, no longer meeting my eyes, which makes me suspicious. "You like painting, and part of this job is painting. But lately . . ." He glances up, studies me. "What do you think, Nicky?"

"I want to quit," I hear myself say. "I want out."

"In order to do what?"

I open my mouth, but I can't find the words. "I don't know. I just want . . . out."

"We moved here for a fresh start. We'd been living in Atlanta, but you said you missed snow. So we did some online research, came up with New Hampshire. Soon there will be plenty of snow here. The question is, will that finally make you happy?"

"Why don't I remember falling down the basement stairs?"

"The concussion wiped it from your mind."

"And I fell outside, months later? Shouldn't I remember that?"

"Another concussion, another blank spot in your mind."

"I don't remember driving around last night. I don't remember putting on my coat, grabbing the keys or climbing behind the wheel. I'm not that stupid, Thomas. I should remember at least one step of the process."

"Maybe not. The doctor said there are no hard-and-fast rules with post-concussive syndrome."

"Did you get me drunk?"

"What?" For the first time, he draws up short.

"Did you pour me the first glass of scotch? That's what the detectives want to know. Did you get me drunk and then put me in the car?"

"Of course not!"

"Who, then? It's not like we have any friends."

Thomas's temper has flared. He rakes his hand through his hair, takes an agitated step forward. "No one poured you a glass of scotch. I never even saw the bottle in the house. You must have purchased it on your own. After you left. Because whether you remember driving off or not, you weren't here, Nicky. I searched high and low through the house for you. You were gone, and so was the car."

"I don't remember —"

"August 24, 1993. We walked to Café Du Monde for fresh beignets. You hadn't tried them yet, so I fed you half a dozen. And then, when you were still laughing and saying they were the best thing you'd ever had, I kissed you. Our first kiss. It tasted like cinnamon and powdered sugar. I've never gotten tired of kissing you since. Do you remember?"

He takes a step closer to me. His eyes are dark, riveting. I say, "Yes."

"Three nights later, in a small hovel of an apartment, single mattress on the floor, not even a TV set for entertainment, we make love for the first time. Afterward you cried, and I panicked, thinking I'd hurt you. You just cried harder and told me to hold you, so that's what I did. Sometimes you still cry after sex. So I still hold you, just like I did that night. Do you remember?"

"Yes."

"September 1, 1993. Production has wrapped and the movie is done. This is it. What happens next? I ask you. But you won't answer me. You won't even look at me. So I grab you by both arms. Stop, you say. You're hurting me. But I don't. I lift your chin; I force you to look me in the eye. I love you, I tell you. I love you and I need you. Stay with me, and I'll give you the world. Anything you want. Just be mine. Do you remember?"

"Yes."

"I will keep you safe, even if it costs me my own life. I promised you that. Do you remember?"

I can't look at him anymore, but there is no way to turn away. He has me pinned against one of the folding tables, and he is right before me. So close I can feel the heat of his body, smell once again the scent of his skin. I feel weak in the knees.

But I also feel trapped.

And just for a second, I want to hit him.

I get my chin up. "We don't have pets; we don't have friends; we move all the time."

"Your requirement, not mine. September 2, 1993. We leave New Orleans. You need to go away, you say. No explanation. You need a new name, you say. No explanation. I should try out a new name, too. Neither of us mentions all the times you wake up screaming in the middle of the night. Neither of us talks about your increasing skittishness, constantly locking doors, checking over your shoulder, breaking out into a cold sweat. You needed to go, so we did. You needed to try on a new identity, so we did. For you, Nicky, I spent the next two years changing out cities and inventing new

161

names on nearly a weekly basis until the worst of the panic left and you finally settled in as my wife. Because that was how much I loved you. Do you remember?"

Loved, I think, noting the past tense.

But he is still bearing down on me, still waiting for an answer. Do I remember, do I remember, do I remember? The moment when this one man agreed to go anywhere, be anyone, for me? The moment I begged this one man to go, and he agreed to follow?

The smell of beignets. The taste of powdered sugar. Thomas, younger, but just as somber, just as intent.

I look at him now. I see him now.

And I whisper, "Yes."

CHAPTER 13

"All right. Let's figure this out."

Eleven A.M., the morning raw and gray, Kevin and Wyatt returned to the scene of the accident. The Audi Q5 had finally been removed. It had taken tow ropes, a pulley system and a great deal of swearing on the part of the state police, but they'd gotten the job done.

Now just the tangle of matted bushes, snapped twigs and dislodged boulders remained to show the vehicle's careening path down the ravine. And of course, the tracks embedded in the mud next to the road. This is where Kevin and Wyatt now stood. Looking down to where it had gone, preparing to head back from whence it had come.

"We know Nicky's credit card was used to purchase the bottle of scotch ten miles from here, around ten P.M. Wednesday night."

"True," Kevin agreed.

"But we have no eyewitness accounts that place her at the store."

"Clerk claims it was too busy to remember one woman in particular."

"And their security system turned out to be compromised."

"When you rerecord over and over again on ancient discs, errors are bound to happen."

"Meaning we know her or someone affiliated with her got the scotch."

"E.g., the husband," Kevin filled in.

"Just don't love that man," Wyatt said. "Three concussions seems less like accidents and more like a pattern to me. But the question remains, if the scotch was purchased around ten, then what?"

"He took the bottle home, liquored up his wife," Kevin offered.

"Once she appears drunk enough . . . which turns out to be a lower threshold than the legal system dictates, but again, given her multiple concussions . . ."

"He probably assumed she was legally intoxicated."

"He loads her into her car," Wyatt continued.

"Drives her out to the middle of nowhere."

"Or maybe to exactly somewhere," Wyatt corrects. "To a spot with the proper grade of descent, ending in a sharp enough angle to the left, while being isolated enough from passing traffic; he can get out of the car, place his wife in the driver's seat, then bump the gear into neutral and let gravity take over. Not just any stretch of road would do the trick. This would take some scoping out, preplanning."

He and Kevin had now hoofed it to the top of the hill. From here, the forty-degree grade looked startlingly steep, especially given the yellow caution sign at the bottom, alerting motorists to the upcoming turn. Accidents on this stretch of road on a rainy night probably happened regularly enough. Meaning with just a little extra effort . . .

"I think he'd have to push the car," Kevin said. "To get the kind of acceleration it would require to fly off the edge . . ."

Wyatt gazed down, conceded his detective's point. "So Thomas positions his wife behind the wheel, puts on her seat belt then knocks the car into neutral. He'd have to move quick: No doubt the Audi is already starting to roll forward as he slams the door. Then he takes three quick steps back, adds his weight to the forward momentum."

The two detectives pantomimed the deed. "Could definitely be done," Kevin said.

"We should try to print the exterior rear

of the vehicle," Wyatt added, studying his open hands, poised instinctively to push.

"Plus the husband's clothes, jacket," Kevin said. "This time of year, cars aren't very clean, especially in a storm. Might have gotten debris, mud, all over him."

"How do you know the car will roll down in a straight line?" Wyatt asked. He studied the hill again, the way the road appeared to travel straight at first glance, except, upon further inspection, had a slight bend to the left, let alone a sloping grade to the right for runoff.

"Could try to tie something to the wheel to keep it straight," Kevin said.

"We didn't recover anything at the scene. Rope, scarf. As our dog handler pointed out, there weren't any personal items in the car at all."

"Maybe she held it."

"Nicky?"

Kevin shrugged. "She's half-drunk but the effects are magnified by the head injuries, someone sticks her behind the wheel of the car. Her husband says, hold the wheel . . . It's not like she knows what's going on. I could see her reflexively following orders. Of course, then the road turns and she doesn't."

"She might take her hands off, hold them

in the air."

According to Nicky's medical records, she hadn't sustained any damage to her thumbs, suggesting she hadn't been holding on to the steering wheel when the airbag had deployed. Some drivers instinctively gripped tighter, as if that would save them. Others let go, a subconscious free fall. There was probably some Freudian interpretation in there somewhere; Wyatt only knew what he'd seen time and time again in auto accidents; a certain percentage of drivers let go, and a certain percentage of drivers didn't.

"All right," he picked back up. "It's dark, it's raining, the road's deserted, Nicky's incapacitated with scotch and an already twice-concussed brain. In this scenario, Thomas would have to physically move her from the passenger's seat to the driver's seat."

Kevin shrugged. "Husband looks to be a strong guy. And his wife isn't that big. Might not be the most graceful maneuver in the world, but I bet he could handle it. My question is, if Thomas Frank wants his wife dead, why fasten her seat belt? Odds are better if it's off."

"Force of habit? Doesn't want the accident to appear too suspicious?"

"Woman's got a fifth of scotch in the car. A drunk driver without a seat belt? Nothing suspicious there."

Wyatt shrugged. "I don't know. Clearly the guy isn't a master criminal. I mean, if our theory is correct, this is the third accident he's staged for his wife."

"Assuming he was behind her first two falls."

"Assuming he was behind her first two falls," Wyatt agreed.

"We got a lot of assumptions here."

"Which is why we're walking through it. To see if some of these assumptions can lead us to some evidence. For example, now we know we should print the rear bumper to see if Thomas Frank's fingerprints or, better yet, palm print is on it. While we're at it, we should examine the seat-belt clasp and gear shift as well."

"None of which proves anything. A husband's fingerprints in his wife's car."

"Gives us grounds for a warrant to test his clothes. That might be more interesting."

"Assuming he hasn't washed them yet."

Wyatt rolled his eyes. "Every now and then we do get lucky. What are the odds of reconstructing the Glenlivet bottle? Testing for prints on that?"

Kevin gave him a look. "Now who's been watching too much TV?"

"Fine, then. What do you think happened here?"

"How'd he get home?" Kevin asked.

"I don't . . ." Wyatt stopped, drew up short, seeing Kevin's point.

"In this scenario," his detective continued, "the husband drives his wife out here in the middle of a storm. Then puts her behind the steering wheel and shoves her down the hill. At which point, he does what? Walks thirty miles home in the rain?"

"Or flags down a ride," Wyatt murmured.

"Which gives us a potential witness. Assuming, of course, a driver is going to stop and pick up a stranger on a dark and stormy night."

"Someone would," Wyatt said, because it was New Hampshire and people did still hitchhike. In fact, many of the locals hitchhiked, as good cars were expensive and not everyone had the kind of job where they could afford to buy their own set of wheels.

"But something like that would stand out," Wyatt continued, musing out loud. "Be a major weakness in the plan. I mean, all we have to do is hold a press conference. Anyone pick up a guy in this area, around this time, on this night? If it was Thomas, how could he explain away being at the site of his own wife's accident? I don't think he'd leave something like that to chance."

"So maybe he left a car parked nearby," Kevin said. "His ride home."

"Where?" Wyatt asked. "Closest gas station is a few miles back, and even then, same problem. How does he get home after parking that car? One way or another, someone would have to give him a ride from here to his house. Either sometime during the day on Wednesday, or later, during a severe rainstorm."

"Phone a friend," Kevin suggested. "Claim to have a flat, need a lift."

"He says he doesn't have any friends."

"That's one way to keep us from questioning them."

Wyatt frowned. "I don't like it," he said bluntly. "As accidents go, staged or otherwise, this leaves too much to chance. What if the Audi veers off the road before it gathers enough speed? Why put on the seat belt if the whole point is to kill the wife? And what does the suspect do, after pushing his own ride down the hill? Walk home in the pouring rain?"

"He would have to have access to another vehicle," Kevin agreed. "An accomplice."

"Which brings us to an important question: Why would a controlling husband suddenly seek to harm his wife?"

"She met someone new, was threatening to leave him."

"Or . . . ," Wyatt prodded.

Kevin got it. "*He* met someone. Wanted to leave his wife, but not halve his assets."

"Meaning maybe we're not looking for a male friend. We're looking for a woman. Who could've parked somewhere on the top of the hill. Headlights out, no one would notice the vehicle — and wait for her lover boy to get the job done."

Neither of the detectives commented on what kind of woman would do that for a man; frankly they'd seen it too many times before.

"We should return to the gas station," Wyatt said after another moment. "Pull their video footage from the last week. Study it for any vehicles that pass by multiple times in a short span of time. Say, because they're scoping out the road —"

"Or it's part of their regular commute."

"Which will be easy enough to rule out during the follow-up interviews. We can also revisit the night in question. See if anyone was hanging out between four and six A.M. Particularly a female, in a nondescript sedan, waiting for a call from her lover."

Kevin nodded. Not a fun plan; reviewing hours of grainy security video was much more difficult than a person might think. But it was a doable plan, and frankly, they needed traction.

"Still think the husband did it," Kevin said as they climbed back into their vehicle. "But I don't think we'll find him on tape. Guy's a pretty cool customer. Feels like the push down the basement stairs, the shove out the front door, were warm-up acts. Now he's getting serious about things."

"Then she shouldn't have been wearing a seat belt," Wyatt muttered.

Kevin didn't answer. They drove in silence to the gas station, got back to work.

CHAPTER 14

I float alone in the darkness. Shades drawn. Yellow quilt pulled up high. Door of the bedroom shut tight. I think my head is on fire, but as long as I keep my eyes closed, I can manage the pain. I like the darkness. It is cool, comforting.

I finger the quilt and think again of the woman who made it. I miss her, have always missed her. Funny, because you'd think the passing of years would make it easier, dull the ache. But if anything, I feel her absence more acutely now.

I don't like to dwell on it, so I call up Vero instead.

Snapshots. Three years old. Six years old. Ten, twelve, fourteen. They blur through my mind, refusing to focus. When I try to slow the parade, I get only her skeleton, asking, *"Why me, why me, why me?"*

A noise. Footsteps, moving downstairs. Thomas, I think, prowling the house. I wonder what he's been doing since the police left. Tending to household chores, cleaning up evidence? The police questions bother me. Just how likely is it for one woman to suffer three accidents in only six months? A woman without family or friends. A woman who, by all appearances, is solely dependent upon her husband. Though he tells me that's my fault, my rules of engagement.

Is it? I honestly don't know. Something about it sounds right, but why would I insist on such a thing? And what kind of man would truly leave everything, do anything, for a girl he's barely met?

I feel there's more here I should know, except the harder I try, the more the details slip away. I don't find my memories welcoming. They don't invite me closer. Instead, they whisper restlessly, *Beware, beware, beware.*

I understand that muscle memory is easier for me. Rote actions, things I do, versus things I think. By those terms, shouldn't I be able to recall putting on a coat, grabbing car keys, before my late-night drive? Or what about climbing into the car or backing out of the driveway? I try, but my mind remains blank. I see only darkness, nothing else.

Which makes me think the police might be right — I'd already been drinking that night.

I consider scotch. Eighteen-year-old Glenlivet. Best of the best. I picture a crystal tumbler filled with liquid gold, feel the smooth taste warming my tongue. On cue, saliva glands water. There's no doubt about it; I could use a drink.

Then something comes to me. An old memory.

Do you know the best place for a wife to hide something from her husband? Not her jewelry box; too obvious. Certainly not under the shared marital mattress. Or in a medicine cabinet, or in a cookie jar or stashed behind the turkey in the freezer.

No, there's one place no self-respecting husband would ever search: his wife's box of tampons, tucked beneath the bathroom sink.

More footsteps below. In my mind's eye, I can follow Thomas's progress to the rear of the house. A faint screech. The back door opening. A slight bang; back door falling shut. He's left the house, headed toward his work shed. I know this without thinking.

The temptation is immediate and overwhelming.

I push back the butter-yellow quilt, rise to

standing. Then — there's no other word for it — I sneak across the hall to the guest bath.

A single sink, undermounted in earth-tone granite, topping a hickory cabinet. Next to it is the toilet, then to the far right the bathtub. My bathroom. I used it to shower without thinking first thing this morning. Moving on memory again; reach for the plate, don't stop to think where the plate is. And sure enough, the top drawer had held my toothbrush, hairbrush, a quilted paisley bag filled with makeup.

Now I open the lower cabinet to discover a collection of bathroom cleaners, a blow dryer and, yes, a box of tampons.

I pull them out. The box rattles slightly; the tinkle of glass. And I know what I'll find inside. As I remove the token six tampons lining the top. As I expose the collection of tiny scotch-filled bottles beneath. It turns out, I have my own hidden collection of nip-size Glenlivet.

The police have it wrong; my husband didn't have to liquor me up Wednesday night, then pour me into my vehicle.

Apparently, I'm already that kind of drinker.

I'm already that kind of wife.

Now I consider the tiny bottles. Six in total. Enough for a bad afternoon or stressful night. I wonder, is it Thomas who drives me to drink? Is it Vero? Or am I my own worst enemy?

There is no muscle memory to call upon for these answers. Only a feeling that if I was smart enough to know why I did what I did, then I'd be smart enough not to do it.

I place the tampons back in the box. I place the box back in the cabinet. I don't destroy the bottles or empty out the alcohol. I'm not that strong. But a new thought has come to me, and it's compelling enough to allow me to walk away.

I know where a wife hides things from her husband. But where does a husband hide his secrets from his wife?

Now, while Thomas is in the work shed. I have to search. It's desperately important.

I creep back into the hall, ears attuned for any sound from downstairs. But the house is settled, silent. I am alone. For now.

I start in the master bedroom, with its massive four-poster bed and oversize dark-wood furniture. His domain, not mine, and when hiding secrets, the first instinct is always to keep them close. I smooth a hand under the pile of pillows, then beneath the edge of the heavy, king-size mattress. I check under the bed but find nothing but dust bunnies, dirty carpet.

Next I hit the nightstand. I can tell which side of the bed belongs to Thomas, as it's more rumpled, and sure enough the nightstand yields a pair of reading glasses, a small roll of antacids, and a collection of magazines: *Guns & Ammo, Entertainment Weekly, National Geographic.* To judge by the diversity, my husband is a regular Renaissance man.

But there is nothing sinister here; at least not his own collection of alcohol.

The bureau boasts a reading lamp, a framed picture of the two of us, and a leather box containing a vintage watch, thick gold chain and simple gold band. His wedding ring, I know without thinking. He doesn't wear it anymore because his job involves tools. But he'd wanted a ring so I'd walked to the neighborhood pawnshop, picking out the cheapest band, which was already the most two poor kids could afford. He'd smiled when I slid it onto his finger. No, he'd beamed, his entire face lighting up.

Now I am yours, he'd said, and I remember my heart pounding in my chest, instinctively scared by that level of responsibility.

The ring has an inscription inside, a date: October 3, 1993. We'd been together barely a month. What were we thinking? From first date to forever in four weeks or less?

And did the fact that we were still together twenty-two years later mean we were a success? Or that simply after so many years, we didn't know any better? Couldn't dream any bigger?

It occurs to me that given the dates, I have been with this one man for more than half of my life.

As I search his bedroom for signs of deception.

The dresser yields nothing, so I move on to the walk-in closet, pausing from time to time to listen for footsteps. But the house remains still. Thomas's job requires concentration, a focused unit of time to create an item from beginning to end. Maybe he'll be out there the rest of the day, or even into the evening. He works a lot, I know without thinking. I spend much of my time alone. But it's never bothered me. I prefer it that way.

The walk-in closet is surprisingly large and features a fancy organization system. Also cherrywood, with shelves and racks and built-in drawers, like something you'd see in a home magazine. Thomas installed it. One of his weekend-warrior projects. He did it to make me happy.

Because at least in the beginning, I'd lived

in this room, too.

Sure enough, some of the clothes in the closet are mine. Dresses, nice slacks, fancier shirts. Not my everyday wardrobe; that I discovered in the guest room closet. But the overflow, clothes I don't need to access regularly, has remained here. A sign we were working things out? Or I was just too lazy to move all of my belongings?

Thomas has rows of cargo pants, stacks of well-worn jeans, an impressive collection of long-sleeved flannel shirts. An overwhelmingly casual assortment of clothes, as befitting a man who spends his day in a work shed. I find three suits, one gray, one black, one navy blue. For funerals and weddings, I think, except if we have no friends, no families, what are we ever invited to?

I start with the drawers, searching each one. I discover socks, underwear, workout clothes, T-shirts, pajamas, pants and nothing else. Next I work my way through the small pile of shoes, mostly sneakers, hiking boots, the obligatory dress shoes, one in black, one in high-gloss brown, to go with the suits.

I try to think of the male equivalent of tampons, but I come up empty. Yet I don't stop looking. He has secrets. I know it. Because twenty-two years later, those secrets have started catching up with us. Even before we moved here. Even before my "accidents." Things have been strained between us.

Then, patting down the dark-gray suit jacket, I feel it. Something thin and flat in the lapel. I stop, search more slowly. Then pull an old, tattered envelope from the inside jacket pocket.

Just as I hear the creak of a board on the stairs.

I freeze, feeling like the proverbial kid caught with her hand in the cookie jar. There is no place for me to run. If he's already up the stairs, he has a clear view of the doorway, would spot me the moment I exit his bedroom. There's only one thing to do, then.

I don't leave the room. Instead, I jam the envelope into the back waistband of my yoga pants. Then I limp hastily across the room, breathing already ragged, and throw myself faceup onto the bed.

A second later, Thomas's voice comes from the hall. "Nicky? Nicky? You all right?"

I don't answer. Don't trust myself to speak without sounding guilty or flustered. But a moment later, I don't have to. Thomas looms in the doorway, his gaze finding me lying coffin straight on my side of the bed.

He doesn't say anything right away. Just makes his approach, eyes upon my face.

"I'm testing it out," I offer.

"And?"

"It feels familiar."

"It should. You used to sleep there." He doesn't come directly to me, but instead loops around the bed. I feel a faint pressure on the mattress as he takes his position. In contrast to my rigidity, he tucks his hands behind his head, crosses his legs at his ankles. I turn my head to study him. It's his bed, his room; he looks as if he belongs here.

"Why did I move out?"

He rolls onto his side.

"Come here," he says.

I don't immediately move.

"More testing," he says, and gestures to the space beside him. I know what he wants; I just can't do it. Then I don't have to. He comes to me, closing the space between us. Until the heat of his body is pressed next to mine. I can smell sawdust, sweat, the residual soap from his morning shower. I hold my breath, not sure what to expect, not sure what I want to happen next.

He reaches out and feathers back my long hair. The pad of his thumb is rough. I feel it trace gently around the first line of stitches, then the second, the third. I flinch, but not because he's hurting me.

"Do you wonder if we have sex?" he asks. "Two decades later, does our marriage still involve intimacy?"

I can't speak. I'm too aware of him, touch, sound, smell. I understand immediately, instinctively, that none of this is new or unfamiliar. I like his touch. Crave it, even. The feel of his body over mine. The intense look on his face as he first thrusts into me. The sound of his heart, pounding wildly in my ear.

"You still want me," he continues. "I still want you. Sometimes, I think it's the only way we still connect. In here, lights out, we find each other again. And I know you need me, want me, love me, even if you remain too quiet the rest of the day."

"Why did I move out?" I whisper. His fingers are still dancing across my face, working the edge of my hairline. Is he trying to distract me? Do I care?

"You have night terrors. Always have. But lately, after your fall down the basement steps, they've become worse. You wake up screaming, nearly out of your mind, sweat pouring down your face. If I try to touch you in any way, reach out, offer a soothing hand, you get worse."

"I hit you."

"Sometimes."

"I smashed your head with a lamp."

"That hurt."

"Then I cried. Because I didn't mean it, I really didn't, and you had blood pouring down your face."

"You thought it was best if you slept alone."

"So I couldn't hurt you."

"You think leaving our bed didn't hurt me?"

My gaze falls. I can't look at him and the vulnerability on his face. I find myself touching his chest, my palm flat, my fingers splayed. I can feel his heartbeat. It's surprisingly steady, given how fast I know my own is racing.

"Do you love me?" I hear myself ask.

"Yes."

"Why?"

He smiles; I can feel the movement of his lips against my hair. I inhale again, the scent of his skin.

"In the beginning," he murmurs, "you were so sad. It was like a tangible presence, all around you. And I thought . . . I wanted to see you smile for real. I wanted to be the man who made you happy."

"Is that love?" I asked him. "Or is that a hero complex?"

"I don't know anymore," he tells me, and I know he's being honest. "Maybe it's something in between. But when I finally did get you to smile, it all seemed worth it. And I just wanted to do it again and again. I figure there are worse ways to spend a life than making the woman I love happy."

"But I'm not happy."

"You were. At least, in the beginning. When we first left New Orleans, we went to Austin. You loved the warm weather, the great music, the dogs frolicking in Zilker Park. But then you got restless. More bad days, fewer good days, so we tried San Francisco. Then Phoenix. And Boulder, and Seattle, and Portland, and Chicago, and Knoxville and Raleigh and Fort Lauderdale and, and, and . . . You would be happy. Then you would be sad. So we would move again. Because to this day, all I want is to make you smile."

I don't speak.

"But you're right: I can't make you happy anymore," Thomas says quietly. "You wear your sadness again, and when I try to ask you questions, you refuse to answer. What do you need, how can I make you happy? Just tell me what you want. But you don't talk to me anymore, Nicky. Hell, I couldn't even get you to come clean about that damn yellow quilt."

"It's mine," I hear myself say. Immediate. Defensive.

"You ordered it on eBay three years ago. Day it came, you locked yourself in the bedroom with it and cried all day. I asked, I waited, I begged. But you've never told me why you need it so badly, what makes it so special. Most of my life I have loved you. And still, there are moments when I'm sure I don't know you at all."

"You have secrets, too," I say, conscious of the worn envelope pressed against the small of my back.

"Silence breeds silence," my husband says.

"Why do you stay with me? It sounds like I'm nothing but trouble."

"Because I haven't given up hope."

"Hope of what?"

"That someday, I can make you smile again."

He rolls away from me. I feel his absence more acutely than I would like. The air is cold, the bed empty, and for a second, my hand actually reaches out, as if I would call him back. It comes to me, what I thought the first moment I saw him. He was looking right at me, smiling right at me. And my first impression was I wished he would just go away.

But then, once he left, I wished he'd come back, because no one had ever smiled at me like that before.

I love him. I fear him. I need him. I resent him. I pull him close. I push him away.

And I have a feeling that it has nothing to do with him and everything to do with me.

"You can stay," Thomas says, rising to his feet. "Rest as long as you'd like. I'll go down, start dinner. Grilled cheese, tomato soup, sound good?"

I nod, not trusting myself to speak.

"We'll get through this," he says. Reassuring me? Reassuring himself? Maybe it's all the same. My husband leaves the room.

I wait until I hear his footsteps descend all the way down the stairs, followed by an echo from the kitchen below. Then, and only then, do I roll gingerly onto my side and pull the envelope from my back. My fingers are shaking. I set the small parcel on the bed, noting the way the edges are yellow, the paper darkened in places from old stains, perhaps the oil from a workingman's fingerprints.

He has handled this often over the years. Obviously revisited it again and again.

I find myself hesitating. A turning point. Do I really want to know? Maybe all couples need their secrets. Apparently, I still hoard mine, from a yellow quilt to a stash of scotch.

But I can't let it go. Having discovered the envelope, I need to know what it contains. So I delicately ease it open, pull out a single item: an old photograph in about as great shape as the envelope.

Faded out, yellow toned, smudged; I still know immediately what I'm looking at. A summer's day. A ten-year-old girl wearing a familiar floral dress and a small, uncertain smile.

I stifle a gasp. Reflexively clutch the picture.

Vero.

I am holding a photo of Vero.

Which my husband had hidden from me.

CHAPTER 15

Wyatt hated security camera footage. On TV crime shows, the quality was always highest resolution. You could blow it up, freeze it frame by frame, zoom in here, zoom out there, read the expiration date on the bread shelved just behind the evil perpetrator.

In reality, gas stations, convenience stores, mom-and-pop shops, were stressed-out businesses with little leftover profit to invest in things like state-of-the-art security systems. They had a tendency to go with the cheapest cameras available, weren't above purchasing used and/or out-of-date technology and reusing the same discs over and over until the results were filled with ghosts of recordings past.

Wyatt and Kevin had wanted one week's worth of security footage. The harried clerk informed them he had three days, which was all they kept in rotation. Wyatt and

Kevin had hoped for decent-quality images. They got dark, blurry footage of endless cars turning in and out of the gas station. As for cars driving by, the cameras were too far away, while the road lacked adequate lighting. They could track twin beams of approaching headlights sweeping by; that was it.

As Kevin pointed out, at least Nicky's Audi had xenon headlights, with their particular crystalline-blue beam, meaning the vehicle that swept by at 4:39 A.M. Thursday morning could very well have been Nicole's car. But could they capture a license plate? No. An image of the driver? Not a chance. A paint color, defining dent, hint of make and model, or anything else that might help them in a court of law? Shit out of luck.

Not like the clerk cared. He'd left them alone in a narrow storage room to sort it all out. From his perspective, security cameras existed to catch the guy who entered the store and placed a gun to his head. Cars idling outside, vehicles passing by on the main road, not his problem.

"Well, at least it tells us what didn't happen," Wyatt said at last.

"What didn't happen?" Kevin asked.

"Nicole Frank didn't fuel up here. Thomas

Frank didn't stop in for an energy drink to perk him up while preparing to crash his wife's car. That's something."

"And no women, beautiful or otherwise, hung out after one A.M."

"Meaning if Thomas Frank did have a lover waiting to pick him up, she didn't wait around here," Wyatt said.

Kevin agreed. "That certainly narrows things down. I can see why you're so happy with this case."

"I like your idea to check his clothes," Wyatt said after a moment. Because when one door closed, another inevitably opened.

"We don't have probable cause," Kevin reminded him. "We'd need a witness who could place Thomas Frank at the scene or, better yet, Thomas Frank personally appearing on one of these video cameras. Without that . . . We can't tell a judge we suspect him solely on the grounds that he's her husband and everyone knows it's always the husband who did it."

"Policing 101: What do we do when we don't have probable cause?" Wyatt asked.

"Stir the pot until we do."

"Exactly. I say we return to the Franks' home. We request a look at his jackets and shoes, and we do it in front of his wife."

"Makes it harder for him to say no," Kevin

acknowledged. "He won't want to look guilty."

"And maybe we get lucky, find something then and there."

"Sediment on the soles of his boots," Kevin deadpanned, "that matches the exact ratio of dirt, sand, minerals, present in the two-foot stretch of road where Nicole Frank's car plunged to its doom."

Both men rolled their eyes. Such CSI matches never occurred in real life. Best you could do in New Hampshire was compare road mixes. As in the newly paved two-mile stretch of road in Albany used a rough patch mix versus the more expensive repaving completed in North Conway. But that narrowed you down to miles, or maybe helped place a guy in a particular town. Still hardly a forensic smoking gun.

Of course, one advantage of TV: people watched the impossible enough times, they honestly thought it could be done. And there was nothing illegal about playing to those expectations. *Why, sir, I see there's sand on your shoes. Very interesting, this sand. We'll definitely be taking a sample. Yep, that's pretty important sand.*

While the sample itself might be bogus, when your suspect chooses to toss the shoes in his burn barrel the second two officers leave his house . . . Even judges grew suspicious of such behavior.

"What if Thomas has already washed his clothes?" Kevin was asking now.

Wyatt smiled. "Perfect. Gives us an excuse to check out the laundry room, scene of his wife's first accident."

"Oh, I like the way you think."

"I'd like it even better if my thinking told us what was going on with Nicole Frank."

"Give it time, my friend. Give it time."

Thomas Frank answered the door after the first ring. Less hesitation this time. Clearly a man growing resigned to his fate.

He looked tired, Wyatt thought. Stressed out. From the strain of caring for a concussed wife, or from the stress of covering his tracks? Either way, Wyatt smelled grilled cheese and tomato soup. He loved grilled cheese and tomato soup.

"Are we interrupting dinner?" Wyatt asked.

"As a matter of fact . . ."

"Then we'll keep it quick. Nicole around?"

Nicky appeared down the hall, by the family room, wearing the same yoga pants and oversize sweater from the morning. Her long brown hair appeared rumpled — maybe she'd been resting — while her face remained a quilted mess of bruises and lacerations.

"Mrs. Frank," Wyatt acknowledged.

"Good evening, Sergeant."

He noticed she didn't immediately approach, but kept her distance. She and Thomas exchanged a glance, and Wyatt began to wonder if they were interrupting more than dinner. Interesting.

"Do you mind if we look at your coats?" Wyatt asked. He and Kevin had rehearsed this on the way over. Rather than go straight after the husband, which might raise his defenses, they would ease their way into it.

"My coats?" Nicky asked in surprise.

"Coat, rain jacket, an article of outerwear you would normally wear to head out at night."

She gazed at them curiously, then looked at her husband again. When Thomas remained silent, she finally approached, opening the entryway closet. "My coats are in here."

"You remember that?" Kevin asked.

"In a manner of speaking. I don't understand. Why do you want to see my coats?"

"We checked with the hospital," Wyatt said. "Morning you were brought in, you weren't wearing a jacket."

"Maybe I left it in the car."

Wyatt thought back to the mint-clean interior of the vehicle, as pointed out by the dog handler. "No," he said.

Nicole appeared confused, but she stepped back, let them do their thing.

He and Kevin took their time. Kevin pulled out each jacket that appeared to possibly belong to a female, while Wyatt made note of all the others. None of the coats were wet or particularly filthy; then again, it had now been nearly thirty-six hours since the rainstorm had ended Thursday morning.

"These all of your jackets?" Kevin asked.

Nicky tilted her head to the side, obviously having to think about it. "I think so."

Kevin looked at Thomas. "This all of your wife's coats?"

"Yes."

"So . . . you weren't wearing a coat when you got into your car Wednesday night."

Even Nicky seemed to understand that was strange. "But it was pouring out. Had been for days."

"Cold, too."

She hesitated, looking troubled. Then, because who else could she turn to, Wyatt thought, she glanced once more at her husband.

195

"Last I saw you," he said quietly, "you were on the couch, wearing jeans, a black turtleneck and a gray fleece pullover."

Which was consistent with what the ER nurse had remembered. She'd also offered the tidbit that Thomas had been very insistent on getting his wife's bloody clothes back, regardless of the fact they were considered biohazardous waste.

"Shoes?" Wyatt asked.

Thomas shook his head. "When I saw her, she was wearing her slippers. Like now."

Kevin and Wyatt glanced at Nicky's shoes. Sure enough, she was wearing a sturdy pair of fleece-lined slippers with black rubber soles. Most likely L.L. Bean, and owned by most households in the North Country.

Now Kevin and Wyatt turned their attention to the line of shoes in the closet. Once again, Kevin drew out the smaller, female models, while Wyatt noted the male equivalents.

"Sneakers are missing," Thomas said at last. "Your running shoes."

Beside him, Nicky nodded. "My old pair. New Balance, silver with blue markings."

"You wore your sneakers out into the rain?" Wyatt asked. He hadn't thought to ask the ER nurse about Nicky's shoes. Now he wished he had.

Nicky frowned, shook her head slightly. "I wouldn't . . . My first instinct is that I'd grab my Danskos. The black clogs, right there. Sneakers soak through, and I wouldn't want to get them muddy. Whereas the Danskos . . ."

One of the most popular clogs in the wintry North, Wyatt thought. And yeah, that's what he'd figure someone would grab on a mucky night as well.

"Picture your sneakers," Kevin spoke up. "Silvery, old, maybe well-worn . . ."

Nicky closed her eyes; she seemed to understand what he wanted from her. "I should throw them away. They're old, starting to smell. But for gardening, household chores, they still come in handy."

"It's Wednesday night," Kevin intoned. "It's dark, raining. Can you hear it?"

"The wind against the windows," she whispers.

Wyatt kept his attention on Thomas, who he noticed made no move to interrupt the trip down memory lane. Because he honestly had nothing to fear from his wife's memories? Or because he was curious for the answers himself?

"I'm tired. My head hurts."

"You're resting."

"On the sofa. Thomas has gone back to

work. I think I should just go upstairs, go to bed. But I don't feel like moving."

"What do you hear? The wind, the rain?"

"The phone," Nicky murmured. "It's ringing."

Kevin and Wyatt exchanged a glance. This was new information. Apparently Thomas hadn't known either, as he straightened slightly, muscles tensing.

"Did you pick up the phone? How does the receiver feel in your hand?"

"I have to go," Nicky whispered.

"You answer the phone, pick it up," Kevin tried again. "And you hear . . ."

But Nicky won't go there. "I have to leave," she said again. "Quick. Before Thomas returns. My tennis shoes. I spot them still out in the hall from earlier in the day. I grab them. They'll have to do."

"You put on your shoes, find a coat —"

"No. No time. I have to go. Now. I need a drink."

Standing beside Wyatt, Thomas flinched but still said nothing.

"You take your car keys," Kevin intoned. "You reach into the basket, feel them with your fingers . . ."

"But that doesn't make any sense," Nicky said abruptly. Her eyes opened. She stared at all three men. "I didn't have to go out

198

into a storm to find scotch. All I had to do was head upstairs."

Thomas was clearly not a happy man. About his wife's confession that she had a secret stash of alcohol elsewhere in the house. That she'd received some mysterious phone call she'd never told him about. But he gamely led Wyatt and Kevin to the handheld receiver in the family room, to check caller history. The phone, however, didn't have any record of a call on Wednesday night.

"Could it have been on your cell phone?" Wyatt asked after a moment.

Nicky hesitated, reflexively patted her pockets. Since her scotch confession, she was studiously avoiding her husband's eyes.

"We recovered your cell phone in your vehicle," Kevin spoke up. "It's currently at the state police lab for processing."

"Oh. I guess so, that the call could've been on my cell phone."

Wyatt made a note. Cell phone records were easy to retrieve, a simple matter of a phone call to the service provider. Which beat trying to trace down the mangled phone from the state police.

"You shouldn't be drinking," Thomas spoke up abruptly.

Nicky didn't reply. She stood with her arms crossed tightly over her chest.

"You said you wouldn't," Thomas persisted. "Dammit! I've been bending over backward, trying to take care of you, ridding the house of any trace of temptation. Where the hell did you even hide it —"

"I don't know. Maybe not far from where you hide your little secrets." Nicky's voice was cool. Thomas shut up, glared at her instead.

Interesting and more interesting, Wyatt thought. Now, as long as both members of the Frank family were fighting among themselves . . .

"Mr. Frank," he said, "mind if we take a look at your shoes and coat?"

"What?"

"Your shoes and coat. You know, whatever you were wearing on Wednesday."

"I already told you, I was here —"

"Which will make our inspection very quick. But we gotta verify your story, you know. It's part of our job. As long as you're telling the truth, I'm sure you won't mind."

Thomas, no dummy, thinned his lips. But with his wife standing there, still regarding him stonily . . . He stalked back to the foyer, yanked open the closet door. "By all means. Have at it."

Kevin and Wyatt helped themselves. They identified a light Windbreaker, a heavy wool jacket, a well-used ski coat, plus a designer leather jacket, the usual suspects for a middle-aged man. Shoes lined up the same. Tennis shoes, old and new, hiking boots, well-worn. Then: a brown pair of slip-on Merrells with their thick soles heavily encrusted with sand.

Kevin pulled them out with a pencil. He gave Wyatt a serious look. "We should have these tested."

Thomas immediately held up a hand. "Wait. Tested? What do you mean?"

"This sand. Of course, I'm just a detective, not one of the lab geeks, but looks to me to be the same color, consistency, of the roadside sand near your wife's crash."

"What? It's just sand. Traditional New England sand, dumped everywhere this time of year to help manage patches of ice. Of course I have it on my shoes. After all those days of rain, damn stuff is washed up into piles everywhere. Hell, step out on my driveway."

Wyatt stared at him. "Sure? We test these shoes, the sand won't come back as matching that stretch of road?"

"Oh, give me a break."

Kevin gave Wyatt a slight shrug. They were

selling their story; Thomas just wasn't buying it.

"These all your husband's shoes?" Wyatt
asked Nicole, who'd followed them back to
the entryway.

"I think so."

"And the jackets?"

She hesitated. "Raincoat," she murmured.
"A black-and-silver raincoat. I don't see it."

Was it Wyatt's imagination, or did Thomas
flinch again?

"Mr. Frank?"

"It was wet. I wore it back and forth to
the work shed during the storm on Wednesday. Of course it became soaked."

"Where is it now?"

No doubt about it, the man's voice was
sullen. "I hung it up in the basement. In the
laundry room, for it to dry."

Wyatt glanced at Nicole. "Mind showing
us to the laundry room? Then we could be
all done here."

Nicole paled. For a moment, Wyatt
thought she might refuse. But then she
squared her shoulders, shot her husband a
look that was hard to interpret and headed
once more down the hall.

Turned out, door to the basement was
behind the entryway staircase, off the family
room. Nicole yanked open the door with

more force than was strictly necessary, snapping on a light. Wyatt made out a downward flight of rough wooden stairs, leading to a bare cement floor below.

In front of him, Nicky took a deep breath in, blew it out, then grabbed the railing and began her descent.

The stairs scared her. Wyatt noted her white-knuckle grip on the railing, the way she took each step one by one. Post-traumatic stress? he wondered. An instinctive response to the site of her first accident? He didn't ask. Just watched her slow but determined progress.

The risers felt sturdy enough, he thought, making his own descent behind her. A little narrow and steep. Coming down them with a laundry basket wouldn't be the easiest task. Day after day . . . Perhaps some kind of fall had been inevitable.

"These days, I slide the basket down," Nicky murmured, as if reading his mind. "It's probably what I should've done from the beginning. Just toss the clothes down, then make my way after them."

"What about coming back up when the clothes are clean and neatly folded?"

"That's Thomas's job now. I wash the clothes; he moves them."

"Why not have him just take over the

laundry duty?"

"He ruins my delicates," she said, and it took Wyatt a second to realize she wasn't joking.

Arriving in the middle of the basement, Wyatt discovered a surprisingly large and open space. Probably meant to be turned into a rec room, man cave, in-law suite, whatever might suit a couple best. One corner had been framed off and finished into a combination laundry room, lower-level bath.

"You guys do this?" he asked Nicky. Kevin and Thomas were still descending behind them.

"One of Thomas's first projects," she volunteered. "I told him I didn't want to do laundry all covered in spiders. So he made me a real room. Said it was his contribution to clean clothes everywhere."

"Nice setup," Wyatt observed, taking in the state-of-the-art front-loading washer and dryer, topped with a long laminate countertop to serve as a folding table. Then, of course, upper cabinets to hold laundry detergents, fabric sheets, cleaning basics.

As a carpenter himself, Wyatt appreciated Thomas's attention to detail. The room was professional grade, no doubt about it. Which made Wyatt wonder, after going through this much work to create a separate laundry facility, why the hell hadn't Thomas taken the time and effort to build a better, safer flight of stairs?

Kevin and Thomas had arrived in the basement.

"Nice work," Wyatt told the husband, indicating the space.

He merely shrugged, but Nicky volunteered: "Thomas is good with his hands."

"Obviously. Must have a good tool collection as well. Miter saw, pneumatic nail gun, cordless drills . . ."

Thomas met his eye. "In my workshop. I craft custom props, remember? A lot of that starts with wooden models, if not finished products."

"Except now you're moving to plastic," Nicky spoke up again. No doubt about it, her tone was disapproving.

Wyatt and Kevin returned their attention to Thomas. "I have a three-D printer," the man said. "Now my clients can send me digital files of their own creations, which I can turn into three-D molds with a push of a button. I call that progress. My wife considers it risky."

He glared at his wife. She glared back at him.

"My coat," Thomas said now, turning

away from Nicky to wave at a drying rack just off to the side of the dryer. Sure enough, a single silver-and-black raincoat hung from the wooden dowels. Kevin fingered the coat first, lifting the front folds this way and that.

"Dry now," he murmured to Wyatt.

"Dirty," Wyatt observed, pointing to a pale smudge marring the front, streaks of sand lining both arms.

"Of course it's dirty," Thomas said impatiently. "I wore it to my workshop. And given that I'd already turned off the heat for the day, I left on my jacket while I worked."

"Not afraid of snagging a sleeve in a power tool?" Wyatt asked.

Kevin was inspecting the left cuff of the jacket, which showed definite signs of wear. What were the chances they'd find a thread from the frayed edge of this coat snagged in the bumper of Nicole's car? Heaven forbid anything about this case would be that easy.

"We should take this for a match," Kevin said, voice deliberately loud.

"Definitely. Mind if we borrow your jacket?" Wyatt asked Thomas, who was looking defensive.

"Of course I mind. It's my only rain jacket. And I already told you. It's dirty and covered in stuff from my workshop; that's all."

"Is this more sand?" Kevin spoke up. "Like the sand on your shoes. Like the sand we found on the side of the road . . ."

"There's sand everywhere! It's New England, for God's sake, and we've already had several mornings below freezing."

"Where are Nicky's clothes?" Wyatt asked abruptly.

"What?" Thomas blinked.

"I understand from the hospital staff you took her clothes from the night of the accident."

"Nothing wrong with that —"

"Where are they? Muddy, bloody, soaked in scotch, sure as hell didn't put them away. So they should be here, right? The laundry room. Waiting to be washed."

Thomas didn't answer right away. "My wife did nothing wrong," he said abruptly.

Nicky's turn to stare at him.

"Dr. Celik showed me the tox-screen results: .06. Below the legal limit. Meaning neither of us owes you answers or explanations. It was an accident. Plain and simple. Dark, rainy night. She drove off the road. End of the story."

"Like falling down the basement stairs?"

"You saw the stairs."

"And stumbling off the front steps? Come on, Thomas. Just how *clumsy* can one woman be? Stairs, steps, driving a car. To hear you talk, your wife can't get anything right."

"Go away. We're done with you now."

"Fine. Then give us your rain jacket. And while you're at it, Nicky's clothes from that night and the tennis shoes she shouldn't have been wearing in the rain, and, oh yeah, the coat she didn't even bother to grab. Provide it all. Give us what we need to prove your *accident.* And maybe, just maybe, we'll leave you alone."

"I want to see it," Nicky spoke up suddenly.

The men stopped, stared at her. She was standing in the middle of the basement, arms crossed defensively over her chest. She wasn't looking at the jacket or at any of them. She was looking at a spot at the base of the stairs.

The spot where she'd landed, Wyatt knew without asking. The site of her first accident, when her headaches and memory loss all began.

Thomas frowned. "What do you want to see?"

"The scene of the crash. I want to visit it. Maybe it will help me."

"Nicky, you have a concussion; you're under doctor's orders to take it easy —"

"I'm going."

"You'll get another headache —"

"I don't care."

"I do! This is exactly what they're trying to do, Nicky. Can't you see that? This whole visit, this farce . . . The police are trying to come between us. It's the only way they think they'll get answers."

"Maybe I want those answers, too."

"Nicky . . ." Thomas reached out a hand toward his wife.

"What are you afraid of? Tell me, Thomas. If our life is so damn perfect, why can't the police have your rain jacket?"

Thomas didn't answer. Nicky shot him one last look, then turned and stalked up the stairs.

"All I've ever wanted," Thomas muttered, "was to keep her safe. Take the jacket, all right. Take whatever you want. Then leave us alone. We were better off without you. You have my word."

He headed up the stairs, chasing his wife.

CHAPTER 16

Thomas follows me up to my bedroom. I think he'll protest more. Maybe grab me by my shoulders, turn me roughly until I have no choice but to face him. Through sheer force of personality, he'll get his way. Do I want him to argue? Manhandle me physically? Pin me against his chest? Is this how our arguments usually end?

But he does nothing at all. Merely stands in the doorway as I pick out a pair of jeans, a heavier sweater, from the guest room closet.

Maybe he didn't come up to argue. Maybe he's simply waiting for me to hand over my stash of scotch.

I close the door in his face so I can change my clothes, finish my preparations. But when I open it two minutes later, Thomas is still waiting for me.

"Are you coming?" I ask curiously, having expected him to update his own wardrobe.

"No."

It brings me up short. Somehow, I'd been sure he'd ride along, if only to continue his role of protective husband.

"I need to work," he says.

"Seriously? Your job is that important?"

"This project is."

The detectives, Wyatt and Kevin, are waiting for us downstairs. I should get moving. But when I go to push pass my husband, he touches my arm, light enough, gentle enough, to draw me up short.

"Why?" he asks quietly. "I've certainly done everything in my power to help you. And still you have a secret supply of scotch?"

I don't say anything, just feel my heart accelerate in my chest. Shame, I think. Remorse. Guilt. Something else I can't quite figure out. I can't look him in the eye. I don't dare pull away. And I still don't volunteer to hand over my stash.

"If you can't dump it," Thomas continues, "at least tell me where it is. While you're gone, I'll take care of it."

"No."

"Nicky, for the love of God, I just got you out of the hospital —"

"It's all I have," I hear myself whisper, and I understand in that moment that it's true. I don't have family. I don't have friends. I don't remember my past; I don't know if I have a future. What I have is a hoarded treasure trove of tiny little bottles. No more, no less.

"You have your quilt," my husband says.

I frown at him, uncertain. He points to the daybed, where I notice the butter-yellow quilt has been folded neatly and placed at the end. Did he do that? Did I do that and already forget?

"You should take the quilt with you," Thomas tells me. "Maybe it'll bring you luck."

"I can't go on a ride along with two cops with a blanky. That's . . . ridiculous."

"Nicky."

The tone of his voice is serious. So serious I pause again, find myself studying him long and hard. A million images flash across my mind. Us laughing, us kissing, us racing across sandy beaches, us scaling rocky mountain cliffs. We lived. We loved. And once, it had been enough. I know all that, staring at him.

I'm sad, in a place way down deep that prior to now, I didn't even know existed. I'm going to lose him. Have known that for a while now. Perhaps even a better reason to hoard secret bottles of scotch. Because for twenty-two years, this man has been my world. He's my sole companion, my best friend, my biggest burr of annoyance, and my largest source of solace. He's been my *everything*.

Except that kind of relationship isn't healthy. For either of us.

"Take the quilt with you," my husband murmurs. "The next few hours are going to be demanding. You might get tired, suffer another headache. The detectives will understand you having a blanket in case you need to rest."

He's already reaching for the quilt as he speaks. He presses the solid square in my arms, where I instinctively clutch it against my chest. I feel the softness of the familiar fabric against my fingers, inhale a scent that is both comforting and lonely.

I cried when this quilt came in the mail. Now I want to cry again.

"You have a picture of Vero," I hear myself say.

"No, I don't."

"Yes, you do. I found it in your closet."

My husband smiles, but it is sad, faint. "No," he repeats quietly. "I don't. Now, if you're really going to do this, time to go downstairs, get it done.

"Just remember," he says, as he moves me

away from him. "The problem with asking questions is that you can't control all the answers. Life is like that. Especially for you and me."

The detectives are clearly surprised that Thomas isn't joining us. They exchange glances but don't immediately say anything. Nor do they comment on the blanket I'm carrying under my arm. Apparently Thomas is right: A woman with a concussion can get away with most anything.

The younger detective — Kevin, the sergeant had called him — is holding Thomas's raincoat. Apparently, my husband agreed to part with it after all. So they could test sand. Funny, I'd never thought about it before, but in New England, there's a lot of roadside sand.

Except not in our driveway or in our backyard. Thomas had lied about that.

I place the folded quilt on one of the lower steps, open the hall closet, and reach automatically for my tan, flannel-lined barn jacket. Next I find my black clogs, because in the backcountry, with mucky roads and sidewalks, clogs are my shoes of choice. Not my tennis shoes. I can't imagine Wednesday night why I grabbed tennis shoes.

Because they were sitting right there and I

had to get out fast.

The phone ringing.

Hello, I said.

And then . . .

My head hurts. I rub my temples unconsciously. I should take more Advil. Or maybe serious painkillers. But I don't want to fog myself even more. I might be the one who ordered this little jaunt, but I'm also the one fatiguing fast. Thomas hadn't been wrong. I really do need to rest.

I reach into the closet for one last thing. Peg behind the door. It isn't there. I finger the spot again, and the older detective, Wyatt, catches the motion.

"What are you looking for?"

I have to think about it. "A hat."

"What kind of hat?"

"Ball cap. Black." With a brim I can pull low. For example, to better obscure my features when purchasing from the local liquor store.

I shake off the memory, feeling unpleasant, vaguely dirty, like I've walked through spiderwebs.

"You're sure your husband isn't coming?" the other detective, Kevin, checks.

"He has to work."

"He works a lot," Wyatt states.

I nod, because what can I say? According

to Thomas this project is important. Except I have no idea what the project is.

The detectives escort me out of the house. They're driving one of the county's white-painted SUVs, the NORTH COUNTRY SHERIFF'S DEPARTMENT emblazoned on the side. I've seen the vehicles parked enough times along the back roads. Sometimes, the uniformed officers engage in traffic stops, but Thomas once told me deputies spent most of their time transferring prisoners around the state. The vehicles I see parked here and there are actually waiting to receive or hand off inmates.

Maybe that's why I feel so uncomfortable when the detectives open the rear passenger door and gesture for me to climb in. My wrists should be cuffed, I think. This is it: the beginning of the end.

I'm surprised when Kevin goes around, gets in the other side next to me. To watch my responses, play more of the memory game? Or do they not trust me alone?

I place the quilt on my lap. The feel of it against my clasped hands helps ground me and I'm glad I brought it.

Wyatt puts the large vehicle into gear, backs out of our drive.

I have one last glimpse of my home. Thomas's dark frame silhouetted in the upstairs window.

Then my husband disappears from me.

We drive for a while in silence. There is a barrier between the backseat and the front, formed from Plexiglas maybe, something scratchy but clear. The rear seat isn't the hard plastic used in so many squad cars for easy cleaning after transporting vomiting drunks. Instead, Kevin and I share the SUV's original gray upholstered bench seat. It's comfortable enough, makes it easier to pretend we're all just friends going out for a drive.

If I look ahead, though, into the front section of the sheriff's transport, I can see the bulked-up dash, with radio, mounted laptop and all kinds of bells and whistles even my cutting-edge Audi never had. Wyatt is murmuring something into the radio, though with the divider closed it's hard to hear. Making further arrangements? Maybe I'll end the night arrested yet.

I try to look out my window, but the impression of rushing darkness makes me nauseous. I wish I were back in the upstairs bedroom, lying beneath my quilt with an ice pack on my forehead. The cool black. The icy oasis to ease the throbbing in my head.

The SUV slows, comes to a stop. Blinker is on. We make a right turn. Off my back road onto a more major thoroughfare. Five minutes pass, maybe ten; then civilization begins to appear. A small strip mall here, a gas station, grocery store, there. A New Hampshire state liquor store.

I feel my body tense. Ready to turn in. Where I buy my supply, I think without thinking. But the sheriff's vehicle keeps on driving.

"Familiar?" Kevin asks me, clearly cuing off my body language.

"I run my errands here."

"Makes sense. Shops closest to your house."

"The bottle of scotch I had that night. Do you know where I bought it from?"

"Yeah, we do."

"Was it there, that state liquor store?" Because in New Hampshire, you can buy beer and wine in a grocery store, but not hard liquor. That's controlled by the state.

"Not that store," the detective says, surprising me.

The vehicle is still moving. This road is nicely paved, which is always a perk in the North Country. I find myself closing my eyes, allowing the movement to lull me. I'm tired. Very tired. That underwater feeling has returned. As if none of this is real, or even happening.

I'm floating along, weightless, senseless. If I could just stay this way, maybe I would never be hurt again.

"Mommy, mommy, look at me. I can fly."

But it's not the flying that's the hard part. It's the landing, always the landing, that gets us in the end.

I hear myself sigh. A long and mournful sound.

Then the vehicle stops.

Kevin says, "We're here."

When I first climb out of the sheriff's SUV, I'm confused. We're not on some darkened back road, but at another small shopping plaza. Local store/deli/gas station, what appears to be a real estate office and, yes, another New Hampshire state liquor store. I don't know this place, is my first thought. Yet I do.

I set down the folded quilt on the backseat, reaching for something instead. Hat, I realize belatedly. I'm still looking for my hat to hide my face from the store cameras. Just as I always do.

Then I feel the first pinprick of unease. Because I'm honestly not sure: Am I trying to keep from being recognized in area liquor stores, or am I trying to keep from being recognized on local security cameras?

Both detectives are now waiting for me.

"Why are we here?" I ask.

"Let's go inside," Wyatt says, "have a look around."

I'm in trouble. I'm not sure where or how, but this isn't what I wanted, what I expected. The police are supposed to take me to the scene of my car accident. I will walk around. I will know exactly what I was doing, thinking, that night. I will fly through the air. I will finally find Vero. She will forgive me.

Instead we are . . . here.

"I don't want to," I stall.

"Just for a moment," Wyatt says.

"I have a headache."

"Bet the store sells aspirin."

I can't move. I just stare at him. Am I begging, am I pleading, can he see it in my eyes? "I bought the bottle of scotch from this store, didn't I? That's why you brought me here. So I'll recognize exactly where I screwed up that night."

"Let's go inside," Wyatt repeats. "Have a look around."

Then he and the other detective are already walking. I feel like I don't have a choice anymore. This is it. Time to confront my fate.

The squat gray building has made some attempt at New England architecture. A covered front entrance, cupola on top, a few false dormers to make it appear more like a house, less like a giant booze-filled supercenter. The automatic doors slide open at our approach. I'm relieved Wyatt and Kevin are in street clothes, because being escorted in by two uniformed officers would've been too much. Still, there's no way to disguise the way they move, assess the scene. They are more than ordinary shoppers, and everyone who looks up seems to realize it. One woman, with a shopping cart piled high with vodka, instinctively looks away. I share her shame.

No one wants a cop in a liquor store, any more than they'd want a priest in a brothel.

I can't look up. I wander the aisles, find myself almost immediately in front of the collection of scotch. But of course. The Glenlivet is shelved at eye level to entice buyers. The store carries an impressive collection of vintages, including the higher-end eighteen-year-old vice of my choice. I can't help it. I want them all. My hands start to tremble; then my whole body shakes.

My head pounds, but I also want to vomit. They shouldn't have brought me here, I think resentfully. Taking a woman with a head injury on an unnecessary side trip. Taking a recovering drinker to a liquor store.

I shoot them both hard stares and have the satisfaction of seeing that at least they're worrying the same.

"You okay?" Wyatt asks.

"I don't want to be here."

"But you recognize this store," Kevin says. "You walked straight to this aisle."

"You already knew that!" I'm still angry. I focus my attention on the dirty gray linoleum floor. Anyplace but at the booze.

"Did you come here Wednesday night?" Wyatt asks.

"I don't know. Maybe. Probably. I guess."

"Why here?" Kevin picks.

"To buy scotch. Why the hell do you think?"

"You said earlier you were in a hurry that night," Wyatt presses. "You had to leave fast."

"Yes."

"So why come here? Forty minutes from your house, when there's another state liquor store much closer."

I blink my eyes, press my hand against my stomach to ease the churn. I don't know. I can't answer his question. He's right. Kevin pointed out the closer store and I knew it, recognized it instantly. So why would I have driven all the way out here?

I shake my head. My nausea won't abate. My headache is worse and the lights in the store are now hurting me. Dozens of sharp daggers, driving into my temples.

"I think I'm going to be sick," I mutter.

The detectives exchange another look. I decide I hate them. I wish Thomas were here. I want to curl up against his chest. I want to feel his fingers working their magic on my hairline. He would make me feel better. He would take care of me.

Because he is my everything. Except I'm about to lose him, because I never deserved him in the first place. Vero tried to tell me, but I wouldn't listen.

Run, she has told me. So many times over the years. Run, run, run. But I don't do it. I can't.

My face itches. The stitches. And for just one moment, I am tempted to reach up, tug at the first ugly black thread. Maybe I can remove the seams, then detach my own face, like a section of quilt. I wonder who I would find, lurking beneath my own skin.

Wyatt has a hold of my arm. He is urging me forward and I realize belatedly they are finally taking me seriously. I've freaked out enough that we're leaving the store. Forget the accident site. I'm going home. I need to lie down. Close my eyes. Up in my little room, the cool black. Like a coffin. An early grave.

Wyatt takes me to the cashier line, as if we're making a purchase. My footsteps slow, grow more leaden. He needs to take me outside. Why isn't he taking me outside? I need fresh air.

The cashier is staring straight at us. She is an older woman with graying brown hair and the face of someone who's already had a hard day, or maybe a hard life.

She still makes an effort: "Honey, you okay?" she asks me gently.

I can't help myself.

I take one look at her, then promptly vomit all over the floor.

CHAPTER 17

As experiments went, this hadn't been the slam dunk Wyatt had expected. Thank heavens for the cashier lady, Marlene, an older woman who'd clearly seen it all. She didn't bat an eye at their puking witness, but bustled around the counter, instructing them to take the poor woman outside while she got the mop.

Not that Wyatt and Kevin didn't have experience cleaning up vomit — that was one of those skills learned quickly on the job — but it was still nice to have some help.

Kevin had gotten Nicky into the backseat. She'd promptly laid down with the yellow blanket clutched in her arms like a teddy bear. Kevin had made the mistake of offering to unfold it, drape it around her shoulders. She'd nearly attacked him.

Mood volatility. Another sign of serious brain trauma.

Now Wyatt headed back into the liquor

store. He'd called in on their way over, to confirm that Marlene Bilek had been working tonight, just as she had on Wednesday night. Even luckier, she'd been the one tending the register when they'd arrived. And now, survey said . . .

Wyatt found the woman in the back, emptying out the contents of the mop bucket. Smelled vile. Given that the Franks had eaten tomato soup for dinner, looked it, too.

"Sorry 'bout that," he said.

The woman shrugged. "Can't work in a liquor store and not deal with barf."

"Same with policing."

She smiled, but it was a tired look. Job couldn't be easy, especially given incidents like this.

"You recognize her?" Wyatt asked.

"I think so. Wednesday night, right? She was dressed differently. Dark clothes. And a hat. Black baseball hat pulled low. That's what made me notice her — thought she was dressed for trouble, and in a liquor store, we gotta pay attention to these things. But she didn't really do anything. Just roamed around for a while. Aisle by aisle. I was about to ask her if she needed help when she grabbed a bottle of whiskey, something like that. Paid for it and was gone."

"How long would you say she was in the store?" Wyatt asked.

"Fifteen, twenty minutes."

Wyatt frowned. That was a long time for a woman who was supposedly in a hurry. Twenty minutes, combined with the long drive out here . . . A woman dressed for trouble and going out of her way to find it.

"Did she talk to anyone?" he asked. "Another customer, store employee?"

The sales clerk shrugged. "Can't really say. It was a busy night. Lot going on. Not like I spent all my time watching her."

Wyatt nodded, wishing once again the state store's security cameras hadn't messed up the recordings for Wednesday night. And yet, these things happened. Unfortunately, more often than a good detective liked. He fished out a card, handed it over to Marlene, who was now tucking the mop bucket in a corner. "Thank you very much. Sorry again for the mess, and if there's anything else you remember, please give me a buzz."

"Sure. She gonna be okay?" Marlene asked. "Poor girl looked pretty sick."

"She's resting; that'll help."

"What'd she do, anyway?"

"What do you mean?"

"You're a detective. You and that other guy escorted her into the store; now you're asking all these questions. So what did she do?"

"That's what we're trying to figure out."

"She lose someone?"

Wyatt paused. "Why do you ask?"

"Because she looks so sad. And I know sad. That girl, she's got one helluva case of the blues."

Wyatt was still churning things over in his head when he exited the store to find Kevin waiting for him.

"Got word from the cell company on the call Nicole received Wednesday night."

"And?"

He followed Kevin to their white SUV, where Nicky remained curled up in the fetal position in the back. She didn't look up when Wyatt approached. To judge by how tightly her eyes were squeezed shut, Wyatt didn't think the woman was asleep, as much as she was purposefully shutting them out.

"Caller ID doesn't belong to a person," Kevin provided, "but to a company."

"Which is?"

"An investigative firm out of Boston." Kevin paused, regarded him intently. "Northledge Investigations," he stated.

Wyatt closed his eyes. "Ah, shit."

Wyatt left Kevin to babysit their charge while he walked across the parking lot, zipping up his coat against the evening chill. Weather service had already recorded a couple of nights in single digits. And it was still only November, meaning at this rate, it was going to be a tough winter. People cooped up by the snow, half-crazed from the cold. Yeah, another excellent season to be a cop.

He dialed Tessa with his back to Kevin. Pick up, pick up, he thought, preconditioned to liking the sound of her voice, even if he worried about what she might say to him next.

Third ring, he got his wish:

"Hey." She sounded breathless. As if he caught her in the middle of something. For a moment, he let himself smile. God, he loved this woman. Which was good, because she was probably gonna ream him a new one.

"Hey yourself," he said. "Busy with something?"

"Just leaving a restaurant. None of us felt like cooking. Headed to Shalimar instead."

Indian restaurant. One of Sophie's favorites. It always surprised him, because when

Wyatt had been nine, he'd been strictly a burger or dog man. Kids these days.

"How'd your lunch with Detective Warren go?" he asked. They'd never ended up catching up last night. Nor this morning, for that matter. Which, now that he thought about it, his bad. Usually they touched base at least once, if not twice a day. But given this case, he'd been preoccupied . . .

Tessa was a grown-up, he reminded himself. Had been on the job, too. She understood these things.

Except when she answered his question, her voice sounded remote, not at all like her. "Oh, fine. I explained investigative services to D.D. She explained why she preferred being a cop. Now we'll both wait for the state of her injury to render the verdict."

"Sophie okay?" Wyatt asked, still trying to get a bead on Tessa's mood. "Have a good week at school?"

"Yeah."

"And your day?"

"Fine."

The sound of car doors slamming shut. Then Tessa's voice, more muffled as she addressed Sophie, probably Mrs. Ennis as well. "It's Wyatt. I need a moment; then we'll be on our way."

They must still be in the parking lot of the restaurant, Wyatt deduced, just now returning to the car. A former state trooper, Tessa hated people who drove while talking on their phones. Ergo, she'd make her family wait for her to finish the call before hitting the road. Which would explain her distraction. She was talking to him but still dealing with her family. Of course.

He decided there was no good way of doing it. In for a penny, in for a pound.

"I got a question for you," he announced.

"Okay."

"Remember my single-car accident? Possible aggravated DWI?"

"Yes."

"Turns out, driver got a call on her cell shortly before she took off that night. Her name is Nicole Frank."

Pause, while he waited to see if Tessa would respond to that name. Of course, she was a seasoned professional, so when she didn't, he continued, evenly enough:

"Number was registered to a company: Northledge Investigations."

More silence now. But Wyatt knew Tessa well enough to imagine the small but significant changes in her body language. Sitting up straighter in the driver's seat. Grip tightening on the phone. Expression smoothing out.

He also understood that right about now, Sophie, sitting in the backseat, would be noticing these changes as well, and also going on high alert.

If Tessa hadn't been irritated with him before, then this oughta do it.

"Why did you call, Wyatt?" she asked quietly.

"Gotta start somewhere."

"So you thought your best move would be to ask your girlfriend to violate the confidentiality of her clients?"

"No. Not what I'm asking."

He was rewarded with more silence. Then Sophie's voice from the back: "Mom, what's going on?"

"Nothing." An automatic reply spoken to the child. Followed by a more direct tone, delivered straight to him: "Wyatt. It's late. It's been a long week. I know you're only doing your job, but I can't help you. You know that."

"She doesn't remember."

"Who?"

"Nicole Frank. The driver. Our perpetrator. Or our victim. Hell, I don't even know. She's suffered three concussions, remember? It's messed her up, deleted some items from the hard drive. Which is starting to scare her. The husband, remember? The one even you worried might be the cause of three accidents? I gather things are a little tense on the home front, and Nicky has decided she needs answers. She's out with us tonight, trying to retrace her final drive. Except she can't remember the details. She knows she received a call. She remembers she had to get out of the house. The rest remains a mystery to her."

"What do you want from me?"

"I know you can't answer my question directly — that would betray confidentiality. But what if I got her on the line? Or had Nicky call in to Northledge? Maybe you could arrange for the right person" — because it was a large firm, with many investigators other than Tessa — "to be there to receive her call. Answer her questions."

"That might be possible," Tessa finally conceded, but he noticed that her voice remained cool. "Assuming she's a client. Could be she was contacted as part of another investigation."

"True." Wyatt hadn't actually thought about that. "You're right. But she received the call late on Wednesday. And afterward, she felt she had to leave immediately. Sounds to me more like someone who

received information — important information — and had to respond to it."

"Where did she go?"

"A liquor store."

"News that drove her to drink?"

"Or maybe news that drove her to meet.
I'm still working on that one."

"She's with you," Tessa asked abruptly.

"In the back of the SUV as we speak. But
she's not in any condition to talk at the moment. Headache, nausea, that sort of thing."

"So you want me to talk to her, but she
can't talk?"

"I have to start somewhere, Tessa."

"Wyatt, I can't deliver potentially confi-
dential information to you. That's not who
I am and not who you want me to be."

"Okay." Wyatt didn't press the point. He
wasn't surprised by Tessa's refusal. She did
take confidentiality seriously, as well she
should. And yet, he did have to start somewhere, and it wasn't unheard of for an
investigator to help out another investigator,
let alone two investigators with a personal
relationship . . .

He was disappointed. But mostly, he was
still trying to understand his girlfriend's
distant tone. Right from the beginning of
the conversation. Even before he'd waded
into forbidden waters.

"You okay?" he spoke up at last.

"Boundaries, Wyatt. Given our jobs, both of us have boundaries. I can respect yours, but if this is going to work, I need you to respect mine as well."

"I understand."

"Do you?"

"Of course. Tessa —"

"It's late. I need to go. We can catch up in the morning. Maybe I can work out something for you then. Good night, Wyatt."

"Okay. Um, thanks. I'll touch base tomorrow."

Wyatt ended the call. But he remained uncomfortable. Boundaries, his girlfriend of six months was telling him. Except suddenly, he was worried she wasn't speaking about professional issues at all.

When he returned to the SUV, Kevin was standing near the driver's door, making notes on his little spiral-bound pad.

"You're still alive," he observed, having no illusions about the dangers of pissing off Tessa Leoni.

"That much faith in my charms? Tessa would be totally delighted to help us out."

Kevin gave him a look.

"Fine. She argued confidentiality, with a sidebar on respecting her professional

235

integrity. But she might be willing to talk to Nicky directly in the morning, assuming Nicky's recovered by then."

Kevin shrugged philosophically. In other words, Northledge was currently a dead end.

"How she's doing?" Wyatt asked, gesturing to the backseat of the vehicle.

"Hasn't moved a muscle."

"Have you checked on her? I'm pretty sure it's bad for taxpayers to die while in our care."

"Checked. Frankly, she's pretty out of it. Probably time to take her home."

Wyatt didn't argue. On the other hand, he had a feeling once they returned Nicky to her husband, they'd never get her out again.

"Why do you think she came here?" Wyatt asked Kevin. "Gets a call. Has such a sense of urgency she grabs her closest pair of shoes, sneakers, even though they're a lousy choice for a rainy night, while forgoing a coat. Then proceeds to drive nearly an hour to a liquor store well beyond her closest shopping center. Then, according to the sales clerk, Nicky spends another fifteen, twenty minutes wandering the store, before finally grabbing a bottle of scotch."

"Didn't know what she felt like drinking?"

Wyatt's turn to give his partner a look.

Then again: "Why an eighteen-year-old bottle of Glenlivet? Pretty specific, not to mention expensive, choice, if you're just looking to get drunk."

"Good memories?"

"She doesn't have any. Except . . ." Wyatt paused, collected his thoughts. "What if she was meeting someone? That's what the phone call was about. The liquor store is the designated spot, so first she looks for the person in the store. Then when she can't find them . . ."

"Buys the person's favorite bottle of scotch?"

"Or something significant to both of them."

"And heads out into the parking lot."

"Where she must ultimately locate him or her, right?" Wyatt continued. "Because she purchases the scotch at ten, but her accident isn't until five A.M. Meaning there's seven hours unaccounted for."

Kevin looked around. At the relatively quiet plaza, near-empty parking lot. "According to cashier Marlene, the liquor store was busy that night. But the plaza as a whole, the mall parking lot . . . Bet it was mostly quiet. Bet you could sit in a car, chat all you wanted without anyone caring."

"So who'd she meet?" Wyatt asked him.

"Lover? Long-lost friend? Used some social media site to reconnect with a former flame, then came out here to take things up close and personal?"

Wyatt shrugged. "What woman grabs old sneakers and a baseball cap for a booty call?"

"One I'd like to meet," Kevin assured him.

"If that's what it was about, they'd pick a hotel, someplace more . . . suitable. This feels more . . . *Magnum, P.I.*"

"*Magnum, P.I.?*"

"You know. Meet with the undercover investigator in the parking lot of the grocery store to receive the surveillance photos of your cheating spouse. That sort of thing."

Kevin rolled his eyes, then gestured with his head toward their out-of-commission charge.

"We should take her home," he said again.

But Wyatt just couldn't do it. They were pushing their luck. With the case, with Nicky's fragile mental state.

He still heard himself say, "Not just yet."

CHAPTER 18

Vero is in the closet. She is wedged back as far as she can go, knees clutched tight against her chest, while the woman piles blankets on her.

"Don't make a sound," the woman orders, voice low, tone fearful. "He's had a bad day; that's all. Temper's a little hot. So be good. Stay out of the way. Understand me, child?"

Vero nods. She's afraid of the dark. She doesn't want to be trapped alone in a cramped, smelly closet. But by now she understands there are worse things than abstract terrors. For example, why worry about the monster beneath the bed when a very real bogeyman sleeps on top of it?

I want to comfort her. I feel her growing dread as my own. But when I reach out my hand, nothing happens. I'm here, but I'm not here. I'm the outsider looking in. And I keep my attention on Vero because the woman . . . the woman hurts too much.

The woman steps back. She's done the best she can. It won't be enough; I know that. But at least she tried, and for a woman leading her life, that's something.

Footsteps, down the hall. The sounding board of my life, I think. Footsteps thudding down corridors, menacing me.

The woman closes the closet door. Not all the way; she leaves a faint sliver of light because once Vero had panicked in the pitch-black and had started to scream. The man hadn't liked that. He'd beaten them both until their faces were bloody and Vero had lost consciousness. The woman had had to wait until he finally rolled over, snoring loudly, before she could ease out of the bed and curl up around her daughter's motionless form.

She'd held her all night long, rocking sound-lessly, begging her baby girl not to die, because she was all she had, her only hope, her one bright light. Without her, she'd be lost in the dark, and though the woman couldn't say it out loud, all of her life, she'd been afraid of the dark, too.

Vero had survived. Another night, another day, another week, another month. The woman survived, too, and so they rolled along in this seedy little apartment, both living in dread of footsteps down the hall.

Tonight, the man staggers into the bedroom.

240

His shirt is already off, his hairy belly rolling over the waistband of his sagging jeans.

"Woman," he roars, reaching for his belt. "Why the fuck aren't you naked?"

In the back of the closet, Vero whimpers.

I'm sorry, I try to tell her. You shouldn't be seeing this. You shouldn't be living this.

But we both know this is nothing new, and the worst is yet to come. Outside these walls. In an entirely different place with scores of footsteps tramping down floorboards. The woman isn't perfect, but at least she tries. Soon, sooner than Vero realizes, the woman will be gone and all she'll have is a rosebush with bloody thorns climbing up a wall. Then this dirty closet will seem like paradise, if only Vero had known it at the time.

The woman strips off her stained blue housecoat. Best to do as he says. No only makes things worse.

The man grunts in approval. Kicks his pants off. Demands the now-naked woman come over, get to work.

Vero closes her eyes. She doesn't like to see, but there is nothing she can do about the sounds. Once she tried humming, but he found her and beat her again.

"Kids are to be seen, not heard!" he'd roared at her, which Vero had found confusing, because best she could tell, she wasn't allowed to be seen either. She reappeared in the apartment only once the man went to work. Then she and her mother were together, and briefly, all was well. Until the sound of footsteps in the outside hall. The jiggle of a key in the apartment's front door.

This is Vero's life. At six, who is she to argue?

The noises finally stop. The woman is crying softly, but that's nothing new. Vero is rocking back and forth. She's hungry. She needs to pee. But she waits for the sound of snoring. That's the all clear, the signal it's safe to come out.

Eventually, after it seems forever has passed, the man falls asleep. The closet door eases open. The woman stands there.

Her right eye is swollen. She moves gingerly, as if her entire body aches. But neither she nor the girl comments. This is the woman's life, too, and she learned long ago not to argue.

The woman helps Vero out of the closet. They tiptoe out of the bedroom, into the cramped family room, the tiny kitchenette. Vero finally pees, but doesn't flush the toilet. For the next few hours she and the woman share the same goal: Don't wake the slumbering beast.

The woman makes Vero a bowl of cereal.

She doesn't eat herself, just lights a cigarette, stares tiredly at the far wall. Sometimes, the woman goes quiet for so long, Vero worries she's dead, eyes open but unseeing.

Then Vero will climb onto the woman's lap and hug her tight. And generally, after a moment or two, the woman will sigh. Long and sad. Like she has years, lifetimes, oceans, of sad to let out. Vero cannot make the sad go away. She just sits there and lets it envelop her, too, until eventually, the woman gets up and lights another cigarette.

Vero eats her Cheerios. She carries her bowl to the sink, rinses it carefully, places it in the drying rack.

"Can we go to the park?" Vero asks.

"Maybe tomorrow."

"Okay, Mommy. Love you."

"Love you, too, child. Love you, too."

She is gone. Six-year-old Vero disappears. Six-year-old Vero never stood a chance. And now it is me and old and wiser Vero, back in the princess bedroom, drinking scotch out of teacups, watching the roses bleed.

"You should've killed me sooner," Vero says.

I pick up my china cup, take another sip of scotch. And I remember. The woman. The park. What will happen next.

"I'm sorry," I say.

Then we sit in silence, one lost child and woman, twice returned from the dead.

A knock on the window. It forces me to open my eyes, get my bearings. I'm lying across the bench seat in the back of the sheriff's SUV. My mouth tastes chalky and foul, and I'm clutching the yellow quilt against my chest. It makes a crinkling sound as I sit up, set it on the seat beside me.

The other detective, Kevin, is standing outside the vehicle, looking in. "You okay?" he asks through the window.

I nod. He pops open the door, and now both him and the sergeant in charge, Wyatt, study me.

"Can we get you something?" Wyatt asks.

"Water." I hesitate. "I think I'll go inside. Freshen up in the ladies' room."

They don't outright exchange glances, but still take a minute to consider my request.

"I'll walk you in," Wyatt says at last. "Kevin can buy you a bottle of water."

"Don't trust me in a liquor store alone?" I ask him.

He says, "No."

When I get out of the car, my legs are shaky. If I'm being truly honest, my head still throbs dully and the glare from the overhead parking lot lights makes me want to scream. I'm weak, faintly nauseous and completely disoriented. I have to focus on the cold to remember I'm now in New Hampshire and not in some tower bedroom. I have to study my shoes to remind myself I'm a fully functioning adult and not a child, still crammed into the back of a closet.

"Headache better?" Wyatt asks, as if reading my mind.

"No."

"What works best?"

"An ice pack. A dark, quiet room."

"Well, we'll get you home soon enough."

We're back at the liquor store. The automatic doors swoosh open. I wince immediately at the influx of too many lights.

Wyatt takes my arm and physically guides me along one wall toward the sign that reads RESTROOMS. I can't help myself; I look for the cashier, the one who was nice to me before I threw up. I want to see her again. I'm running low on acts of kindness tonight.

But I don't detect any sign of her. Some bored kid is manning the register now. I wouldn't buy scotch from him, I think immediately. I wouldn't want to deal with his knowing snicker.

Wyatt stands outside the family restroom while I clean up. My color is horrible, completely washed out, except, of course, for the nasty patchwork of stitches and bruising. I look like a crack addict. This is your brain on scotch, I think. Except I haven't had a drink in at least . . . forty-eight hours? I wonder, if I'm truly an alcoholic, shouldn't I be detoxing? Maybe that's why I got sick, why my head hurts so damn much.

But I associate sweating and trembling with detox, and I don't see any beads of moisture dotting my skin. I'm mostly tired. A woman with a battered brain who should be resting, not gallivanting through liquor stores.

I rinse out my mouth. Splash water on my face. Wash my hands again and again. Then, this is it. I open the door, face my police escort.

"Are you going to take me home now?" I ask Wyatt.

"We'll work our way there," he says.

Which means he's not.

Kevin sits in the back of the SUV with me again. He purchased three bottles of water, one for each of us. Wyatt has his unopened in the cup holder up front. Both Kevin and I sip our bottles, riding in silence. From time to time, I run my hand through the folds of the yellow quilt, feeling the edges of something that shouldn't be there.

But now is not the time or place. Later, when the detectives finally leave me alone . . .

We wind our way through long, looping back roads. No streetlights. No guardrails. No center divider. Welcome to northern New Hampshire. None of us can see beyond the glow of the headlights. We could be driving through deep woods, past scattered houses, through tiny villages. Anything is possible.

Wyatt is talking on his cell phone, but the words are too muted through the barricade for me to follow. I'm uncomfortable, though. The longer we drive, the deeper we head into the night, the more I think nothing good will come of this.

Finally, a gas station looms ahead. The vehicle slows. In the rearview mirror, Wyatt glances at me.

"Gonna top off," he says.

He turns off the road, eases in front of a pump.

"Hungry?" Kevin asks me. "Want a snack or anything?"

Then, when I hesitate:

"Come on. Let's see if they have anything good inside."

They're testing me, I realize. Just how many places did I stop that night? And will I vomit at all of them?

I climb down from the SUV, leaving my quilt only reluctantly. Wyatt goes to work with the gas pump. I follow Kevin into the gas station, wincing once at the bright lights, wishing I had my hat.

Inside is nothing special. I don't puke or grab my head and scream in agony. Instead, I follow Kevin up and down snack aisles. He settles on Pringles; I go with a pack of gum.

Up front, the bearded guy manning the register glances at me, studies Kevin, no doubt recognizing a county cop, then takes Kevin's money without comment. Sitting on the countertop is a hunting magazine. As we leave, he picks it back up and resumes reading.

"Did I pass?" I ask Kevin as we return to the vehicle. Wyatt is already waiting for us, the SUV having obviously not needed that much gas.

"Nothing familiar?" Kevin presses. "Lights, smell, beer stains all over the floor?"

"I've never stopped here," I tell him with certainty.

"Then where'd you go? Wednesday night. You purchased the bottle of scotch around ten P.M., from that store, eighteen miles back. You don't drive off the road for another seven hours. So where'd you go, Nicky? What did you do for all that time?"

Wyatt has joined us. He pins me with a matching stare. But I don't have anything to offer either detective. I open my mouth. I close my mouth.

"I have no idea," I say at last.

"Who'd you meet?" Wyatt asks.

"I have no idea."

"Lover? Private investigator? Why so many secrets, Nicky? If you and Thomas are leading such a charmed life, why all the subterfuge?"

"You'd have to ask him."

Wyatt shakes his head. "You're sure you've never been here before?"

"I'm sure."

"But the liquor store . . ."

"I stopped there."

"Then what, Nicky? Where'd you go?"

I still can't answer.

Finally, Wyatt gives up. He says, "Let's drive."

We pile once more into the car.

Vero is learning to fly. I think of her. Can nearly feel her sitting in the SUV next to me. Vero is learning to fly. Because by the time she's six, she already understands this isn't the life she wants to live; this isn't the place she wants to be.

So she dashes around the cramped family room, childish hopes giving her wings.

The woman will take her to the park. There, she'll take a seat on a nearby bench. And then, because she's exhausted, beaten down, or maybe because she had two shots of cheap whiskey for breakfast, she'll fall asleep. She'll never see the other girl who appears in the park. Who joins Vero on the swings.

This girl is fourteen, fifteen, sixteen. She's dressed today to look like any other kid on the playground. Maybe an older sister, or a babysitter, entertaining her charges.

She strikes up a conversation with Vero. You like coming to the park? Me, too. What's your favorite thing to do, game to play? Do you like dolls? I have two dolls. Why don't you come with me? I'll grab them from the back of the car.

Vero is learning to fly.

But it won't help her in the end. She's no match for a strung-out girl, ordered to return with fresh meat or else. She doesn't expect the light-haired woman who suddenly appears, plunges a needle in her arm.

Vero never screams. She doesn't run.

She stands there. A lonely six-year-old girl who just wanted to play with dolls.

Then she's gone.

Later the woman will rouse herself from the park bench. She will scream. She will run. She will tear that park apart, trying to find the child who was her only reason to live. Police will come. Locals will rally. Dogs will search.

But by then, Vero will already be too far away, headed to a tower bedroom and a life of ruffled dresses and bleeding rosebushes.

She will cry. In the beginning, morning, noon and night. She will plead for her mom. She will beg to return to that terrible little apartment. She will fly off the bed, crash into walls. None of it will help her.

One day, Vero won't cry anymore. She'll sit at her table, sip teacups full of spiked punch and do exactly as she is told to do.

But inside, deep, deep inside . . .

Vero still longs to fly. And she hasn't completely given up dreams of flight just yet.

The SUV slows. The SUV pulls over.

Wyatt says, "We're here."

Kevin comes around to open my door.

The night is dark, cold and thick all around us.

I take one moment to inhale deeply. Then I feel myself die, all over again.

Vero wants to fly, I think.

And suddenly, I'm terrified of what will happen next.

CHAPTER 19

"I think she's taken one too many hits to the head," Kevin murmured to Wyatt. They were out of the SUV, watching Nicky walk agitated circles at the edge of the road. She was mumbling something under her breath. It sounded like *Vero wants to fly . . .*

Kevin had a point. Their suspected felony DWI driver was currently falling a little low on the sanity spectrum. Most likely, Wyatt should have driven her straight home from the liquor store. Yet, they had learned something:

"Got a hold of Jean while we were driving here," he informed Kevin now. "Had her check the Franks' credit cards for the last time Nicole fueled up her Audi. We got lucky: appears she hit a gas station Wednesday morning."

"Within twenty-four hours of the accident."

"Exactly. Now, I wrote down the trip

odometer on the Audi while at the scene of the crash. It read two hundred and five miles. Assuming she reset the odometer when she fueled up, the way a lot of folks do to monitor their gas mileage . . ."

"She drove over two hundred miles between fueling up Wednesday morning and plunging off the road Thursday, five A.M."

"Yeah. Wanna guess the number of miles from her house to the liquor store to here?"

Kevin glanced at Wyatt. "I'm going with eighty."

"Damn, you are the Brain. Answer is eighty-three."

Kevin frowned. Nicky's circles were starting to widen out. A sign she was less manic? Or about to bolt on them?

"That leaves a hundred and twenty-two miles unaccounted for," Kevin said.

"Give or take. Now, maybe she drove around all day Wednesday —"

"Doubt it. Husband implied he didn't like her driving, given the head injury. I thought his story was that she spent the day resting at home."

"In which case . . . ," Wyatt prodded.

"She logged the miles Wednesday night. Meaning she didn't drive a direct route, from house to liquor store to here."

"I think we can all agree she was at that

state liquor store but didn't stop at the gas station up the road."

"We could return to the liquor store," Kevin suggested. "We lost focus with her getting sick, maybe left too soon. Instead, we pick back up in the parking lot. This time, we put her in the front seat with you and start driving; see if any landmarks trigger any memories, help her resurrect the route she drove that night."

They both glanced at Nicole, who'd made it to the edge of the road. She'd stopped walking. Now she appeared to inhale deeply. Wyatt did the same, in case he was missing something. He smelled wet leaves, churned-up earth, decaying grass. The scent of fall, he thought, hiking through woods, raking up leaves, bedding down less winter-hardy plants.

But apparently, Nicky had a different association. "Smells from the grave," she informed them, her pale, patched-up face nearly glowing in the dark. "You can't leave. That's the problem. Even if you age out, grow ugly, waste down to nothing, it doesn't matter. You can't leave; you just move lower down the food chain."

"Leave where, Nicky?"

"It's a lifetime plan," she continued, as if Wyatt hadn't spoken. "Only way out is to die. But Vero wants to fly. You understand, don't you? You believe me?"

"Understand what, Nicole?"

"Why I had to kill her. She never should've gone to the park that day. Want to play with dolls, little girl? I *fucking* hate dolls!"

"Nicole." Wyatt took a slow step forward, the edge in her voice starting to worry him, not to mention the glassy sheen in her eyes. "Why don't you take a deep breath, then start from the beginning. Take us back to the park. Which park are you talking about? What happened there?"

"Vero is learning to fly," Nicky whispered.

"I thought Vero didn't exist," Kevin spoke up.

"Then why does my husband have her picture?"

Wyatt was still processing that bit of information as Nicole Frank turned away from them.

Then flung herself down the ravine into the darkness below.

Wyatt hated this damn hillside. The slippery, sliding descent, with mud that not only oozed over the soles of his boots but splattered up around his legs. Let alone the hidden rocks, random twigs, prickly bushes, just waiting to trip up a man and send him flying.

He didn't even have a flashlight on him. No, that would've been too smart, too prepared. And if there was one thing Wyatt was learning, chasing a barely seen woman through a barely lit half-moon night, it was that dealing with a thrice-concussed woman was a lot like dealing with the mentally ill. Maybe she was all there. But maybe she wasn't. Either way, he should've started this night prepared for anything. Including vomit, midnight confessions and possible murder charges.

Kevin had caught up to him. The detective was breathing hard, stumbling awkwardly as his foot slid out on a patch of wet grass.

"Head right," Wyatt ordered. "I think she's going for the crash site. We can cut her off."

Kevin grunted his agreement; then both men went back to focusing on their footing. Even though the rain had finally ended yesterday, the ground remained saturated from the weeks of precipitation before that. One of the rainiest falls on record, Kevin had announced the other morning.

Wyatt hated this damn ravine.

He caught sight of Nicky's form again. She appeared to be veering around one of the prickly bushes. Briefly, her hair tangled. She jerked the strands free, kept on trucking. Wherever she was going, she was determined to get there.

She'd killed Vero? Had to kill her, she'd said. Shouldn't have been in the park that day.

Except last Wyatt had known, Vero was the post-concussive version of an imaginary friend.

He was beginning to get a bad feeling about this evening, from Nicky's strong reaction to the liquor store, to now this escapade. Seemed to him, her brain might be even more scrambled than she and her husband realized. But he was also beginning to wonder if somewhere in that wreckage of gray matter, new and important information was finally coming to light.

I thought Vero didn't exist.

Then why does my husband have her picture?

Why indeed.

Having seen Nicky's encounter with the bush, Wyatt knew enough to cut around it. Which allowed him to gain several more footsteps. This close, he could hear Nicky's ragged breathing, choking sobs. A woman on the edge.

Had she really killed a little girl in the

park? Nicole Frank, with no known criminal record, had murdered a child sometime between 10 P.M. Wednesday and 5 A.M. Thursday, then transported her body all the way out here?

But as soon as he thought it, Wyatt knew that couldn't be the case. The searchers would have found it. The dog would've hit on the scent. No way Nicky had a child's corpse in the back of her Audi. So what, then?

Nicky hit another tangle of bushes. She slowed. Tried left, then right. Just before she could make her choice, Wyatt launched a flying tackle.

"Hate this damn ravine," he grunted as they both went down hard.

"You don't understand, you don't understand. I have to save her."

Kevin came crashing over, barely stopping himself before he tumbled over their fallen forms. He planted his feet for balance, then helped pull Wyatt to standing. Next they got Nicky up, positioning her between them, each of them holding an arm. They were all out of breath. And, Wyatt was surprised to see, a mere thirty feet from the accident site.

"Stop," Wyatt ordered, keeping his attention on Nicky.

Kevin looked at him curiously, Nicky more blearily.

"No talking, no running, no crying."

Nicky sniffled.

"You're injured, hell, three accidents in six months and now you're tearing down steep embankments and fleeing from police officers, which just earned you yet another knock on the skull. Stop. Breathe. Focus."

Nicky took a deeper breath, though her chest was still heaving, and a hiccupping sound came from her throat.

"Now: Walk with us."

Kevin followed as Wyatt led them the rest of the way to the former scene of the Audi's last flight. Why not, if she wanted to get here so damn badly. The car was gone, of course. Now all that remained were twisted bits of plastic and metal, shreds of rubber from the tires and glass. Dozens of feet of brilliant shards, twinkling in the moonlight. And maybe it was just his imagination, but he thought the stench of scotch still laced the air.

Nicky stared at the sea of glass, mesmerized. While her breathing continued to slow, and the manic glaze finally left her face.

"Tell us about the park," Wyatt demanded.

She glanced at him, appearing genuinely puzzled. "What park?"

Ah yes, composed Nicky versus crazed Nicky. One clammed up; the other couldn't stop talking. The question was, which of them was actually telling them the truth? Or, perhaps more accurately, which one of them was living in the present? Because Wyatt was growing suspicious that one of the mixed-up elements in Nicole Frank's head was time line. Today, yesterday and a long time ago were playing out with equal intensity. Meaning maybe it wasn't so much *what* she was talking about, but *when* she was talking about that mattered.

"What do you see when you stand here?" he asked now.

She shook her head lightly. "It should be raining."

"Like it was Wednesday night."

"The rain was pouring down. Inside my car. On my cheeks, soaking my clothes. I could smell the rain, the mud, dug-up dirt."

"What did you do?"

"I had to get out of the car. I had to find Vero."

"When did she go missing?"

A pause. Aha, Wyatt thought, now they were getting somewhere.

"Vero is six years old," Nicky whispers. "Then she's gone. It's a terrible thing, Sergeant, when a child disappears."

"When did this happen, Nicky? Last year? Five years ago? When you were young?"

"A long time ago."

Bingo, Wyatt thought. And abruptly, he felt goose bumps. A detective on a precipice. This had started with an auto accident. But he suspected it was about to get much, much worse.

"Nicole," he prodded gently, "I want you to take a moment. Focus. Think. Do you know what happened to six-year-old Vero?"

"Vero wants to fly," she murmured. "And then, one night she did."

He gave her a few minutes. Watched as Nicky's breathing continued to ease, her face regained some color, her eyes some focus. Relax, Wyatt thought. Let it all go. He wanted his witness to slow down, absorb, process. Then they'd talk.

Beside him, Kevin thrust his hands in his pockets and practiced his patience. Kevin was the Brain, absolutely the guy you wanted for stats or technical questions. But Wyatt was their resident people person. That's what made him a good cop.

"Nicky," he spoke up finally. "I want you to go back to Wednesday night. You're at home. Your head hurts. You're resting on the couch. Your phone rings."

"I have to leave," she says immediately.

Wyatt and Kevin nodded, having heard this part before. Kevin gestured to a fallen tree. They moved over, had Nicky take a seat. As comfortable as one could get in a muddy ravine, Wyatt figured. Anything to keep the suspect talking.

"You step outside. It smells like rain," Wyatt continued levelly. He tried to remember her phrase. "It smells like dug-up dirt."

Scent was one of the biggest triggers of memory, and in Nicky's own words, Wednesday night had smelled like a grave.

"Yes," she whispered.

"You feel the rain on your face."

"I hurry to get in my car. I don't want to get too wet."

"Where is Thomas?"

"Out back, working."

"Do you tell him where you're going?"

"No. He didn't want me to start asking questions. It was so long ago, he keeps telling me. Isn't our life good enough? Can't we just be happy? But of course, it's November."

"What happens in November?" Wyatt asked curiously.

"It's the saddest month of the year."

Wyatt and Kevin exchanged glances. While Wyatt was doing the talking, Kevin

263

was doing the note taking. And no doubt already formulating search criteria. For example, any six-year-old girls that went missing and/or were murdered in the month of November. Question was, going back how many years?

Wyatt took a shot in the dark: "So you contacted Northledge Investigations with your questions. To help you learn what happened . . . in November, so many years ago."

Nicky didn't say yes, but she didn't dismiss his statement either.

"The investigator called you back, right? Wednesday night, you're at home, resting on the sofa, and the phone rings. What did you learn, Nicky? What was so important you had to leave right away?"

"She gave me an address. Employment records list a state liquor store, but I've never been there before."

"Who is she? The investigator from Northledge?"

"I have to leave. Go there quickly. Before I lose my courage."

Interesting, Wyatt thought. Because up to this point, they'd assumed the urgency behind Nicky's sudden exit Wednesday night had to do with getting away from her husband. But now it would appear there was a different spin on the evening. Nicky had been contacted with information regarding someone who worked at the state liquor store. And she had to find that person before she lost her courage.

"Who are you meeting?" Wyatt tried again.

"I have to go."

"Who did you pay Northledge to track down? Is it Vero?"

"I have to save her. I never save her. Every time I fail in the end." Nicky's voice picked up, growing agitated again. Wyatt took the hint and dialed things back down.

"You put your Audi into drive," he prompted.

"The night is dark. No moon, no stars, just the thick storm clouds. I should turn around, head back home, but I can't. God, my head hurts."

"What do you do, Nicky?"

"I drive. I just keep going. What choice do I have? I see her everywhere; I hear her everywhere. Vero is having tea. Vero is braiding my hair. Vero is standing before me, maggots pouring out of her skull."

Wyatt paused, sparing a glance for Kevin, who'd gone positively wide-eyed. The detective quickly scrawled another note. While Nicky's breathing quickened once more.

"But Vero's not with you right now," Wyatt offered gently. "You're alone in your car.

You're out of the rain, driving for the state liquor store."

"My hands are shaking. I think I could use a drink. But I've been doing so well. My headaches, you know. Thomas tells me alcohol is no good. I need to get healthy again. Then maybe we could be happy again. We were happy once. God, I loved him so."

"So you're driving to the liquor store. Do you make any turns, any stops, before you get there?"

"No, I must get there. Before I change my mind."

"Okay. You arrive. The parking lot is huge. Filled with burning overhead lights."

Nicky immediately shook her head, shuttering her eyes. "I don't like them. They make my headache worse. I thought I'd just park. I don't know. Maybe hang out. But there's no place to put the car where I won't be seen. And the lights, they're killing me."

"What do you do?"

"I park in the back. As far away from the store as I can get. Then I step out into the rain."

Nicky paused. Her eyes were open but had that glazed look again. Wyatt was about to bring her back, refocus her attention, when she started on her own:

266

"I shouldn't go in. I have to go in. I should just let it go. Thomas is right. What good will come of this? Oh my God, I think I'm going to barf. No, I can do this. Because it's November and even the sky is crying and if I'm ever going to be happy . . . Thomas says I'm strong. He says he believes in me, he's always believed in me. I was sad from the very beginning, you know. He said he just wanted to be the man who finally made me smile . . .

"I get out of the car. I'm trembling. I don't feel good. Maybe I will throw up. But I like the rain. It drips from my hat brim, dances across my cheeks.

"I go inside the store," Nicky murmured. She wasn't looking at them, but staring straight ahead. "I'll just look around. She might not even be working tonight. I never asked that question. Plus I might not recognize her. It's been so long, decades, people change, you know. But then . . . What if she recognizes me? I hadn't even thought of that. Or maybe I have, because I have my cap pulled low. Why bring the hat, if I hadn't already known I'd want to hide my face?

"I can do this. I walk by the cash registers. The store is very busy. Three lanes open, crowded with people. One cashier is tall, a man. I can see him. The others . . .

267

"It's too crowded. I shouldn't have come. This was stupid. Better to let it be. But I can't leave. I'm this close. So close. The closest I've been in God knows. Then . . . I can't see her, but I *feel* her. I know she's here."

"Who's there, Nicky?" Wyatt asked. "Who are you looking for?"

But she shook her head, agitated again. "I'm going to throw up. I think my head is on fire. Oh God, I gotta get out of here. I make it to the bathroom. I turn off the light, close the door. I stand in the pitch-black until finally I can breathe again. I like the dark. I used to hate it once, but since the headaches . . . I find the sink, turn on the cold water. It feels nice against my wrists. I wish I had my quilt. Then I would curl up on the floor. I would stay here.

"Knocking. Someone else wants in. It takes me a moment, but I pull myself together. I open the door. A guy is waiting. He doesn't say anything. Just moves in as I move out.

"Now what? I don't want to go home, but I can't just stand here. I wander. Up and down the aisles. I pretend I'm looking at wine or flavored vodkas, but really, I'm try-ing to check out the store clerks. Then from the back, I see her."

"See who, Nicky?"

"That's her. I know it. I'm staring at the back of her head and even that's too much. I can't breathe. I can't move. If she turns around . . . I panic. I march into the scotch aisle, grab a bottle. You don't understand; I need it. Fuck the concussion and my stupid headaches. I *need* this.

"I go straight to the nearest checkout line. It's her line, but I refuse to think about that. This is normal, nothing special. I'm a customer; she's a cashier; end of story. Nothing to see here. Then it's my turn. She's busy, barely even glances at me. Is it better this way? Do I want her to truly look at me? Do I think . . . Do I think she'd really know?

"She rings up one bottle of Glenlivet. I swipe my card.

"We're done. Just like that. Thirty seconds or less, and now she's moved on to the next person. I'm shaking so hard I'm afraid I'll drop my bottle. I clutch it against my chest like a baby. Then I leave the store. I walk into the parking lot. I climb into my car. And I . . .

"I should call Thomas . . . ," Nicky whispered. "Tell him what I have done. He'll be angry but he'll help me. Poor Thomas, still trying to save me after all these years. I should dump out the scotch, drive home. So many things I should do. Things I know I should do. But I open the bottle instead. The smell. My God, it's like a long-lost friend. And the second I smell it, of course, I have to take a sip. I don't understand, I've never understood, how something so evil can taste so good.

"I'm bad. I'm weak. But then, I already knew that."

"What do you do next, Nicky?"

"I sit. I wait. I drink. Eventually, by the time the store empties out and the lights turn off, my limbs are loose, my face is rubbery. I'm not nervous. I'm not shaking. I'm not scared. I'm happy. Is this really the only time I'm happy?

"She comes out. Just like I knew she would. It's still storming. I can't see her that well, raincoat pulled over her head. But I recognize her, even though she hadn't recognized me. No, she'd stood three feet from me, not a flicker of realization on her face. Not even a sense of déjà vu, hey, haven't I seen you once before? Nothing. Nada. Nope.

"That pisses me off! She should know, dammit! I never forgot her. How dare she forget me!

"Her car. It's pulling out of the parking

space, headed for the road. I don't know what I'm going to do; I just do it. Jerk my own car into gear, head out after her. I'm not driving great. The night is very dark. My headlights bounce off the raindrops, which makes me dizzy. It's hard to find the road.

"At least there are no other cars around. I follow her taillights. I don't know where I'm going or what I will do once I get there, but I can't stop either. I can't . . . turn away. I drive. I grip the wheel, I force my eyes to focus and I stay behind her.

"Around and around we go. Along this road, then there. And here, and there and everywhere. A dark and stormy chase. We drive through one town, then another. Then she turns off the main road and now we're bouncing and heaving along some little side street. It needs to be repaved. I keep hitting the potholes and my stomach heaves.

"Brake lights. She's slowing before a house, probably going to turn into the driveway. I don't know what to do. There is no place for me to go, no place for me to hide. I can't just stop in the middle of the road. I can't turn in after her; that would be too much. So I . . . hit the gas, pass her right on by, just another driver with places to go and people to see. But then, when I'm

271

far enough way . . . I hit the brakes, loop around.

"I backtrack down the road. The second I see the right house, I kill my lights. The night goes pitch-black. Out this remote, there are no streetlights, not even porch lights glowing from surrounding homes. No, I'm in back-of-the-closet dark. Don't-make-a-sound dark. One-false-move-and-the-monsters-will-get-you dark.

"But I don't care."

"Nicky, where are you?" Wyatt asked carefully. Nicole's eyes were unfocused again. Staring not at him, but at things only she could see.

"Shhh," she murmured to him. "I don't want her to hear; I don't want her to know. I pull over. Get out of my car. Immediately, I'm soaked. But it's okay. I creep carefully forward toward the little house. It's nothing fancy, but I like the color; she's painted it yellow with white trim. I always liked that shade of yellow. I wonder if she's happy here. It makes my chest feel funny. I want her to be happy. Right? But maybe it's not that simple. Maybe I'm jealous. I'm almost at the side window now. Step, step, step."

"Where are you, Nicky?"

"Vero is learning to fly."

"Who are you trying to find?"

"Six years old. She is gone. November is the saddest month of the year."

"Nicky, stay with me, honey. It's Wednesday night. You've been drinking. You followed a woman home from the liquor store. Now you're standing in the rain outside her home. What do you see?"

"I see the impossible. Vero. All grown up. Sitting on a couch in the family room. I see Vero, back from the dead."

CHAPTER 20

What is happiness? I feel like I've been chasing it my entire adult life. I study it in commercials, watch it on other people's faces. When Thomas and I first married, he took me on vacation to Mexico. We tried on fake names, invented wilder and wilder character histories. He was a runaway circus clown, I was a burned-out Vegas showgirl. We laughed hard, we drank too much. Then we woke up and did it all over again. I remember lying on a warm, sandy beach after one particularly crazy night, feeling the sun on my closed eyelids and thinking, this must be happiness. I can do this.

Except I woke up screaming, night after night after night. Regardless of the rum. Regardless of my new and improved backstory. Regardless of Thomas's strong arms around my waist.

Happiness, it turns out, is an acquired skill, and I've had problems learning it.

Just be happy, the song says. I tried that, too. Especially all those mornings, waking up to find Thomas studying me so intently. Knowing I must have dreamed again, or maybe shouted out, or hit him. He learned quickly not to touch me once the thrashing started. That in fact, I'm stronger than I look.

Meditation, yoga, juice fasts. It's amazing how many tricks are out there. I took up painting. Art therapy, because Thomas and I both knew talking to someone was not an option. Those first few years, Thomas was very good about burning the canvases. The images I created, the color palette . . . These were not pictures to hang on your wall.

Fake it till you make it. So I studied photos of flowers and serene landscapes. I dissected petals and leaves and dandelion fluff. I recreated each image on canvas down to the tiniest detail because maybe if I didn't feel happiness, I could at least copy it. Then it would be mine. I could point to it and say, I made that happiness.

Then November wouldn't make me cry. And I wouldn't spend my free time lying with a yellow quilt talking to the skeleton of a little girl covered in maggots.

Maybe happiness is genetic. Maybe it's something your parents have to gift to you.

That would certainly explain a lot.

Or maybe it's contagious. You have to be exposed to it, to catch it yourself, and given my small, isolated world . . .

I want to be happy. I want to not only see my husband's warm smile, but feel it in my chest. I want to hold up my face to a clear summer sky and not already notice the clouds on the horizon. I want to sleep, the way I imagine other people sleep, deep and uneventful, and wake up the next morning feeling refreshed.

But I am none of these things. Only a woman twice returned from the dead.

By the time I'm done talking to the detectives, I'm exhausted. They ask me more questions, but I can't answer. My eyelids are sagging; I can barely stand without stumbling. You'd think I'd spent the evening drinking, and not just retelling my last drunken misadventure.

Vero.

The name comes and goes from me. I lost her. I found her. I killed her. I know where she lives.

These concepts are too much for me. They overwhelm my battered brain. Each possibility seems more improbable than the last. Vero is my imaginary friend; Thomas told me so. Vero and I sit together and indulge in scotch-laced tea, but only in my concussed head.

Vero is six years old. She is gone. Disappeared.

She never existed.

Except my husband had her picture hidden inside his jacket pocket.

The detectives are trying to help me up the ravine. It's slow going. My legs don't want to work; my feet stumble over twigs, sink deeper into the mud.

I remember this ravine, the blood on my hands, the rain on my face. Pushing myself past the pain, forcing my way through the mud and muck, because I had to save Vero. That's the key to happiness for me, I think. Whether the girl is real or not, it's my duty to save her. So I keep trying, again and again, because even the worst of us wants to be able to sleep at night.

"I don't get it," the younger detective, Kevin, is whispering to the other. "I thought we agreed Vero didn't exist."

"Technically speaking, the husband told us she didn't exist. Doesn't mean we have to agree with him."

"But if Vero's real, doesn't that mean our suspect just confessed to killing her?"

"Only if she's dead. Our suspect has also

just claimed to have found the girl alive."

"Remind me never to get a concussion," Kevin says.

"It would be a waste of a great Brain."

I stumble. Both detectives pause, Wyatt bending down to help me up.

"Northledge Investigations," he tells me. "That's the firm you hired, right? I want to talk to them, Nicky, which would happen quicker if you granted permission. Do you think you could help me with that? Give them the okay?"

I stare at him blearily. I don't nod yes and he finally frowns at me.

"I thought you wanted answers." His tone is faintly accusing.

"Shhh," I tell him.

"Nicky —"

"It's not the flying; it's the landing," I inform him soberly.

But he doesn't get it. How can he? He has yet to understand the yellow quilt and the real reason Thomas wouldn't come with us.

He doesn't understand this night isn't over yet.

The detectives pull me up the ravine. They tuck me back into the SUV. They hand me my precious quilt.

I sit in the back of the vehicle. I think these are two good, hard-working men.

They deserve better than to get involved in my messed-up life.

I'm sorry.

Then I close my eyes and let it all go.

I'm on the basement floor. The concrete is hard against my neck and shoulders. I try to move, sit up, roll over, something. But I can't. There is pain, radiating everywhere, but mostly in the back of my skull.

Distant footsteps, moving quick.

Footsteps down a hall, I think, and feel immediate panic.

No. Stop. Focus. I'm in a basement. Cold floor. Surrounded by discarded clothes. Laundry. That's it. I'm a grown adult, doing laundry in my own home, and then . . .

Floorboards, creaking above me. "Nicky?" a man's voice calls. "Nicky? You all right?"

I wonder who Nicky is. Is this her home?

"Honey, where are you? I thought I heard a car in the drive. Nicky?"

My brain throbs. I have to squeeze my eyes shut against the pain caused by the overhead lights. I try to turn my head, but that makes my head groan. I should say something. Cry out, call for help. But I merely lick my lips helplessly.

I don't know what to cry out. I don't know who to ask for. Where am I again? Who is that upstairs?

Nicky, Nicky, Nicky, he says.

But Vero is all I think.

Footsteps sounding closer. A man's form appears above me, silhouetted at the top of the stairs.

"Nicky, is that you?" Then: "Oh my God! What happened? Nicky!"

The man hammers down the stairs. He drops to his knees beside me. Thomas, I think, but then frown, because I'd swear that name isn't quite right. Tim. Tyler. Travis. Todd. A man with a hundred names, I find myself thinking. Which makes perfect sense, as I'm a woman with a hundred ghosts.

He's touching me. My shoulders, my knees, my hips. His touch is light and feathery, trying to check me out, afraid to land too hard.

"Nicky, talk to me."

"The light," I whisper, or maybe groan, my eyes going overhead.

"I think you hit your head. I see some blood. Did you fall down the stairs? I think you may have cracked your skull against the floor."

"The light," I moan again.

He scrambles up, hits the overhead switch, casting me into blessed darkness. He throws on a different light, somewhere behind me, probably in the laundry room, ambient glow for him to see by.

"Honey, can you move?"

I manage to wiggle my toes, lift an arm, a leg; the rest is too much.

"How did I get down here?" I ask.

But he doesn't answer.

"Tell me your name," he demands.

"Natalie Shudt."

He blinks. Maybe it's my imagination, but he appears nervous.

"How did I get down here?" I try again.

"Can you count to ten?"

"Of course, Theo."

That strange look again. I count. I like counting. It actually soothes the hurt. I count up to ten, down to one and then . . .

"Toby, your name is Toby."

"Thomas —"

"Tobias."

"Shhhh. Just, shhh. I gotta think for a minute."

I'm on the basement floor. The concrete is hard against my neck and shoulders. I should call out, get some help.

Oh look, there's a man here. Tyler.

"Your name is Nicole Frank," he tells me.

"Natasha Anderson," I reply.

"I'm your husband, Thomas. We've been married twenty-two years."

"Trenton," I singsong.

"We just moved to this area. We're very

happy together. And" — he stares at me hard — "we have no children."

"Ted, Teddy, Tim, Tommy. Ta-da!"

"I think I have to take you to the hospital." He's clearly worried about this. "Nicole —"

"Nancy!"

"Nicole, I need you to do something for me. Just . . . be quiet, okay? Let the doctors do their thing. You concentrate on feeling better. I'll answer all their questions, handle everything else."

"Vero!" I call out.

He closes his eyes. "Not now. Please." Then: "Honey, why were you down here anyway? It's not laundry day."

I stare up at him. I don't say anything. Who is this man? I think suddenly. Then, even more poignantly, who am I? Nicole Natalie Nancy Natasha Nan Nia Nannette. I am everyone. I am no one at all.

I am November, I think. The saddest month of the year.

"It's going to be okay," Thomas Tyler Theo Tim Trenton tells me. "I'll take care of you. I promise. I just need to know one thing. When I was out in my workshop, I swore I heard a car. Did someone come to visit, Nicole? Did you let someone into the house?"

Then, when I don't answer:

"Oh my God, it was the investigator, wasn't

282

it? After I asked you not to."

I still don't say anything. I don't have to.

This man I love. This man I hate. What is his name, what is his name, what is his name? Ted Tom Tim Tod Tyler Taylor Tobias . . .

This man sighs heavily and whispers, "Oh, Nicky. What have you done?"

We smell it before we see it. The acrid smoke wafting into the SUV's ventilation system. I can't help myself. I reach out my hand. But of course Thomas isn't here. Instead, I clutch my quilt. And I will myself forcefully to be in this moment.

I must be in this moment.

Because the smell of smoke, the smell of smoke . . .

These poor two officers, I can't help but think. They haven't even begun to see crazy yet.

We had been driving steadily since leaving the crash site, sixty, seventy minutes of winding our way along dark ribbons of country roads, Wyatt driving, Kevin checking his phone, me. Now, as the smell intensifies and a dizzying array of lights starts to come into view . . .

Wyatt hits the gas, both men on high alert.

Stay in the moment, I remind myself. No smell of smoke, no heat of fire.

No sound of her screams.

This is now. This is this moment. And tonight, I am merely the audience. The main event happened hours ago.

Thomas handing me the quilt while the officers waited for me downstairs. Telling me I had to take it.

A final gesture of love, because a boyfriend brings you flowers, but a husband of twenty-two years gives you what you need most. The depth of all of our years together. The way we have come to know each other, despite our lies.

Thomas gave me my quilt, pinned with one last item he knew I couldn't bear to lose: Vero's photo. The secret I stole from him, then stashed beneath my own mattress. I have felt its shape several times this evening, attached to one edge of the blanket.

A parting gift from a man with too many names to a woman with even more.

The smell of smoke.

Myself, still reaching for my husband's hand.

I'm sorry, I'm sorry, I'm sorry. Oh, Thomas, I am so sorry.

As my house comes into full view. Already surrounded by fire trucks, flames shooting up everywhere.

"What the hell," Wyatt begins, jerking to a

stop behind the line of emergency vehicles. He twists around from the driver's seat, eyes me angrily. "Did you know about this?"

I shake my head, only a partial lie.

"I don't see Thomas's vehicle . . . Dammit! He did this, didn't he? Your husband torched your house to cover his tracks, before disappearing into the wind."

I nod, only a partial lie.

The smell of smoke. The heat of the flames.

The sound of her screams.

I close my eyes. And I think, while I'm still in this moment, that my husband was right. I should've let it go. I should've tried harder to be happy.

I should've told Vero once and for all to please, just leave me alone.

But of course, I did none of those things. Have been capable of none of those things. Now . . .

"What the hell is he so afraid of?" Wyatt thumps the steering wheel.

So I finally tell him the truth. I say: "Me."

CHAPTER 21

Tessa couldn't sleep. Her phone call with Wyatt had left her unsettled, let alone D.D.'s disturbing revelation yesterday at lunch. Now, instead of tucking in for some desperately needed rest, she was mostly lying in bed, feeling the weight of her own silence.

Tessa was highly compartmentalized by nature. She'd never told anyone, not even Wyatt, everything that had happened three years ago. At the time, she'd committed herself to doing whatever it would take to get her daughter back. One thousand ninety-five days later, she didn't regret those choices.

The discovery of Purcell's gun, on the other hand. A possible incriminating fingerprint . . . She should do something, most likely. Say something? But all these years later, what? She'd done what she'd done. If three years later some tech in the state police lab managed to prove it, well, not even Wyatt could help her undo those consequences. She would simply have to face the music. While counting on Mrs. Ennis to take care of Sophie.

As for Wyatt . . . They'd been together only six months. And maybe she did love him, and maybe he did love her. But he didn't need to be connected to a felon. Not good for his professional future, not good for his personal reputation.

Compartmentalization: She couldn't undo what she'd done, but she could at least limit the collateral damage.

The skill had certainly helped her stand out as a top security specialist. Clients paid dearly for discretion. A good investigator such as Tessa got in, got out, and didn't ask a lot of questions along the way. Or volunteer information to the local police. Even if she was sleeping with the investigating officer.

Wyatt should've known better than to even ask if she had knowledge of Nicky Frank. That wasn't how her job worked, and he knew it. A Hail Mary pass on his part, plain and simple.

Then again, Nicole Frank had suffered three concussions. As Wyatt had pointed out, she might not even remember she was a Northledge client. In fact, she might not remember what Tessa had called that night to tell her.

Boundaries, she thought again. Their jobs required boundaries.

She required boundaries.

Because D. D. Warren had been right yesterday: Tessa still was a lone wolf. Even after getting her daughter back. Even after falling in love.

Tessa gave up, got out of bed. She padded through the darkened house into the kitchen, opening the refrigerator door, not because she was hungry, but because it was something to do. She pulled out a bottle of orange juice.

When she turned around, Sophie was standing there.

Tessa gasped. Dropped the container. Splattered OJ all over the floor.

"Dammit!"

"Darn it," Sophie corrected automatically.

"Oh, don't just stand there. Help me clean it up."

Sophie yawned, reached for the paper towels. Tessa did the honors of flipping on the overhead lights. It was one thing for her to be alone in the dark, but all these years later Sophie still required light.

"What brings you to the kitchen in the

middle of the night?" Tessa asked finally. According to the digital display on the stove, it was 1:22 A.M.

"I heard you."

"Problems sleeping?"

Sophie shrugged. In other words, no more than usual. She worked at the spill with the sponge. Tessa followed up with damp paper towels.

"Warm milk?" Tessa suggested shortly. "At least I didn't spill that."

Sophie smiled; Tessa pulled out the milk.

She warmed it on the stove top, low heat, adding vanilla to taste, an old ritual from the first few months after the incident, when neither she nor Sophie had slept. They'd been a ragged pair of survivors then, barely functioning, each nursing her own scars. They were a curious little family now. Both more comfortable with firing ranges than polite conversation, both still prone to roaming the house at night.

"Do you still miss him?" Sophie asked. She'd taken a seat at the kitchen island, where she could watch Tessa work. Tessa didn't need an explanation to know who Sophie was asking about. It had been months since they'd last talked about him. But from time to time, Sophie had questions about her stepfather, which Tessa did

289

her best to answer.

"Brian? Sometimes."

"I don't remember him much."

"He loved you."

"You always say that."

"Because it's true."

"But he was sick. A gambling addict. He hurt us."

Tessa stirred the milk carefully, then glanced up at her daughter. "Why do you ask about him, Sophie? What's keeping you awake tonight?"

"I don't know." Sophie looked away. "I like our family," she said abruptly. "You, me, Mrs. Ennis. It's perfect."

"Even without a dog?"

Sophie flashed a faint smile. "But that's kinda the point, I guess. Families change. Once we were three. Then we were two. Then we became three again. And now . . ." She glanced up at Tessa. "You like him, don't you? Wyatt's not just a stupid fling—"

"Sophie!"

"He's going to become our fourth. Do you love him?"

"Well, there's the question of the day," Tessa murmured.

"Do you?" Sophie demanded.

She was always honest with her daughter:

"Yeah. I do."

"So that's it. He'll move in. I'll have to call him Daddy."

"You don't have to do anything. And I don't know about this moving-in thing. One step at a time."

Sophie's turn to look curious. "Why not? If you love him."

Because I'm afraid, Tessa wanted to say. Because happily ever after never looks the way you think it will from the movies. Maybe it's not an ending at all, but the beginning of the next terrible misadventure. The future is unreliable, and three years later, the past can still come back to haunt you.

"Relationships take time," Tessa said at last.

Her daughter nodded but didn't appear convinced.

"Sophie," Tessa said at last, leaning her hip against the counter. "What are you most afraid of?" She thought given the mood of the evening, it was a good question for both of them.

"The dark," her daughter said immediately.

"I mean with Wyatt. Do you think he'll hurt us? Do you think he's a bad man?"

"No."

"Do you like him?"

"I like the cop stuff," Sophie said at last.

"I like that he's honest," Tessa supplied. "He says what he's going to do, and he does what he says. A man of his word — that's how people describe him. You know, he thinks we should get a puppy."

"I think we should get a puppy!" Sophie sat up straighter.

"It's a lot of work. Especially for Mrs. Ennis. You and I aren't even home most of the day."

"I'll help. I'll help first thing in the morning, and I'll help again at night. The puppy can sleep in my room; then I can help even more."

"I asked Mrs. Ennis about it," Tessa said, a dog being a potential source of comfort and security for Sophie. And, say, something that would still be there for Sophie, even if Tessa had to leave for a bit. "She wasn't dramatically opposed. Maybe it would be a nice first step. We could all pick out a puppy together."

"Including Wyatt?" Faint scowl threatening.

"It was his idea."

"I guess."

"Do you plan on hating him forever?" Tessa asked curiously.

"I don't know. I guess he's nice enough. And a puppy is good. I'll have to wait and see."

"Fair enough."

Tessa thought that would be it. Sophie would finish her warm milk. They'd both go to bed. But instead, her daughter once more grew serious.

"What are you afraid of, Mommy?"

Tessa had to smile. Other than a recently recovered firearm and a single latent print . . .

Tessa set down her mug. She regarded her daughter as soberly as Sophie regarded her. "There's an old saying," she began, "the only thing there is to fear, is fear itself."

"That's stupid! There are plenty of things to fear."

"I know, Sophie. You and I both know. And I guess that's what scares me. We spend so much time, you and I, preparing for the worst, I worry we'll miss out on the best. I'll meet a good guy like Wyatt. You'll get a perfect puppy. And yet . . . we'll still be waiting for the next bad thing to happen. That's not a great way to live, you know. We need to not just see the good, but trust in it a little more. Learn some faith."

Stop being a lone wolf, she supposed. Talk a little more. Let go of the boundaries. And yet some habits were hard to break.

"That's why I should get a puppy," Sophie was saying. "A puppy will definitely help me learn trust."

"As well as how to scoop poop."

"Mom!"

Tessa smiled, ruffled her daughter's hair.

"Thank you for the warm milk, Mom," Sophie said.

"Thank you for the company."

Tessa cleared their mugs. She walked Sophie back to her room, tucked her daughter into bed.

Then it was back to her room, where she lay in bed and once more stared at the ceiling.

For all of her wise words to Sophie, the truth was, the next bad thing did loom on the horizon. Three years ago, she'd shot a man. It was not an act she regretted. Though she was sorry the police now had that gun.

And she remained a woman who struggled with trust. Because why not simply tell Wyatt what was going on? Why not show some faith in a man who'd never been anything but honest with her?

Funny, the things that scared a woman like her. Enter a room full of hostile gunmen, check. Talk openly and honestly to the man she loved . . . maybe later.

There was one thing she knew she should do, however, first thing in the morning. She would reach out to Nicole Frank, Wyatt's DWI suspect, and see how the woman was doing. Because Tessa knew something even if Nicole didn't remember it.

The past was never completely the past.

It had a way of catching up with you. Especially a past filled with as many sins as Tessa's.

Or with as many secrets as Nicole Frank's.

CHAPTER 22

Wyatt ordered Nicky to remain in the county's SUV. Did he have the authority to do that? Nope. Did he have probable cause to arrest her for anything? Not really. Couldn't nail her for the house fire, as she'd been with him and Kevin the entire time. Even an arrest for Wednesday's crash was problematic, given her blood alcohol reading didn't meet the DWI threshold of .08.

Technically speaking, Nicky Frank could walk away from him and Kevin, not to mention the burning embers of her house, and be well within her rights.

Like hell, Wyatt thought, for the third time in as many minutes. She was his only link to something larger, murkier and far more criminal than a lone car accident.

He left Kevin in charge of babysitting, while he went in search of the fire marshal.

"What can you tell me?" Wyatt asked the older man, Jerry Wright, who'd been called out from several towns over. All in all, three separate volunteer fire departments were on the property. It was that kind of blaze, deserving that kind of response.

"Started in the outbuilding," Wright answered crisply now. They had to stand well back, not just because men were still working hoses, but because the flames were throwing off tremendous heat. "Definitely an accelerant, and lots of it. Metal buildings don't normally like to burn. But this one. Shi-it."

Wyatt had checked out the rear of the property, where the gray shed was now a charred, twisted shell of its former self. The shed that had once housed Thomas's tools of the trade. Interesting.

"Who called it in?" Wyatt asked.

"Neighbor, eventually. But given the distances between the properties out here, it had probably already been burning for a bit. Call came in a little after eight. Response time was solid, first unit rolling in by eight fifteen. Still, shed was a goner from the start, I'm told, house already fully engulfed. Whoever wanted this done didn't mess around."

"Any reports of a man on the scene?"

"Negative. House is too hot to enter, so can't swear to what we'll find inside. But from the time we've been here, no signs of life."

Wyatt nodded; he strongly doubted Thomas was anywhere on the property. The man's silver Suburban, which had been in plain sight in the driveway four hours earlier, was now conspicuously missing. Wyatt's best guess, Thomas let the police take his wife away, then torched his own place and split.

But why?

Nicky claimed he was afraid of her, and Wyatt was a smart enough man to understand she didn't mean in the literal sense. More likely, Thomas feared her fickle memories. Three concussions in a row seemed to have unlocked some doors in Nicky's mind. And not all the contents were pretty.

Meaning, what had Thomas and/or Nicky done in the past that at least Thomas was still desperate to hide? More important, how did it relate to the existing, nonexisting, probably dead, possibly still alive mystery girl, Vero?

"Fire's too hot," the fire marshal informed Wyatt now. "You want more info, gotta wait till morning."

"All right, keep me posted."

Wyatt left the man, taking a few steps back

to once more consider the blaze. The roof of the house was fully engulfed. It was an impressive sight, an entire home being consumed alive. Windows shattered. Metal groans. A singular type of destruction that was both awesome and terrifying.

He wondered what Nicky saw when she gazed upon it. Was she horrified by what her husband had done? Had to be photos, family mementos, favored possessions, that were even now turning to ash before her eyes.

Yet, when he returned to the car, she simply sat in the backseat, staring at the inferno, blank faced.

"We got an APB out on Thomas's vehicle," he informed Kevin. " 'Bout all we can do for now."

Kevin nodded.

"She spoken at all?" Wyatt asked, gesturing to the backseat.

"Not a word."

"Checked her phone?"

"She doesn't have a phone. Lost it in the car wreck, remember?"

"Meaning Thomas has no means of contacting her," Wyatt murmured.

"Unless they have a predetermined meeting place."

"That's it. We're taking her to the station.

As long as Thomas Frank is missing, she's our bait."

Nicky didn't protest when they pulled out of the driveway and once more hit the road. She didn't ask where they were going or complain of hunger or thirst. She simply sat, eyes out the window, quilt on her lap.

From time to time, Wyatt would study her in the rearview mirror, trying to decipher what she was thinking. She looked exhausted, as she should be. She looked unwell, as she was. Too thin, too pale, as if a good stiff wind would knock her off her feet. But her face was shuttered, flat affect.

Hadn't someone mentioned shell shock once before? At the accident, the passing motorist who'd stopped to assist. He'd been a war vet and reported she appeared shell-shocked, as in the literal definition of the word. Watching her now, Wyatt saw the man's point. Nicky Frank had gone somewhere inside her head. Question was, when would she come back out again?

The North Country Sheriff's Department was housed in a two-story brick building not far from the county jail and even closer to the county courthouse. It offered a parking lot, fingerprinting and lots of buzzing overhead lights. But no food. For that, Wyatt

300

and Kevin made a detour to McDonald's, one of the only joints open after midnight. Wyatt and Kevin ordered with gusto. Quarter pounders, large fries, large coffees, all the calories, salt and caffeine a good detective needed to stay up all night.

Nicky requested another bottle of water, in a voice that was perfectly monotone. Wyatt would've thought she'd been turned into a statue, if not for the way her fingers stroked the top layer of her quilt. Touching it over and over again. Like she was working the rosary, he thought. A woman lost in prayer. Or offering penance.

They took the food to the station house. This time of night, you could count on headquarters for a little action. County dispatch worked out of the building, meaning there was plenty of noise coming from down the hall, in terms of both phone calls and the operators entertaining themselves between the calls. Of course, bookings happened at all hours, with 2 A.M. being prime time for collared drunks.

Wyatt and Kevin carefully steered Nicky through the lobby, then down the narrow hallway, around one twitchy meth addict, around another. The station lighting always felt glaring to Wyatt, as if trying to compensate for something. It was enough to make him squint. He couldn't imagine how much Nicky was suffering with her condition.

In the end, they set her up in the conference room. Not an interrogation room, because that might have seemed aggressive, and again, technically speaking, Wyatt couldn't make the woman stay. But nor did he want her in their offices, because she needed to feel the pressure. Her life was imploding. For all their sakes, time to talk.

She didn't look at them when Kevin pulled out the chair. She took a seat, gaze forward. Quilt back on the lap. Bottled water on the table. Then she waited.

She's done this before, Wyatt thought. Police stations, interrogation; none of this was new to her. Just as he had his strategy, she had hers.

Wyatt took his time. He set down his Mc-Donald's bag, let the room fill with the unmistakable fragrance of fries. Kevin did the same. Next, Wyatt removed the cover from his large coffee, adding yet more aroma to the mix. Unwrapping his burger, taking his first greasy bite. Yeah, he'd regret it in the morning. A man his age couldn't afford to eat like this regularly, but for the moment, it was a salt-fat-carb explosion in his mouth. Two A.M. eating didn't get any better than this.

Kevin made a show of squeezing out ketchup onto the burger wrapper, then dipping his fries.

Still Nicky didn't say a word, though they all sat so close, Wyatt thought they'd be able to hear her stomach growl at any moment.

"Sure you don't want anything?" he asked at last, voice conversational.

She shook her head.

"We got vending machines, you know. Maybe chips, a candy bar? More gum?"

She shook her head.

"Lights too bright?"

She finally looked at him. Her eyes were tired, he thought, but more than that they were flat pools of resignation. She didn't want. She didn't need. She was simply a woman awaiting her fate.

Wyatt felt a chill then, uncomfortable enough that he got up, wadded up his wrappers and threw away the remnants of his dinner. He kept his coffee. He paused long enough to murmur to Kevin, "Check on the APB. Any news at all, we could use that."

Kevin nodded, disposed of his own wrappers, left the conference room. Wyatt stood alone with Nicky. Their prime suspect. Witness. Victim? Maybe that's what really bothered him. Forty-eight hours later, he still had no idea, and it pissed him off.

When he took his seat again, he deliberately placed his elbows on the table and leaned forward.

"What happened at your house tonight?" he demanded.

Her face finally flickered to life. "How would I know? I was with you."

"Your house is gone, you know. Total loss, according to the fire marshal. Meaning everything inside, photos, your paintings, favorite pillow . . . poof."

She didn't say anything.

"Same with the work shed," Wyatt continued. "Gonna be a bummer for the family business. All those tools, projects, supplies. Gone. Orders that now won't be fulfilled. Clients that will be unhappy. Three-D printer that'll never be used again."

She didn't flinch. The business hadn't been her bailiwick anyway, Wyatt thought. It had been Thomas's.

"First house fire?" he asked now.

She frowned, seemed to come slightly out of her fog. "What do you mean?"

"I mean, all the cities, states, houses you've lived in over the years. Come on, you and Thomas give new meaning to rolling stones."

She frowned again, rubbed her temples. Then held out her hand as if reaching for something. Someone.

Wyatt waited. She didn't say a word. Just her hand, suspended in the air. After another moment, she seemed to realize what she was doing. She replaced her hand on her lap. A single tear rolled down her face.

"Shame it was this house," Wyatt pressed. "You'd put some effort into this one. Repainting the door, working in the garden. Did you think that maybe this was the place you'd finally stay?"

"I missed snow," she murmured, gaze still fixed on the table.

"Where is Thomas now?"

"I don't know."

"You should. You're his wife, his business partner. If you don't know him, who does?"

"Ted Todd Tom Tim ta-da!" she whispered.

"What did you just say?"

"He has no family. He has no friends. He has no place to go." She finally glanced up, met his eyes. "I have no place to go."

"Damn selfish of him, don't you think?"

"You should take me to a hotel."

"First I want you to tell me about New Orleans. When did you meet?"

"At work. A movie production set. I was working craft services. He was in set production. He told me he waited three weeks to

305

get me to say hi." She spoke the words automatically. Wyatt thought he'd heard that story before, because he had: almost word for word from Thomas that first day at the hospital.

"Is Thomas from New Orleans?" Wyatt asked.

"No."

"What brought him there?"

"I don't know."

"You don't know? Twenty-two years together, and you never asked him what he was doing in New Orleans?"

She peered at him blearily. "Why did it matter?"

"Are you from New Orleans?"

"No."

"You two . . . just met up there."

"Yes."

"Helluva courtship. Four weeks, then that's it? You two hit the road, never looked back. You live together, work together, travel together, everything together."

"There's nothing wrong with that."

"He burned your house alone."

"I wrecked my car alone. Drank alone. See, maybe it's best if we stay together."

"You ever meet his family? In all your travels and wanderings, he ever take you home?"

"No."

"Why? Ashamed of you? Scared of something? Who doesn't bring their spouse to meet the family? Mom. Dad. Sister." Wyatt didn't actually know about the sister part. He was baiting her, though, waiting to see if Nicky would react, ask any questions of her own.

But she merely shook her head, said nothing.

"Who are you, Nicky? What really brought you and Thomas to New Hampshire?"

"We wanted a change."

"You're looking. You want something, are trying to find it so badly you contacted a private investigative firm even after your husband asked you not to."

She didn't answer.

"Then you took off in a storm Wednesday night, while your husband was otherwise occupied, just so you could go looking again. You followed a woman home from a liquor store. You stood out in the rain. You spied on her house. Why? What do you need to find so badly you're willing to go behind your husband's back? And what did you do that made him so angry he torched everything you own?"

"Not everything." She tapped her quilt, still folded neatly on her lap.

Wyatt stilled, studied her. "You're right. The blanket. You've been carrying it around all night. He gave that to you, didn't he, Nicky? He told you to take it with you."

To his surprise, her eyes filled with tears. "I didn't know what he was going to do. I didn't. But in hindsight, he must've already had the plan. That's why he told me to take the quilt with me."

"Why? What's so special about the quilt?"

She shrugged. "I need it. On the sad days. I can smell her. I hold this close, and I can smell her and it comforts me."

"Smell who?"

"I don't know."

"Vero?"

"I don't think so."

"Who, then? Dammit, Nicky!" Wyatt pounded the table. "Enough with the half answers. Who are you looking for? And what the hell did you finally find that scared your husband enough to do this? It's time for answers. Start talking."

"But I don't know!"

"Yes, you do! Somewhere in that mixed-up head of yours, you know everything. Think. Remember. Your husband's gone, your house is ashes. It's just you, Nicky. All alone. No place to go. You wanna keep being the victim here? Then stop stalling and think!"

The conference room door opened. Nicky jumped at the sound. Wyatt turned, annoyed by the interruption. Then he caught the intent look on Kevin's face. Wyatt rose immediately, as his detective walked over, handed him a stapled sheaf of paper.

"Came in earlier today," Kevin said softly. "But we were already out, so Gina left it on my desk."

Wyatt glanced down at a report run by the state on the bloody prints recovered from Nicole Frank's car. The top sheet didn't even make sense at first blush. It wasn't until he digested the second piece of paper, then the third, the fourth . . .

He looked up at Kevin, as if waiting for the obvious denial.

Instead, his detective was nodding slowly. "Yeah. My first reaction, too. But it's all in there. The pieces fit."

Together, they turned, studying Nicky, who was staring at them expectantly.

"It's true," Kevin whispered. "By God, it's true."

Wyatt didn't speak. He returned to the conference table. He pulled out his chair. He took a seat. Then he placed the report before him and slid it across the table toward her.

"Nicole Frank," he said steadily. "Meet Vero."

CHAPTER 23

"Did you know?" Vero asks me. We are back in her tower bedroom, drinking scotch out of teacups.

"I think some part of me must have," I tell her.

"Will you stop visiting me now? Finally let me go?"

"I'm not sure it's as simple as that."

"True. Not to mention, you've left out a lot of details."

On cue, more skeletons begin to appear in the room. Pop, pop, pop. One, two, five, more than I can count. They jam into all available spaces, huddling on the gauze-draped bed, pressing against the walls, climbing up the rosebush. All of them wear flowery dresses draped over their gleaming white bones. One of them grins toothlessly at me. She waves a hand in my direction, like a long-lost friend, like a promise from the dead.

"I can't do it," I whisper frantically. The teacup in my hand begins to tremble. "I can't. It's too much. I don't *want* to remember! I just want it all to go away."

Vero adds more scotch to my china cup.

She says, "I'm not sure it's as simple as that."

"Did you know?" Wyatt asks me.

I am staring at a flyer for a missing child. VERONICA SELLERS. AGE 6. LONG BROWN HAIR. LIGHT BLUE EYES. LAST SEEN IN A PARK IN BOSTON.

Hey, you like to play with dolls? I have a couple in my car . . .

The poster includes a blown-up photo of a smiling little girl. I touch her hair — I can't help myself. I peer deep into her gray eyes.

One of the only photos her mother had, I know without asking. Shot with a Polaroid after they'd baked cookies. Her mother had been in a curiously good mood all afternoon. Picked up the camera, said, 'Hey, sweetie, smile!' Vero had giggled at the unexpected attention, then marveled at the developing process.

Right before footsteps started down the hall.

VERONICA SELLERS. AGE 6. LONG

312

BROWN HAIR. LIGHT BLUE EYES. LAST SEEN IN A PARK IN BOSTON.

I turn to the next page. Three photos now. The first from the missing persons poster, then a second, age-progressed to ten years. Features crisper, more defined. But still the big smile, the light in her eyes.

No, I want to tell them. They have it wrong. Vero never smiled at ten. Her eyes had not looked like that at all. By ten, she'd been a hardened pro.

A third and final photo. Age-progressed to sixteen. Nothing more, because finding a missing child that many years later was already a long shot. But someone, a case worker, a computer technician, had made this effort.

She looks beautiful at sixteen. Brown hair softer, waving around sculpted cheekbones, a smattering of freckles across her nose. Wholesome. The girl from down the street. The teenager you'd hire to watch your kids.

I touch this photo, too. I think of pouring rain and the smell of dank earth and the weight of it against my chest. I remember the feel of the dead.

VERONICA SELLERS. AGE 6. LONG BROWN HAIR. LIGHT BLUE EYES. LAST SEEN IN A PARK IN BOSTON.

"Do you recognize these photos?" Wyatt

asks me.

I can't answer. Confronted by the evidence, I still can't state the obvious.

Eventually, Wyatt does it for me.

"You're the girl in these photos, Nicky. The fingerprints recovered from your car prove it. Your name isn't Nicole Frank. You are Veronica Sellers and you've been missing for over thirty years."

The detectives have questions for me. The FBI will want to speak to me, too, Wyatt says. I'm not sure if this is a warning or a threat. Better to speak now, in the company of "friends"? Or wait for the swarm of suits, endless streams of strangers who will demand to hear my story again and again, all while claiming to have my best interests at heart?

Kevin has taken a seat. Again they ask me if I need anything. Food, snack, another bottle of water?

I think a bottle of Glenlivet would do nicely. But mostly, I hold my quilt on my lap. I concentrate on the soft feel of the fabric beneath my fingerprints. I wonder what she will say when she finally hears the news.

Happy, happy, joy, joy? Or thirty years later, is it too late to welcome your dead child home again?

"Do you remember the name Veronica?" Wyatt asks me, after I refuse all their requests, after I sit there, still doing nothing, because what is there for me to do?

I shake my head.

"When was the last time you used that name?"

"Vero is six years old," I whisper. "She is gone. She disappears."

"From the park," Wyatt provides.

"An older girl invites her to play dolls. Vero knows better. Her mom has told her not to talk to strangers. But the older girl seems nice, and Vero is lonely. She would like to play with dolls. She would like to have a friend."

The detectives exchange glances.

"What happened to Vero next?" Wyatt asks.

"A woman appears. Her blond hair is pulled back; she wears such pretty clothes. Much nicer than anything Vero's mom can afford. She is holding a needle. Then she jabs it in Vero's arm, while she stands there, still waiting to see the dolls. And that is that. The older girl is a recruiter. And now Vero is recruited."

"This woman and the girl, they kidnap Vero?"

"They drive her away in the car."

"And no one sees," Wyatt mutters, but he speaks this to Kevin. Information they must have from the original case file, because Vero has no way of knowing this. From the first instant the needle pricks her skin, Vero is gone. She disappears.

"Where do the woman and the girl take Vero?" Wyatt asks.

"Vero moves to a dollhouse. Deep red walls, beautiful stained-glass windows, floral carpets. She gets her very own tower bedroom with a rose mural climbing up the wall. She cries at first, when the woman leads her inside, then turns and locks the door. But of course the room is the prettiest she's ever seen. A bed that is all hers, surrounded by yards of gauze. A wooden table already set with a real china tea set, and surrounded by four chairs filled with a stuffed bear, several dolls. Even the carpet is soft and fluffy. Vero wonders if she's been adopted by her fairy godparents. They've come to take her away, and while she wished they hadn't sent a woman with a needle, she likes this room. She likes this house. Maybe, if she prays really hard, she and her mom can stay here."

"Does Vero's mom arrive?"

"No. The first woman returns. Dressed all

in black now, frosted hair upswept, fat pearls around her neck. She's beautiful but scary. Like a china doll you can look at, but never touch. She tells Vero that Vero is their new guest. Her name will now be Holly. She will wear dresses at all times. She will do as she's told. She will speak only when spoken to. Then the woman gives Vero a new dress. Flounces of pink silk. Vero . . . Holly? . . . likes the dress. She thinks it's very pretty. But she's nervous. She doesn't know what to do, so she doesn't move.

"The woman steps forward. She slaps Vero across the face. Then she rips Vero's shirt from her body. She tells Vero she stinks. She tells Vero she is stupid and ugly and filthy and what kind of ungrateful child refuses such beautiful clothes? Then she holds up the new dress and rips it in half, too. If that's the way you're going to be, she tells Vero . . . Holly . . . then you can wear nothing at all.

"She takes all of Vero's clothes, even her panties. Then she leaves. And Vero sits in the middle of the pretty bedroom, naked and alone. For days and days and days.

"Vero cries for her mom," I whisper. "But her mom never comes."

"What happens?" Wyatt asks softly.

"Vero learns. She wears what they tell her

to wear. She answers to the names they call her. She speaks only when spoken to. There are daily lessons. Some are like school, reading, math, the basics. Others are in clothing, hair, makeup. Then there's music, culture, art. She studies, every day. She tries, because the room is beautiful and the dresses are nice and when she does well, the woman praises her. But when she messes up . . .

"She's alone. Except for lessons with the woman, she sleeps alone, wakes alone, sits alone. She starts to tell herself stories. Of where she once lived. Of the woman who once loved her. Of life before these walls. As days become weeks, become months, become years? It's hard to tell time in the dollhouse. There is just now. Everything else ceases to exist."

"What happens?" Wyatt asks.

"Eventually she passes her lessons. She is old enough, educated enough. Then the men come. And she's sorry she ever studied at all. But she doesn't fight, doesn't protest, doesn't complain. She already knows the men aren't the real danger. It's Madame Sade she has to fear."

"The woman, Madame Sade, runs a brothel?" Wyatt asks bluntly. "She trains the girls, then brings men into the house for sex."

"Our job is to make them happy."

The detectives exchange glances. They are no more fooled by Madame Sade's euphemism than I was.

"What can you tell us about Madame Sade?" Kevin asks.

My lips tremble. My grip on the quilt tightens. I can't speak.

"Describe her," Wyatt prompts more gently. "What does she look like?"

"A china doll. Beautiful but scary."

"Is she as old as Vero's mom?" Kevin presses.

"Older. Fifties maybe."

"Does she have kids, a husband, a special friend?"

I look at him, the memories heavy. "Some of the men want her. But the girls, they whisper: *Be careful what you wish for.*"

"Are there other people in charge?" Wyatt asks.

I shake my head. "It is Madame Sade's house. She makes the rules. She doles out the punishments."

"How many other girls are there?"

"I don't know. Until Vero is twelve, she stays locked in her tower room, a precious flower, a rare commodity."

Kevin looks away. Wyatt's face is too shuttered to read, but that's okay; I'm too lost in the murky corridors of my mind to focus on him anyway.

"What happens after twelve?" he asks at last.

"There are other floors in the dollhouse. Vero moves downstairs, to a smaller room she shares with another girl. Chelsea is older and not happy to see Vero. She steals Vero's makeup, cuts holes in her dresses. She won't allow Vero to sleep on a bed. Instead, Vero is given a spot on the rug. Vero is no longer alone, but she's still lonely. She has her stories, though. She whispers them, night after night. Once upon a time, in a secret realm, there lived a magical queen and her beautiful princess . . ."

"Do the men still come?"

"Madame Sade likes nice things. We make the men happy; she gets more nice things."

"Can you describe the clients?" Wyatt asks.

I shrug. "They are men who have the right jobs and wear the right clothes and grew up with the right connections. Madame Sade doesn't allow just anyone to come over to play."

"Would you recognize these men if you saw them again?"

"Do you really think I was looking at their faces?"

Wyatt flushes, sits back.

"What can you tell us about the house?" Kevin asks.

"Vaulted foyers, marble parlors. Levels and wings and towers that go on and on."

"A mansion? Something castle-like or more Victorian in style?"

I rub my temples. "Victorian," I whisper.

"Were you ever allowed out of the house?" Kevin continues. "Can you tell us about the surroundings? Were there street signs, other homes nearby? What about neighboring woods, water, mountains, other distinct geological features?"

I shake my head. My forehead is on fire. The telltale nausea is back. I don't want to have this conversation anymore. I don't want to have these memories anymore.

"Vero . . . Nicky." Wyatt tries to regain my attention. "What you're describing sounds like a very high-end sex-trafficking ring. This is a big deal. Do you understand that? Some of these people could still be actively exploiting children. Organized operations such as the one you're describing have a tendency to grow larger and more sophisticated with time. Think of the mafia. Thirty years later, the original don might be retired, but he has a whole new generation of lieutenants running the show. This place . . . We need to find it."

I stare at him. He doesn't understand. His words mean nothing to me. They can't mean anything to me. If not for three hits to the head, I never would have allowed these memories to return in the first place.

I sigh. I can't help myself. I'm tired. I'm so very tired and my head hurts and all these things he is asking of me . . .

"Vero is six years old," I whisper. "She is gone. She's disappeared. You can't help her anymore."

Wyatt studies me. "Then why are you still looking for her?"

And just for a moment, my eyes sting with tears.

They're not going to let me go. They want what they think I know, details and memories that will bolster their investigation even if it destroys my sanity. Thirty years ago, a little girl vanished. Now a grown woman stands in her place. The cops can't just let it be. Thomas understood this. So he lit a fire.

The problem with asking questions, he tried to tell me, is that you can't control the answers.

The smell of smoke. The heat of fire.

My hand reaching out, still trying to find him.

"Vero is twelve years old," Wyatt prods now. "She no longer lives in the upstairs room. Where is she?"

But I can't play anymore. The memories are too hard, and I am too done.

"Shhh," I tell them. "Shhh . . ."

For a moment, I don't think they'll listen. Or maybe they won't care, being detectives on a case. But then Wyatt sits back. He eyes me carefully, maybe even compassionately.

"One last question?" he negotiates.

"One."

"How did you get out of the house, away from Madame Sade?"

I stare at him. I think the answer should be obvious. But since apparently it's not, I give him the truth.

"Vero finally learns how to fly."

CHAPTER 24

Wyatt and Kevin exited the conference room. Whatever questions they still had would have to wait. Nicky had placed her quilt on the table, then her head on top of the quilt, and that was that. The poor woman was out cold.

Now the two detectives took a moment to pull themselves together.

"Ladies and gentlemen," Wyatt said, standing just outside the door in the hallway, "we are not in Kansas anymore."

"I need aspirin," Kevin agreed.

"Well, start popping, because it's gonna be a long night."

They couldn't very well leave Nicky unsupervised in the middle of the sheriff's department. On the other hand, they weren't getting any further with her until she got some rest. So being practical men, they took a seat in the hall, just outside the door, backs against the wall.

"Let's start with what we know," Wyatt suggested. "One, Nicole Frank is indeed Veronica Sellers, as proved by the finger-prints recovered from her crashed vehicle."

"According to her," Kevin picked up, "she was kidnapped by a high-end madam thirty years ago and held for at least six years until she finally got away."

"What did you think of her story?" Wyatt asked him.

Kevin didn't hesitate. "The flat affect? The way she refused to engage in the first-person singular, instead everything was in third-person omniscient . . . Vero did this, Vero did that. Consistent with acute trauma. Frankly, not even a serious actress could make that up."

"She implicated herself," Wyatt mur-mured. "First you are recruited; then you are a recruiter."

"Which we know from other victims' testimonies is exactly how these organiza-tions work. Further proof Nicky's probably telling the truth, because someone just try-ing to play victim would never think to go there."

"So we now have a possible lead on a thirty-year-old brothel–slash–sex-trafficking organization. Very sophisticated to judge by what Nicky remembers. Very high-end."

Kevin was more philosophical. "A lead that comes from a woman with a history of one too many blows to the head. Look, I'm not saying I'm doubting her; I'm just saying, this is hardly a slam dunk."

"Post-concussive syndrome cuts both ways," Wyatt said. "A good lawyer can argue the fact she's suffered multiple TBIs proves her memories are suspect. But, on the other hand, it's most likely because she's suffered multiple TBIs that she's now regaining these memories at all."

"Lawyers hate recovered memories," Kevin said flatly. "Judges hate them; juries hate them. Remember in the eighties, when all those kids magically 'recovered' memories of being victimized by satanic cults? Innocent people went to jail, good people eventually realized a bunch of pseudo experts had messed with their heads."

"Then we're in agreement," Wyatt said. "Nicky's 'memories' alone won't be good enough."

"No. We're going to have to corroborate each and every detail, starting with the dollhouse. Thirty years later, that won't be easy."

Wyatt nodded. His thoughts exactly. "How old is Nicky again? Thirty-six, thirty-seven?"

"According to Veronica Sellers's DOB,

right around in there. So we're still within the statute of limitations on sex crimes, if that's what you mean."

The statute of limitations on sex crimes didn't run out until twenty-two years after the victim's eighteenth birthday, if the offense happened before the victim turned eighteen. In this case, that would give them until Nicky/Vero's fortieth birthday to file charges. Not that the statute of limitations was a driving parameter. Wyatt personally felt duty bound to investigate any allegations of wrongdoing, regardless of how long ago the alleged incident occurred. While Joe Public had a tendency to focus on the primary offense — say, kidnapping or sex trafficking — truth was, it took crime to commit crime. For example, chances were any major sex-trafficking organization was also involved in drugs, falsifying documents, witness tampering, and/or transporting victims across state lines. If, say, invitations to these private "parties" were sent using US mail, yet another slew of charges.

Wyatt had had cases where in the end, he couldn't prove the major offense but nailed the perpetrator on dozens of minor charges, which worked just as well.

"All right," he said briskly. "We've identified Veronica Sellers, who's been missing for thirty years. We have allegations of kidnapping and sex crimes. That alone warrants pulling together a task force, while also contacting the National Center for Missing and Exploited Children. Second we make those calls, this place is gonna get hopping. So now, while it's still just you and me, what don't we know?"

"The cause of the initial auto accident," Kevin rattled off without hesitation. "Why had Nicky contacted Northledge Investigations, and who was she following Wednesday night?"

Wyatt studied him. "You haven't figured out who Nicky followed home from the liquor store? Seriously?"

Kevin's turn to look confused. "You have?"

"Absolutely."

"Who?"

"Marlene Bilek, our favorite New Hampshire liquor store clerk. Who also happens to be Veronica Sellers's mother."

"What?"

"The case file, Brain. Mother's name is given as Marlene Sellers. Who I'm guessing has since remarried and taken on the last name Bilek. But that's who Nicky hired Northledge to find. That's the information she got by phone on Wednesday night.

Northledge had finally located her mom. At which point, Nicky took off to see her. Before she lost her courage, remember?"

Kevin scowled at him. "All right, if you're so genius, then have you figured out why Thomas Frank torched their home? I mean, if Nicky's story is true, she's the victim. Even if she's starting to remember her past, no obvious reason for the husband to toss a match and head for the hills."

"That's a problem," Wyatt agreed.

"Didn't Nicky say that her husband had a picture of Vero?" Kevin asked.

"Something like that."

"How? If she disappeared when she was six from Boston and didn't meet him until many years later in New Orleans, how could he have such a picture?"

Wyatt paused, considering the matter. "Maybe they didn't magically meet in New Orleans. Maybe he knew her from before. From . . ." He hesitated. "The dollhouse."

"If he has ties to the sex-trafficking operation," Kevin said, "he'd have reason to run. Clearly, the walls are coming down in Nicky's mind. Meaning the more she remembers . . ."

"The more he has to fear," Wyatt filled in. "The story of how they met always sounded rehearsed to me. Maybe it is. Maybe Thomas's real job has been to keep tabs on Nicky. As long as she wasn't talking — or at least not remembering — he's had nothing to report, and they've been allowed to live and let live. But then, six months ago, after that first fall down the stairs . . ."

"She started looking for Vero."

"And hiring private investigators."

"And moving further out of Thomas's control."

Wyatt nodded. "Never let it be said our job is boring. Okay, we have a boss to get on board, some calls to make, a case team to assemble." He rose to standing, brushing off his pants, but then found himself hesitating.

"Kevin, one last question."

"Yeah."

"The Veronica Sellers case file. She went missing in May, right?"

"Yeah."

Wyatt stared at his detective. "Then why is *November* the saddest month of the year?"

Wyatt assigned one of the female deputies, Gina, to keep an eye on Nicky Frank in the conference room. In the meantime, he had work to do. And not just bringing the sheriff up to speed or filling out paperwork or harassing the locals on why they hadn't managed to locate Thomas Frank yet.

It was 4 A.M. He was dog tired and more than a little confused by a case that refused to be nice, neat and orderly.

But he also was a decent guy, and truth was, he couldn't just leave poor Nicky Frank with no place to go. Not to mention he was an above-average boyfriend who currently had unfinished business with his girl.

So he did what a guy like him did. He picked up the phone and dialed.

Tessa picked up by the second ring. Years of midnight phone calls had that effect on a person.

"Hello." She didn't even sound tired. He couldn't help himself; he was proud of her.

"You talking to me?" he asked her.

"Apparently. You okay?"

"Yeah. Been thinking about your boundaries."

"At four A.M.?"

"That's the kind of world we live in. I love you, you know. I respect you. Admire your job. Appreciate your ethics."

"Okay."

"Having said that, fuck boundaries."

"Excuse me?"

"I mean, you can have them if you want. Feel free. You're right; some kind of limits are implicit in our jobs. But see, you want everything hard lined. Solid walls, this fits over here, this fits over there, bing, bang, boom. I don't buy it. World's too complicated. Our jobs are too complicated. *We* are too complicated. Personally, I like dashed lines. Boundaries with a bit of flexibility built in. Hence I'm calling you right now, even though I don't have to."

"Damn right you don't have to call me at four A.M. —"

"Your client needs you."

"What?"

"You don't want to talk, so just listen. Nicole Frank received a call from Northledge Investigations Wednesday night. Ergo, Nicole Frank is most likely a client of Northledge. Knowing the way your highfalutin firm works, I'm assuming that meant she put down some hefty sort of retainer —"

"I can't comment —"

"Dashed lines, remember? Nicole's house burned down tonight. Her husband has vanished. She's currently all alone, no place to go. As in she's sleeping with her head on our conference room table. I'm assuming her retainer with your firm is still valid. I'm assuming if that's the case, her best interests are in your best interests. I'm assuming . . . Dammit, Tessa, the woman could use help. I can only be an investigating officer. She needs an ally."

Tessa didn't answer right away, but he could nearly hear the gears turning in her mind. "It would be in your own best interest if she was dependent on you," she murmured at last. "She'd be more likely to tell you everything. Even help you find her husband."

"Yep."

"You owe me nothing. Your job. Your case. Your boundaries. Eventually, she might have thought to call Northledge, but you would've had that much more time to isolate her, press your advantage."

"True."

"You didn't have to do this."

"Exactly."

Another pause. Tessa doing the math. Which would always be one of their differences, Wyatt knew. He was a big believer in going with his gut. But for a woman with Tessa's history, it would never be that simple.

"What do you want, Wyatt?"

"The truth. It's why I became a detective. I like answers. And trust me, this woman is a whole lotta questions."

"What if she tells me some of those answers but doesn't allow me to share them with you?"

"Dashed lines are still lines. I know that."

"Do you know why her husband has gone AWOL?"

"No. But I know her real name."

Pause. "Is it Veronica Sellers?"

Wyatt's turn to be surprised. "You didn't know?"

"No. Not what she hired us for. But once I did some digging, I suspected. Only thing that made any sense. It's not my job to report suspicions, however. I can only do what the client employs me to do. Do you think the husband is trying to kill her? The multiple falls, the accident Wednesday night?"

"I have no idea. But I think if half of what Nicky just told us about her abduction thirty years ago is true, her life is about to become very dangerous."

"All right. I'm on my way. And Wyatt . . ."

"Yes?"

"Thank you."

CHAPTER 25

I jerk awake. My legs kick out. My head flies up. Maybe I scream? At the last second, I do my best to choke off the gasp, old habits dying hard.

Round wooden table. Gray linoleum floor. Ugly drop ceiling. The sheriff's department. I have fallen asleep with my head on the conference room table, still clutching the pale yellow quilt.

Wyatt and Kevin are no longer sitting across from me. Instead, Wyatt stands near the door and there's a dark-haired woman beside him. She wears dress jeans, black leather boots and a tailored navy-blue jacket that brings out the color of her eyes. There is something about the way they are standing that captures my attention. Together, but separate. I have a sense of déjà vu. Thomas and me.

"Nicole Frank?" the woman asks. Her voice is low and firm, a voice of authority.

"Yes."

"Do you remember me? My name is Tessa Leoni. We spoke on the phone. Wednesday night."

Something clicks in the back of my head. I glance at Wyatt.

"Sergeant Foster contacted me on your behalf," the woman provides, as if reading my mind. "He thought, given present circumstances, you might appreciate some assistance."

"You're not a lawyer."

"No. I'm a private security specialist."

I can't help myself; I smile. "My life is so bad I require a specialist."

The woman returns my smile. She's not beautiful, I think, but striking. Hard angles. Strong jaw. Her smile is not soft, but reassuring. Her stance is not relaxed but confident. She doesn't look like a person who was given a private security title. She looks like a woman who's earned it.

Now she turns to Wyatt, and there is something in his gaze . . .

He would stare at her forever if he could. The way Thomas once looked at me.

"Are you filing charges against my client?" she asks him.

"We have some questions —"

"Which I'm sure can wait until she's had

a chance to clean up, eat a meal."

"We did offer her bread and water," Wyatt deadpans.

"Please, I've seen your vending machine."

They have a history. I want to tell them to stand closer. I want to tell them to talk less, listen more. Hold this moment. I think I'm going to cry. It's the mood swings, I tell myself, just another side effect of multiple head traumas.

It's not that I've woken up for the first time in twenty-two years in a world without Thomas.

Both of them are looking at me. The woman doesn't ask questions; she tells me what we're doing next.

"You're coming with me. I'm going to get you situated in a hotel, order you some food, find you some clothes. You're my client, so please know anything you tell me will be kept in strictest confidence. This guy, however, can't say the same, so I'd advise waiting on the rest of this conversation until we're alone."

She turns to Wyatt. "How watertight is your department these days?"

"Now, now, don't piss me off."

"We need time." Tessa's voice softens. "She needs time." She jerks her head toward me. "Twenty-four hours?"

"Can't make any guarantees. Missing kids belong to the feds. And kids who magically reappear after being gone thirty years . . ."

"There are cable news execs getting fluttering feelings in their heartless chests as we speak," she fills in.

"Exactly."

Tessa doesn't talk again until we've left the building. She leads me straight to a dark Lexus SUV with a beautiful tan leather interior. I think of my Audi, and it already seems so long ago, a vehicle for a different woman in a different life that never could've been me.

When we get in the car, she locks the doors.

"How are you?" she asks without preamble. "I understand you've suffered from multiple concussions. Do you require medical attention? Do we need to pick up any ibuprofen, painkillers, Band-Aids, chocolate doughnuts, whatever, to help you?"

"I like ice packs."

"I can make that happen. When did you last sleep?"

"What time is it?"

"Nine A.M."

"Then I slept the past few hours at the station."

Tessa nods, pulls out of the parking lot.

338

"Do you remember me?" she asks as she pulls onto the main road.

"We talked on the phone Wednesday. But you weren't the investigator who first took my case . . ."

"No. Originally you met with Diane Fieldcrest. But she got hung up on another assignment. I just happened to be having a slow week, so I offered to help her out. To be honest, I don't normally handle such routine assignments. But once I realized who you were looking for . . ."

I don't say anything.

Tessa glances at me. Her hands are sure on the wheel. "You don't owe me anything," she continues matter-of-factly. "You hired Northledge to locate a woman. I ran the background, discovered the requested information and reported back to you. After that, what happens is your business, not ours."

I don't say anything.

"You don't owe me anything," she repeats. "You do, however, need to understand exactly what you're about to be up against."

"What do you mean?"

"Fact one, you're a missing person who is essentially, thirty years later, returning from the dead."

I wince.

"The media loves this stuff. As in, if we

339

can keep reporters at bay until after lunch, I'll be shocked."

I stare at her. I haven't considered any of this.

"They're going to ask questions," Tessa continues. "Starting with, why didn't you come forward before now? If you were abducted at six, but somehow got away . . . Why have you waited this long to find your family? What have you been doing all these years?"

I can't speak. My heart is pounding too hard. I can feel a tremendous sense of pressure building in my chest. Like a grave, I think wildly. They have no idea.

"Nicky, you're in trouble."

I open my mouth. I close my mouth. Finally, I nod.

"I know it, you know it, Wyatt knows it. Frankly, that's why he called me. Now, I'm going to start with the obvious. I'm going to check you into a hotel under an assumed name. I'm going to find you clothes, including the proverbial oversize sunglasses and bulky hats. Also, we're going to find you a lawyer, and I mean ASAP. But even then, Nicky, you're in trouble.

"You have thirty years to account for. You have a husband who might be an arsonist. You have a motor vehicle accident that may be the result of a felony DWI."

She turns to me. "You have a family, Nicky. You have a mom, who's lived forty miles from you for the past six months, and you never even let her know you were alive.

"Nicky, on behalf of all the reporters and really bored community members who are about to zero in on your life: What the hell do you have to say for yourself?"

I don't have any answers.

I hold my quilt. And I find myself thinking once again, flying is not the hard part; the landing is.

Tessa finds us a hotel. Not a major chain, but a smaller operation near a ski resort where hotel rooms outnumber the local population ten to one. This will make it harder for the reporters to track us down, I realize.

She leaves me in the car to book the room. When she returns, she drives to the back of the hotel, where it turns out she's gotten us a second-floor walkup. There are no buildings across from the hotel, meaning there is no way for anyone, say, a photographer with a telephoto lens, to find us. I realize I'm starting to think the way she thinks, or maybe I've known these things all along. Back of the hotel is more secure than the front. Lower level too accessible, second floor easier to control.

The room is basic but nice. Two queen beds, relatively new beige carpet, flat-screen TV. There is the obligatory picture of a moose on one wall, a photo of a snow-capped mountain on the other. Could be any hotel in the North Country, I think, which makes it perfect.

Tessa has a small overnight bag with her. Obviously, I have my quilt.

She places her bag on the bed closest to the door, so I set the quilt down on the other bed.

"Are you staying?" I ask. By which I really mean, are we sharing a room? The thought already has me uncomfortable. Like I traded in one set of jailors — Wyatt and Kevin — for another.

Tessa doesn't answer, just takes a seat at the foot of the bed. She's already drawn the curtains. Now she turns on the TV, finds a cable news channel, sets the volume on low.

"All right, we have some basics to cover."

I don't know what else to do, so I sit.

"Are you hungry?"

"I think so."

"I'll bring you food. Write up what you want; I'll take care of it. But no room service. Not yet. Draws attention."

"How long are we staying here?"

"I have no idea. My turn: Where is your husband?"

I decide to play along: "I have no idea."

She smiles. "Let me clarify some things. I imagine Diane had this initial conversation with you, but given the post-concussive syndrome and the fact you barely remember employing Northledge at all —"

"I'm pretty sure I did," I interject.

"Can you describe our Boston office?"

I try, come up blank.

She nods. "Exactly. So when you hired Northledge to track down Marlene Bilek, you handed over a large deposit, a retainer check to be used to cover the expenses of that search. In your case, you handed over a cashier's check."

She pauses a beat. I fill in the rest. "I couldn't use a personal check. I didn't want Thomas to know."

"Fair enough. The firm never minds being paid in cash. But the truth is, tracking down Marlene Bilek took about fifteen minutes of my time. Meaning, we didn't come close to burning through the retainer. You are, by virtue of your money sitting in our account, a client in good standing."

"Okay."

"This makes me the investigator handling

your case. Couple of things you should know. The first principle of our firm is that your privacy is our most important asset. I need you to be honest with me. I can help you best if you are honest with me."

I study her. I think I'm getting good at this game: "But?"

"But while a private investigator can offer her client confidentiality, our relationship still doesn't rise to the level of privilege. For example, anything you say to a doctor or a lawyer is automatically protected in a court of law. I'm *only* your investigator, not a doctor or lawyer."

"Meaning you can be forced to disclose what I tell you."

"I can be subpoenaed, yes, much like a reporter. At which time I can protect my source, so to speak, and be found in contempt of court, or I can disclose the information."

"Contempt of court equals jail time. Why would you want to go to jail for me?"

Tessa tilts her head to the side. "I don't know, Nicky. Why would I want to go to jail for you?"

"You need me to be truthful," I say at last. "But you also need me to be careful. For both our sakes."

"If it makes you feel any better, I'm going

to try to make it easier for both of us."

"How so?"

"Wyatt . . . Sergeant Foster —"

"Wyatt. You know him. You have a relation-ship."

"We've worked together before."

"This isn't a court of law," I tell her. "You're not under subpoena."

Tessa smiles, still doesn't take the bait. "Wyatt says you claimed you were kid-napped and held as a sex slave. In a fancy home, maybe a Victorian, probably some-where in the greater Boston area. You referred to it as a dollhouse."

"Yes."

"There were other girls there. At least one roommate, but most likely dozens more."

"It was a big house."

"And the clients who frequented, we're talking successful men, well-to-do. This was an elite operation."

I shrug. "Perverts come in all socioeco-nomic classes."

"Trust me, I know. This was a sophisti-cated operation, yes? You weren't the first girl taken, nor the last."

I can't look at her anymore. "No."

She nods. "The police are going to look for the dollhouse. This kind of sex-trafficking operation, the resources it would take, the players involved. I bet they already have a few ideas of where to start. Given your situation, however, I have a different idea."

"What do you mean?"

"Nicky, has it ever occurred to you that maybe you're not the first girl to have gotten away?"

I can't help myself. I stare at her blankly. No, I've never thought such a thing.

"Maybe," Tessa continues now, "there are more of you out there. And that would be a good thing, Nicky. There's strength in numbers. It bolsters your story. It takes some of the pressure off you. It would mean, by definition, you're not alone."

I can't speak; I can't breathe. Another girl. Would that be a good thing? Sisters in arms? Or . . . I can't sit anymore. I get up and pace.

"Thirty years ago," Tessa is saying, "the investigative landscape was very different. ViCAP, a database for linking criminal cases from around the country, was just getting started. The National Center for Missing and Exploited Children had barely been founded. All in all, it was very difficult for law enforcement agencies from different jurisdictions to compare notes. Meaning a six-year-old girl could be kidnapped from a park here, while a twelve-year-old runaway disappeared from a shelter there, and an eight-year-old delinquent never came home from the mall, and no one would necessarily connect the dots. We know better now, and I'd like to use that to our advantage."

"What do you mean?"

"I have a friend. A Boston detective who currently has some time on her hands. I'm going to ask her to go back through thirty years of missing-kid cases, from all over New England, to see if she can connect some dots. If we can establish just how many girls they were taking, and how, and from where, that would enable us to corroborate your story. It might also help identify the players involved."

I walk away from her. Check out the flatscreen TV. I'm rubbing my arms, though I'm not sure why. I'm not cold but I'm covered in goose bumps.

I miss Thomas. I wonder where he is right now. Where is he going and what is he doing? Right or wrong, I wish he was here.

"Why are you hiring someone else?" I mumble. "Can't you just ask around yourself?"

Tessa doesn't answer right away. When she does, her question takes me off guard.

"Do you know what a Chinese wall is?"

I shake my head, already confused. I need more sleep. My head hurts.

"A Chinese wall is an informational barrier constructed within a firm for the sake of ethical integrity. For example, in a law firm, if investigating one client's case might result in identifying information that was detrimental to another client, the firm could construct a Chinese wall. Essentially, the company would establish two separate investigative efforts, operating independently and not sharing information, thus enabling itself to serve both clients without compromising ethics."

I frown, still confused. "But I'm your only client. How is hiring someone not to tell you what they learn helpful?"

"She would tell it to you, just maybe not to me." Tessa hesitates. When she speaks again, her tone is careful. "Northledge is a top-notch investigative firm. With an impressive list of wealthy and respectable clients. Now, according to you, the customers at the dollhouse . . ."

"Wealthy and respectable clients." I spit out the words.

"Exactly. I could do the research. But what I might find and have to present to my own bosses . . . It's cleaner this way, for both of us. And trust me, this detective I'd like to hire, D. D. Warren. If she identified the governor himself exploiting young girls, she'd slap him in handcuffs. If there's something to find, any kind of trail to be picked up from thirty years ago, she can do it."

I nod, but I don't feel reassured. This Chinese wall protects Tessa and her firm's roster of wealth and privilege. What I need is a Chinese wall for me. Some kind of defense to protect who I am now from what I once did. Except maybe there is no protection for that. Which is why I spend most of my days both forgetting who I am and yet still searching for Vero.

"One last thing," Tessa says quietly.

"What?"

"Your mom. Nicky, Thomas may be gone, but you still have a family. Don't you think it's time to finally call them?"

"You don't understand," I whisper. "Vero is six years old. She is gone. She disappears."

But then I remember something else. A view from outside a house on a rainy night. A young girl sitting on a sofa.

I open my mouth. No words come out.

Tessa is waiting for me to speak. She is patient. Wyatt is patient. The whole world is waiting for me.

I want to lie down in the dark, ice pack on my head. I want to cover myself in the quilt. I want to close my eyes and be alone with Vero.

We will sip scotch out of teacups. I will watch the maggots crawl around her shiny white skull.

I will apologize once more for everything I've done.

Maybe this time, she will forgive me. Because no one ever got out of the doll-house alive.

"Nicole?" Tessa asks quietly.

The memories are shifting again. Cold, dark shadows that heave and menace. Nothing comforting, nothing enlightening.

I understand for the first time, the truth is not all out yet. And maybe not even the kind of truth that will set me free. Thomas had tried to warn me, but I hadn't listened. Now here I am. Shivering in dread. Nearly choking on the bile of my own fear. Something, something in that darkness looms.

All these years later, is still waiting for me . . .

"Nicky?"

Tessa's voice comes from a distance. I use it to anchor myself, pull myself back to the present.

She must see something in my eyes,

because she takes my hand, helps me take a seat on the edge of one of the beds.

"Nicky, picture the dollhouse. A room, a piece of furniture, some aspect of that home, then breathe in deep and tell me what you smell. Nothing too scary or overwhelming. Just an association that comes immediately to mind."

Funny, I don't have to think too hard. As she said, a fragrance comes immediately to mind.

"Freshly mowed grass."

Tessa doesn't question or debate my choice. She simply rises to standing. "I need to run a few errands for us. I recommend using the time to freshen up. Because the moment I return, we are getting to work."

CHAPTER 26

Wyatt had started to feel the burn of an endless night. He sat in his boss's office, head sagging, as he did his best to talk his way through a case that posed way too many questions and not nearly enough answers.

"You're sure this woman is Veronica Sellers?" Sheriff Rober asked now. "A missing girl from thirty years ago?"

"According to her fingerprints, yes."

"You think she was kidnapped by some high-end madam, imprisoned in the woman's home-slash-brothel until she eventually escaped. At which time she made it to New Orleans, where she married this guy Thomas, and, what, started over? Lived happily ever after for twenty-two years, until six months ago, when Thomas decided to kill her, resulting in three accidents and now a house fire."

Wyatt nodded, though something about hearing his case as a laundry list of crimes . . .

"Can one girl be so unlucky?" the sheriff asked bluntly.

"I have no idea, sir."

"Seems to me, you really got two cases. You have what happened thirty years ago. The kidnapping, followed by the sex crimes. Then you have today. The single MVA followed by arson. I guess followed by the missing husband."

"We have an APB out on Thomas Frank now, as well as a trace on his cell phone. One way or another, we'll find him."

"But you don't have him yet. What you have is a bunch of stories from an injured woman's mind."

"We know the car accident was more than an accident," Wyatt interjected. "The stability system was disabled, the vehicle placed in neutral and most likely given a shove down the hill. That implies a second person had to be present at the time of the accident."

"The husband again?"

"Who was very reluctant to turn over his rain jacket and went out of his way to retrieve his wife's own clothes from that night, I believe to further conceal any evidence of his actions. Add to that him torching his own home and running for it the second we homed in on him, and yeah, he looks pretty guilty to me."

"Why?" Sheriff Rober asked. "Twenty-two years later, what changed? Forget the wild stories of brothels and missing kids. Return to the basics. Why does a husband kill his wife?"

"Insurance money, revenge, wanting out of the marriage but not wanting to divvy up assets." Wyatt shrugged. "We have looked at the basics, trust me. At the moment, there's no sign of a large life insurance policy, nor any sign that either of the Franks was involved in extramarital activities. Honestly, sir, my best guess is that whatever's happening now ties back to what happened thirty years ago."

"You think Thomas Frank was part of this so-called dollhouse?"

"Maybe. Of course, thirty years ago, he was just a kid himself. Which makes things more complicated."

"Fellow victim? Sex trafficking isn't just about girls."

"I don't know. Kevin is running a deeper background on the Franks now. According to Thomas, he and Nicky met and married twenty-two years ago in New Orleans. Upon further investigation, however, Thomas Frank doesn't show any activity under that name until twenty years ago. As in he never had a credit card or a driver's license until 1995. Same with Nicole Frank."

"Fake identities?"

"Most likely. Well done, deep enough to stand up to cursory inspection, but when you start filling in the details . . . Sure, Thomas Frank has a birth certificate. But he still never lived until the past two decades."

"Ask the wife about it?"

"Given the state of her memory, not sure how productive, or reliable, that conversation would be."

"Meaning, all the more reason to find Thomas and grill him."

"Agreed."

"So what's your game plan?" the sheriff asked. "You got a missing suspect and a scrambled victim. What next?"

"I need to contact the National Center for Missing Children, of course. Let them know about Veronica Sellers. Thought I might see if they could send over the original documents on the missing persons case. Maybe by going through the original witness statements, I can find something that will give me some traction on what's going on now."

"You could," the sheriff said, but he was

nodding in a way that Wyatt already knew meant he disagreed. "You have to call them, true. And maybe they'll agree to give you access to some old case file. But consider this. Moment you call, they're assembling a task force in a conference room. That task force is then going to locate northern New Hampshire on a map. By evening, they'll be on a plane. First thing tomorrow morning, they'll be walking through our front door. At which time, maybe they'll hand you a box of paperwork. But definitely they're going to take your best witness, Nicky Frank, as well as this entire case, away from you. Just like that."

Wyatt sighed, then nodded heavily. The sheriff was right, of course. The recovery of a kid, missing thirty years, was big news. Hold-a-press-conference-wearing-their-best-federal-suits, taking-full-federal-credit kind of news. A mere county sheriff's department didn't stand a chance.

"Can you locate this brothel?" the sheriff asked now. "You got a description, something concrete that puts it in our county, gives us half a chance?"

"I got nothing," Wyatt confessed. "Nicky described the home as a Victorian mansion, driving distance from Boston. Run by a madam who looks like a china doll, and also

356

occupied by an evil roommate named Chelsea. That's what we know."

"Please don't tell the feds that."

"Yeah."

"What do you have?" the sheriff pressed.

Wyatt was tired. He'd been up all night, and the coffee was wearing off. He stared at his boss blankly.

"You got Nicky Frank," the sheriff spelled out for him. "Or Veronica Sellers, or whatever the hell her name is. That's what you have; they don't."

"You mean the world's most unreliable witness?"

"Whatever's going on here, she holds the key. Get a doctor. Get a hypnotist, a therapist, whatever it takes. But start pushing, and don't stop until you get some real answers out of her, including what's up with the husband. You have less than twenty-four hours to find answers, Sergeant. Time to make your play."

Wyatt turned over the matter in his mind as he walked down the second-floor corridor to his own modest office. He didn't like the idea of a hypnotist. He agreed with Nicky; her mind was messed up enough. But a therapist? Maybe an expert in PTSD? Could someone like that possibly coax

Nicky into a walk down memory lane that finally ended with some answers? Of course, how to locate such a therapist and get him or her to his office ASAP? Clock was ticking, so definitely no rest for the wicked on this one.

He'd just made it to his office door, was debating whether more coffee would help or hurt at this point, when Kevin burst through the stairwell ahead of him.

"We got him."

"Who?"

"Thomas Frank. Patrol officer spotted his vehicle parked behind a strip motel, Route 302, forty minutes north."

Wyatt forgot all about caffeine. Quick swipe of his car keys off the corner of his desk; then he and Kevin were hammering down the stairs toward the parking lot.

"Did the officer approach him?" Wyatt asked as they hit ground level.

"Nah, called it in. Since you were tied up with the big boss, I instructed him to lay low, keep eyes on, but remain out of sight. He's gonna work on getting the exact room number for us."

"Perfect. All right. Mobilize the troops. We're gonna want patrol cars north and south in case he runs for it. In the meantime, this is our party. We make the first contact."

They clambered into the county SUV, Wyatt behind the wheel, Kevin working the radio. Forty minutes north. Wyatt figured he could make that thirty. And he did.

Kevin had just spotted the long, white-painted strip motel on the left, when Thomas Frank's silver Suburban turned out of the parking lot right in front of them.

"There, that's him!" Wyatt called out. The driver didn't appear spooked, but was driving at a moderate pace. Wyatt hit the sirens, however, and all that changed.

The Suburban shot forward, V8 engine gunning. Apparently, Thomas Frank wasn't done running just yet.

"What the hell did you do, man?" Wyatt muttered under his breath. "Because you're about to go down the hard way."

Wyatt hit the accelerator, easily closing the gap. Beside him, Kevin was already alerting the two patrol cars five miles north that the chase was on. They careened past a gas station/local deli, a diner and a campsite; then civilization thinned out, and it was full speed ahead.

Sixty, seventy, eighty miles an hour on the winding road. The Suburban took one corner too fast, rocking onto two wheels.

For one second, it remained suspended in precarious balance, then slammed back to four tires on the ground, lurching awkwardly forward. Another sharp left, followed by a winding right. As the Suburban slipped from eighty to sixty to eighty again.

Wyatt felt calm and focused, the way he always did on the hunt. His hands were steady on the wheel, his breathing controlled. This was his element. The moment a good officer trained and, frankly, lived for.

In contrast, the Suburban was beginning to weave erratically. Panic, exhaustion, impairment, but Thomas Frank appeared to be losing it.

The Suburban swung wildly into the left-hand lane. An oncoming car blared its horn, then belatedly spotted the pursuing police vehicle and pulled over. Better late than never, as the saying went.

Now the Suburban overcorrected to the right, skidding almost sideways across the road, two wheels crunching into the soft shoulder and making it fishtail wildly.

Wyatt backed off his speed, frowning at the Suburban's out-of-control maneuvers. Suddenly, he wasn't feeling so good about things. In fact . . .

A tractor-trailer appeared ahead. Logging truck, just coming around the corner, a little wide with its long, heavy load bearing down upon the Suburban.

"Don't you dare, don't you dare!" Wyatt shouted at Thomas Frank.

Who'd just swung his Suburban back into the path of the oncoming semi, as if playing chicken with a tractor-trailer was a good idea. In fact, better than surrendering to the local cops.

Wyatt could think of only one more thing to do. Not a great idea. Not his best idea. But in the spur of the moment . . .

He shoved the accelerator to the floor, fully committing 202 horsepower to his bidding. As he pulled alongside the lumbering Suburban's dark-tinted passenger window. No view of Thomas. Wild-eyed with desperation, or dead set with determination, Wyatt had no way to know. And no time to find out.

The logging truck hit its brakes, sounding its deep horn. As Wyatt drove his own vehicle into the side of the Suburban. The crunch and grind of metal. A frozen instant of time, when neither vehicle gave way, but remained locked together with the other, a twin-size target for the oncoming semi. Wyatt lifted his foot from the gas, swerved one last time into the side of the Suburban. Then . . .

The Suburban was knocked left. Veered off the road onto the tree-lined shoulder just as the logging truck squealed through the space it used to occupy. Wyatt fought with his own vehicle, steady, steady, snap, back into his own lane, blowing by the logging truck as Kevin roared a few words the Brain rarely said.

Wyatt hit the brakes. His vehicle stopped. The logging truck stopped.

The world stopped.

"Shit," he muttered.

Kevin got on the radio and called for backup.

The silver Suburban had done a face-plant into a tree. The hood was a crumpled mess, steam rising, fluids flushing down, as if in its last moments, the vehicle had lost control of its bowels.

Wyatt looped around to the driver's side door, Kevin assuming cover position. In the distance they could already hear the sound of approaching sirens.

Driver's side window wasn't broken, which put Wyatt at a disadvantage. He couldn't completely see inside, but it appeared the driver was slumped over the wheel. He gestured to Kevin, then did the count with his fingers. On three, Wyatt took one fluid step forward, jerked open the door, then twisted behind it for cover.

As the driver toppled out of the car onto the ground.

"Thomas Frank, you're under arrest," Wyatt barked out loudly.

Except when he stepped forward, it wasn't Thomas Frank who lay before him.

It took another thirty minutes to work it out. Despite the first officer's best intentions, Thomas Frank must've made him. Rather than run for it, he'd knocked on the door of the room next to his. Introduced himself to Brad Kittle, who, it turned out, had spent most of the morning doping up. When a strange dude offered him the keys to his car, that had seemed the best thing that had ever happened to good old Brad. He'd taken the keys. When the dude suggested he go for a test drive, even better.

Except, of course, then there had been sirens. Things got a little fuzzy for Brad after that. Mostly, he was high, he knew he was high, and, oh yeah, he was driving a car that wasn't his while having a suspended license. Even his baked brain had understood that could be a problem.

So he'd run for it. Real exciting, like Hollywood, he'd informed them, as the blood had poured from multiple cuts down his face, and yet, thanks to his morning binge, he still wasn't feeling any pain.

"Didn't even know a Suburban could drive that fucking fast," he'd exclaimed. "I mean, it's like supercharging a rhino, man. A beast, swerving around this corner, that corner. Dude, I thought I was gonna die. Cool!"

Wyatt and Kevin gave up on the pothead, returned to the motel. The original reporting officer had greeted them in the parking lot, very excited to hear how things had turned out. Wyatt and Kevin didn't talk. They got Thomas's room number. They crashed through the door, and they discovered exactly what they expected to find. An empty room, Thomas Frank nowhere in sight.

"Door-to-door," Wyatt had instructed the uniformed officer. "Get everyone out of their rooms. Thomas didn't just disappear. He stole a car, copped a ride, something. Get everyone talking until you know exactly how he left this property. Then report back to me immediately. We gotta update the APB."

A very subdued officer went to do as he was told.

Kevin called for the evidence techs to

process the room; then they returned to what they did have: one wrecked Suburban, their lone link to Thomas Frank. They both started searching.

Wyatt took the front seats, Kevin the rear bench seat. Like his wife's, Thomas's tastes ran toward the neat and tidy. No food wrappers, crumpled-up receipts or discarded maps.

Glove compartment yielded the normal vehicle operations manual, insurance card and valid registration in the name of Thomas Frank. Wyatt picked up a black baseball cap from the floor, still slightly damp to the touch. From Wednesday night's storm, maybe wearing it when he followed, pursued, somehow tracked down his wife?

He also discovered an E-ZPass toll transponder; unfortunately, the only tolls in New Hampshire were to the south, so it couldn't help them track local movements.

"Is it just me," Wyatt muttered to Kevin, who'd moved on to the rear cargo area, "or is it almost as if the Franks were trained to leave no mark behind?"

"I got something."

"Thank God."

Wyatt gave up on the front, moved to the rear doors of the Suburban, where Kevin was currently standing.

"In the spare tire well. First item of interest." Kevin held it up in gloved hands. "A collapsible shovel" — he gestured to the sales tags — "recently purchased."

"Interesting. Thomas on his way to bury something?"

"Which brings us to item number two, a brown paper bag. Which . . ." Kevin started coughing heavily. "Smells like scotch. Blech."

"The clothes." Wyatt grabbed the bag. "Betting you now, Nicky's clothes from Wednesday night."

He donned gloves to open up the sack, which absolutely reeked. Of whiskey, wet earth and something worse.

He and Kevin weren't talking anymore as Wyatt drew out a pair of mud-encrusted jeans, a black turtleneck, a gray fleece.

He gagged slightly as the odor became more pronounced. Blood. Definitely. Dried. Soaked into the fabric, now permeating the bag. From Nicky's injuries that night? Or something else?

"Wyatt." Kevin gestured to a crumpled object that had just fallen from the jeans. Wadded, sticky, nearly black in color. Except not black, of course, but a deep, dark red.

Wyatt used a pencil and took his time. As

bit by bit, he unwrapped the blood-encrusted latex, until a familiar shape lay before them. Ripped, tattered, but nonetheless distinct.

The proverbial bloody glove.

"Just what the hell were they doing Wednesday night," Kevin whispered, "that involves a collapsible shovel and bloody gloves?"

Wyatt didn't say a word.

CHAPTER 27

Vero is braiding my hair. We aren't in the tower bedroom anymore. Maybe it's her mood, maybe it's my mood, but we've downgraded to the little room. With the one narrow window and the twin beds shoved tight together because that's all the space will allow. At the foot of the bed is a tattered blue area rug. Neither of us look at the rug.

I'm sitting on one of the beds. Vero is kneeling behind me, efficiently plaiting my long dark hair into braids. She is lecturing me as she works.

"You can't trust them."

I don't say anything. Nor do I move. Every now and then, the flesh disappears from her hands, and I feel her skeletal fingers rake across my scalp.

"Where were the police thirty years ago? If they're so good, they should've found you then. If they're so hardworking and trustworthy, they should've rescued you then. Even cops have appetites. You know it's true."

In the distance I can hear the sound of a lawn mower. I don't know why, but it makes my expression soften, my shoulders relax. If I wasn't here with Vero, I would get up now, climb across the beds to the tiny window. I would look out and see . . .

"You need to pay attention!" Vero tugs my hair. Hard. I wince. She doesn't care. "Time is running out; don't you get that?"

I can't turn my head to look at her, so I shrug.

"I'm trying to help you. You still won't see what you need to see. You still don't know what you need to know. How long do you plan on being so stupid?"

"What are you?" I ask. "My childhood ghost, my guilty conscience?"

She yanks my hair, definitely annoyed. "I know what I am, but what are you?" she taunts back.

"I think you're a tool."

She gasps, clearly surprised by this mundane description, maybe even put off.

"You are the gatekeeper of the memories I can't face," I continue, thinking out loud. "Whatever happened all those years ago . . . I boxed it up. Put it away with a sign that read 'Keep Out.' Except things don't like to stay boxed up, do they? Even the past wants to be heard. I think you're its avatar, the face of all the memories trying to break free."

"If you're so fucking smart," Vero informs me, "then why are you so stupid?" She drops my hair, steps off the bed, clearly done with me.

But I don't let her go. I'm running out of time. Something worse is lurking out there. I've started a process that can't be undone, and now, if I don't figure out everything, and fast . . .

The past doesn't just want to be heard. Sometimes, it wants revenge.

The smell of smoke. The heat of the flames.

The sounds of her screams.

Even in my own mind, I automatically reach out a hand for Thomas.

"Why does Chelsea hate me?" I ask Vero now. "This room . . ." I drift my fingers across the threadbare brown coverlet. "There was just the two of us. I thought we'd be friends."

"She can't be your friend," Vero says immediately. She is standing on the blue carpet. Her skin is back on her face, but her hands remain skeletal.

"Why not?"

"There are no friends in the dollhouse. You survive in this place. You endure. You *don't* make friends."

Vero's voice sounds funny. I study her carefully and discover she is crying.

"You're sad," I whisper. I don't know why this surprises me. Of course she's sad. The memory of a kidnapped little girl. She should be devastated.

"The secret realm, the magical queen," she singsongs now. Her hair is starting to fall out in clumps, the white of her skull showing through. "Once I had a life. Once I had a story. I told you those stories. Over and over again. Because someone had to know. Someone had to remember what was real."

"I understand."

"Chelsea doesn't have a story. Even before the dollhouse. There was no magical queen, no secret realm. No one has ever loved her, not even you. No one wants to be her" — she eyes me slyly — "not even you."

"She was jealous."

"I stole her room, the best room, the tower room . . ." Vero's voice is no longer sad, but smug. A look flitters across her face. Not little girl at all, but devious. Suddenly, I'm nervous.

"Once, she was the princess, but when I came, I was younger, more beautiful." She preens. I step back, even more uncomfortable.

"I took it. I claimed the tower. I commanded all of Madame Sade's attention. I was the youngest, the brightest, the best. Of course she spent all her time on me. I was worth it!"

"You were a little girl —"

"A diamond in the rough. But I learned. I learned everything. And when I was twelve and the time came, she gave me to her most special of friends, the richest, the most powerful, the most commanding of them all. The others knew. Of course they hated me for it." But Vero's not complaining; she's boasting.

Maybe she should. For six long years she was locked away, all alone except for her teacher's company.

"Who are the other girls?" I ask, for things are shifting again in the back of my mind. Except this time, I don't turn away. I step closer.

"You know. You know you know. We are a family. A fucked-up, twisted family, fashioned by the world's most fucked-up, twisted mother, Madame Sade herself."

And for a second, I can almost picture it.

Family dinners, yes. All of us sitting around the formal dining table. Except Madame Sade's family only has girls — yes, no? — four of us. Two older, two younger. Chelsea and I are the younger pair, positioned at the far end of the table. Where we watch the two older girls, with their carefully polished faces and poofed-up hair, whisper between themselves. Every now and then, almost on cue, their heads rotate to stare at us. Their expressions are harsh, knowing. We quickly look away. We're scared of them. They are our future, and we know it.

Vero whispers in my ear, "No one ever leaves the dollhouse. Only way out is death, death, death."

But there is something else here, something else I know I need to grab on to, study harder.

I hear myself say: "You didn't keep the tower bedroom."

Vero jerks back. More patches of hair fall from her skull. Followed by pieces of her face.

"There is no one younger and prettier than me!" she snarls.

"You moved into the room with Chelsea."

"Jealous. No one ever loved her. Not even you. No one wants to be her, not even you!"

"But she . . ." I hesitate; then the words

simply come out. I don't know if I'm speaking the truth, as much as I simply have to speak. "Chelsea loved you. In the beginning, she was jealous. No, she was afraid. But by the end, she loved you very much. Living in this room with you; it was the first time in her life she didn't feel alone."

Vero won't look at me anymore. She spins away, half flesh, half bone. Half girl, half ghost.

She is dancing on the rug, I realize. As if daring me to see it.

Outside, the sound of the lawn mower, moving closer. I want so badly to go to the window. I don't want to be trapped in this room anymore with Vero. I want to peer out over the vast, sweeping lawn. I want to feel the sun on my face. I want to see him.

But I don't move. I stay where I am, watching Vero, and I realize for the first time, she is holding a needle in one hand. As I watch, the insides of her arms fill up with track marks. Identical to the marks on the older girls, I realize now. Our future selves. Because in the beginning Madame Sade offers a beautiful bedroom, a roof over your head. But by the end, it's not enough. It takes a more compelling incentive to keep the girls working.

To keep them dependent.

Vero catches my stare. She laughs louder, spins more wildly.

"Please," I try to tell her. "It wasn't your fault. Whatever happened, whatever you did. You shouldn't have been put through this; you shouldn't have —"

"Loved to fly?"

I can't talk to her anymore. There is a look on her face . . .

I'm afraid again. More frightened than I think I've ever been, my fingers sinking into the edge of the mattress. I don't want to be here. I don't want to talk to her; I don't want to remember.

But I still don't leave. A process has been started. It's too late to turn back now.

"There's only one way out of the dollhouse," she cries now, twirling on the rug, dancing on the rug, toe-tapping across the rug. "Death, death, death!"

"But I didn't die," I protest.

She stops moving so suddenly, the skin flies from her body. She stands before me, a bone-white skeleton, proud of her decay.

The look on her face is once more smug. "Then how did you get out? Or did you escape at all?"

Then she goes toe-tapping once again across that terrible, awful, moldering navy-blue rug. And now I shiver.

■ ■ ■ ■

I wake up to the smell of freshly mowed grass. For a moment, I'm completely bewildered. Thomas, I think. He must be outside, mowing the lawn. But then the ceiling comes into focus, as well as the framed picture of the moose hanging on the wall. I register the familiar feel of my favorite quilt against my fingerprints, but a strange pillow under my head.

The hotel room, of course. I blink a few more times, but the smell of cut grass remains. I sit up and find Tessa Leoni positioned in a chair, eyeing me intently.

"What are you thinking of right now?" she asks me.

I answer without thinking. "Thomas."

"First thing you noticed about him."

"His eyes. They're kind."

"Describe him."

"Tall. Lanky. All arms and legs and thick dark hair that's always rumpled. He has big hands, calloused, capable. You can tell just by looking that he knows how to do things. He's strong."

"First thing he ever said to you."

"He didn't. He watched me. But I didn't want him to notice. I didn't want him to

376

see. Every now and then, though, I'd glance up and he'd be studying me. He would smile. And I'd feel . . . warm. Like I'd been cold for a very long time. But I always looked away again. Before we got in trouble."

"Nicky, where are you?"

But I'm awake now, aware enough not to take the bait. Such as the answer is not New Orleans. It's different, it's earlier, and it's a memory I'm still working on myself. I need to know what I need to know first, I think. Then, and only then — maybe then? — I will share it with others.

But Vero had been telling the truth; I can't trust anyone, not even the cops. If they were so great, where were they thirty years ago?

"You bought a candle," I say, finally having identified the source of the smell. There, on the round table in the corner of the room, a fat glass jar filled with light green wax sits, burning merrily.

"Yankee Candle Company," she informs me. "They have a scent for everything. I brought you food, too. And some supplies."

She lets me eat first. A Greek salad topped with grilled chicken. I didn't realize how famished I was until I wolf it down. There are also new clothes, an oversize navy-blue pullover, dark ball cap, glasses. An ensemble meant to disguise rather than flatter. Finally there's a large sketch pad topped with an assortment of pencils and pastels.

Tessa outlines the game plan, as the room steadily fills with the scent of freshly cut grass.

"I want you to draw. The house, room, yard, people, places, things. Anything that comes to mind, really. Just close your eyes, focus on the smell and sketch away."

"You want to know if the dollhouse is real," I tell her.

"I need you to make it real. Right now, you're a woman with a history of brain damage and imaginary friends. If this investigation is going to get off the ground, we need details. You're going to have to go to the places you don't want to go, Nicky. It's the only way."

I understand. I'm even intrigued. Talking about the past is hard. Trying to get the memories to focus, then lock in my mind using words; I grow too tired and over-whelmed. But I'm an artist. I can draw. And maybe, much like muscle memory, if I just let my hand move across the page on its own . . .

I open the sketch pad. I pick up a charcoal-gray pencil. I get to work.

I close my eyes. Tessa's right; it's easier

this way. I inhale deep, pulling the scent all the way into my lungs, into my stomach. I feel sun, the promise of an outside world. I feel the yearning of a young girl, locked up for too long inside.

My hand moves across the paper.

From time to time, Tessa asks me questions. She sits at the table across the room, leaving me be. I can hear the clack of a keyboard, her own fingers busily at work. But she's in her world and I'm in mine, and even her questions blend with the pictures opening up before me.

"What are the names of the girls?"

"Vero, Chelsea, CeeCee, Renita."

"How old are they?"

"CeeCee and Renita are older. Madame's first girls. They scare us."

"Why?"

"They're . . . cold. Know things even we don't know yet. Madame is hard on them. They're getting too old for the dollhouse, and everyone knows it."

"Do you talk to them?"

"Never."

"Who do you talk to?"

"Vero tells stories. Of the time before. When she was a real girl and someone loved her. Chelsea listens. They hunker together in their side-by-side beds. They whisper and dream of Someday. Other Places. Outside. Then night falls. Madame unlocks their door. And it's time again."

I draw a room. Not the narrow bedroom, but a parlor. With a marble-trimmed fireplace and brass sconces on the wall. A room that had once been grand. But it's worn now, frayed around the edges. Like Madame. Once beautiful, now clinging desperately to what used to be and might have been.

I draw her next, my hand stuttering over the grim set of her mouth, the harsh lines at the corners of her eyes. I can't help myself; I shiver.

"What's her name?" Tessa asks me.

"Madame."

"Does everyone call her that?"

"Anything else is a sign of disrespect. We must respect." I pause. "She wants us to love her. Maybe some part of her even wishes we actually were her daughters, that we are one big happy family. But if we don't love her, she will settle for us fearing her instead."

"Is it her house?"

"Been in the family for generations. We're lucky she lets us live here."

"Like you're lucky for the clothes on your

back, the food on the table?" Tessa asks sharply.

"Without her, we would have nothing," I say simply. "Without her, we would be nothing."

I move on to the dining table. A long rectangle, capable of hosting a party of sixteen. An elaborate crystal chandelier dangles in the middle, while a faded crimson floral print adorns the walls.

"Who cooks, who cleans?" Tessa is asking.

"She takes care of us; we take care of her."

"And at night, when the . . . guests arrive."

"Dinner parties. She's the hostess. We're her daughters. We must be considerate of the guests. Engage them in conversation, entertain their every need."

I leave the dining room. The wraparound front porch, where we could sit as a reward for good behavior. The vaulted foyer, where she would stand to greet every new arrival. The tower bedroom, with the rose-painted mural. Where it all began. Where it all ended.

Where Vero and I still sit and drink a cup of tea.

One room left. I know it well; the twin beds shoved together, the narrow window on the wall. Where Chelsea and Vero spent their last years, whispering stories together in the dark.

Small, cloistered, should be the easiest to sketch. And yet my hand skips over it time and again.

Vero braiding my hair, her skin falling off in chunks.

Vero dancing across that awful frayed blue rug.

My hand is shaking. I can't get the tip of the pencil down on the paper. I try to focus, will my own fingers into action. My arm shakes harder.

I'm aware of Tessa watching me, which only makes it worse.

"Nicky," she asks quietly, "was it your or Thomas's idea to return to New Hampshire?"

I don't answer her question. I'm too busy staring at my trembling hand. Her cell phone rings. Tessa checks the display, then excuses herself, taking the phone and stepping out of the room into the hall.

Alone I think I can do this. Draw the rug. Just draw the rug.

But I can't.

When my hand moves again, it doesn't draw the room. It draws a face. One as familiar to me as my own. With deep, dark eyes. Laugh lines crinkling the corners.

Dark hair, tousled around his forehead.

Except this Thomas is younger than my own. With fewer lines and thicker hair. His jaw is not fully fleshed out, his face still babyish around the edges. A teenager, full of promise but not yet grown into himself.

And he's not smiling at me kindly. Or flirting with his gaze. Or winking at me slyly.

My fingers move again. Mud splattered across his brow. The smell of wet-churned earth, the feel of the grave. Or maybe it's soot, smeared across his cheek. The smell of smoke, the feel of the flames.

I don't know this Thomas. The look on his face. So grim, so horrible.

The things he has done, I think, automatically. The things he's about to do next . . .

I drop my pencil. Grab the sheet of paper. Quick, before I can think twice, I rip it from the pad.

I can hear Tessa's voice, still talking on her phone in the hall. As I cross to the hotel bed, lift the mattress and shove the sketch beneath it, disappearing it from sight.

My heart is still beating wildly. I can barely sit. My head throbs. Thomas, young Thomas, clearly not from New Orleans.

Vero is laughing in the back of my mind. Or maybe she's taunting. *"How does someone so smart get to be so stupid?"*

Then: *"Run, baby, run."*

But I can't run. There's no place for me to go. Only worse things for me to remember. Fresh dangers for me to face.

I need to pull myself together. The scent of grass. Trying to draw it in, find my center again. But it's not happening.

Vero is whirling around in my mind. Dancing across that awful rug as hair and flesh fly off her bones.

I'm on the edge, I realize. The furthest I've ever gotten in my memories. Maybe even now standing right outside the shuttered-up box. All I have to do is lean forward, remove the sign that says "Keep Out," then tug hard on the lid . . .

The door opens. Tessa walks into the room. The look on her face is stern and immediately foreboding. "That was Wyatt. We need to return to the sheriff's office. They've recovered Thomas's vehicle. Nicky, you have some serious explaining to do."

CHAPTER 28

Wyatt took his time. For too long things had been moving too fast. He'd been playing catch-up. His officers had been in reaction mode. Now, with less than twelve hours to learn everything he needed to know from one woman regarding two crimes, he was slowing things down. Getting his ducks in a row.

For the upcoming interrogation, he'd commandeered the conference room. He and Kevin had hung a map of the North Country on one wall. They had blown up photos of the liquor store, the gas station, an outside shot of Marlene Bilek's home, and the crash, which they placed at key points around the atlas. He had odometer readings. And last, but not least, he had laid out on a table one recently purchased collapsible shovel and one pair of bloody gloves.

The gloves fascinated Kevin. He'd spent a

solid hour meticulously uncurling them, careful not to further damage the shredded material. They were thicker than traditional latex gloves, he reported, but thinner than rubber garden gloves. He'd done a presumptive test on a carefully scraped sample of the dried brown substance, which had been positive for human blood. Yet another i dotted, t crossed — *don't try to tell me you wore these gloves to bury Fido or tend to an injured deer. We know this is human blood, now start talking.*

The sheriff had been right; no more messing around. Wyatt wanted answers and he wanted them now.

Because, yeah, he'd made his call to the National Center for Missing and Exploited Children and they were very excited to learn of Veronica Sellers's recovery. Definitely fly-to-New-Hampshire, take-over-the-case kind of excited.

Four in the afternoon, going on thirty-six hours without sleep, Wyatt figured he had one chance to get this right. He didn't plan on screwing it up.

He glanced through the window. Spotted Tessa pulling into the parking lot. He motioned to Kevin to wrap things up; then both took their positions.

When Nicky Frank aka Veronica Sellers

walked into the room, Wyatt's first thought was that she looked better than she had seven hours ago. Sure her face was still a pale canvas overlaid with a patchwork of black stitches, purple bruises and brown lacerations, but she had her chin up, blue eyes clearer. She carried herself stronger. A woman with a purpose. Looked like she'd made some resolutions of her own while she was away.

Coming in behind her, Tessa was her normal shuttered, efficient self. She didn't so much as glance at Wyatt, but helped usher Nicky into a hard plastic chair. Rather than sit beside her, Tessa took up position a few seats away. A neutral party, trying to keep her distance from the fray.

Wyatt noticed for the first time that Tessa was carrying a sketch pad. She set it on the table in front of her. Her gaze, like Nicky's, went to Wyatt, then waited.

He cleared his throat, suddenly nervous and resenting it.

"Thanks for coming," he started out. He kept seated, determined to remain relaxed. "As Tessa most likely explained, we have some more questions for you."

"We've been busy, too," Nicky started out. "Tessa came up with this candle trick. She burns a familiar scent and I draw pictures

from the dollhouse. I've been able to remember half a dozen rooms —"

Wyatt held up a hand. "No."

Nicky sputtered, stared at him. "No?"

"I'm not interested in the dollhouse."

"You're not interested? You don't care
what happened thirty years ago?"

"No. I care about Wednesday night. You
wanna make up stories about what happened thirty years ago, be my guest. Tell
fanciful tales about madams and kidnapped
girls and evil roommates, have at it. I can't
solve thirty years ago, Nicky. Hell, I'm
beginning to think the whole thing is just
one more wild-goose chase, like getting us
to search for Vero on Thursday morning.
You have issues. We know you have issues,
and still we took your bait. Not anymore.
We're talking Wednesday night. Every hour,
every minute, every second, and we're starting with a pair of bloody gloves, recovered
from the pants pockets of the jeans *you* were
wearing Wednesday night. What did you do,
Nicky? And why did it require a shovel?"

He'd definitely caught her off guard. She
appeared genuinely baffled, her mouth
opening, then closing. A fish struggling for
oxygen. A liar fresh out of excuses. Wyatt
made no move to fill the silence. Neither

did Kevin.

Even Tessa sat quietly. She'd been through such rodeos before, and while she was Nicky's hired investigator, she wasn't legal counsel and she knew it.

"Gloves?" Nicky whispered at last.

Wyatt rose to standing. He didn't move immediately to the gloves or the shovel; better to keep her off-kilter. Instead, he moved to an oversize map of New Hampshire, where he and Kevin had done their best to resurrect her drive on Wednesday night, based on a conversation with Marlene Bilek and Nicky's odometer reading.

"You drove to the New Hampshire state liquor store Wednesday night. You had a call from Northledge. From Tessa Leoni."

He glanced at Tessa. She provided a curt nod.

"She informed you of the employment information for Marlene Bilek, your long-lost mother, whom you'd hired Northledge to locate."

"I wasn't planning on bothering her," Nicky said immediately. Her eyes were glued on the map. She already appeared stressed. "I just wanted . . . I wanted to know."

"You bought the yellow quilt from her," Wyatt said, a statement, not a question.

"I Googled her name on and off over the years. But she'd remarried; her last name is different. Then I found an old posting, showing the marriage photo with both their names in the caption. So I searched again with last name Bilek. And . . . and I found her. In New Hampshire. She sold quilts online. I bought one."

"As Nicky Frank?"

"Yes."

"You never told her who you were? Never gave out one shred of personal info?"

Nicky shook her head. "I never even spoke to her. It was an online transaction. I used PayPal. We never spoke at all."

"But you've been tracking her."

"The website only had a PO box. No street address was listed. Not under her name. Not under his. I think her husband . . . he's a cop, right? A retired officer. He must monitor their personal information online."

"So you hired Northledge. With Thomas's blessing?"

Nicky shook her head wildly. "No, no. Absolutely not. I did it on my own. Used a cashier's check and everything. I didn't want him to know. Not after . . ."

"After what, Nicky?"

She looked away, head down. "I think he

figured out about the quilt. I never told him, but the first time I held it, I cried and cried and cried. I couldn't help myself. I think he guessed where it came from. He grew shorter with me, less patient. 'Aren't we happy?' he'd say, over and over again. 'We have each other; isn't that enough?' I didn't want to hurt his feelings. I didn't want to upset him after everything he's done for me . . . But no" — she looked up slowly — "it's not enough. I'm still sad even when I know I shouldn't be."

"Wednesday night, you went in search of Marlene Bilek," Wyatt stated firmly.

"Yes."

"You drove to the liquor store." He tapped it on the map. "You went inside, hoping to see her."

"I recognized her. Even from the back. Then I panicked. I saw her, but I wasn't ready for her to see me. What if she didn't remember me? Worse, what if she didn't want me? Thirty years later, what kind of daughter simply reappears from the dead?"

"You bought a bottle of Glenlivet."

Nicky didn't look away. She held his gaze while she nodded miserably.

"And then you followed her." Wyatt returned to the map. "I spoke with Marlene Bilek this afternoon —"

"You told her about me?"

"I spoke with Mrs. Bilek this afternoon," he continued brusquely, "determining her usual route home. It's a forty-mile drive, mostly back roads, passing through here, here and here." He traced the red line with his finger. "Leading at long last to her house."

He tapped the blown-up picture of the Bilek's front porch. Taken during daylight, not at night, when Nicky would've viewed it, but close enough.

Her gaze remained locked on the tiny yellow house. As if she could drink it up.

"Did you tell her about me?" Nicky whispered. "That I'm Vero. What . . . what did she say?"

"Don't think that's my story to tell." Wyatt gazed at her hard. She couldn't return his look.

"According to Mrs. Bilek," Wyatt continued, "her daughter was also home that night. Sixteen-year-old Hannah Veigh. Look like anyone you remember?"

"Vero," she whispered.

"What did you do, Nicky?"

The sternness of his question seemed to catch her off guard. "What?"

"What did you do? You've been up half the night. You've been drinking; you've been driving. Now you're at a cute little house, peering in the window, and there she is: your long-lost self. Vero. What did you do?"

Nicky sat back, pushing against the table with her hands. "Do? I didn't. I don't think. How could I?"

He crossed swiftly to the table. "Tell me about the collapsible shovel, Nicky. Tell me about the gloves. Covered in blood. *Human* blood. We know; we already tested it. You're drunk, you're alone, and you've just discovered your long-lost mom hasn't been pining for you after all. In fact, she's remarried, has a new kid, Vero 2.0. Your mother has gotten on with her life. She doesn't miss you at all."

"You don't know that. How can you know that?"

"You're stalking her."

"I just wanted to see her. To find out how she was doing —"

"You couldn't call? You couldn't write? *Hey, Mom, I finally got away from an evil madam. That was twenty-two years ago, but, hey, better late than never to finally reach out. Wanna do lunch?*"

"It's not like that," Nicky protested weakly.

"Like what? Like you're a mixed-up, fucked-up woman, driving drunk and stalking your own mom? Tell me about the shovel. If you were just going to find out how she was doing, why'd you need a shovel? Tell me about the gloves. If you were just following along, why are they covered in blood? What did you do Wednesday night? Come on, Nicky. I'm tired of your lies and your stories. What did you do Wednesday night?!"

"I called Thomas." The words blurted out. Nicky blinked her eyes, as if even she was surprised to hear them.

"You called your husband?"

"From a pay phone. I was crying and I was hysterical. I'd just seen Vero. She was dead except now she was alive. I didn't know what to do anymore. And my head hurt so much. I know I shouldn't have been drinking. I know I shouldn't have been driving. And Thomas was going to be mad at me, because he'd asked me, begged me, to please let it go. 'We can be happy,' he would say. 'Once we were happy; I know we can be happy again.'

"But I don't think I can continue being this sad anymore. I need to change. Except to change, I need answers. Why is November so bad? Why do I spend my afternoons talking to a ghost girl in my head? Thomas knows how to live. I . . . don't. So I asked to move here —"

"You asked," Wyatt interjected sharply.

"Yes."

"Thomas didn't refuse."

"He suggested Vermont. But I kept at it and eventually he caved. Then once I was here . . . I felt closer. Marlene's post office box had been New Hampshire. Now we were in the same state. Except it wasn't quite enough. I wanted to see her, just . . . look. So I hired Northledge. Then Wednesday night . . ."

Nicky's voice trailed off. "Looking in the window, seeing Vero. My head exploded. So much bright light. Flames. I saw flames everywhere. *Vero learned to fly.* I wanted to run into the house. I wanted to hold her so badly. Tell her over and over again that I was sorry. She mustn't hate me. I didn't mean . . . Except she wasn't Vero, right? Couldn't be Vero. I was crying too hard to function. No cell reception, so I made my way to a pay phone and called Thomas."

"He came to you."

"He told me where to meet him. Right after that gas station. Bend in the road. Pull over there."

"You went to meet your husband. Were you wearing gloves, Nicky?"

She shook her head. "No, I was driving,

focusing hard. My head, the alcohol. I had to concentrate to stay on the road."

"When you got to the meeting spot, Thomas was waiting for you. Was he carrying a shovel?"

Nicky closed her eyes, seemed to be trying to think. "No."

"Gloves?"

"He . . . he handed me gloves. Told me to put them on. 'Do you trust me?' he asked. 'Do you trust me?' "

Nicky opened her eyes. She peered up at Wyatt. "I said, 'Yes.' "

"Then what?"

"Then . . . he . . . he disappeared. And I was flying through the air. And I died again. A woman twice returned from the dead."

Wyatt kept on her. He made her walk over to the gloves, examine the shovel. Revisit each photo of her stops that night.

"Is she . . . is she okay?" she asked, looking at the picture of Hannah Veigh Bilek, who, frankly, with her long dark hair and light-blue eyes, looked exactly like Nicky's younger sister. "Nothing happened to them, right? I mean, there's blood on the gloves. But I know I didn't. And Thomas . . . He couldn't. He wouldn't. Right?"

"Sounds like you have doubts."

"He's a good man," she said, but the words sounded more automatic than convincing.

"Where is he, Nicky?"

"I don't know."

"Does he love you?"

"He's never left me."

"Not even now? Burned your house, disappeared into the wind."

She hesitated. It occurred to Wyatt immediately what she couldn't say. Thomas wasn't gone. At least Nicky didn't think so. Even now, he was around, somewhere local, waiting for her. Such was the power of their bond.

A husband who most likely engineered her auto accident and burned down their home. And yet still, in her heart of all hearts, Nicky knew he loved her.

One of those kinds of relationships, Wyatt thought. Cops saw them all the time. Yet he remained troubled.

He made her review the night, over and over, but he couldn't get her to crack. She'd worn the gloves. Maybe the blood was her own, from the accident, all that glass everywhere, hence the shredded remains. She had a vague recollection of taking them off, shoving them in her back pocket. They were too awkward to wear and she didn't want to litter. The shovel was a mystery to her. She didn't know why Thomas had it.

And, yes, she'd followed Marlene Bilek. She had wanted to speak to her, but she'd lost her courage. Wanting to change wasn't the same as changing. Trying to remember your past wasn't the same as being able to confront it.

Finally, Kevin led her away for fingerprinting. While technically they had Veronica Sellers's prints on file, they were thirty years old. Wyatt, not to mention the evidence techs, would prefer a fresher, cleaner set for use when comparing her prints against others collected from the shovel, gloves, et cetera.

After Nicky and Kevin left, Wyatt and Tessa took a minute to catch their breath. He pulled out the chair next to her, swiping a hand through his already mussed-up hair. God, he could use a shower. Not to mention a nap.

"Get any sleep?" she asked him.

"No more than you."

"Then you must be very tired."

He grimaced. "Sorry to pull you away from Sophie for the weekend."

"Not the first time. I mentioned the puppy to her. I believe you had her at hello."

"I get to help pick it out?"

"I hope so."

She was smiling softly, saying the right things. And yet he felt it again. That something was off. A shadow in her eyes that didn't quite match the curve of her lips. Maybe he was simply too tired. Or maybe that was the problem with dating a woman like Tessa. She would always be a bit of a mystery to him.

"Sophie doing okay?" he asked now.

"As far as I know."

"Just . . . you seem" — he wasn't sure how to term it — "preoccupied."

"D. D. Warren told me something interesting at lunch," she said at last, gaze on the sketch pad. "I'm still processing it."

"Good interesting or bad interesting?"

"I'm still processing it. Wyatt, you know I'm not perfect, right?"

"I would never say such a thing."

"Three years ago . . . some things went down. I can't say I regret them."

"Having met Sophie, I don't regret them either." He paused. "Are you in trouble, Tessa? Because you know I'm here for you, right? Whatever you need . . ."

She smiled again, that smile that didn't dispel the shadows from her eyes. "Let's not get ahead of ourselves. So far, I've heard some interesting news —"

He stopped her, took her hand because it seemed the least he could do. She startled at the contact but didn't pull away. "I'm here for you, Tessa. As in solidly, absolutely, one hundred percent. I know you have a past, but personally, I'm vested in our future."

It might have been his imagination, but he thought for a moment, her eyes glistened with tears.

"D.D. says I'm a lone wolf," she whispered.

"I think Sophie and Mrs. Ennis would argue otherwise."

She nodded, didn't speak right away. "Nicky wants to be free," she said abruptly. "I know you have doubts about the dollhouse story, but having spent the afternoon with her, I think she also has a past, and a pretty horrible one at that. Where not only things happened, but I have a feeling . . . You don't survive in that kind of environment without doing some things yourself."

Wyatt's turn to nod.

"Maybe twenty-two years seems like a long time. She should've come forward sooner, contacted her mother sooner, but she's trying now. Isn't that what matters?"

"She says she drew some pictures this afternoon?"

"My own attempt at memory therapy. Here." Tessa lifted the cover of the sketch pad, withdrew half a dozen oversize sheets. "As you can tell, she's a good artist, with a great eye for detail."

At first, Wyatt wasn't sure what he was looking at. A rounded room with a rose mural and gauze-enshrouded bed. A marble fireplace in a formal parlor. But the third sketch presented the big picture: a vast, wood-shingled Victorian, the kind built by wealthy families in the nineteenth century as summer homes for their families away from the heat and stench of cities. The house included a gorgeous wraparound front porch, a three-story turret, and an expansive right wing dotted with multiple dormers. Impressive house. Expensive house. And indeed, given the diamond-paned windows and gingerbread trim, a dollhouse.

He looked up from the sketch, eyed Tessa thoughtfully. "You think it's real?"

"I think she thinks it's real."

"That's not very helpful."

He flipped a page, coming to a portrait of an older woman, hair up in a bun, face stern, eyes cold. He couldn't help himself. He shivered.

"Madame Sade," Tessa provided.

"Looks like a woman who could kidnap small children," he agreed.

"I asked D.D. to examine past missing-kids cases," Tessa mentioned. "I'm curious. Given the databases we have now, maybe we can determine if thirty years ago there was a spike in missing-girl cases in the greater New England area. It would give Nicky's story some weight."

"It would."

"And as long as we're entertaining the notion this house exists, look at the background. The view through the window of the tower bedroom."

He had to flip back. He hadn't noticed it at first, still getting his bearings and all, but sure enough, the round room included several impressive windows. Nicky had meticulously drawn in each diamond pane of the glass. Then, behind that . . . the mountains. A view so familiar he felt that if he studied it just a minute more, it would come to him.

"The White Mountains. You think this is New Hampshire." He glanced at Tessa.

"She asked to move here, not Thomas."

"Because Marlene Bilek is here."

"Maybe. But you heard her talk. She's looking for answers. I think instinct brought her here. Closer to the truth."

"Sheriff asked me a good question this morning," Wyatt said abruptly. "If Thomas is the one responsible for the accidents against his wife, why? Only a few reasons a husband tries to kill his spouse. Revenge, money, power. After twenty-two years, what changed in their marriage?"

He knew the answer, but Tessa did the honors: "Nicky decided it was time to move forward. She was tired of being sad."

"A move toward independence can be threatening to any man, but especially to a husband who likes to tend as much as Thomas wants to tend," Wyatt agreed.

"I don't buy the story of them meeting in New Orleans," Tessa stated.

"Me neither. Always sounded rehearsed."

"I tried to get her to talk more about Thomas while she was sketching. It sounds to me like there is part of her that loves him. But more than that, she believes she *needs* him. He takes care of her. I'm guessing for his own reasons. Think of their pattern: always on the move. That seems less like a couple who's living happily ever after, more like a pair on the run."

Wyatt turned back to the picture of the madam. "If Nicky was truly kept in this dollhouse, and Thomas was somehow part of it, I can think of at least one person who'd never want them talking to the police." He tapped the cold-eyed woman. "Tessa, if this is all true . . . How'd Nicky, Vero, get out? That's what bothers me the most. An operation like this, a woman like this, she didn't simply let one of her girls go. Something happened. And I'm not just talking Vero learned to fly, and all that nonsense."

Tessa hesitated. "I have a theory. Maybe I'm biased, having my own . . . past and all. But I think Vero was kidnapped thirty years ago. I think she was held by this woman in this house. And I think . . . I think something really terrible happened that enabled her to escape. No. I suspect Vero *did* something really terrible that got her out. And all these years later, that's what she can't stand to face. Except." Tessa shrugged, that sad smile back on her lips. "The past has a will of its own. It wants to be heard. Her own purposefully blocked memories are starting to break free."

"November is the saddest month," Wyatt murmured. "A woman twice returned from the dead."

"I think Nicky's trying to remember. I think some part of her even wants to tell us what happened, get it off her chest. She just needs a push."

"Another scented candle?" Wyatt arched a brow.

"No. I think we put her face-to-face with her mom. Let them finally speak."

Wyatt thought about it. "All right. I'll call Marlene, break the news. She's already taken an interest in Nicky. I can't imagine she wouldn't want to see her missing daughter after all these years. We'll need to keep it under wraps, though. God knows the press is about to descend upon us any minute."

"True."

"But it's gotta be tonight. And I don't just mean because the feds will change everything in the morning. Thomas Frank fled from his burning home nearly twenty-four hours ago, yet we pinged him only forty miles from here. Know what that tells me?"

Wyatt paused.

"He still considers Nicky a threat. And he isn't finished with her yet."

CHAPTER 29

Vero and I are sipping cups of tea. The rosebush mural has been obliterated on the wall, scribbled over in angry black marker. The pink gauze that once surrounded the bed is now sliced into ribbons. The mattress has been reduced to a gutted pile of shredded foam.

I can't even look at what she did to Fat Bear.

"You're scared," I tell her knowingly, though it's my own heart pounding in my chest.

"Fuck off." Vero hasn't bothered with clothes. Or the memory of skin. I sit with a grinning skeleton, bits of hair and decaying flesh plastered to her skull. When she drinks, I can watch the scotch cascade down her moldering spine.

"She's your mother," I try again. "You've dreamed of this moment for years and years. Remember?"

"I liked this room best," she says abruptly. "Of all the places in this stupid house. This room looked like it was meant for a princess. All little girls dream of being a princess."

"Your mother still loves you," I tell her.

She suddenly smiles. "Don't you mean your mother?"

"It's okay," I hear myself say, to her, to me, to the sad remains of eyeless Fat Bear. "Everything is going to be okay."

Vero smiles again, tosses back another shot of scotch.

"Ah, Nicky," she assures me. "You always were an idiot."

By 9 P.M., I can't stay on the bed anymore. I get up, pace around the hotel room. Sitting on the second bed, Tessa does her best to give me space. She is checking all the news channels, trying to see if the story has gone national. There were news cameras arriving when Wyatt hastily shuttled us out of the back of the sheriff's department hours earlier, word of the discovery of a missing child, thirty years lost, having finally leaked out.

I'd just returned to the conference room, mesmerized by my black-stained fingerprints, when Wyatt dropped his second bombshell: Marlene Bilek wanted to meet

with me. Immediately. Tonight. Not a discussion, not a debate. He'd already set it
up. End of story.

I would speak with my mother. After all
these years, doubts, wonderings . . .

Tessa got us back to the hotel, using every
back road and evasive-driving technique she
knew. Once we were safely ensconced in the
room, she advised me to eat a good dinner,
then rest up. It was going to be a long night.

Now Tessa works the remote. So far, a
startling break in a thirty-year-old cold case
seems to be local fodder only. The news
producers are most likely in a holding pattern, Tessa informs me, waiting for the right
confirmation, interview, photo op, to blow
the story to the next level. Lucky me.

I pace around the beds again, my mind
going in a million directions.

I think of that tiny, desperate little apartment. Of the woman who once tucked Vero
in the closet for her own safekeeping. The
mother who brought her ice cream and
played hide-and-seek and would sleep, when
he wasn't around, with her arms holding
her daughter tight.

I pause to finger the yellow quilt, inhaling
a fragrance my head knows can no longer
be there, though my heart still hopes for
otherwise.

And I miss Thomas. I wonder what he's doing right now, even as I struggle to understand what happened Wednesday night. I did call him. And he came, because he always came. For twenty-two years, he's been my anchor, my rock. I might scream in terror at night, but he greeted me each morning with love. At least, that's what I thought it was.

Or was it? For all of his talk of our closeness, I'd moved into the guest bedroom. More proof that at least some part of me knows more than I'm ready to consciously face? When I first woke up in the hospital, my initial response wasn't love but anger. I wanted him gone, away. I loved him; I hated him. The concussions may have scrambled my brains, but maybe there were head games going on way before that.

Why haven't I ever called my mom, made some kind of contact with my family? I got out. Somehow, someway —

Vero learned to fly.

But I never went home. I stayed with Thomas. Always Thomas.

Do you trust me? he asked Wednesday night, handing me the pair of gloves.

Except why did I need to wear gloves? And why did I say yes?

I'm angry with him, I think. For torching

409

our home, for disappearing in the middle of the night, for leaving me with so many unanswered questions.

"Run," Vero speaks up in the back of my head. And I know she isn't talking about the upcoming meeting with my mother. She's talking about Thomas.

Ten fifteen. The sound of a car engine breaks the unbearable silence. I pop off the bed, follow the noise of the vehicle approaching, the crunch of tires as it turns into the parking lot. Instinctively, I head toward the door. Tessa gives me a stern look and orders me to sit back down. I notice her hand has gone to her side, as if reaching for a gun, and the nervousness officially becomes too much.

I rush back into the bathroom to vomit. When I return, voices are now in the hall, followed by the sound of a key jiggling in a lock. The door of the room next to ours. This is what they planned. Tessa has reserved this room here; then, under a second name, the adjoining premises.

Nothing to trace back to the sheriff's department, which the press must be watching like a hawk. Nothing to suggest my presence. Or Marlene Bilek's.

Now, when no media vans suddenly scream into the parking lot, when no photographers suddenly bound down the hall, when the midpriced hotel remains just its normal level of off-season quiet . . .

The connecting door slowly swings open. Sergeant Detective Wyatt Foster steps into the room.

Then . . .

Marlene Bilek appears before me.

We don't speak right away. It's one of those moments . . . What do you say? Instead, we stand, we stare, we absorb. I'm holding her quilt. Her eyes go right to it; then she smiles.

"I knew that quilt was going to where it needed to be," she whispers.

I'm crying. The tears pour down my face. I can't stop; I can't move; I can't even wipe them away. I just stand there, staring at this woman, with water coating my cheeks.

Not everything is as I expect. The image I've pictured in my mind all these years is of a twentysomething mom, a little lost, a little resigned to her fate even before her beloved daughter was snatched from her. I thought of her as softer, her body rounded in a comforting mom sort of way. This woman, on the other hand: Her face is drawn, features stamped by years of tough decisions. Tessa mentioned that she kicked her abusive ex to the curb, stopped drinking, turned her life around.

She still carries an unmistakable air of sadness. A woman who's lost much and knows she can never get it back.

"Why don't we, um, take a seat," Wyatt says. He gestures to the two beds. "Make yourselves comfortable."

He and Tessa exchange a glance. Tessa has her iPhone out. She is recording us, I realize. But of course, even this "private" reunion is still the subject of much scrutiny.

Marlene enters the room slowly. She is wearing her dark-red uniform from the liquor store, as that was the ruse they devised to throw off the press. But I'm surprised she didn't bring a change of clothing, something more personal for her first meeting with her long-lost child. It unsettles me further. I'm looking for Mom but mostly seeing state liquor store cashier Marlene Bilek.

I take a seat on the edge of the bed closest to the door. She takes a seat on the bed opposite me. Wyatt and Tessa move to the small circular table shoved in the corner of the room, trying to give us privacy, while still very much part of the space.

"Your hair is exactly as I remember," Marlene murmurs now, her gaze raking over my face. I find myself rounding my shoulders self-consciously. "Long brown waves. Once a week, I used to bathe you in the kitchen sink. Then, if it was sunny outside, we'd sit by a window and I'd brush your hair until it dried. You had such gorgeous locks, much nicer than my own."

She touches her short, graying brown curls as if embarrassed. I'm trying to remember exactly what her hair looked like back then, long, short, curly, straight, but coming up blank. She looked like Mom; that's what I've preserved after all these years. Not an image of a specific woman, but a generalized ideal.

"It's funny, though," Marlene says now. "Your eyes were much grayer when you were a child. Now they look more blue. I guess that's the way it is with some kids. I had a friend whose son was a blond until he was eight or nine. Now he's a brunette."

"You have another daughter," I hear myself say. Is my tone accusing? Surely I don't intend that.

"You mean Hannah?" Once again Marlene's expression falters. She glances down at the carpet. "She has brown hair, gray eyes, like you did. First second she was born, my heart nearly stopped in my chest. It's Vero, I thought. My God, I've gotten my daughter back!

"I had to work hard on that, to let Hannah be Hannah. Because there is only one Vero. Lord, child, I've missed you so much."

She bursts off the other bed. I'm not prepared. I can't get my hands up in time. Her arms go around me, hold me tight.

She is hugging me, I think, nearly bewildered. This is me, being hugged by my mother.

I should open my arms. I should hug her back. I should declare, "Mommy, I'm home."

But I can't move. I can't say a word.

I'm too aware of Vero, who's back in my head, laughing hysterically.

"You make quilts," I say finally, two, three, ten minutes later. Mine is setting next to me on the bed, one more thing I suddenly don't know what to do with.

"I started twenty years ago," Marlene tells me. In contrast to my constantly ping-ponging gaze, her eyes remain locked on my face, as if mesmerized. "I, um . . ." She takes a deep breath. "The years, right after your disappearance. They were a dark, dark time. And Lord, I'd already thought I'd been through some dark times. I'm sorry I took you to the park that day. I'm sorry I fell asleep. I'm sorry, I'm sorry, I'm sorry."

"You'd been drinking." My voice is sterner than I expected. I don't soften it. "You were drunk."

"I'm sorry." She speaks the words automatically, the syllables nearly worn out from thirty years of utterance.

"The moment I realized I couldn't find you," she says. "When I'd been all around the park, calling your name over and over, and you still weren't coming . . . I knew. I knew immediately the worst had happened."

"Vero just wanted to play with dolls," I murmur. I've switched to third person. I can't help myself. I don't know how to tell the story any other way. For too many years, Vero has been a little girl inside my head, one prone to shedding her skin in times of distress. Even knowing she is me, or I am her . . . It feels too surreal. Vero is Vero. I'm just a gatekeeper. I know things because she tells me things. A way of disassociating myself from the horror, I guess, a quirk of coping. But it has worked for so long, I don't know how to magically undo it now. Even sitting face-to-face with this woman — my mother, I keep telling myself — feels strange. She is Vero's mom, I think. I've always wanted to meet her. But my mom . . .

I'm just not ready for that.

"Vero followed the girl away from the

park," I continue now. "But Madame was waiting for her. A stab of the needle, a quick shove into the car. By the time you missed her, Vero was already gone."

Marlene's fingers dig into the edge of the mattress. But she nods. I'm not telling her anything she hasn't already imagined over the years.

"I tried so hard to find you," she assures me now. If my use of third person bothers her, she doesn't show it. "I answered all the police's questions, went around to the neighbors. I was sure it was only a matter of time. They'd find you wandering down the street. Maybe you'd followed a stray dog or an ice cream truck, who knew? But the police were on it; even all the locals turned out to search. You were mine, but after you were lost, you became everyone's. Except we still couldn't bring you home."

"Madame Sade took Vero to a house," I tell her. "A beautiful mansion where Vero was given a room fit for a princess. Soft bed, beautiful hand-painted rose mural. Her very own china tea set."

"The first few days, I didn't drink a drop," Marlene murmurs. "I was sober. Stone-cold for the first time in a decade. No sleeping, no drinking, no eating. I waited. I waited, waited, waited, because at any moment, the

416

phone would ring, and it would be the police returning you to me."

"Madame gave Vero new clothes, then took them away when Vero couldn't stop crying. Madame left Vero alone in this huge cold room for days and days. No sleeping on the bed. Vero found a closet instead. She curled up naked on the floor and cried for you."

"Ronnie beat me the first night," Marlene whispers, her eyes locked on mine. "Called me a stupid whore for losing you. Then he beat me the second night because I wouldn't stop crying. Then the third and the fourth. The fifth night, the officer who'd come over to update me on your case ended up taking me to the emergency room. They had to screw my jaw back together. That officer, Hank, told me I should never go back to that apartment again. The first step to saving my daughter, he told me, was saving myself."

"There were classes. Madame Sade came every afternoon. 'Girls can't afford to be stupid,' she said. So Vero learned reading and math and geography and history. Then there was dancing and fashion and makeup and hairstyling. She told Vero she was her mother now. They were family. She would live in this beautiful house forever; she just had to do as she was told. Then Madame Sade would leave again and Vero was alone. Every morning, every evening. Hours and hours and hours, all night long, so very alone.

"Vero wanted to be brave," I whisper. "But the isolation . . . It became harder and harder to remember who she was. And easier and easier to be whatever Madame wanted her to be. Especially once she turned twelve and the first man arrived. When it was over, she didn't cry. Vero simply locked it all up, something that happened to someone else, and stuck it way back in her mind. None of that could've been done to the real Vero, because the real Vero was a princess from a secret realm, whose mother was a magical queen who'd vowed to keep her safe from the evil witch."

I stare at Marlene. "Vero made up stories. Or maybe she did her best to remember her story. It is very hard to be yourself in the dollhouse."

Marlene can't look at me anymore. I'm not sure that I blame her.

"I returned to Ronnie," she continues now, for this is as much her confession as mine, and thirty years later, there's much to get out. "Second they released me, of course I came back. I didn't know how to live alone. I'd been a young, stupid girl, already pregnant when we met. I couldn't support myself, had never managed to hold down a job. Ronnie took care of me. And if he had a temper, sometimes drank too much, hit too hard, well, at least he put a roof over my head.

"But after you were gone, things got worse. Six trips to the emergency room later, the responding officer, Hank, said he'd had enough. I was coming home with him. He'd take the sofa. I got the bed. But in return, no more boozing, no more crying, no more dying. It was hard enough, one year later, to know he'd failed some little girl he'd never met. He'd be damned before he failed her mother, too."

"Girls grow up. Even a beautiful princess . . ." I grimace, feel a spiderweb of memory brush across my mind. *He doesn't want you anymore; now what good are you?* Madame Sade was angry. You didn't want her anger. You couldn't afford for her to be angry.

I shiver, struggling to shrug off the recollection. When I speak again, the image is gone, safely locked back up, and my voice is matter-of-fact. "Vero moved downstairs. She gained a roommate, a girl several years older than her, Chelsea. Chelsea also had dark

419

hair, blue eyes, because that's what Madame's best customer preferred. Vero was happy to have a roommate, thinking that finally, she wouldn't be alone. But Chelsea hated her on sight. No one had ever loved her the way Vero had been loved. Chelsea's own mother had sold her to Madame Sade for a quick fix. At least at the dollhouse she had been the favorite, living in the pretty tower bedroom. Until, of course, Vero came along. Now Chelsea ripped Vero's clothes, ruined her makeup.

"She made Vero sleep on a rug on the floor. She told Vero she was nothing more than Madame Sade's pet. Except Madame Sade never kept her pets for long. Soon enough, she told Vero, they'd come for her. The only way out of the dollhouse was death, and Vero's time was up."

"The nights were always the worst," Marlene says. "Watching the sun set, knowing another day was gone and I still didn't know where my baby was. I wanted to drink. All the time. Instead, I dreamed of you. I'd sit on Hank's sofa and I'd remember your first birthday, your second birthday, your third. Then, after a bit, I imagined your seventh birthday, your eighth, your ninth. But for your tenth birthday, I made a vanilla cake with blue frosting because you were older

420

now, and I had to believe you were growing up. I had to believe you were okay."

"Vero slept on the rug. She did her best not to make Chelsea angry. And every night, she whispered her stories to herself. Of the secret realm and the magical queen and the evil witch. Except one night, she discovered Chelsea listening. So Vero told another story, of a closet that was a portal between the worlds, and if she could just find the right door, she could escape again. Chelsea kept listening." I close my eyes, and for a moment, I see it clearly. Two girls, both with dark hair, heads bent close as they huddled together. A happy memory, like freshly mowed grass. A moment when the dollhouse almost felt like home. I hear myself whisper: "Vero didn't sleep on the rug anymore. She moved to the bed, right next to Chelsea, and they began to talk and trade secrets and exchange dreams. They became sisters. And Vero wasn't alone anymore."

I'm crying, slow, silent tears. Why am I crying? Then I see Vero again, twirling across that terrible blue rug, needle in her hand, track marks on her arm. An unbearable pressure grows in my chest.

Marlene takes my hand. I feel her fingers trembling within mine. Giving me strength. Drawing strength. We are in this together.

She goes first: "One day, I fell off the wagon. Just like that. I was out taking a walk and I passed a liquor store and I . . . I went inside. I bought a fifth of whiskey. Then I took it back to Hank's place and downed the whole thing. When I finally came to in the emergency room, Hank was a wreck. He made me swear to never do that again. He . . . He told me he loved me. He asked me to become his wife. But there was a condition: I had to make it sober for an entire year. I had to want to live, he told me, because otherwise, I would only break his heart."

"Things in the dollhouse started to change," I say. I'm back in my head, walking down the shadowy corridor, steadily closer to Keep Out, Keep Out, KEEP OUT!!! "No more younger, fresher models entered the home. Instead the entertaining became less frequent, Madame Sade more desperate. She needed money. 'Do you think a house like this supports itself?' she'd say. And the food we ate and all the clothes we demanded. We were nothing but ungrateful girls; no wonder no one wanted to play with us anymore. She drugged us. The first time, she simply strolled into the room and jabbed us with the needle. I thought this was it; she'd sedated us again, only this time our bodies would be taken into the woods and left there to rot. Only way out of the dollhouse, right?

"But it wasn't a sedative. Instead it was . . . melting and floating and bliss. We giggled; we smiled; we danced. And within a matter of weeks, we'd do whatever Madame wanted, party, chat, entertain, live it up, more men, lots of men, whatever she wanted, as long as she kept the happiness coming." I pause and it comes to me, what I've been half remembering for a long time now: "Vero learned to fly."

"I took up quilting as part of my sobriety," Marlene says. "In the mornings, I'd visit craft stores, pick up scraps of fabric. I'd pick out the gray of your eyes or maybe the chestnut brown of your hair, or the pink of your first dress. I sewed my grief into quilts, and before I knew it, people were asking if they could buy them. So that became my first job, first honest dollar I earned on my own, selling a quilt to my neighbor. Later, Hank helped me figure out how to sell on the Internet. Then I learned I was pregnant."

"Life in the dollhouse . . . unraveled. You could feel it. The rooms became more frayed. Madame Sade angrier, edgier. And we became . . . tired. We didn't talk anymore, didn't huddle together and tell stories for comfort. We were either up, up, up or passed out cold as part of the down, down, down. Dinnertime became more strained. Looking at the two older girls sitting at the other end of the table. Harsh. Gaunt. *Knowing.* Vero and Chelsea know they must escape. But how?"

"I made a family," Marlene whispers. She sounds embarrassed, having finally put together a life just as her first daughter faced the abyss. "I married Hank. I gave birth to a beautiful little girl. I got a real job at the liquor store. And I haven't touched a drop of alcohol in twenty years. I'm so sorry I didn't sober up sooner. I'm so sorry I didn't learn my lessons quicker. If I could go back in time, if I could undo what I did —"

"You failed Vero."

"I'm sorry —"

"But what I did was worse."

She doesn't talk; her fingers tremble in my own.

I have arrived at the end of my mental corridor, outside the largest door of my memory banks. The one clearly marked "Keep Out." But my hand is on the knob and I'm going to do it. I have to do it. Right now, this moment. There's no turning back.

"I stopped shooting up the drugs. Bit by

bit, day by day, I took less, stashed more. I couldn't do it anymore. The life, the slow decay. We had to get out. Maybe if I could just think straight.

"I stuffed the vials in a hole in my mattress, where Madame Sade wouldn't find them. My roommate watched me do it, but I didn't worry. We were in this together, her and I. We were sisters. I tried to get her to stop, too, but it was harder for her. She was tired by then, even more tired than me. Even if we got away, she would say, where would we go?

"I tried . . ." My voice breaks. I'm turning the handle now. I can see the door opening, watch the dark crack yawn open before me.

"I knew," I say flatly, staring at no one, my gaze locked on the sight of this woman's hands folded in my own. "I told myself I didn't, but I knew what she was going to do."

"I'm sorry," Marlene whispers, as if she already understands what's coming next.

"She took my stash. Every single vial. One afternoon when I was down in the kitchen, my turn to cook. By the time I returned, she was dead, collapsed on the rug. I didn't know what to do." *Screaming, begging, pleading. Don't leave me, don't leave me, don't leave me. I can't do this alone.* "Madame came. We'd never had anything happen like that before. She was incensed, furious. Nothing to be done, she announced. Just have to wait till nightfall when the caretaker could deal with the body. Then she left her. Just like that. And I was all alone in the room with my best friend's corpse.

"I brushed out her hair, long dark locks so much like my own. I closed her eyes, a pale blue like my own. And then . . . I knew what I had to do."

Marlene is still clasping my hand, willing me to finish. The cops, Tessa and Wyatt, have moved from the corner table, are standing now, waiting with baited breath.

I will myself to look up. I will myself to stare them all in the eye as I say what I have to say next.

"I switched our clothes. I wrestled her into the bed, tucked her in. Then I took her place on the rug." *Wet with vomit, rank with urine.* "Rolled myself up. Ordered myself not to move again.

"Eventually, the door opened. Footfalls sounded as the caretaker arrived. I couldn't see, only hear, as he heaved me up, tossed me over his back. Thump, thump, thump, down the stairs, his shoulders digging into my stomach. I'm going to vomit. I can't vomit. I'm already dead.

"Outside, he heads into the woods, striding heavily over rocks and tree roots. It's raining. I can feel it through the rug. A dark and stormy night. Perfect for digging a grave. Shortly, he stops. Tosses me to the ground. I want to scream. But I don't. I'm already dead.

"Then, suddenly, he lifts me up. He heaves me in. Just like that. No last visit from Madame Sade, no final words from the so-called family. Just . . . whomp. I am garbage and now I'm gone. Then, of course, he picks up his spade and begins refilling the grave."

Marlene's grip on my hands is so tight now, our knuckles have gone white. I've lost all feeling in my fingertips. But I don't draw back. I stare at her, and I realize for the first time how truly angry I am. Because six-year-old Vero had believed in her, the power of a mother's hugs. Six-year-old Vero had fought to be brave for her, the eternity of a mother's love. Except six-year-old Vero never should have been in that house at all.

It comes to me for the first time. I shouldn't have had to save Vero. This woman, Vero's mom — that was *her* job.

"The dirt is heavy," I tell her now, my words hard, clipped, biting. "Wet and solid.

I can't move my legs. I can't move my arms. I'm trapped. Pinned. Suffocating. I really am going to die."

"I'm sorry," Marlene whispers.

"Just when I think I can't take it anymore, the weight settles. The caretaker leaves. His job is over. Now mine begins. As I wriggle and wrestle and tug and pull. I fight, fight, fight my way out of the grave. I burst out of the dirt into the middle of the storm, gasping and heaving and covered in mud. I return from the dead."

Lightning forking across the sky. The feel of rain upon my head. And air, pure, blessed air, which I draw into my lungs over and over again. I laugh, I cry, then I curl into a ball and completely break down. Because I am alive. And all it cost me was my best friend, my only friend. The sister of my heart.

I let go of Marlene's hands. Suddenly, violently, I push away from her. "I knew what would happen."

She doesn't know what to say. Standing near the table, Wyatt takes a step closer, as if thinking he should intervene.

"I knew she would overdose. She was tired, depressed. She was an addict, unable to help herself. And still I let her see where I hid my stash."

"Baby," Marlene begins.

"Don't! You knew there were dangers in a park. You knew what could happen to unattended children. Still you drank and took Vero there."

She shrinks back, doesn't say a word.

I'm wild. My head is on fire, but worse, my heart is breaking. I've let the memory in, and now it's that day all over again. "Just like I knew, if I hoarded the drugs, of course she might take them. Only one way out of the dollhouse, and she'd had enough. I knew. And still I did it. Because her death gave me the best shot at freedom."

"Vero —" Marlene tries again. I shake off her hand.

"I'm not Vero! Don't you get it? She's not me. She's just a ghost inside my head. She's a past I'm still trying to save, a mistake I'm still trying to face. I don't know; I don't completely understand it. I wanted to see you, but I never wanted to talk to you, because I can't do this. I can't . . . go back. I can't . . ." Words fail me; I don't know what I'm trying to say. I take two steps forward, rustle beneath the pillow and grab the photo I'd found in Thomas's jacket. "Here." I practically throw it at her. "You want your little girl? This is all that's left."

Marlene takes the photo. She holds it closer, then frowns. "Who is this?"

"Vero, of course. Surely you recognize —"

"No, it's not."

"What?" My turn to draw up short. I blink my eyes, scrub at my temples. Finally remembering what I once worked so hard to forget has hurt me. I know I'm disoriented; I know I'm not functioning on all cylinders. But still.

"That's Vero," I insist. "Taken at the dollhouse. I found it in Thomas's pocket." I say the last sentence without thinking. Now both Wyatt and Tessa have closed the gap between us, studying the photo intently.

"No, it's not," Marlene insists. "I understand this picture was taken later, but that girl still isn't Vero."

"Are you sure?" Wyatt asks Marlene. "It's an old photograph, not the best resolution, but the hair, the eyes . . ."

"Look at her left forearm," Marlene instructs him. "There's no scar."

"What scar?" Me again, my voice strangely high-pitched.

All of a sudden . . .

Vero is back in my mind. Vero is grinning at me with her gleaming white skull. Vero, who has always felt separate from me.

"Wait for it," she whispers. *"One, two —"*

"Vero has a scar," Marlene says. "From, um, an accident, when she was three. She

430

was pretending to be an airplane. She um, hit the coffee table."

Except that's not how Vero tells the story. In Vero's story, told night after night to her roommate, Chelsea, Ronnie the wicked knight tossed the princess into the air. He hurtled her into the table: *"You wanna cry, little shit? I'll give you something to cry about . . ."*

Marlene turns to me now. Real time. Real life. No memory to forget.

"Show him," she instructs me. "Your left arm. The scar."

I move in slow motion. I raise my left arm. I roll back my long sleeve.

I expose what I already know will be there: a long, pale expanse of perfectly unblemished skin.

I realize at last, the final secret remaining in that yawning black box of memory. The tidbit I withheld even from myself, because all these years later, I still didn't think I could handle it. Vero lives inside my head, not because she is some dissociated version of my past. Vero lives inside my head because I'm the one who killed her.

As Marlene gasps. "You're *not* my daughter."

And Vero, triumphant as ever, yells: *"Surprise!"*

CHAPTER 30

"Who are you?" Marlene Bilek had her hand wrapped around Nicky's wrist, gripping tight. Across from the older woman, Nicky winced in clear discomfort. "You know things. How do you know such things? What did you do with my daughter?"

"Ma'am, please." Wyatt hastily inserted himself between the two women. He had to forcefully pry Marlene's fingers from Nicky's wrist.

The older woman turned on him. "What kind of sick game is this? You told me you had found my daughter. You said you had proof!"

"We have fingerprints, Mrs. Bilek. Fingerprints that match your daughter's —"

"But she's not Vero! She doesn't have the scar. Vero has a scar —"

"Okay, okay. Everyone, deep breath. Let's take a step back for a second."

Wyatt got Marlene to one side of the

room, Nicky to the other. Marlene appeared nearly wild-eyed with grief, rage, betrayal. Nicky simply looked bewildered. And she was already rubbing her temples, a telltale sign of an impending migraine. Wyatt could feel a killer headache coming on himself, and he hadn't even suffered three concussions.

Tessa took over Nicky, helping the woman into one of the wooden chairs to one side of the room, while Wyatt positioned Marlene Bilek in a chair on the other side. Tessa retrieved cold bottles of water from the mini-fridge. She handed the first to Nicky, the second to Marlene.

Both women took a long drink.

Wyatt used the minute to regain his own composure. It was creepy to him, but watching the two women, sitting in one hotel room, not just their similar coloring, but the way they moved, the way they held themselves. He could believe they were mother and daughter, no problem.

Except according to Marlene Bilek, that was impossible.

"Let's start at the beginning," he said, after another moment had passed. He turned to Marlene. "You're saying Veronica has a scar."

"Left inside forearm. Right below the

elbow. Two to three inches long. From the coffee table."

"Ronnie threw her into it," Nicky intoned. "Picked her up. Vero was just a little girl and he tossed her into the wooden table like a piece of trash. The table broke. One of the legs gouged her arm."

"How do you know that?" Marlene demanded.

"Vero wants to fly," Nicky whispered. "She just wanted to fly. How could you stay with him? How could you let her suffer like that?"

Marlene paled. She didn't say another word.

"You're sure about the scar?" Wyatt asked again. He couldn't help himself. Vero couldn't have a scar. Because if Vero had a scar, none of this made any sense.

"Check the missing persons report," Marlene informed him crisply. "It's listed under identifying marks."

Tessa did the honors. She pulled her copy of the report from her computer bag, gave it a quick perusal. When she glanced back up, Wyatt saw the answer in her eyes. She nodded once, an affirmation that, yes, they had passed into the land of crazy.

He turned to Nicky. "Who are you?"

"I'm lost. No one wanted me, even before the dollhouse. No one loved me, even before the dollhouse."

"You're Chelsea," Wyatt put the pieces together. "You're the roommate." He thought he got it: "Who killed Vero in order to escape."

"Except I've been trying to save her for the past twenty-two years."

Wyatt shot a glance at Tessa. She'd tried to warn him there had to be a reason Nicky had buried her past. This sounded good enough to him.

"Chelsea —"

"Nicky."

"Nicky. Did Vero die that night?"

"There is only one way out of the doll-house."

"Are you sure?" he asked carefully, aware of Marlene Bilek's sharp intake of breath.

Nicky didn't answer. The anguished look on her face was proof enough.

"Then how did her fingerprints wind up in your car?"

"She didn't die!" Marlene picked up immediately, leaning forward in her chair. "She was with you! You've seen my daughter. You know where she is."

Wyatt turned to Nicky. She was frowning, scrubbing at her forehead again. "Shhh," she whispered. "Just . . . shhh . . ."

"Are you all right?" he asked her cautiously.

"She's laughing at me. I hate it when she's in this mood. I wish she would put on clothes. Or at least skin."

Wyatt and Tessa exchanged another glance.

"Nicky," he commanded briskly. "Wednesday night. You're in your car. You're driving to the New Hampshire state liquor store. You came to see Marlene Bilek, Vero's long-lost mother. Who is with you?"

Nicky opened her eyes. She appeared miserable, but not misleading. "Vero's with me. She's always with me. But not like you think."

"You're looking for her."

"Always."

"You want to keep her safe. You failed her once, and now you're stuck trying to get it right."

"Yes!"

"Nicky," Wyatt took her hand, held it between his own. Her fingers were ice-cold, in sharp contrast to the beads of sweat forming on her brow. They didn't have much time left, he realized. Regardless of his concerns about the rest of the case, Nicky's concussions were real enough, and the stress of the situation was taking its toll.

Any minute now, she'd be hammer-smacked by a migraine, and that would be that.

"Once and for all, did Veronica Sellers, did your friend, your roommate, make it out of the dollhouse?"

"Vero learned to fly."

"The drugs, she OD'd on the drugs."

Nicky stared at him. Stared at him, stared at him, stared at him. And for the first time, Wyatt got it. It wasn't that she couldn't admit these things to the police. It was that she couldn't admit them to herself. Chelsea, who'd been unloved before the dollhouse, but who'd found a sister while living in it.

"Yes," she whispered. Then she closed her eyes, which suited them both, because he wasn't sure even he could handle the pain he saw there.

"Nicky, I have to ask you another question."

She swallowed heavily.

"The fingerprints, the ones we recovered from your car . . . How did they get there?"

"She had to be with you," Marlene spoke up urgently. "My daughter. You're lying about her death. She was with you that night in your car."

Nicky shook her head. "No, it's not like that."

"It's not," Wyatt agreed. "We had a search

437

dog on the scene. And according to Annie, there was only one occupant of the vehicle, the driver who hiked up to the road."

"But then how do you explain the fingerprints?" Tessa pressed. Her brow was furrowed. It made him feel better to know this was as perplexing to her as it was to him. "You can't fake fingerprints. No two sets are alike. Not even with identical twins."

"True." Wyatt's gaze fell to Nicky's hands. They had recovered prints from Nicky's car, but until this afternoon they'd never printed Nicky herself. They'd questioned her, visited her home, taken her on a road trip, but printed her . . . No, it had never come to that.

Meaning at the end of the day, they had recovered Veronica Sellers's fingerprints from Nicky Frank's car. But that didn't mean they were Nicky Frank's prints.

Of all the stupid, idiotic, rookie mistakes. He'd have to call Kevin immediately and have him perform a comparison of Nicky's prints from this afternoon and Veronica Sellers's childhood prints from thirty years ago.

"Nicky," he said now, "those prints were left in blood. I saw them for myself. They weren't old prints. They were made that night. Left in blood, *your* blood, on the car seats and dash of your vehicle."

"Vero wants to fly," she whispered. "And the car flew, so weightless. I can feel her smile. I can feel her laugh with me."

"What happened?"

"Nothing stays weightless forever."

"What happened?"

"It's not the flying; it's the landing that's the hard part."

"Nicky!" he commanded firmly. "Look at me. Consider the photo. That's *not* a picture of Vero. Do you understand me? That's a picture of you! You. Meaning however Thomas got that picture . . . This isn't about Vero. It's always been about *you.*"

"You're wrong." Nicky looked up abruptly, stared Marlene straight in the eye. "It is about Vero. She never should've been in the dollhouse. She never should've died there. Twenty-two years later, she still wants her revenge. And we will all pay in the end."

Wyatt escorted Marlene Bilek back into the adjoining room. Having made her grand announcement, Nicky had collapsed on the nearest bed. For her part, Marlene seemed to have gotten over the worst of her anger and now seemed shell-shocked instead.

Wyatt made Marlene review the details of Vero's description once again, but she had nothing new to offer. Her Vero had had gray eyes. Nicky Frank's were blue. And her Vero had a scar on her left forearm. Yes, the coffee table accident had happened exactly the way Nicky described it, and no, she wasn't proud of it, but the fact that Nicky knew the details didn't change anything in Marlene's mind. Nicky Frank might know all the stories from Veronica Sellers's life, but she still wasn't Marlene's long-lost daughter.

As for the fingerprints retrieved from the woman's vehicle . . . They just didn't make any sense. If Vero was still alive, why hadn't she contacted her family? For that matter, why had Nicky gone to the trouble to track down Marlene through Northledge Investigations? It wasn't like Marlene had come into a large inheritance since her daughter's disappearance. She and her family were strictly working class, meaning there was no financial gain to posing as Marlene's missing child.

"She's sick," Marlene said at last, seeming to have finally talked herself into some semblance of empathy. "And I don't just mean the way she keeps rubbing her forehead. Nicky, that woman . . . she's a little crazy, isn't she?"

Wyatt hesitated, unsure how to answer

that question. "I think she's honestly confused."

"She thought she was Vero," Marlene said.
"I mean, buying the quilt, tracking me
down. It's like she really thought she was
my daughter."

"She seems to feel a strong connection to
Vero," Wyatt said at last, which was the most
he could understand the subject.

"Why?"

He found himself hesitating again. "Mrs.
Bilek . . . For everything that comes out of
Nicky's disjointed mind . . . I don't think
she's delusional. In fact, I suspect many of
her recollections are genuine memories. If
that's the case . . ."

Marlene grew quiet. "You think she's telling the truth about this dollhouse. Those
stories she told me in the beginning. They
really did happen. To Vero. And to her."

"I think we owe it to Nicky and Vero to
find out."

She looked up at him. "My daughter died
there. This Chelsea girl, she found the
strength to get off the drugs. Whereas my
Vero . . ." Her voice broke; she swallowed
heavily. "That's why Chelsea can't let her
go. She used my daughter's death for her
own escape, and she's been feeling guilty
ever since."

"I don't think we should rush to any more assumptions."

Wyatt retrieved the sketches Tessa had provided earlier. "Do you recognize this house?" He showed Marlene Bilek the picture of the dollhouse. The woman's face shuttered. She eyed the drawing stonily.

"That's the place?" She flashed him a look. "It's big. It's . . . grand. You'd think the people lucky enough to live in a house that nice were good people. You'd think the kids there, the little girls, were happy."

Wyatt continued to hold the drawing. After another moment, she shook her head.

He moved on to the sketch of Madame Sade. Much like his initial reaction, Marlene flinched. Then she did the unexpected. She reached out and jabbed the image.

"This is the woman who killed my girl?"

Wyatt didn't say anything.

"Whatever happened, it was her fault. You heard Nicky, Chelsea, talking. This woman took Vero from the park. This woman locked her up, never let her go. This woman killed my child."

"You recognize her from the park?"

"No."

"Ever see her before? In your building, around your neighborhood?" Because Wyatt didn't believe a woman like Madame Sade

442

abducted girls at random. Especially given the physical similarities between Vero and Chelsea, it was clear she was looking for a specific type. Perhaps even filling a client's request, which would take scouting on her part.

But Marlene shook her head. "No."

"You're sure?"

She regarded him sharply. "You think you could forget a woman this cold? Just looking at her picture churns my stomach."

Wyatt had another thought. "Notice any boys in the park that day?" He did his best to describe a younger version of Thomas Frank, who had to fit into this puzzle somehow. But once again Marlene shook her head.

"It's been a long time, Sergeant. And Nicky wasn't lying. I was drunk that day. I shouldn't have taken my girl to the park. I shouldn't have sat on that bench. That's on me. And I paid for it, paid as dear as any mother can."

He tried a different tack. "Who knew about Vero's scar?"

"Anyone who read the missing persons report, of course."

"By that, you mean the official police report? Because it's not on any of the flyers. Those just have her picture and the basics, height, weight, age."

"True."

"Friends and family?" he asked her.

She grimaced shamefully. "Didn't really have those. It was just me, Vero, and Ronnie."

"So Ronnie knew. Police ever question him about Vero's disappearance?"

"Sure. But that was a long time ago, and he had an alibi — he was at work when she disappeared."

"Okay." But Wyatt was thinking again. In terms of general age and description, Nicky Frank really would make the perfect long-lost Veronica Sellers. If not for that scar, as Marlene said.

Which made him very curious. Because not many people would have the information on that particular detail. Certainly, police reports weren't available to the general public. Meaning, if you wanted Nicky Frank to be Veronica Sellers . . . Even went so far, say, as to plant a missing girl's fingerprints in Nicky's car in order to try to get away with something . . .

Except how? And why?

Thomas had met Nicky that night. His half-drunk, thrice-concussed, extremely distraught wife. He'd handed her gloves. He'd put her car into neutral and shoved it down a hill toward a ravine. Had he some-how planted the prints? Because he wanted her to live as Veronica Sellers? Or die as a long-lost child? But why?

A collapsible shovel, a pair of bloody gloves. What the hell had the man been up to that night? And when would any of this case make sense?

Wyatt thanked Marlene for her time. Got the woman's assurances she wouldn't be talking to the press, then arranged for a deputy to drive her home.

Moment she left, Tessa appeared in the adjoining doorway. This room was a twin to its neighbor; she took a seat on the bed directly across from him.

"Well," she said at last. "That didn't go as planned."

"Let me ask you something: Can you fake a fingerprint?"

"Don't I wish." Her tone was dry. He shot her a glance, but she merely smiled at him. "In theory, I guess it could be done. Lift it from one surface, maybe with tape, then try to transfer it to another. But . . . a latent print is nothing more than a microscopic film of skin ridges and natural oils. Transfer-ring it back onto a second surface and managing to recapture the entire print . . . feels like something that might work better on a TV show than in real life."

"You know what struck me about the vehicle?" he asked her now.

Tessa shook her head.

"How lucky we were to have such obvious prints. Think about it — most cars, you can't even print. Surfaces are irregular, have been handled so often, all you get is a smeary mess. But Nicole Frank's car. With my plain eyes, I could make out a thumb print left behind in blood. Lucky us."

Tessa stared at him. "You're thinking it was planted."

"Annie the search canine swears there was only one person present at the crash site, and I don't argue with a good dog's nose."

"But why?"

"I have no idea."

"How would you get such a print?" Tessa continued. "Three decades later, who even has access to her case file?"

"Don't need her case file for her fingerprints," Wyatt said. "The Center for Missing and Exploited Children digitized all the records years ago for national distribution. To assist with matches."

"So we don't know why or how, but under the who column, you're thinking someone with access to the national database."

Wyatt stared at her. In the back of his

head, something finally clicked. "Of digital prints," he stated. "*Digital* files."

"Yes?"

"You know what else you can do with digital images?"

"Um . . . . E-mail them, text them, share them —"

"Import them into AutoCAD and create a digital model."

"A digital model of fingerprints?"

"Yes. Which could then be downloaded to a three-D printer, which would create a three-D mold of the distinct ridge patterns, used to, say, create a latex glove cast from a perfect handprint."

Tessa's eyes widened. "A glove alone can't leave fingerprints. You'd have to spray it with an oily substance such as cooking spray —"

"Or blood."

Tessa shuddered slightly, but nodded. "The bloody gloves, the ones you collected from Thomas Frank's car."

"That's what he handed Nicky that night. A pair of . . . fingerprint gloves . . . he'd made himself on his three-D printer. So she'd cover the car in Veronica Sellers's fingerprints. So she'd be mistaken as Veronica Sellers."

Tessa asked the next logical question. "But why?"

Wyatt shook his head. "I don't know. He's got to be part of it, right? According to Nicky, she found that photo of . . . herself, I guess, in Thomas's possession. Taken while she was in the dollhouse."

"How'd she get away?" Tessa said suddenly. "I mean this whole, got Vero to OD then took the place of her roommate's dead body. So Nicky gets herself buried alive, then heroically claws her way back to the land of the living in the midst of a storm . . . and then what? Walks all the way to New Orleans?"

Wyatt saw her point. "She must've had help. Enter Thomas Frank?"

"In that scenario, he saved her. And he must've cared for her to end up spending the next twenty-two years together. Just rescuing her one dark and stormy night doesn't require a lifetime plan. And if he's in cahoots with Madame Sade, maybe assigned as, what, Nicky's watcher all these years, that doesn't necessitate marriage. It feels like . . . he must genuinely care for her, at least in some manner."

Wyatt remained skeptical. "He crashed his wife's car, with her in it. He burned down their house, with all their belongings in it. If

448

this is love, I'm sorry I've been wasting my time buying flowers."

Tessa rolled her eyes. She rattled off their case: "Thirty years ago, six-year-old Veronica Sellers was abducted from a park and locked away in a high-end brothel. Twenty years ago, roughly, she died in that same house, but her roommate, Chelsea, managed to escape and, all these years later, has kept Vero's memory alive."

"Chelsea spent all her time in the dollhouse internalizing Vero's stories. Which she now has a tendency to confuse as her own? Or maybe just wishes were her own?" Wyatt decided it was a moot point. "Either way, Vero is always with her. She can't let her go."

"Which leads us to six months ago, when Chelsea, who's been trying to live happily ever after with her husband, I-will-always-take-care-of-you Thomas Frank, decides she can't keep running anymore. She wants answers to her troubled memories, trauma, depression, et cetera. She demands they move to New Hampshire."

"And suffers her first accident almost immediately. A fall down the basement stairs of her new home. Followed by wiping out on her front steps."

"Followed by," Tessa continued, "Wednesday night. When she meets Marlene Bilek, who she's obsessed with as a living link to Vero. Unfortunately, Nicky then discovers Vero's beloved mom has a whole new family and isn't mourning Vero nearly as much as Nicky-slash-Chelsea is."

"Nicky calls Thomas. And he puts his own plan in gear? Turn his confused wife into Veronica Sellers?" Wyatt stared at Tessa. "Now, see, this is where things break down for me."

Tessa nodded. She eyed him thoughtfully. Opened her mouth, paused, then shook her head. "No. I agree. It makes no sense."

"I'm gonna get Kevin on the phone. Have him start comparing prints and analyzing those rubber gloves. Then you and I are gonna run through this all over again. We're missing something." Wyatt glanced at his watch, noting it was now nearly midnight. "We have about nine hours left to find it."

Tessa nodded in agreement. "Where do you think Thomas is now?" she asked him.

Wyatt had no doubt: "Somewhere close."

CHAPTER 31

Vero and I are fighting.

"I don't want to do this anymore," I tell her. "I want my life back."

"What life? You don't have a life." Vero sits calmly at the wooden table in the tower bedroom. She has finally put on clothes, that dreadful floral dress, though her skin is hanging from her skull in leathery flaps.

"I didn't know about the scar!"

"Should've. Lived with me long enough. Not my fault you weren't paying attention." She holds out her left arm, but she's gone all skeletal again, revealing only the twin bones radiating from her elbow down to her wrist. "Oops," she says. "Maybe I forgot something after all. But again, not really my fault. I am you, you know."

I rub my forehead. In my mind's eye, in real life? The lines are too blurred; I don't know anymore.

"I want to be free."

"No. You want to be me. Always have. Again, not my fault you're so jealous. First time I told you about my mother, that someone out there actually loved me, that someone out there actually *cared* about me." Her tone is mocking. "You're the one who set out to make my life miserable."

She's right. There are other images in my mind. Deeper, darker memories I never visit, because I prefer Vero's stories. From the very beginning, hearing about the magical queen, the evil witch. Vero might have ended up in the dollhouse, but for six years prior to that, six long, glorious years . . .

A mother who hugged her. A mother who let her crawl on her lap. A mother who once slept with her on the floor and begged her to live.

I have none of those memories. Not even three concussions later. I have only Vero, whom once I hated and then . . . grew to love in my own way. Incarceration can have that effect on people. Her stories became my stories. Her hope, my hope. Because all those years we were together, Vero never stopped talking about one day seeing her mother again.

Except, of course . . .

"You shouldn't have killed me," she says now, voice conversational. She is pouring herself a cup of tea, a shot of scotch. "If you hadn't killed me, maybe you would've escaped me in the end."

"That's not fair."

"Who hoarded her drugs? Who left them someplace you knew your roommate was bound to find?"

I finally stop pacing, do my best to take a stand.

"Vero wants to fly," I state flatly. "And that's what you did. *You* gave up. *You* shot up, anything, everything, the entire supply. If you hadn't done that . . ."

Vero grins at me. "If I hadn't done that . . . ," she goads.

I try to stay on track. "You had someone out there who loved you. You should've put the drugs back. If not for yourself, then at least for her."

She is definitely in a mood now. "Then what? I would've lived happily ever after? You and me, best friends forever in the dungeon of the dollhouse?"

Abruptly, the room grows hazier. The rose mural nearly disappearing. As if the room is suddenly filling with smog. Or smoke.

In my mind, in real life, I feel myself automatically reach out my hand.

But of course, Thomas isn't there.

"Tell me," Vero demands now. "Tell me

what would've happened if I hadn't taken the drugs."

"I don't know!"

"Yes, you do."

"I don't! I never —"

"Yes, you do. Yes, you did!"

And of course she's right. More dark shapes shift. Memories I can't afford to have. Willful ignorance I'm still waiting to bring me bliss. Except now I can feel them, looming larger, darker, chilling the very corridors of my mind. Sergeant Wyatt had been right; none of this is about Vero. It's about me. It's always been about me and, three concussions later, the past I'm still not ready to face.

"Go away," I order now. "I don't want to talk to you anymore!"

"Can't. I'm you. Only one talking here is you. Only one arguing here is you. Only one who can't handle the truth is you. I'm not just a pretty little ghost, you know. I'm your fucking conscience."

She holds out her arm. Her skin is back, and now the left arm's scar stands out prominently, a thick, jagged pucker ripping savagely down smooth white skin. Proving once and for all what I did know, even if I later chose to forget. Vero smiles, except this time her mood isn't antagonistic. Her ghost, my conscience, appears sad.

"I wanted to fly," Vero says quietly. "Once. A long time ago. A little girl who didn't know any better. Then Ronnie picked me up and hurtled me into a coffee table. There are many ways to die, Chelsea. And not all of them happened in that dollhouse."

"I'm sorry."

"You wanted the princess to have a happy ending. You wanted her to reunite with the magical queen and everything to turn into sunshine and rainbows. In your own way, you believed in me long after I stopped."

I don't say anything.

"But you also know, Chelsea," she continues soberly, "deep down inside, why that couldn't happen; my story was only a work of fiction. Now you can visit me as much as you want and resurrect me in your head for as long as you'd like. But there's still no going back. There's just you: the lone survivor."

"I loved you," I whisper.

"I know. But take it from me, love alone can't save you in the end."

Abruptly I feel more shifting in the dark corridors of my mind. Memories I swear I didn't stir up, and yet . . . I look up sharply. Vero is watching me, her look cunning.

"Stop," I tell her.

"Can't. I'm you, remember?"

"I'm not ready for this."

"For what? The smell of smoke? The heat of flames. Fire, fire, everywhere. Why'd your husband burn your house, Nicky? Why? And better yet, when did Thomas get so good with flames?"

"Shut up!"

But she won't. Vero shoves away from the table. She marches across the room. Her dress is gone. Her skin is gone. Now she is nothing but decaying flesh, marching closer and closer, reaching out with her bony hands.

"Thomas," she singsongs. "Handsome Thomas. Caring Thomas. Thomas who's *always* been there. Is it your past you're trying to escape, Nicky? Or is it the man you married?"

Her skeletal hands reach my neck, scrape across my collarbone.

Abruptly, the door to the tower bedroom crashes open behind me. But I don't turn. I keep my eyes on Vero's grinning skull. Because I already know I don't want to see who's standing there.

"What have you done, Nicky?" Vero whispers to me. *"Who else do you have to fear?"*

I jerk awake with a gasp. My head is on fire;

my entire body aches. For a second, instinctively, reflexively, I lock down each muscle. Willing myself not to move. Old habits, back from the days when you never knew who else might be present. Waiting to hurt you next.

A first careful inhale. Followed by a long, slow exhale. I listen, registering voices, coming through the wall, from the room next door. I search closer, for the sound of another person's presence nearby. Only when I'm absolutely, completely convinced that I'm alone do I finally open my eyes, allow my muscles to relax.

The room is dark. I can see a thin streak of light on the far wall, coming from the cracked doorway between the two hotel rooms. Bits and pieces return to me. My current hideaway in the form of a nondescript New Hampshire hotel room. The disastrous meeting with Marlene Bilek, who turned out to not be my mom, because of course, my real mom died of an overdose years ago, before I even escaped from the dollhouse. Someone I once looked up to, only to forget again, because what was the point? I was never the princess with a magical queen. My entire life, I've only ever been in the service of an evil witch.

My eyes burn. Stupid tears, I think as I

roll over, eye the second bed. It's empty, as I'd suspected. Tessa must be in the adjacent room, talking to Wyatt.

They are probably rehashing the case. Trying to understand why I went to the trouble to track down Marlene Bilek, when she isn't my mother. Why I cling to a quilt handcrafted by a woman I'd never met.

How I ended up with Vero's fingerprints in my Audi.

I don't know the answer to the last question. It confuses me as much as it does them. As for the first two issues . . . I guess I was just trying to keep Vero alive, shore up her memory. Our imaginary visits weren't enough to ease my pain, so I went to the next step of establishing a tangible connection in the form of her mother.

Maybe, if I could make Vero real enough, her family real enough, then she wouldn't be gone and I wouldn't have to feel so guilty.

Because twenty-two years later, I still haven't figured out the business of living. I survive, I suppose. I exist. I even got married and moved all around the country. But was that truly living or just another form of running? All those nights I woke up screaming. All those memories I suppressed time and time again, until my mind was a

458

mixed-up mess way before the concussions began.

I got out of the dollhouse but never escaped the past. The weight of my own guilt, a skill set I never learned? I don't know. I feel like I want to be something more. I want to do something more. But I don't know how to get there.

I could run again, I contemplate now, curled up on the hotel room bed. Pick out a new state, new town, new identity. It's what I've done before. Especially the first two years after my escape. Dragging Thomas from place to place, name to name, often on a weekly basis. Less a strategic bid for freedom than a clear case of hysteria. Thomas had begged me to slow down. At least try out a new location before casting it into the wind. At least pick one name, one identity, so we had some shot at building a normal life.

Under his guidance, we'd done one last professional do-over, paying good money for proper IDs, vetted history. We'd become Thomas and Nicole Frank, identities he swore would keep us safe. And yet still, every two years I'd had to move again. Because the weight of November still became too much.

Maybe I can take up drinking seriously

this time, I ponder now. Brain trauma be damned. I'll throw back scotch, burn out these terrible memories once and for all. I'll tell myself I'm free and happy and independent. Fuck Thomas; fuck Vero. I will escape both of them. I will be a woman who has it all.

A woman who is no one at all.

Except that's not completely true, I find myself thinking. More shadows, shifting and lurching in the back of my head. The taste of dirt. The feel of earth giving way beneath my fingertips. And that moment, that one savage moment when I realized I had done it. I was out; I was alive. I was free of the dollhouse.

That moment, right before . . .

Smoke. Heat. My house burning down in New Hampshire. Why did Thomas torch it? His workshop maybe, but our entire house? Why the need to burn it to the ground?

How did Thomas become so good with fire?

Vero, laughing in the back of my mind. *"Is it your past you're trying to escape, or the man you married?"*

I rein it all in. Force my eyes to focus on the here and now. The darkened hotel room. The empty bed beside me. I don't want to feel so helpless anymore. Or lost or confused or overwhelmed.

This is it. The moment of truth.

I can spend the rest of my life being a dead woman's roommate or a missing man's wife.

Then, in the next heartbeat.

No. I'm more than either of those two things. I'm the one who wanted to move to New Hampshire, even when Thomas tried to convince me otherwise. I'm the one who hired a private investigator, even though Thomas tried to tell me to let it be.

I'm a woman twice returned from the dead.

And I'm not finished yet.

CHAPTER 32

While Wyatt worked with Kevin on the fingerprint riddle, Tessa got on the phone with D. D. Warren.

The Boston detective was her usual charming self. "Do you have any idea what time it is?"

"My watch says midnight."

"I haven't even agreed to work for your high-and-mighty investigative firm yet —"

"But you did agree to a freelance assignment."

"I already achieved the high score on Angry Birds."

"You, an angry bird? Who would've thought?"

"Shut up," D.D. said.

Which made Tessa smile. Because as interactions with the temperamental detective went, this was par for the course, and so far, the most normal conversation Tessa had had all night.

"I'm sorry to call so late," Tessa acknowledged. "But if memory holds, you're one of those round-the-clock workers. As in you'll sleep when you retire. Or the day you drop dead."

"Same diff," D.D. replied.

"Perfect, because this case feels like it's spiraling out of control and we definitely could use some answers sooner versus later."

Wyatt had wrapped up his call. Tessa waved him over to join, putting her phone on speaker. Wyatt and D.D. had worked together on the Denbe case, so no introductions were required.

"How's your arm?" Wyatt asked.

"Getting there."

"Got a date for the fitness-for-duty test?" he asked.

"Getting there," D.D. said, and this time her voice indicated end of discussion. "So the Veronica Sellers case. According to the always-in-the-know-and-never-wrong nightly news, you found the missing girl. Albeit thirty years late."

"Um . . . we're not so sure about that," Tessa said.

A moment of silence. Then: "Well, I'll be damned. Guess I'm happy I took your call after all."

Wyatt explained about the fingerprint

confusion, filling in now: "Kevin just examined the latex gloves using a magnifying glass, and sure enough, there appear to be ridge patterns at the end of each finger. As in, Thomas Frank somehow fashioned a pair of fingerprint gloves, designed to leave Veronica Sellers's prints all over his wife's car."

"He wanted his wife identified as a missing girl from a thirty-year-old cold case?" D.D. asked in confusion. "But why?"

"That's the million-dollar question. Got any ideas?"

"I've been reviewing the whole sorry case file," D.D. said. "Can I just say, when you asked me to look into all the missing-kid and runaway-youth cases from thirty years ago in New England . . . What a shit assignment."

"It's a major investigation," Tessa informed her. "Is there any other kind of assignment?"

"Touché. Look, I gave it my best go, but you have two fundamental issues when trying to track down a major sex-slave ring from that far back."

"Okay," Wyatt prompted.

"One, the National Center for Missing and Exploited Children was still in its infancy. So we don't have one central database. I mean, kind of. Major departments, such as Boston, took the time to send in their documents. But if you consider all the small-town offices, remote sheriff's departments, out there who were already way understaffed, the information collection in the beginning was hit or miss, particularly for the years you're looking at."

"Then you go department by department," Tessa stated, which was definitely a shit assignment, and yet, as all three of them knew, how things got done.

"Yeah, yeah, yeah. Which brings us to problem number two. Garbage in. Garbage out."

Tessa was still contemplating that one when Wyatt got it.

"You mean were the missing kids ever categorized as missing?"

"Ding-ding-ding, give the man a prize. Ask any cop who works vice. Most of the underaged working girls are runaways. Some might have been declared missing, but the vast majority —"

"Aren't even in the system," Tessa finished for her.

"Exactly. So yeah, I can kill the next week begging and pleading for every backwoods law enforcement agency to search their archives for missing persons cases going back at least thirty years, or I can actually do something productive with my time."

"I presume you're going to dazzle us with your brilliance?" Wyatt spoke up hopefully.

"Please. I fractured my arm, not my head. So first thing's first. For the sake of argument, I did a broad-strokes statistical analysis. You want some numbers to keep you awake at night? There's been a roughly sixfold increase in the number of missing persons cases in the past twenty-five years, from one hundred and fifty thousand to nearly nine hundred thousand. Now, a significant portion of that increase can be attributed to greater law enforcement attention and better national databases, much like improved cancer diagnostics lead to an increase in the number of cases of cancer. It's not great to see those numbers go up, but it's not as bad as it sounds either.

"Breaking those numbers down, only so many of those cases involve youths under eighteen, and of those, two hundred thousand are considered custodial situations. Basically, boil it all down, and only about a hundred missing children's cases each year are categorized as stranger abductions. Speaking as a mom, that's still a hundred too many, and yet . . . that wasn't as many as I would've thought."

Tessa considered the matter, had to agree. She and Wyatt shared a nod.

"But that's nationwide," Wyatt spoke up. "It's rare for a sex-trafficking ring to span that much geography."

"Exactly. So if I'm focusing on the New England region, I'm guessing I should find records for maybe a dozen, two dozen missing kids. But those are today's numbers. Remember, in the nineteen eighties, our police departments weren't as well versed in this game. So I'm thinking if I can find as many as a dozen missing children's reports, then maybe there is some proof of an active sex-trafficking ring in that time period. Plus, I open it up to look at runaways, too, for obvious reasons."

Tessa found herself nodding; Wyatt, too. Neither of them spoke, simply waited.

"I found three cases," D.D. announced. "Of those, Veronica Sellers is one. But that's it. Three kids went missing in that time frame. Two girls, one boy, Veronica Sellers being the youngest at six, the others being a twelve-year-old girl and a fourteen-year-old boy."

Tessa couldn't help herself. She frowned, stared at Wyatt beside her.

"So assuming there's this dollhouse, filled with dozens of working girls," Tessa spoke out loud.

"They'd have to be runaways," D.D. answered. "Most likely recruited from back alleys, bought off other pimps. Except, you described a pretty high-end operation, right? A Victorian house, oriental rugs, crystal glasses, an elite clientele. I would think customers like those would have a certain expectation of the merchandise, so to speak. A young, fresh-faced girl, sadly, fits the bill. A washed-out runaway, on the other hand . . ."

"Doesn't seem the right match," Tessa filled in. She considered the matter. "Nicky claimed she spent the first few years locked away in a tower bedroom, taking classes. Madame Sade appeared every day, educated her in both basic studies but also culture, entertainment, et cetera. Maybe she groomed the runaways, polished them up for her clients?"

"Maybe," D.D. conceded. "Time-consuming, though. If she's spending all that time on one girl, how could she be recruiting any others?"

Tessa and Wyatt didn't have an answer for that.

"I got another theory for you."

"By all means," Wyatt prompted.

"I'm a homicide detective. You want to

know our secret to success? Play the odds. A wife meets a brutal end. Arrest the husband. Or, if you're feeling frisky, the pool boy she just dumped because while he might've been good in bed, she still wasn't givin' up her mansion for him. Either way, you got a victim, odds are you got the perpetrator in the same room with the body."

"You mean Thomas Frank?" Wyatt asked. "Because trust me, I suspect the husband."

"Who's Thomas Frank?" D.D. asked. "Look, my assignment was to investigate Veronica Sellers and other missing kids going back thirty years. I found three cases, which means either there was definitely *not* a sex-trafficking ring that specialized in abducting fresh-faced young girls. Or . . ." Long pause. "The other girls who disappeared were never listed as missing because they were never *declared* missing by their parents."

It took Tessa a moment to understand. Then she closed her eyes and leaned closer to Wyatt, simply because she needed to.

"If this was a high-dollar operation," D.D. continued, "discreet location, wealthy clients, high expectation for merchandise . . . Well, then, maybe the madam went about things the smart way: Why risk kidnapping your product when you can simply buy it instead?"

"Children," Wyatt said. "Madame Sade didn't just abduct kids. She purchased them?"

"Sure. It happens. Sadly, anywhere in this country, most days of the week."

"If the parents were the ones selling," Wyatt finished the thought, "naturally they wouldn't report their own child missing."

"Absolutely. Can't call attention to their own crime. And if you're a family living on the edge, or maybe a single parent, no family support network of your own, who's gonna ask questions? You tell the neighbors little Sally went off to stay with your ex or is visiting your grandparents or, hell, got sick and died. You'd be amazed how few people will really push the issue, ask the pertinent questions. By and large, people don't want to know what they don't want to know."

"Vero's abduction was the exception, not the norm?" Tessa asked. "Madame Sade grabbed her maybe because she fit a general type, brown hair, blue eyes, but probably even more to the point, was clearly unguarded in the park, as her mom was passed-out drunk. Vero's abduction was a crime of opportunity, but for other girls, the madam took a more direct approach?"

"Well, now, just to make matters more interesting," D.D. said, "Vero's mom wasn't the one who reported her missing."

"What?" Tessa sat up straighter. Now D.D. had her and Wyatt's complete attention.

"I pulled the original file. Because frankly, it got me curious. I mean, so *few* missing children's cases from that time period, and now here is one, suddenly back from the dead, and yet she never looked up her mom. Didn't that bother you? 'Cause again, being a paranoid homicide cop, it bothered me."

"She said she wasn't ready, looked nervous and scared on the subject . . ." Tessa shut up. Nicky Frank wasn't even Veronica Sellers in the end, so what did it matter?

"Report says Vero and her mother, Marlene, went to the park. Mom ended up falling asleep on the park bench. When she wakes back up, her six-year-old daughter is gone. Uproar ensues, cops are called. But here's the deal. According to the individual witness statements, Marlene wasn't calling her daughter's name. She was just walking around the park. It wasn't until another woman approached her, asking about her daughter, saying she'd seen Vero leave the park, wondering what had happened . . . That's when things got off and running. Police came, Marlene gave a statement, a reward was hastily assembled, a local case was born. But you tell me, mom to mom" — D.D. was speaking to Tessa at this point — "would you walk around a playground, never calling your vanished child's name?"

Tessa didn't have an answer. It was unfathomable to her.

"Hold on," Wyatt spoke up. "This was nearly thirty years ago. Missing children's cases didn't have the publicity they do now. It might not have occurred to Marlene to assume the worst."

"True. And the investigating officers at the time apparently agreed with you. Case was worked, ran out of steam, put away, taken back out, reworked, ran out of steam, and eventually, ten years ago, pulled again as a cold case. Because you never know, right?"

"Sure," Tessa and Wyatt agreed.

"Now, that detective, in his notes, raises some questions right off the bat about Marlene Bilek. And not just her behavior, or lack of urgency in the park. No, what caught his attention was that six months later, Marlene opened her first-ever savings account with five thousand dollars cash."

"What?"

"Yeah. Now, by this time, Marlene had taken up with a fellow officer, Hank Bilek.

He swore the money came from her abusive ex. Basically, this Ronnie guy had bashed in her face one too many times. Hank did the noble thing, stopped by, told Ronnie if he ever laid a hand on Marlene again, Ronnie would spend the next six months assembling all his broken body parts. To make it official, Ronnie would cover Marlene's moving expenses, hence the five grand so she could leave him and get a place of her own."

"Okay," Tessa interjected, "I gotta say I like Hank's style."

"Sure, what's not to love? One problem, though . . . Ronnie's account never showed a five-thousand-dollar debit. And he had the money. He'd just finished up some major plumbing job. But while Marlene has a record of cash coming in, Ronnie has no record of cash going out. So where'd the money come from?"

"You think Marlene might have sold her six-year-old daughter for five thousand dollars," Wyatt said slowly.

"It's a question worth considering."

"But Marlene didn't even get the money until six months later," Tessa protested.

"Case was front-page news. That kind of cash appearing in Marlene's name within twenty-four hours of her daughter's abduction? Please, they would've had her in handcuffs for sure. Six months later, however, with no leads, no suspects, no theories . . . Press had moved on. And so had the police."

"Any proof," Wyatt asked now, "linking the money to Vero's disappearance, or, say, a person of interest?"

"Not that lucky. The deposit was in the form of cash, so no way to trace. And for that matter, Marlene has a clean record. A history of alcohol abuse, yes, but criminal mischief, no. So . . ." Tessa could hear the waffling in D.D.'s voice. "Marlene hardly made for a great suspect. Especially given the grieving-mother act that had already been filmed on TV."

"What about her new life with her new family, new daughter?" Tessa quizzed.

"Clean as a whistle," D.D. reported. "By all accounts, Marlene is a law-abiding citizen. The worst may have happened to her thirty years ago, but she turned things around."

"Well, a mysterious cash infusion of five grand doesn't hurt," Wyatt muttered.

"Now," D.D. spoke up, "you're saying Nicky Frank is not Veronica Sellers, right? So who is she?"

"We're running her fingerprints now," Wyatt provided. "We believe she was Vero's roommate in the dollhouse, first name Chelsea. But we don't have a last name or any other information as of yet."

"She looks like Vero, right? Same general description, brown hair, blue eyes? Same general age?"

"Sounds like she arrived in the dollhouse first, so maybe a few years older."

"Got it. I'll go back through the runaway reports. See if I can find a record of any girls with that name and description. Never hurts to try."

"Appreciate it," Wyatt said. They wrapped things up, ended the call.

Tessa set down her phone. She recognized the look on Wyatt's face. He was tired and pissed off but still thinking hard.

"I feel like we're being played," he stated abruptly. "Nicky who's Vero who's Chelsea. Marlene who's a tragic mom who's maybe the kind of woman who sold her own child. Thomas Frank who's a caring husband who's an accomplished arsonist who's a criminal mastermind. They're all knee-deep in this, but how to make the pieces fit?"

"We need Thomas Frank," Tessa said quietly.

"Trust me, I know. I got uniformed patrol officers sweeping every hotel and motel in a fifty-mile vicinity. We're monitoring any and all cell phone and credit card activity. Unfortunately, the man's a ghost. We don't even know what vehicle he's driving. The one he stole from the hotel he ditched ten miles away, where his trail stops cold. It's almost as if he's done this before."

Wyatt raked a hand through his hair. "Here's a question," he said abruptly. "Given that Nicky isn't Vero, how'd she recognize Marlene Bilek Wednesday night?"

"What d'you mean?"

"I mean, you told Nicky Marlene worked at a New Hampshire state liquor store. Now, according to Nicky, minute she entered the store, she recognized Marlene as Vero's mom. How? Based on stories told to her more than twenty years ago?"

"Nicky said she looked her up online."

"Maybe, but the way Nicky spoke, her reaction was more personal, even visceral. She *knew* Marlene to be Vero's mom."

"You think she saw her before?"

"Why not?" Wyatt was off the bed, pacing. "If Marlene collected five thousand dollars, she had to get the cashier's check somehow; it's not the sort of thing you send through the mail. Dammit! I showed her Nicky's sketch of the house. I showed her the picture of Madame Sade. She looked me right in the eye and told me she didn't recognize either one. But I bet you now, she was at that house one day. She personally picked up that check, and Nicky saw her there. That's why Nicky's been hell-bent on tracking her down. Marlene isn't just some link to Vero. She's another trigger for Nicky's suppressed memories. That's it, we're picking her up."

"Marlene Bilek?"

"Absolutely." Wyatt was already crossing to the room's round table, grabbing his keys. "And while we're at it, wake up Nicky, too. We're taking them both for a ride."

"You think Marlene can lead us to the dollhouse?" Tessa was up off the bed now as well.

"Dollhouse, Madame Sade, I want it all. Bet you anything" — Wyatt turned, eyes gleaming — "we find them, we find Thomas Frank. And we get to the bottom of this once and for all."

Sounded good to Tessa. She crossed to the adjoining room to rouse Nicky.

Except . . .

"Wyatt," she called urgently.

Rechecking the first bed, the second, rounding to the bathroom, the small closet. But the room was small enough, the truth unavoidable.

"What is it?" Wyatt stalked into the room,

jiggling keys.

"She's not here. Wyatt, Nicky Frank is gone."

CHAPTER 33

It's not hard to sneak out of the hotel. Middle of the night, off-season in the North Country. Summer, a hotel like this one would be overflowing with families eager to jump in the pool, hike the mountains, raft down the rivers. Early fall, tour buses would cram the parking lot with aging leaf peepers, armed with cameras and heavy knit sweaters. Of course, December brought snowfall, teenage boarding dudes, and impeccably clad ski bunnies. But now, mid-November, when the mountains were denuded of leaves, covered in nothing but dirt . . .

Not even the locals enjoyed November in the North Country. This was a time of waiting. Which is exactly how the night felt to me. Expectant. With just enough chill in the air to prickle the hair on the back of my neck.

Slipping out of the room was easy enough.

First I found Tessa's computer case, where she'd left it next to the table. Then I rifled through it in the dark, until my fingers discovered the rectangular shape of her key fob. Next it was a simple matter of waiting for her and Wyatt's voices to pick up, become louder, more focused on their phone call next door. Six quiet strides and I stood next to the exit.

Tessa asking a sharp question. Me opening the door. One muffled click. Another exclamation from the adjoining room. Me slipping out, closing the door behind me. Second muffled click.

I didn't wait after that. Just headed straight down the hall to the stairs. Down one flight; then I was striding out into the darkened parking lot, armed with keys and hopped-up on determination.

Of course, where to go, what to do . . .

Is knowing who you aren't the same as knowing who you are? Is knowing you're sick of running the same as knowing how to fight?

Is knowing that you're tired of forgetting the same as knowing how to remember?

I stride across the parking lot in search of Tessa's black Lexus SUV. Cloudless night above. Half-moon in the sky and so many stars. I can't help but stop and stare. In all the places I've lived, the cities, the coasts, the deserts, there's still nothing like the night sky in the mountains of New Hampshire.

I should count the stars, I think. So many, so vast. I could count and count and each one would make me feel smaller, less significant. Until I'd disappear once and for all, standing in the middle of a hotel parking lot. No more decisions left to make. No more past left to escape.

Then, in the next instant, I smell smoke.

And that's how I know he's here.

I can't help myself. I take one step forward. Then another. There are only six cars in the dimly lit space. But I already know he's not in any of them. He's the shadow, right there, leaning against a tree. The man slowly straightening, unpeeling himself from the branches.

My husband walking toward me.

It's funny the things you know after so many years together. I can't see his face. He's too far away and it's too dark. But I don't need to see his eyes or his nose or the slash of his mouth or the set of his jaw. I know my husband simply from the way he moves.

And the corresponding tightness in my chest.

He has his hands in his pockets. Non-threatening, I think, and yet already my nerves are on edge. I hold Tessa's key fob tight in my fist, just in case.

He stops four feet back. I can feel his gaze on my face, assessing me, even as I try to gauge his mood.

I feel too much at once. An urgent desire to rush forward, throw myself at him. Because I'm alone and I hurt and I wanted a family and I lost a family and he's all I have. All, maybe, I've ever had, and God, I've missed him. The steady comfort of his voice. The feel of his fingers, massaging my temples. The strength of his resolve, day after day, week after week, month after month.

I love you, he told me, all those years ago. *Wherever you want me to go, whoever you need me to be, whatever you need me to do . . . I will always be there for you.*

Now I stare at my husband of twenty-two years, and I realize that for the first time, I'm afraid.

"Where are you going?" he asks. In the faint light cast by the moon, I can see that he's frowning. "Should you even be out here?"

"Funny, I was going to ask you the same."

He frowns again. Takes another step

forward, before something about my expression brings him up short. He rocks back on his heels. Nervous, I think. Uncertain, which doesn't make any sense.

"You met with her, right?" he presses. "Marlene Bilek. I saw the cops bring her."

"You're spying on me."

"Of course. What did you expect?"

I shake my head, fight an instinctive need to rub my forehead. "You burned down our house." Then, perhaps more important: "You were with me Wednesday night. You asked me if I trusted you. Then you fastened me into the driver's seat and shoved my car down a hill."

Thomas doesn't say anything. He's eyeing me intently. Waiting for me to speak more? Or waiting for me to remember more?

Sergeant Wyatt has it wrong, I realize abruptly. This has never been about Vero. And it's never been about me. It's about us. Thomas and me. Because that's marriage, right? It's never about one person or the other. It's always the dynamics between the two.

And Thomas and I, we go way, way back. The longest relationship I've ever had. To the smell of freshly mowed grass. And a lonely girl's view from a tower bedroom.

All these years, my husband hasn't been

waiting for me to tell him the truth. He's simply been waiting for me to remember it.

I step forward. Testing out my theory, I hold out my left arm, push up my sleeve to reveal smooth skin. "Vero had a scar," I say.

There, just for a second, a flash of recognition in his eyes.

"On her left forearm," I continue, eyes still on his face. "I don't have it."

He knows. He knows exactly what I'm talking about.

"But the fingerprints," he counters, "recovered from your car. The police identified you as Veronica Sellers. I saw it on the news."

"I'm not Vero. Marlene Bilek knows it and so do I."

He frowns, disappointed, frustrated, annoyed? I can't tell and it makes me angry.

"You did this." My conviction is growing, and with it, my sense of power. "You handed me those gloves. Did you tamper with them somehow, etch Vero's fingerprints into the tips? But you did it. You made me put them on. And then . . ."

Rain, mud. I'm cold; I'm hot. I'm crying, but I don't make a sound. I've consumed too much scotch. I've followed the woman, the magical queen from all the stories. And I've seen Vero, who was once dead but is now alive, and my world is imploding and I can't put the pieces together again.

Thomas, responding to my frantic call. Thomas, once more riding to the rescue.

"Do you trust me?" he asks me, standing in my open car door. "Do you trust me?"

He bends down, presses his lips against my cheek. Soft, featherlight. A promise already laced with regret.

Suddenly, in the midst of the rain and the mud and the smell of churned-up earth.

The smell of smoke. The heat of fire.

I sit, fastened into my Audi in the middle of an empty, rain-swept road. I stare at my husband, and I can almost see the flames dancing around him.

I remember.

In that moment, I remember everything.

And he knows I know.

My husband reaches across my lap. My husband puts my vehicle in neutral. My husband steps back, closes the door, shuts me in. And I realize, belatedly, what he's about to do next.

His lips moving in the rain.

"Do you trust me?" Thomas says again. He's standing right in front of me. So close I can feel the heat of his body, the bulky softness of his overcoat.

"You tried to kill me."

"I love you."

I shake my head. Order myself not to listen to his words, but focus on his actions. "Something happened back then. Worse than Vero OD'ing, worse than being buried alive. What can be worse than being buried alive, Thomas? What did you do?"

"I love you," he says again.

I realize then that I'm doomed, for I can already hear the undertone. *But it won't save you in the end.* Vero had tried to warn me. Maybe it wasn't my past I was trying to escape, but the man I married.

"I am not Veronica Sellers," I hear myself say. I need the words out. Thomas's fingerprint trick had briefly disoriented me, my own confused state and guilty conscience making me that much more vulnerable. But Vero is Vero, and I am me, and I owe it to both of us to get it right.

"I know."

"My name is Chelsea Robbins. My mother sold me to Madame Sade when I was ten. And I hated her for that and I loved her for that because the house was nicer, the food better, and at least Madame Sade pretended we were family. Then Vero came along and kicked me out of the tower bedroom and I hated her for that, but I loved her for that because she became the sister I never had

486

and spun our world into a fairy tale."

I look at him. "And I met you, the boy I watched in the distance, walking free about the property. And I hated you for that and I loved you for that, but mostly . . ." My voice breaks. "I loved you. From the very beginning, I've loved you and I've never forgiven myself for it."

Thomas smiles. I think it's the saddest expression I've ever seen on a man's face.

"It's time," he says simply. "She's waited long enough."

He holds out his hand. This time, I take it, following him across the parking lot. Because there is nothing else to do. There is nothing else to say.

Thomas had been right: I never should've returned to New Hampshire; I never should've hired an investigative agency; I never should've tried so hard to discover the memories I'd worked even harder to forget.

But what is done is done.

And now, twenty-two years later, for both of us, for all of us, there is no going back.

CHAPTER 34

"My car keys are gone," Tessa reported ten minutes later. She and Wyatt had snapped on the lights, giving the room a cursory glance, before tearing outside to the parking lot. With no sign of Nicky inside or out, they'd returned to the room and summarily ripped it apart. Senseless, really, given they were looking for a full-size female, which wasn't exactly something you could lose beneath a sofa cushion.

"She doesn't have wheels of her own," Wyatt commented.

"But where would she go? She doesn't have a house of her own either."

Wyatt nodded. He straightened, took in the wreck of the hotel room and finally exhaled in defeat. "All right. Time to regroup. We're reacting. This whole damn case, frankly, has been one reaction after another, and it's not getting us anywhere. From the top, what do we know?"

"Nicky Frank is missing," Tessa supplied sourly. She'd stripped the covers from both beds. Now she was on her hands and knees, peering under the first, then the second, as if locating a missing witness was no different from finding a lost pair of shoes.

"Nicky Frank who is *not* Veronica Sellers," Wyatt emphasized, "the girl who went missing thirty years ago."

"Meaning she's probably not running to Marlene Bilek's house," Tessa muttered, still crawling on the floor. "Her only contact in the area remains her husband, Thomas."

"Who most likely engineered her car accident and set things up for her to be falsely identified as Vero."

Tessa finally paused, sat back on her heels. "Could they be in this together? A joint ruse to pass Nicky off as a missing girl? Maybe as part of that, Thomas and Nicky set a predetermined rendezvous point for if things got too dicey, and that's where Nicky's headed now?"

Wyatt grimaced. "Except what is this ruse? What could Nicky possibly gain as Marlene's long-lost daughter that would justify the risk of a major auto accident, let alone Thomas burning down their home?"

Tessa had to think about it: "Revenge? Marlene failed her daughter, maybe was even part of Vero's abduction? Nicky wants payback, and what better way to get it than masquerading as the lost child?"

"I think Thomas is behind it."

"Okay." Tessa resumed her search, slipping a hand beneath the box spring and top mattress of the bed closest to the door.

Wyatt ticked off on his fingers. "Nicky's concussions are real. Her memory loss certainly appears real. Then there's the multiple accidents, house fire, et cetera. In all those scenarios, Nicky's a victim, not a perpetrator. Given all this started when she decided to move to New Hampshire and search for answers, I think her desire for the truth upset the apple cart. Meaning Thomas is the one with something to hide."

"Hang on." Tessa paused. "What do we have here?" Her fingers worked between the mattresses; then she slowly withdrew an oversize piece of paper, top edge ragged where it had been torn from the sketch pad. Tessa eased it carefully from where it'd been stashed, between the mattresses on Nicky's bed.

Wyatt immediately crossed the room to study the black-and-white pencil sketch. "That's Thomas Frank."

"Little young, don't you think?"

"She must've drawn this earlier, when you

had her working, because you're right; this isn't the Thomas Frank from present day. This is him, easily twenty years ago."

"The time of the dollhouse. My God, look at his face."

Wyatt understood her point. The Thomas he'd interviewed had been a stressed-out middle-aged male. Clearly tired, maybe a bit frayed from caring for his ailing wife, but not the kind of man you'd look at twice.

Whereas younger Thomas — teenage Thomas? He looked haggard. Haunted. Hard.

A kid who already had plenty to hide.

"Nicky never showed this to you?" Wyatt asked.

Tessa shook her head. "No. I left to take a call. Bet she stashed it then."

"She's sitting here. Candle's lit, the air smells like grass. She draws the house. She draws rooms in the house. She sketches Madame Sade, and then: this." Wyatt turned over the matter in his mind. "She didn't expect it. I bet that's why she hid it. Of all the details to start returning to her, that Thomas is part of the dollhouse, that she knew him before, better yet, *he* knew *her* from before, must've rattled her."

"He was part of it," Tessa whispered. "And judging by his expression, not a nice part of

491

it either. You think she contacted him somehow, set up a meeting time? But how? She doesn't even have a phone."

Wyatt shrugged. "If she really wants answers, Thomas is the next place to start."

"Except . . ." Tessa's voice trailed off. "I don't think this boy" — she tapped the sketch — "has anything good to tell her."

Wyatt nodded. He was worried about the same. If even half of what Nicky had said about the dollhouse was true, then there were plenty of secrets worth killing to protect.

"We need to get eyes on your car. Immediately."

"Shit! We're idiots. It's my vehicle, dammit. And I have OnStar!"

Tessa made the call. Once given the password, the operator of OnStar was more than happy to be of assistance. In fact, he pinpointed the location of her Lexus in less than thirty seconds as sitting in the hotel's parking lot.

"What the hell?"

She and Wyatt walked out together, discovering Tessa's black SUV, sitting beneath an energy-efficient lamppost.

"Why take my keys if she wasn't going to take my car?" Tessa exploded. She sounded genuinely insulted.

"Slow us down, keep us from following her?" Wyatt reasoned. "She already hid Thomas's sketch. Clearly, she wants some privacy."

Wyatt took his hands out of his pockets, walked the space. One A.M. Lot held four vehicles, which made for a quick inventory. Bushes, trees, shrubs, nothing.

"She didn't walk out of here," he stated. "We're too far away from civilization, let alone any major roads. So if she's not here, but your car is, then she found another mode of transportation."

"Maybe she didn't have to drive to meet Thomas. He met her here."

"She called him from the hotel room?" Wyatt tried on.

"Can't. I asked the hotel manager to block all incoming and outgoing calls. Containment issue. Plus, I have my cell. We didn't need anything else for making contact."

Wyatt was impressed. "You didn't trust her?"

"Hey, just because she's my client doesn't mean I'm stupid. Plenty of people ask for help, then maneuver around your back, which, of course, gets the savvy investigator in trouble. One form of contact means I always know what's going on. For example, she didn't call Thomas."

"Maybe he followed us from the sheriff's department to here," Wyatt theorized. "Or even tracked my vehicle while I was picking up Marlene Bilek. Easy enough to guess she'd want to meet with Nicky, given the story on the nightly news." Wyatt's voice trailed off. If Thomas had known Nicky was here, then the moment she walked out of the hotel into the darkened parking lot . . . They hadn't kept her safe at all, he realized. More like delivered her straight to the lion.

Wyatt glanced at his watch again. He needed to get on the radio, mobilize a fresh search. Except be on the lookout for what? They'd already been hunting for Thomas Frank for more than twenty-four hours. The man was a fucking ghost.

"We need cameras," Tessa muttered, as if reading his mind. "Search like this in Boston, we'd have toll records, traffic light cameras, business surveillance and/or ATM security on every block. One click of a video screen, and Thomas would be ours."

"Hang on. We might not be in a big city, but this hotel has a security system. Check it out." He pointed back at the hotel roofline, where at least one camera was clearly visible. He turned on his heels, already heading for the front office. "We might have some tricks up our sleeves just yet."

The nighttime hotel clerk identified herself as Brittany Kline. Blond, bubbly, and extremely excited to assist with an official police investigation. Yes, the hotel had an excellent security system, she informed them. Installed six months ago, great cameras, great imaging, tons of stored footage. She liked to peruse it herself on slow nights. You know, in order to augment her online classes in criminology. She led them toward a back office, where she immediately proved herself to be adept at retrieving video from the system. With Brittany's assistance, they sorted out which security camera had the best view of the parking lot; then backtracked through the various video feeds in one-minute intervals. It took only four tries to get it right.

"There!" Tessa exclaimed excitedly, pointing at the screen, as Brittany manned the digital controls. "That's Nicky, walking toward the parked cars."

"And there's person number two, pushing away from the tree," Wyatt provided.

They watched the figure approach. Clearly a male, but his back was to the overhead lights, casting his face in shadow. Still, neither one had any doubt.

"Thomas," Wyatt stated.

"She doesn't seem afraid of him," Tessa commented.

"And yet, no welcoming hug."

"Can you zoom in?" Tessa asked Brittany. The night clerk did her best, but the resolution remained grainy. After a bit more playing around, they decided the footage was best in broad view. Brittany resumed normal screen size, hit replay.

Wyatt watched the screen. Thomas's rapid approach upon spotting his wife, followed almost immediately by an obvious hesitation. Nicky's instinctive lean toward her husband yet also drawing up short. Love and fear, he thought. Twin companions in any relationship.

Even his and Tessa's.

Thomas held out his hand to his wife.

Nicky stood there. Doubt? Wyatt wondered. Hostility? Wariness? Did she still see her husband of twenty-two years, a man who'd pledged to take care of her? Or did she see the grim-eyed youth from the dollhouse, a boy clearly conditioned to do what had to be done, regardless of the cost?

Another moment passed. Two. Three.

Thomas stepped closer. Nicky tilted her face up. The lighting was wrong. Wyatt couldn't see her expression, and yet what she did next didn't totally surprise him.

She placed her fingers within her husband's grasp. She handed herself over to him.

Brittany sighed heavily, as if watching a romantic movie.

While Tessa exclaimed, "Oh my God, they're in this together!"

"Maybe," Wyatt murmured. But he wasn't thinking of joint criminal activity. Mostly he was thinking that love is like that.

Thomas led Nicky to the last vehicle in the row. Low-slung hatchback. Subaru, dark green. In a matter of seconds, he was backing it out of the parking space. Heading toward the exit.

Standing behind a seated Brittany, Wyatt and Tessa both leaned forward, willing the parking lot light to illuminate the back license plate, give them what they were looking for.

"Come on," Wyatt whispered, grabbing a notebook and pen from his pocket. "Come on . . ."

One digit. Two, three . . .

He was hastily scribbling them down, when Tessa suddenly grabbed his arm.

"Stop!" she ordered Brittany. "Freeze that frame. Look. On the right. Another car is pulling out. Wyatt, someone is following them."

CHAPTER 35

Thomas and I drive in silence. He has both hands on the wheel, his gaze ping-ponging from the front windshield to the rearview mirror. Checking for what, I'm not sure. But I can feel his tension.

Outside the car windows, the darkness rushes by. There are no streetlights out here. No road guards, traffic lights. We are in the mountains, carving our way up through vast wilderness. It should be raining, I think. Then it would be exactly as it was before.

"For the longest time," Thomas says at last, "I thought if we just stayed away, if you just had more time to heal. There were moments, you know, entire months, sometimes even a year, when you seemed to be better. I'd catch you smiling at a bird, a flower, a sunrise. Your face would brighten when I walked into a room. You'd even sleep at night."

I don't say anything.

"But then the wheels would come off. Abruptly. Without warning. I read book after book on the subject. Tried to identify the triggers. Some PTSD sufferers can't handle noise; for others it's a smell, a color, the feel of the walls closing in. For you . . . I couldn't figure it out. Ocean, desert, city, country. I tried it all. But no matter where we went, your nightmares found you again."

My husband turns to me. It's hard to see his expression in the dark, but I can feel the seriousness of his gaze. "I tried, Nicky. I tried everything. I believed for the longest time that I could be the one who saved you. But then . . ."

He pauses, returns his attention to the road.

"I fell down the stairs," I fill in.

"Vero," he states. He sounds bitter, though I understand, somewhere in the back of my head, that his feelings regarding her are as complex as mine. He found a way to move forward, however. I didn't, and therein lay the difference.

"Days on end," he says now, "you laid on the couch with that damn quilt and whispered under your breath. Long, involved conversations with Vero. Vero flies. Vero cries. Vero only wants to be free. If I interrupted, you flew into a rage. If I tried to comfort you, you slapped my face and screamed at me it was all my fault. You hated me. Vero hated me. Go away."

I can picture it, exactly as he says. My need, my all-consuming need, to commune with the past. Thomas, walking into the room. Thomas, daring to interrupt. The sharp feel against my palm as I connected with his face.

It's all your fault, I screamed at him. *I know what you did. She told me, you know. She tells me everything!*

Thomas, not even bothering to argue. Thomas, walking away.

"The day you fell down the basement stairs, when I returned from the workshop and couldn't find you . . . I ran around the house frantic. I thought you'd left me, Nicky. I thought, this was it. Given a choice between a future with me or a past with Vero . . . you'd left. The ghost girl had won."

I don't say anything.

"Then I finally discovered you sprawled on the basement floor . . . You wouldn't respond to your name. Any of them. Trust me, I ran through the whole list. All the places we'd been, the names we'd initially tried on. Finally, I called you Vero. And you opened your eyes. You stared right at me. And so help me God, I almost walked away right there and then. You, her . . . I just can't do this anymore."

I can't help myself. I shiver slightly because I know he's right. There's a thin line in my mind, and it's been that way for a long time. *"I am you,"* Vero tells me. But I wonder what she really means. As in, she's a piece of my subconscious, maybe even the voice of my guilty conscience? Or . . . something else entirely?

I would like to say I don't believe in ghosts, but I can't.

"I only ever wanted for you to be happy," Thomas says now, his hands gripping the wheel. "I fought a good fight for twenty-two years, thinking if we can just keep moving forward, once more time has passed. But I'm wrong, aren't I, Nicky? You can't go forward. You have to go back. Given a choice between Vero and me, Vero has won."

I don't speak. I can't tell my husband what he wants to hear, which makes it easier to say nothing at all.

Instead, I study the dark night rushing behind him. I smell smoke. I feel flames. But I don't reach out my hand to him.

We have both come too far for that.

I feel Vero then. She is standing in the back of my mind. Not speaking, not sipping tea, not even sitting in the dollhouse, but more like a lone figure, waiting in a black void. I can't see her face; more like I feel her mood.

Somber. Tired. Sad.

She is not coming to me, I realize, because for the first time in twenty-two years, I am coming to her.

She finally opens her mouth. She utters a single word: *"Run."*

But we both know it is much too late for that.

Thomas slows the car. For the first time, I see it. A dirt road has appeared on the right. Nearly overgrown, it would be difficult enough to spot during the day, and almost impossible at night. Except, of course, that Thomas already knows that's it there.

"Run!" Vero whispers again.

But there's no place to go. I'm trapped in this car now, just as surely as I was trapped in my Audi three nights ago.

As my husband takes the turn, headlights slashing across a tangle of shrubs, tiny car heaving up the first divot.

"All I ever wanted," Thomas repeats, "was for you to be happy."

As he forces the four-wheel-drive vehicle up the rutted road.

Returning to the dollhouse.

Thomas's childhood home.

CHAPTER 36

They struck out on the green Subaru. Kevin was able to trace the partial license plate to a vehicle that had been listed as stolen the day before. Being an older model, it didn't carry such modern-day amenities as GPS for tracking, and they had no hits on sightings of the vehicle.

Two A.M., Wyatt sat back in frustration, scrubbing his face with the palm of his hand. "We're still reacting. Thomas runs, we give chase. Nicky taunts us with half a puzzle, we batter our brains trying to deduce the missing pieces. Just once, I'd like to be ahead in this game."

"As in knowing where Nicky and Thomas went?" Tessa asked him.

"Oh, I know where they went. Can't find it on a map, of course, but I know where they went."

"The dollhouse."

"Who's in the second vehicle?" he barked

impatiently. They were still in the back hotel office, surrounded by the security video they'd watched again and again. Wyatt had sent Brittany out of the room, ostensibly because they no longer required her assistance, but mostly because it was never good to appear stuck in front of an adoring member of the public. "What the hell happened way back when, what the hell is going on now and who did we miss? Because if Nicky is with Thomas, and according to my deputy, Marlene Bilek was returned safely home three hours ago, who's left to follow our favorite two suspects in a separate vehicle?"

They'd tried zooming in on the security footage of the second car, but that vehicle had stuck to the dimly lit edges of the parking lot. They had a recording of a small, dark compact. Not even a blur of the driver's face, let alone something truly helpful, such as a glimpse of the license plate. "Madame Sade?" Tessa guessed now.

Wyatt nearly growled in frustration. He'd gone almost forty-eight hours without sleep. Combined with a sense of his own stupidity, the night was wearing on him.

He picked up Tessa's sketch of the woman, held it up. "We take this picture to the press, we gotta tell them why."

"Police have some questions for her regarding the disappearance of a child thirty years ago," Tessa provided immediately. "Don't call her a suspect, but imply she's a witness. People feel better about ratting out their neighbors when it won't get them in trouble."

"Excellent plan for the morning news cycle. Problem is, we need answers now, and press conferences don't work well at two A.M. Mostly because the target audience is asleep."

"Maybe you should take a nap," Tessa informed him.

He nearly growled again. "I want the dollhouse. Thomas, Nicky, our answers. All at the dollhouse."

"We have that sketch."

"Fed it to local Realtors this afternoon. No hits. Kevin ran specs through a New Hampshire property tax database, too many hits. Historic homes, even grand old Victorians, are lousy in these hills."

"What about Marlene's hubby?" Tessa asked now. "If Marlene's safe at home, what about him, because I bet he has opinions about a long-lost daughter appearing from the dead."

"Except Nicky's not Vero. No threat to him or the new family order."

Tessa frowned, plopped down in the office chair across from Wyatt.

"Nicky and Thomas are both connected to the dollhouse," Tessa stated. "We can't prove it, but that makes the most sense."

"Agreed."

"Meaning their relationship didn't start in New Orleans, but here. Meaning both of them most likely know things about a former brothel that plenty of people wouldn't want known."

"Agree times three," Wyatt assured her. "Unfortunately, it leads us back to the same conundrum. Dollhouse holds the key. Except we can't find the dollhouse."

"Track down Nicky-slash-Chelsea's real identity?" Tessa asked him.

"No hits off her fingerprints as of yet. Assuming Chelsea is a runaway or was sold to Madame Sade, it's possible her prints aren't in the system at all, meaning we may never get that answer."

"Thomas Frank's real identity?"

"No prints to run. The fire destroyed such evidence from his home. Latent prints attempted to work his car, hotel room, et cetera, but recovered nothing usable. Guy's either that lucky or that good. You can guess my vote." Wyatt expelled heavily, wrapped his knuckles against the top of the office desk. "Case is starting to piss me off."

"Not your fault," Tessa said mildly. "You started with a single-car accident. Who would've guessed it would lead to an old child abduction case and Victorian brothel?"

"November is the saddest month," he muttered. Then paused. Repeated the phrase out loud: "November is the saddest month. That's when Nicky escaped. Must've been. November. The saddest month. When she had to kill Vero in order to save herself."

"Okay . . ."

He looked up at Tessa, feeling the first traces of excitement. "That's a variable. We're not just looking twenty-two years ago. We're looking for something that happened in November twenty-two years ago."

"Would Madame Sade have filed a missing persons report?" Tessa asked. "I mean, if she was pretending they were family, or even needed to keep up pretenses with the neighbors after her teenage 'daughter' disappeared . . ."

"I doubt she'd want the police on her property, especially given another girl had just died." Wyatt paused, reconsidered the matter. "That's a good question, though. One night in November, two girls from the same home vanish. One dies; one ostensibly runs away."

"Maybe three kids disappeared," Tessa prodded. "What about Thomas? Assuming he was part of it, maybe he bolted with Nicky."

They regarded each other thoughtfully.

"Madame Sade would have to smooth it over somehow," Wyatt mused. "Explain the new world order to her neighbors, maybe even local authorities. Otherwise people would get suspicious."

"She could declare them runaways."

"Three kids. From the same house." Wyatt gave her a look. "Speaking as a former officer, wouldn't you definitely check that out?"

"Definitely."

"But no one did." He said it with more certainty now. "Because if she had filed a report, D.D. would've run across it as part of her search, right? She just explored all missing-kids cases from the past thirty years. No way three teenagers from New Hampshire wouldn't have made her radar screen. It's too odd a case not to call attention."

Tessa picked up his train of thought. "Madame Sade never said a word. Maybe the situation spooked her. I mean, first she thinks Vero is dead and buried in the woods. Except, of course, eventually she must've figured out it wasn't Vero's body that was

508

carried out, but the roommate's instead. Now she has at least one missing girl, not to mention one dead girl. Maybe that was too much. She bolted herself. Makes some sense."

Wyatt agreed. Given the intensity of that night, the fear and uncertainty for all concerned, it made sense the madam might have panicked and shut down operations. It came to him, the new variable to search: "What about the house? Girls are gone, owner has bolted, what happens to the house?"

"Depends on if the owner continues to pay mortgage, property taxes, that sort of thing."

Wyatt raised a brow. "If you were running from past sins, would you continue to mail in your property taxes?" He sat up straight, tapped the desk top. "That's our search requirement. Tax lien. On a historic Victorian, going back to November, twenty-two years ago. Why not?"

"I'm on it."

"You're on it?"

"Sure." Tessa was already digging out her computer. "What do you think us private investigators do? Death and taxes. Only two things no one can avoid, making them the best source of records."

Her fingers started humming across the keyboard. Wyatt watched her work without asking any more questions. His job was biased toward search warrants. He didn't want to know about hers.

"Most towns give you at least a year before they get too antsy," Tessa informed him now. "Costs money to file a lien, so they opt for mailing out overdue notices for a bit. Not having an exact town makes it harder, of course, which is why search engines are worth their weight in gold . . ." She tapped more, frowned, tapped more. "I got homes, all right. Old homes, rich homes, valuable homes. But I'm not seeing any Victorians. Okay, let's try twenty years ago. Nineteen. Eighteen."

Fingers still tapping, face still frowning. "Shit." Tessa paused, glanced up. "I'm not seeing anything. And yet . . . we have to be on to something. November, twenty-two years ago, Vero dies, Nicky disappears, maybe even a young man named Thomas takes off. It had to have affected operations at the dollhouse. It had to have sparked some sort of reaction by Madame Sade."

Wyatt shrugged. "Search that. November, twenty-two years ago, historic Victorian. What the hell. Someone had to be called out for something, maybe even a report of a runaway?"

Tessa, typing away again. "Holy . . . No way. You've got to be kidding me!"

"What?" Wyatt was up, out of his chair, leaning over her shoulder in the cramped space. She gestured to her screen and he got it. Headline article. Not of a missing teen or a dead girl.

But a fire.

A hundred-year-old Victorian, one of the last grand summer cottages in the area, burning to the ground. November. Twenty-two years ago. With an unidentified body pulled from the smoldering ruins.

"The dollhouse," Tessa murmured. "Gotta be."

"You know what this means, don't you?"

"We're heading forty miles north."

Wyatt already had his keys in his hand. "Absolutely, but that's not what I meant. Thomas. A husband who burned down his own home two nights ago. A man clearly experienced with gas cans."

She got it. "He was definitely at the doll-house all those years ago. He's the one who burned it to the ground." Tessa hesitated. "And now he's taking Nicky back there? But if it's gone, totally demolished, what's left for them?"

"I don't know. But I have a feeling for

Nicky's own sake, she'd better start remembering."

CHAPTER 37

By the time the car crests the washed-out drive, my stomach is heaving and my head is on fire. Motion sickness, I try to tell myself. But of course it's more than that. It's dread and nerves and sadness and fear. It's every dark emotion rolled into one, and my hands are shaking so badly, I can't open the car door. I fumble with the latch again and again.

I swear I smell smoke, though I know that's impossible. And I'm terrified that the moment I step out of the car, it will start to rain. I don't think I could handle that. I don't think I can handle this.

Thomas climbs out of the driver's side. He fiddles for a minute with the rear passenger door, extracting something from the backseat. When I don't immediately exit the vehicle, he comes around to assist me. I have to hold his arm to stand. I don't look up, can't bring myself to see his face.

Instead, I keep my gaze on the sleeve of my husband's coat; I am shaking uncontrollably.

I can feel them already. The shadows in the back of my mind. Slippery shapes and chilling whispers that scare me even more than Vero. I would have her back, grinning skull and all.

But she is quiet now. She gave me her best advice and I ignored it.

Or maybe, faced with this place once again, she is also too terrified to talk.

For just one moment, I wish love really did heal all wounds. I wish Thomas's genuine care and nurturing had been enough to heal me. Somehow, he'd found the ability to move forward.

But I never have. He's right; I was losing my mind even before I suffered three blows to the head.

Thomas takes the first step, my hand tucked beneath his arm. Slowly, I force myself to follow. I realize for the first time that he's holding something in his left hand. A shovel, which he'd pulled from the backseat. Thomas is carrying a shovel.

I don't speak. I march with this man who is my husband. It occurs to me we never had a formal wedding, never walked side by side down church steps, officially pronounced man and wife.

But now we have this.

A man. His wife. And our shared secret.

These grounds had been beautiful once. In the back of my mind, I know this. I could see the rolling green lawn from the house, especially from the tower bedroom, which had offered a two-hundred-and-seventy-degree view. I'd spent hours alone, gazing at the vast grounds in back, not to mention a sweeping circular drive in the front, punctuated by a gurgling fountain. Rose-bushes in the summer, mounds of rust-colored autumn sedum in the fall. The carriage house had stood to the left, already converted by that time to a three-bay garage. Another outbuilding had been slightly behind it. Caretaker's cottage, or maybe a playhouse for the privileged kids of the family who'd first built the home a hundred years ago.

I used to picture a boy and girl, bouncing blond curls, a stiff blue playsuit for him, a flouncy pink dress for her, as they chased an old-fashioned leather ball across the lawn. There was a pond in the back as well, a swimming hole for those hot summer days.

I never walked to it. Never stuck a toe in the stagnant water. I simply watched the rippling green surface from the third-story window, trying to imagine the family who had once built this summer home. Wondering what they'd think if they'd lived to see what it had become.

Thomas has a flashlight. He lets go of my arm to illuminate the circular drive, but it's gone, nothing but more weeds and brambles. He searches for the center fountain next, but it's either collapsed or lost under more vegetative growth.

The wilderness likes to take back its own. In this case, it really should.

"What do you remember?" Thomas asks me quietly. We push forward, following the narrow path that's all that's left of the drive.

"When I first got out of the car . . ."

It's April, the sun is setting, I'm already feeling the chill. I'm hungry, I'm tired, I'm scared. But I don't let these things show. Game face, fighting to be brave. Until I step out of the vehicle. Look up and see . . .

"It was beautiful," I whisper. "Like something out of a fairy tale. Especially for a city girl like me. I only knew cramped apartments, tenement housing. Then to come here, see this."

"It was already falling into disrepair," Thomas says. His voice is apologetic. He hefts the shovel in his left hand. "After my father's death, there wasn't enough money

516

for upkeep. Even after my mother's . . . business idea . . . the house was never the same. I used to wonder. Maybe homes have souls. It's not enough to paint and repair. You have to refresh them. Love, laughter, life. I don't know. But after my father died, what my mom did to this house, in this house . . . I don't think it was ever the same."

We move deeper through the vegetation.

Once, there was a beautiful wraparound front porch. White-painted rails, gingerbread trim. If I close my eyes, I can still see it in my mind. But when I open them again, follow the beam of Thomas's flashlight, I'm startled to see nothing is as large as I remember. The porch is gone, of course. The house as well. All that remains is the foundation, a pile of enormous granite blocks such as the type favored back in the day . . .

Thomas was skilled only with fire. To destroy this foundation would've taken dynamite.

"When my mother first brought you home," he says now, "she claimed you were a new foster child. That was her big scheme after my father's death. We had a large house, so many empty rooms. She'd decided to take in foster kids. For the money, of course. She was never one to pretend to care."

"A car came to our building," I tell him now. "My mom told me to get in. Do whatever the woman said. It wasn't the first time."

"I'm sorry."

"I didn't expect to be taken away. Yet, when I first saw this place . . . It was so much nicer than anyplace I'd ever been. Better food, too."

"In the beginning, I believed her," Thomas said. "It made sense. State pays for foster kids and I knew we needed cash. It was all my mother talked about. My good-for-nothing father who'd promised her this and promised her that but had proved to be nothing but a loser who'd then gone and dropped dead . . ."

Thomas looks at me; his face is hard to read in the dark, but when he speaks next, his tone is flat, frank. "I hated her. Surely you must know that. She did this, all of this, purely out of greed. Because she was owed a life of luxury. When my father failed her, well, this was the next logical step. She took in 'foster kids,' all of whom were young, pretty girls. Then she started throwing lavish parties. Getting to know the neighbors, she told me. I was so young myself, it took me years to realize the party guests were only older, wealthy men. And none of them went home after dinner."

We are close enough now to climb onto the first enormous granite block. I don't want to peer down into the pit of what used to be the home's cellar, but I can't help myself. I swear I can smell smoke again, but any charred remains of wood are long gone. I see only thick green vegetation, vines and weeds that have overgrown the bones of this once grand house.

Heat, I think. If I close my eyes, I will feel it again on my cheeks.

I will hear her screams.

I backpedal sharply, slipping off the granite slab. Thomas reaches for me, but is too late. I go down hard, banging my shin against the hard rectangular slab. Blood. Pain.

Smoke. Fire.

Screams.

I can't help myself. I reach up my hand. I beg, I implore.

"Save her. For the love of God. Please!"

Thomas doesn't move. His face is set in a grim line as he stands there, flashlight in one hand, shovel in the other. He knows. What I'm asking. What I'm finally remembering.

But whereas I am crying, his eyes remain dry.

"I'm sorry," he says, but I'm not sure what he means. For what happened then, or for what must happen now.

"The first two girls who arrived," he tells me, stepping off the granite slab, "were older. Fifteen, sixteen. I was maybe five? I didn't think much of it. Mother said they had no families. We would host them. So we did.

"Looking back now, I think it started with them. Maybe they already were prostitutes. Or simply girls who came from . . . situations." He glances at me. "My father might not have been the breadwinner my mother desired, but he still came from a long line of people who knew people. My mother mined those connections. Small, intimate dinners at first, inviting the neighbors, family acquaintances. Mother kept things simple. Cocktail hours, small cookouts to show off the house, introduce her new 'daughters.'

"Maybe she was trying to reposition herself, us, in the community, but I think from the very beginning she had a plan. She knew what older, bored, wealthy men really wanted. So she started with a couples event, then later, the husbands might 'drop by,' to see if my mother needed any help, maybe stay for a few hours. I didn't understand the full implications, but I still noted the new patterns. More and more male visitors. Two 'foster daughters' who spent most of their time giving male guests tours of the house, including long stays in their bedrooms. I don't even remember their names anymore, but those first two girls, that's when it all started."

I have pictures in my head. A middle-aged woman in elegant linen trousers escorting me out of her car. Leading me through a tired but obviously once grand home. Taking me up a long flight of stairs in the south-facing turret.

This will be your room. The tower bedroom. *You can make yourself comfortable. I'll bring you clothes.*

She closed the door. Was it locked? I'm not even sure anymore. Maybe, in the beginning. But it hardly mattered. Living out here, stuck in a mansion perched on a mountainside, thirty, forty miles from civilization. Where would I have gone? Where could any of us have run?

Madame Sade had not relied on armed guards or overt controls. She had a cold smile and indomitable will that served her just as well.

I look up now. I can't see it, but I feel like I should know where it is, the three-story, wood-shingled turret, rising against the night sky.

"I loved that room," I whisper.

"I spotted you in the window," Thomas says. "You were ten years old, the first young girl she brought —"

"Bought," I say bitterly.

He doesn't correct me. "Close to my age. I'd been out in the yard, mowing, because everyone, even me, had to earn their keep. I looked up. Saw your face pressed against the glass. Your expression was so serious. Then you held up your hand, as if reaching out to me . . .

"And I . . . I don't know how to explain it. I was only twelve myself, but I took one look at you and I was struck. I wanted to talk to you, become your friend. I wanted to *know* you, even though it wasn't allowed. The rules had already been established. Foster kids were separate. Mother managed you. Guests visited you. I, on the other hand, was never to mingle."

"You waved at me." For a moment, I'm ten again. Lonely and overwhelmed by this fancy house and well-dressed woman who already terrifies me. I'm in the prettiest bedroom I've ever seen, in an honest-togoodness princess tower, but I already know nothing in life is free. This room will cost me. This house will cost me.

Then I look down. I see the boy. A flash of smile. A quick wave. He quickly tucks his hand behind his back, glancing around self-consciously. But I don't put my hand down. I keep it pressed against the window. I imagine, just for one moment, that I'm standing on the lawn with him. He's still smiling at me and I'm not so scared or lonely anymore.

Thomas was right: We hadn't been allowed to mingle or interact. But in his own way, he had become my lifeline, a point of interest in an otherwise monotonous existence of sitting in a gilded cage, waiting for nightfall. Madame Sade called the shots: First she isolated us in this mansion; then she extolled her own virtues. *Look at this fancy house where I brought you to live; look at this new dress I found just for you. Aren't you so lucky to have me to take care of you, so fortunate to have this opportunity to get ahead in life.*

She'd flash that cold smile, the one that never reached her eyes, and the smart girl did as she was told. The smart girl didn't dream of life beyond these walls.

Or Madame Sade would take away your

food, shred your clothes, slash one of your new toys, maybe the one she'd just given you the day before. She'd twist your arm behind your back, so hard you could barely breathe, and she'd remind you of everything she'd bought and paid for. Oh yes, including you. So you'd better wise up, shut up and entertain that man over there, because it wasn't like anyone would miss you if you didn't show up one morning for breakfast. Lots of things disappeared in these deep, dark woods. Including ungrateful little girls.

I wised up. I shut up. I entertained that man over there.

But I also watched the boy out mowing the lawns. I studied him from beneath my lashes as he strode across the grounds. I caught his eye from time to time, as we passed in the hall.

Vero had the magical queen and the lost princess from the secret realm.

I had entire fictional conversations with a young boy I'd never officially met. Until, of course, I lost my place in the tower bedroom.

Now I look back at the sky, to the blank space on the horizon where there had once been the three-story turret. She's close, I think. Very close. No longer just a presence in my mind, but here in these overgrown ruins.

"Vero took my room," I hear myself say. "She arrived, and I was booted downstairs."

Thomas doesn't say anything.

"I hated her for that. I didn't have to. I could've felt bad for her. She was so young, just this poor little girl torn from her family. I could hear crying night after night, you know. But I didn't feel any pity. I hated her instead."

"Divide and conquer," Thomas provides gently. "My mother was no dummy."

I can't look up anymore. I smell smoke, and what's going to happen next . . . The real reason Thomas brought me here.

"I just wanted my room back," I murmur now. An apology? To him, to her, I don't know. "I wanted to pretend to be a princess. Because of course, I knew by then, I was nothing but a whore."

Thomas steps in front of me.

"It's not your fault. Don't you understand? That's why you need to remember, Nicky. Because in forgetting what happened, you're also forgetting the reason you're not to blame."

"No." I shake my head, then force myself to look at him, take a steadying breath. "You don't understand. Vero is my fault. I'm the one who killed her. From the first moment I started hiding the drugs, I knew she'd find them. I knew she'd take them. Worse, I loved her. By then she had become the little sister I'd never had, the closest thing to a best friend. She was family. My only family. And I killed her. Consciously, deliberately. I let her die, so I could live."

Thomas studies me. He stares and he stares. Then he says the most curious thing. He says: "And then what, Nicky? Vero took the drugs. But what happened next?"

CHAPTER 38

"No cell reception," Tessa reported, holding her phone closer to the passenger window, as if that might help. "Damn mountains."

"Do you know where we are?" Wyatt asked her. Because it felt to him like they'd already been driving forever, and Tessa had a point. So far, all he saw was dark, endless mountains.

"No, only where we've been."

"Gotta be getting close."

"Can I just say one thing? This road alone proves one of our theories. We've been driving forever without even a bear for company. If this is truly the location of the infamous dollhouse . . . no way Nicky Frank magically crawled off the grounds and hitched a ride to New Orleans all by her lonesome. She had to have help."

"Thomas isn't just her husband; he was her getaway," Wyatt agreed.

"Interesting basis for a marriage."

"And yet they've lasted twenty-two years."

"Until the past six months," Tessa grumbled. "When Nicky decided she wanted the truth about her past and immediately became expendable."

Wyatt didn't comment right away. He'd been the first to doubt Thomas. Any man whose wife had mysteriously suffered three accidents. Let alone that Nicky herself had placed him at the scene of the car accident. And yet, the video. Something about the video. The way Nicky still walked right up to him, placed her hand in his own.

Fear and love.

Wyatt was making an investigator's worst mistake and he knew it: He was contemplating two suspects, Nicky and Thomas Frank, and seeing himself and Tessa.

"Come on," Tessa prodded him now. "You're telling me you're suddenly a fan of Thomas Frank? At the very least, he met his distraught wife Wednesday night, handed her a pair of fake fingerprint gloves, then seat-belted her into her vehicle before pushing it down a ravine. Hardly the actions of an innocent man."

"Fan would be a big statement. Just gotta say, for the record, the vehicle in question was a new Audi Q5 with airbag this and safety feature that. Hardly a death trap.

Plus, he put on her seat belt."

"Better to cover his tracks, make it look like an accident."

"Nicky was already drunk. She'd done that on her own. An investigating officer wouldn't have questioned the lack of seat belt."

"He's not an investigating officer."

"True. It's just that . . ."

She stared at him. "Spit it out."

"I don't know. The cop in me agrees with you. Clearly here's a man with plenty to hide. And yet, two decades of marriage later . . . You said it yourself. Just because he saved her that night didn't mean he had to marry her. And even if his job was to somehow keep tabs on her, watch her for Madame Sade. Twenty-two years later, how do you fake that kind of relationship? I don't know. I watched that video tonight, and . . . There's something there, some kind of dynamic we don't understand yet."

"You're a romantic," Tessa informed him.

"I prefer the term *open-minded.*"

"The picture she drew of him. Thomas was at the dollhouse. The expression she sketched on his face. Thomas was not a happy kid. Meaning he was definitely part of what was going on back then. Nicky starts to remember *everything,* those memories put him at risk."

"He would've been young himself. Possibly a victim as well."

"The look in his eyes was hard."

"I thought he looked determined."

"Wyatt!"

"Tessa!

"You know I love you, right?" he said abruptly.

In the passenger's seat, Tessa stilled. He could tell his words had caught her off guard, and yet they hadn't. Love and fear, he thought again. Except not Nicky and Thomas's, but their own.

"I'm not good at this," Tessa murmured.

"Tessa, what's wrong?"

"Can't we just . . . solve this case? You like arresting people; I like arresting people. We'll be fine."

"Is it Sophie?" he asked steadily. "Because I can be patient, Tessa. I know she hasn't fully accepted me yet. That's okay. I'm in this for the long haul."

She didn't answer.

Sharp turn in the road. Forcing himself to focus.

"John Stephen Purcell," she stated abruptly. "Police just located the gun used to kill him. I'm told they recovered a single latent print."

Wyatt couldn't help himself; he exhaled sharply. "That's it? A gun? A recently recovered gun? That's why you're so distant?"

"You don't understand. John Stephen Purcell, the man who *shot* Brian, my husband . . ." Her words were weighted with meaning.

"No, no, no," he interjected hastily, hands flexing on the wheel. "I understand plenty. And we're not married, so this doesn't fall under privilege, and there's definitely no need to say more. God, Tessa. I thought you were breaking up with me."

Her turn to frown. "It doesn't bother you? I'm not just talking about what the police might discover; I'm talking about what I once did."

He didn't even have to think about it. "No. You saved Sophie. Tessa, I know who you are. It's why I love you so much."

She fell silent again. Not ominous this time. More pondering.

He reached over and took her hand. Heard her own heavy exhale.

"Tessa," he said, keeping his voice light, "you're not getting rid of me that easily."

"What if I don't have a choice? One fingerprint; that's all it will take."

"We'll figure it out. Two smart people with

lots of law enforcement and legal connections. You really think we can't figure this out?"

"I can't lose Sophie."

"I know."

"One thousand ninety-six days. I told myself it should be enough. It isn't."

"I know."

"Plus, you know, the puppy. I haven't even met the puppy, and I can't leave the puppy. Our family is changing; that's what Sophie said. Our family, my family. I can't give it up, Wyatt. I can't lose all of you."

"Then we'll figure it out. Together. Because that's what families do. That's what *we* do."

And suddenly, he got it. How far a man might go for the woman he loved. Or what Thomas Frank had been doing that night, at the scene of his wife's accident, bearing a glove with fake fingerprints.

A desperate husband, taking one last desperate chance . . .

"Stop!" Tessa shouted. She twisted away, pointing at a spot along the darkened road just as their headlights swept by. "That's our turn. The road to the dollhouse. Wyatt, we're here!"

CHAPTER 39

I can't stand still anymore. Thomas has the light, but I don't want to see. I walk away from him. My head hurts. My heart hurts. I put my hands over my ears as if that will help, but it's no use. I can still hear the screams.

She's here. I feel her. In the wind, in the vines, in the hardness of the granite foundation. And it makes me shiver. Because I could handle the Vero in my head. The girl who came to visit. The skeleton who stayed for tea. But this Vero . . .

This Vero can hurt me.

"The first five years," Thomas says from his perch on the granite blocks, "Mother kept things simple. We fostered a couple of girls at a time. Always teenagers; they'd stay a year or two, then leave. Aged out, right? But eventually, Mother became greedier. By then, she'd made some other . . . connections, in the industry. Now no more fostering. She simply brought in young working girls. Got them directly from their pimps. Or, as in your case, purchased them from their own families. No witnesses, no fuss. Everyone's equally guilty, right?

"I think she also started taking requests. Maybe from several of the clients, or just the wealthiest. I'm not sure. But the girls became younger. For example, she brought you in at ten. But that also made things trickier. Younger girls might seem easier to control, but some of the new charges . . . Their backgrounds were more hard-core. They grew up lying, stealing, hitting, punching. I remember my mom slapping one of the new girls. I'd just walked into the room; I was maybe thirteen, fourteen. I stopped in my tracks, shocked. But then the girl, half the size of my mom . . . she slugged my mother back.

"So my mother upped the ante. She drugged them. Claimed they were addicts anyway. She was simply doing them the favor of avoiding the horrors of detox."

Thomas paused, smiled faintly. "Funny the way you can know things aren't right, but still not allow yourself to think of them as being wrong. For example, if I acknowledged my mother was criminal to supply drugs to addicts, then I'd have to also know she was sinful to have a ten-year-old girl shut up in the tower bedroom. Or worse, little Vero, only six years old when she walked through our door.

"I couldn't . . . She was my mom. And I was just a kid. Like the rest of you, I had no place else to go."

Thomas leaves his granite block. He moves to standing in front of me, trying to get me to look at him. But I can't. Too many things are exploding in my head, and the memories are both simpler and more horrible than I want them to be.

The new girls were mean and awful and cruel. Before, we had each kept to ourselves. Now I had to watch my back. It wasn't enough to hate the men. I had to hide my hairbrush, hoard my dresses, watch my stash of sweets.

The girls were older and wiser. Especially compared to Vero and me. Madame Sade ended up pairing us up in a single room.

Otherwise you'll be eaten alive, she'd informed us coldly. *Seriously. Wise up.*

I hated Vero. Whatever mean things the other girls did to me, I turned around and did to her. The trickle-down theory of pain. And maybe that did make us a family. A large dysfunctional family where each member competed to dish out the most hurt.

Vero started telling stories. Whispering them under her breath. Secret realms. Magical queen. Kidnapped princess.

At first, I think she was simply comforting herself. But eventually . . .

I made her keep talking. *Tell me more about this mother who loved her daughter. Tell me more about this daughter who knows one day she'll make it home again.*

We slowly but surely became allies, as the dollhouse darkened and twisted around us.

"I couldn't pretend things were normal anymore," Thomas says now, as if reading my mind. "At a certain point, even I understood most foster families didn't have kids locked in towers, and normal deliverymen didn't look so shady, nor lick their lips every time a girl walked into view.

"I confronted my mother. At least, I tried. I said we shouldn't be a foster family anymore. I was worried about the girls. Couldn't we just . . . go back to the way things used to be.

" 'What?' My mother laughed at me. 'You mean poor?'

" 'If you want to help the girls,' she told me, 'then the least you could do is assist with their medicine.' Which is how at the age of fourteen, I started driving our car into town, meeting with 'business associates,' then returning to the home with drugs. I wasn't even legal to drive. Meaning that of course I was extra careful every inch of the way, terrified that I'd be pulled over by some cop. My mother had no patience for fools, not even her own son."

I look up at him. "You became a dope dealer. You made all the purchases. You kept us drugged out of our skulls!"

Thomas doesn't deny it. "Where would I have gone, Nicky? What would I have done if my mother turned me out? Her gift was equal culpability. She turned us all into her partners in crime. Then none of us could escape, because all of us were too terrified of the consequences."

I want to argue with him. I want to yell and scream because it would be easier to blame him. Maybe once, I even did. But now I have an image in my head. A teenage boy with a mop of brown hair, all arms and legs, striding down the front steps of the house, moving with purpose. At the last moment, turning, looking back. The expression on his face. Frustration and longing and rage. Before turning once more toward the vehicle.

He was a prisoner, too. I remember thinking it then. The irony that he was her son, her actual son, and he was just as much a victim as the rest of us.

Vero once said she felt the sorriest for him. The rest of us didn't belong here. But Thomas had been right: Where else could he go? Madame Sade was his family. This was his home. How do you escape that?

Vero and I lasted longer than most. But eventually, years and years of hopelessness took their toll. Vero talked about the magical queen less and less. I no longer imagined long, quiet conversations with the boy I'd once watched mow the lawn. We succumbed. Depression. Fear. Anxiety.

Then, when we refused to turn out at night, do as we were told — because what did it matter? — Madame Sade shot us up. First me. Then Vero.

I should've protested. I should've run, fought, anything. I would've liked to have been the girl who at least hit back.

But I didn't. I stood there. I held out my arm. And when the meth first hit my vein . . . the rush. Suddenly I was alive for the first time in years.

While Madame stood there smiling with the syringe.

She didn't just victimize us. She taught us to victimize ourselves. Go along to get along. So we did, so we did, so we did.

Until the day I started hoarding my drugs instead.

"I figured out what you were doing," Thomas says now, with his uncanny ability to read my mind. "It took me a few days to notice it; that your eyes weren't as glazed over, your expression was more alert, your responses quicker. I kept handing over your supply, and you kept accepting, but clearly . . . I didn't say a word. If you wanted off, I wasn't going to rat you out. I admired you, Nicky. You were up to something. And I thought it was about time someone had a plan."

"I'd had enough," I say simply. "And I don't mean of being an addict. I mean of living. My first plan wasn't to sober up and escape. Once, I'd thought about it. But even sober, walking out the front door . . . I had no hope in the woods; they're too thick, the terrain too steep. That left the driveway, but she'd simply send you to fetch me."

Thomas doesn't argue. That's what would've happened, and we both know it.

"My first thought wasn't escape; I was going to OD. Which meant, of course, I needed to build up a certain quantity. Then I'd take it all at once. Vero watched me. She knew what I was doing. Then one day . . .

"She's the one who told me what to do. And you want to hear something funny?" I smile at Thomas, and even now, all these years later, my eyes well with tears. "My first thought was that she just wanted my stash. She was looking out for herself, manipulating me. Of course, I wouldn't hear of it. She'd OD on *my* drugs? Then I'd simply take her place in the body bag. No way!

"But Vero . . . she always had a way with words. An ability to tell a story. 'Vero wants to fly,' " I murmur. "All those years later. Vero wanted to fly; she knew she was never going home again.

"She hurt, you know. We all hurt. But she really was dying on the inside. She kept at me. Telling me what needed to happen. There is only one way out of the dollhouse." I look at Thomas. "We'd been there for so long," I say softly. "The other girls, they passed through. But Vero and me, did you think your mother would, could, ever let us go?"

Thomas doesn't say a word.

The wind is blowing. Or maybe it's Vero's breath, whispering across my cheek. She's here. I know she is. Because Vero got it only half right. She died; but she still didn't escape the dollhouse.

"I weaned myself off the drugs. I hoarded the stash. Then, after a particularly bad night . . . Vero took it. I watched her walk over to my mattress, dig into the box spring. I watched her take it all out. I watched her shoot it all up.

"Protest. Intervene. Take it away. Throw it out. So many things I could've done. But I didn't. 'Vero wants to fly.' And so I watched her take flight."

"None of the girls had OD'd before," Thomas says softly. "Mother didn't know what to do. She sent me in to check Vero again and again. I remember you sitting curled up in the corner. You'd been crying."

Young Thomas, the mop-haired boy, bending over Vero's body, checking her pulse. Young Thomas glancing over at me. Our eyes meeting. And for just one moment, I'm sure he knows what I did. But he never says a word.

He leaves the room. When he returns, a decision has clearly been made. He positions her body carefully on the old blue rug. He rolls it up, slowly, even gently. I have to look away because it hurts too much to stare.

"I'll take her out later," he tells me. "After dark. Will you be okay until then?"

I don't speak, only nod. When I glance up, he's staring right at me. He knows what I did,

I think again. The question is, does he know what I'll do next?

I wait most of the afternoon. Maybe something will change. Thomas will return early. Madame Sade will demand to see Vero's body. There are only two other girls in the house; they are both eighteen, older than Vero and me. Maybe they will want to visit. But nothing happens.

All day long, the house is quiet. Just the sound of the rain against the glass.

November, the saddest month of the year.

When the sky starts to darken, I finally move off the floor. I unroll Vero's body, not as slow, not as gentle. My heart is beating too fast. Her limbs flop and my limbs shake. I don't think either of us can take it. Finally I have her out of the rug, onto the bed. Swapping out our clothes, pulling up the bedcovers.

Putting Vero to sleep in my bed. And placing myself inside death's shroud.

It smells of her. Of vanilla lotion and almond soap. Of the smile she used to flash before the days grew too short and the nights too long. Of the stories she used to tell, when she still hoped to see her mother again.

I'd hated her. But then I'd loved her. She became the only family I ever had. The younger sister who was prettier and wiser and funnier, but I forgave her everything because she loved me more than I deserved and we both knew it.

I wonder if she's already escaped. Up to some bright light in the sky. Or maybe back into her mother's loving arms.

Then I cry, but I keep it silent because that's how you learn to cry in a dollhouse; without ever making a sound.

Eventually, footsteps down the hall. The door opening. A long pause.

Thomas, I remember now. Returning to fetch the corpse, to do his mother's bidding.

I feel myself tense. Force myself to relax. I can't be afraid, I remind myself. I am already dead.

The sound of footsteps slowly approaching. I can hear his breathing as he leans down.

Don't unwrap. Don't check. And if he does?

I think of the way his eyes met mine just hours before. I think of the way I've seen him stare at this house. And I'm not frightened anymore.

As Thomas lifts me up into his arms. As Thomas carries me out of the room, down the stairs, into the hall.

"Wait!" Madame Sade's imperious voice.

"What, Mother?"

"Surely she's not still dressed. Clothes are not cheap, you know. Isn't that a sock I see?"

"You don't need these clothes."

"Don't be ridiculous. Set her down. Losing a girl is bad enough. We might as well keep the clothes."

"No."

"What?"

"I'm not setting her down. I'm not stripping off some dead girl's clothes. You told me to take care of her. That's what I'm doing. Now, get out of my way or you can dig the grave yourself."

A long pause. I try not to breathe, not to hear the thunder of my own heart. Because I can feel the tremors in Thomas's arms. I understand what this conversation is costing him. What it might yet cost me.

Then . . .

Thomas advances forward. Out the front door, down the steps, into the rain, though I don't feel it right away. I am protected by the rug, lost in a dark world of muffled sound.

He walks forever. At least it feels that way. Wet leaves, tree limbs, smack against my foot, and I realize he has carried me into the woods. Of course, where else to dig the grave?

It comes to me slowly, and with growing horror. If he's carrying me with both arms, then by definition, he can't be carrying a shovel. Meaning he's already been out in the woods. He's already dug the trench.

Now he'll drop me straight into it. No more time for me to prepare. No more somedays, maybes, eventually. This is it.

Sure enough.

He stops. His breathing hard and heavy. Then.

I fall down. Down, down, down, into the deep, dark earth.

Do I scream? I can't scream. I'm already dead, I'm already dead, I'm already dead.

But I am screaming. Deep inside my mind, I'm screaming Vero, Vero, Vero. I'm so sorry, Vero.

The first heavy thump of wet earth. Followed by another, then another.

I close my eyes, even though I can't see. I fist my hands, even though I can't move. I am dead, I am dead, I am dead. I am Vero, tucked in the back of the closet, willing myself not be afraid of the dark.

Shovelful after shovelful of earth.

How long does it take to bury a body? I don't know. I'm too lost in the blackness of my mind. Vero. Vero. Vero.

But the sound stops. The weight of earth settles, remains the same.

Then . . .

I panic. I can't take it one second more. I wiggle and twist and thrash to and fro. And I scream. Out loud. Full throttle. Long and frantic and high-pitched and wailing.

I was dead, but now I am alive. And my lungs are bursting, crying out frantically for air.

Suddenly, the night sky is above me. I don't know how I've done it, but I'm free. I can feel the rain on my cheeks. I can taste the mud on my lips. I open my mouth and inhale greedily.

Just in time to hear the gasp. As Thomas stumbles back, his hands still clutching the edge of the death-shroud rug.

"You!" he exclaims. "Oh my God! You. I knew it!"

Thomas does not run away.

Instead, he listens to my story. Then he threads his fingers into my own.

And he says, "This is what we're going to do next."

"Ouch . . . yikes, dammit! Is this road over yet?"

Wyatt's SUV hit another rut; Tessa's body bounced up, her head banging off the window.

"I don't think this is a road," he said. "More like a washed-out drive."

"Which clearly hasn't been used in years."

"Not true. Look at that." They jounced by another low-hanging tree, its limbs screeching across the vehicle's roof overhead.

"Freshly broken branch."

"Nicky and Thomas?"

"That would be my first guess."

"Wyatt, there's no way another car followed them all the way out here without them noticing. The road is too deserted, this driveway too difficult to find."

"The second vehicle would have to be right on their tail," Wyatt agreed.

"In which case, they'd know they had company."

"Third partner in crime?" Wyatt asked.

Tessa shrugged. "Gotta be someone who already knew how to find this place."

"So either a third partner in crime, or a less welcoming blast from the past." He glanced over at her as the vehicle hit another massive rut. "Which'll make this very interesting, very fast."

CHAPTER 40

"You saved me." I stare at my husband, the memory so real, so vibrantly alive, I feel as if I should be able to reach out and touch it.

"Did you just hear something?" he asks me sharply. Thomas turns, the beam of his flashlight bouncing along the ruins, but I can't focus.

I'm breathing hard. My whole body is trembling, which I don't understand. I'm safe. I'm out of the grave. Thomas pulled me out. Thomas saved me.

Twenty-two years ago, we found each other in the dark.

So why is my heart already constricting painfully in my chest?

"You told me to stay in the woods," I murmur now. I'm talking to air. Thomas has left me, walking closer to the jumble of granite blocks. He still holds the shovel. Why did he bring a shovel? "You told me to stay out of sight. And that's what I did."

It comes to me. Slowly. Like a whisper. The wind against my cheek.

"Smoke." I turn toward my husband. "There's smoke in the air."

The smell of smoke. The heat of fire.

Screams in the air.

Smoke.

I reach out my hand, but once again my husband isn't there to take it. He stands too far away, the flashlight trembling in his grip.

"When I returned to the house, my mom was waiting for me in the foyer," he says. His voice sounds funny. Strained. "She started with her usual snapping demands. Don't track in mud. Don't do this. Don't do that. Is the body taken care of? Well, is it?

"And . . . I saw her. I finally saw her. She wasn't my mother. She wasn't even a person. She was a monster. Like something out of an old horror movie. She would devour all of us. And it would mean nothing to her in the end.

"I told her I was done. I told her I was leaving, taking the car. That was it.

"She laughed at me. Where would I go? What would I do? I was just a kid. I knew nothing of the real world. Now, upstairs.

"But I didn't. I stood there. I didn't move

549

a muscle. So she walked up and slapped me. *'Go to your room!'* she screamed. Like I really was a little kid, and not the son she'd turned into a drug dealer and a gravedigger and God knows what else. I still didn't move. She slapped me again, then again.

" 'Enough,' I said, finally blocking her hand. 'We're done.' I pushed past her, up the stairs to my third-floor room. I would grab my clothes and, of course, my stash of cash. Then I planned on doing exactly what I'd said. I'd throw everything in the car and take off down the drive. Then, once I was safely out of sight, I'd pull over and double-back through the woods to grab you. It would be perfect, I thought. She wouldn't chase me; I was her son. And nor would she chase after you, as she couldn't afford any more trouble, especially with Vero's death to still handle.

"But she wouldn't let me go. Instead, she followed me the whole way up the stairs. Enraged, shouting, screaming. The older two girls came out to see what was going on. On the second-story landing, Mother caught up with me. She smacked the side of my head; then when I still refused to stop, she threw herself at me. Literally tackled me. It was as if she'd gone crazy. Guess that's what happens when nobody has ever told you no before. We struggled. And then . . ."

Thomas pauses. He stands six, seven feet away. Too far for me to see his face in the dark.

"She fell down the stairs," he says flatly. "Landed on her neck. We all heard the crack. She was dead."

I open my mouth. I close my mouth. I don't know what to say.

"I told the girls to leave. They were the only people left in the house, and it's not like they were sorry she was gone. I gave them the keys to the car. On their own, they ransacked the china, silver, crystal. Why not? It was the least they deserved.

"Then . . ." Thomas hesitates, seems to be composing himself. "If I just took off, left the body, of course there would be a major investigation. So I figured I needed to do something. It had been an accident; her neck was broken. Maybe if it looked like she'd been rushing out of the house. You know, because she was escaping from a fire."

"No." The second he says the words, my hands close over my ears again. I can't hear this. My heart, rapid before, is now beating triple, quadruple time. The smell of smoke. The heat of fire. Her screams. "Please stop, please stop, please stop."

The wind is blowing harder, feeding off my agitation. Battering both of us.

But Thomas doesn't stop.

"I didn't know, Nicky. Trust me. I never imagined . . . I grabbed the cans of gasoline from the garage. I poured them all over the second-floor bedrooms, landing, beginning with one of the fireplaces so it would look like, I don't know, a log had rolled out, starting the fire. Four cans of gasoline I used, because it was raining out, and I needed the place to burn. You pulled yourself from a grave. Well, now I was helping us get a fresh start.

"When I was done, I returned the empty gas jugs to the garage. Then starting in the rear second-story bedroom and working backward toward the door, I tossed matches. Lots and lots of matches. Next thing I knew . . . whoosh! I had no idea. The exterior of the house might have been wet from the rain, but apparently, over the course of a hundred years, the wood on the inside had dried to kindling. I seared the hair off the back of my hands stumbling my way across the foyer and out the front door.

"It was magnificent. It was terrifying. Then I heard her scream."

"No. No. Please, stop." I doubled over, hands still covering my ears. Tears streaming down my face.

But Thomas doesn't. He walks closer and closer. He won't stop talking. And now, after all these years, I finally can't stop remembering.

"She must not have been dead," he whispers. "I mean, I was just a kid, checking a kid, and we'd never had an OD. Maybe she'd been unconscious, like in a coma. I don't know. But the fire started and she woke up."

I'm in the woods. I smell the smoke. It makes me crinkle my nose. Who would light a fire in a rainstorm?

Then I hear the first scream. Vero's scream.

"She couldn't go down. The second-floor landing was already completely engulfed. So she must've headed up. To escape the flames."

I'm running now. Through the woods, wet branches smacking against my face. I don't care anymore about Madame Sade's wrath or Thomas's pretty promise. I have to get to Vero. She's screaming my name.

"I could see her," Thomas says, the flashlight shaking uncontrollably in one hand, the shovel in the other. "Up in the tower bedroom, beating one of the windows with her fists. I tried, Nicky. I rushed back toward the front door, but already the heat was too much. Then I bolted for the garage, to where we kept the work ladder."

From a distance, I spot her. Vero in the princess bedroom. She's looking down at me. Already I can see orange flames dancing behind her head.

Vero doesn't scream anymore. Vero presses her hand against the glass. Vero reaches out to me, as surely as I reach my hand toward her. Running still. So hard, so fast. Trying to . . . I don't know what to do.

I simply race my way toward her, calling her name.

Now I'm the one screaming her name.

She disappears. The next instant, glass shatters. A chair comes flying through. One of the small ones from the child-size table. The fire roars its approval, inhaling fresh air, reaching hungrily for it.

Another chair; now both panes are broken. Then Vero is back, standing in the opening of jagged glass. She is bleeding. Her hands, her feet, her face.

She doesn't care.

The smell of smoke. The heat of fire.

As she raises her arms above her head. Closes her eyes. Lifts her face to the night sky.

Vero wants to fly.

I scream once.

She makes no sound at all.

As she launches herself into the air. Away from the heat. Away from the flames.

Her dark hair ripples behind her. Her flowery nightgown sprouts like wings.

Vero wants to fly.

Another shout. Thomas, running up behind me. But it's too late. Nothing either of us can do.

It's the landing that's the hard part.

As Vero comes down, down, down. Plowing into the earth. A pale, crumpled heap that moves no more.

"By the time I returned, it was too late. I didn't know a house could go up like that," Thomas murmurs. "I didn't . . . We were just kids, Nicky. There were so many things we didn't know."

I can't look at him. My heart is breaking. Like it broke that day. Because he's right. It was all our fault. It wasn't our fault at all. We were just trying to survive what we never should've had to survive in the first place.

Thomas took me away that day. He loaded me in his mother's personal car, where I curled into a wet, shivering ball in the passenger's seat. The house burned. Vero died. Thomas drove us to New Orleans.

In the days and weeks that followed, I could barely function. If I slept, I woke up screaming. If I was awake, I spent it crying.

Thomas found a place. Thomas purchased food. Thomas got a job on a movie set during the day, then held me in his arms at night. As I tried to put myself back together, but failed over and over again.

Until, four weeks later, attempting to do laundry, I found a picture in Thomas's pocket. One he must've taken when no one was looking. Of a ten-year-old girl in a flowered dress. Of me.

And I broke. I know of no other way of saying it. I looked at myself, I saw Vero. I remembered Vero, I saw myself, and I couldn't . . . I just couldn't.

Thomas came home. I greeted him with the news that I was gone, leaving, out of there. I had died, and now it was time to be dead. No more Chelsea. No more Vero. I would move, new name, new town, new experience. It was the only way for me.

And he said yes.

I didn't even understand at first. Then he walked to the dresser, tossed his few items of clothing in a bag, and declared he was ready. If I needed to leave, then we would go. If I needed a new name, he'd get one, too. If I needed a fresh start, he'd take it with me.

He loved me. He would go wherever, do

whatever, be whomever, as long as he was with me.

And that's what we did. Have been doing for twenty-two years.

"How did you do it?" I ask him now. Because this is what I don't understand. How that night could break me completely, while making my husband so strong.

"You were what I wanted, Nicky. I'd been watching you, waiting for you, I don't even know for how long. I failed Vero. I know that. I failed all of us by not acting sooner, by not turning on my own mother. Trust me, in the beginning I replayed it in my mind over and over again. All the coulda, woulda, shouldas. But in the end, I couldn't go back. So I resolved to move forward. I vowed to make you happy if it took the rest of my life. And that's what I've been doing. Loving you. If only for you, that was enough."

"I miss her."

"I know."

"I should've gotten us both out," I exclaim in a rush. "I should've been smarter. She was lost by then, so sad. She wouldn't even tell her stories anymore. But maybe, if I could've gotten her out. Returned her to the secret realm, the magical queen. She was just a little girl who missed her mother."

"It wouldn't have worked."

"It might have —"

"No. It wouldn't have. Nicky, turn around."

The tone of his voice is sharp. It catches me off guard, like a slap to the face.

The wind is not blowing anymore, I realize. The night has gone totally still. Totally quiet.

I turn. Very slowly. To discover Marlene Bilek standing in the beam of Thomas's flashlight.

Her hard-worn face is stamped with a grim expression I've never seen before. And she is holding a gun.

Chapter 41

"We got a problem." It was Kevin, reaching them via the radio as they bounced up the steep, rutted drive.

"What kind of problem?" Wyatt shouted over the noise of the SUV's engine straining.

"Marlene Bilek has disappeared. Sent a uniform to pick her up, per your request. House is dark, vehicle not in the drive. She's gone off the range."

Wyatt turned to Tessa. "Maybe wanting a private chat with the last person who saw her daughter alive."

"Circled back to the hotel, spotted Nicky with Thomas and decided to follow?" Tessa frowned at him. "But why? She already knows Nicky isn't Vero."

"No, Nicky is something more powerful. She's Vero's memory, a walking legacy of Vero's young life."

"You think Marlene's worried that Nicky

might know about the money she received after Vero's kidnapping? But why not pry a little more earlier in the evening?"

"She couldn't. Not with both of us sitting there. But I can imagine her attempting to return later to ask more questions. Maybe she spotted Nicky meeting with Thomas and decided to follow."

Tessa shook her head, still not buying it. "But she couldn't have followed right behind them without them noticing . . ."

"Nope. Which proves my earlier point. If she's the one driving the second vehicle, Marlene Bilek has definitely been here before."

"You killed my daughter." Marlene stands back from the foundation, closer to the circular drive. Her face is illuminated by the beam of Thomas's flashlight, but the night is too thick to reveal much more. Her car. Where she might have come from. If she's here alone.

Clearly, she's been listening to our trip down memory lane.

"It was an accident," I hear myself say. Is it strange to be apologizing to a woman holding a gun? Or maybe, the most natural response?

"She burned. Here. Where the fancy

560

house used to be."

I don't say anything. Vaguely, I'm aware of Thomas trying to ease closer without capturing Marlene's attention.

No such luck. "Stop. One more step, I'll shoot her first. Trust me, this gun isn't for show. First thing Hank taught me was to use a firearm. Good exercise for a woman, he said, who'd already spent too much of her life as a punching bag."

"Vero loved you."

I offer the words in comfort, but if anything, Marlene recoils, appears struck.

"What did she tell you?"

"What do you mean?"

"Did she know? Did she ever figure it out? After everything you said, hearing about her life. Sweet Lord. The woman said it was a good home. How was I supposed to know any different? She had fancy clothes, a nice car. I never imagined. I never imagined!"

For the first time, I think I get it. Or maybe it's simply because the wind has finally picked up again. And it's cold now. Icy shivers fingering up my spine.

It's Thomas who does the honors. He's halted eight feet back, but his grip on the flashlight is now steady. "You sold your daughter."

The wind whisking more briskly. Rustling

our hair.

I stare at Marlene as if seeing her for the first time. She doesn't deny it. But of course, Madame Sade was a business-woman. And what kind of woman risked kidnapping children, when buying them was so much easier?

"I needed out! Ronnie, the beatings . . . I just couldn't take it anymore. You don't understand what it's like to be that helpless —"

I laugh bitterly.

Marlene flushes. "I had no money. I couldn't take care of myself, let alone Vero. Not to mention, the way Ronnie had taken to looking at her. It was for her own good. You don't have to believe me. But one day, through a friend of a friend, I heard of a woman who sometimes took in young girls. Lived in a fancy house, not enough kids of her own. Would even kick a little money your way. She took pity on single moms; that's what I heard."

I can't help myself. "You mean from other addicts, alcoholics? Women willing to sell their own kids for their next fix?"

"Vero would be better off. I could leave Ronnie, get on my own two feet. Except, that day at the park . . . One of the other women noticed Vero wasn't with me anymore. I didn't have any choice. I had to cry kidnapping. Otherwise the police would've figured it out."

"I remember that," Thomas spoke up abruptly. "My mother was furious that afternoon. Muttering the whole evening if you wanted something done right you just had to do it yourself."

"It wasn't my fault! Worked out, though. The police investigated, found no leads; it all went away. She still got Vero, and eventually, when the dust settled, I got my money."

All of a sudden, it comes to me: "I know you!"

Marlene frowned at me. "I don't know what you mean."

"That's how I recognized you at the liquor store. The second I saw you, I knew you. Memory, I thought. I was half right. Except it wasn't Vero's memory, it wasn't the vision of you hiding your little girl in the closet. It was here. Right here. You came to the house to collect the money in person. Madame Sade yelled at you."

"I came to get what I was owed!"

The wind, sharper now. Colder.

"Did you see her?" I hear myself whisper. "Back then, she would've been standing at the tower window. She could've peered straight down the circular drive. Seeing the taxi pull up. Watching her mom step out, walk up the stairs. After all her nights of crying and begging. Finally, you came to rescue her."

My hair whips around my cheeks. Goose bumps up and down my arms.

As I see things I've never seen before. As I know things I have no way of knowing. "She beats the glass with her little fists," I hear myself whisper. "She calls your name, excited, hopeful. Vero is six years old. Vero is *found*. Vero will go home again.

"Except no one ever unlocks her door. Eventually, you come out of the house. Down the steps. Back into the waiting cab. You leave without her.

"Vero wants to fly. She wants to open the window and fly right over the sill. Because nothing matters anymore. Her mother has come. Her mother has gone. She loved you with all her heart. And you broke it."

"It wasn't my fault!"

"You sold your own daughter!"

"And I paid the price. I returned to Ronnie. I spent another year getting the shit beat out of me. Doesn't that count? I screwed up and I paid for it."

"Not as much as she did! What about after you left Ronnie? Why not go to the police then? Why not rescue your daughter then?"

Marlene doesn't answer. She doesn't have to. We all know. Because she would've been arrested, too. And what kind of woman wanted to go to jail, when she could start over with a new man, five thousand dollars richer and no one else the wiser?

I step toward her. The gun wavers in her hand. I don't care. I take another step, then another. I don't have a gun, a flashlight, any kind of weapon. I have only my outrage, and it's enough.

"What will they think of you, your new and improved family? Once they realize what you really did to your first child? You're not the victim at all. You're the monster Vero feared in the dark."

"I don't know. And I don't plan on finding out."

Marlene raises her gun. She stares me straight in the eye.

Just as Thomas yells, "Run!"

He hurls the flashlight. I feel it rush by my ear, the second before it connects with Marlene's face.

She cries out, reaching up instinctively with her left hand, even as her right pulls the trigger.

A bullet. I swear I can see it. I can watch it spiral through the night, homing in on my chest. For a fraction of an instant of time, I don't care. I throw open my arms. I embrace my own death.

Because this was how it was always meant to be. I knew it from the first moment I set foot on this property. I would die here.

Such is life in the dollhouse.

And then . . .

I fall down. I don't know how or why. Then I don't have time to consider it. Another shot is fired. Thomas yells, at me, at her, I can't tell. He rushes by, shovel overhead, a man on the attack.

"Run," he screams at me. "Run!"

And I find myself racing across the rolling hills I used to contemplate from the tower bedroom, cutting a path straight for the woods.

Another scream of frustration from Marlene. Another explosion from the gun. Followed by a heavy grunt, distinctly male. Thomas, I think; she's shot Thomas.

But I can't go back. The wind is carrying me now, cold and determined. Into the woods I go.

"Vero!" I cry out.

And I know she is here with me. We run together, two little girls finally escaping. I hold out my hand, and she is there.

"Shots fired, shots fired!"

Wyatt's SUV had just crested the hill when he heard the first exchange. He grabbed the radio; Tessa was already unclipping her seat belt.

"There," she reported, pointing through his window. "Lights. Near that mound of vegetation."

He careened his own vehicle to a stop, identifying Marlene Bilek's car, dead ahead. A quick request for backup while unholstering his sidearm; then he and Tessa had both doors open, using them for momentary cover. Whatever was happening was playing out beyond the beam of the headlights. They couldn't see as much as hear the action.

Dark bobbing shapes as two people struggled. Then a woman's shriek of frustration, followed by a fresh crack of gunfire. A muffled grunt; then the second shape dropped to the ground.

Thomas Frank, Wyatt guessed, given the larger size.

"Marlene Bilek!" Wyatt called out. "This is the police. Drop your weapon!"

He leveled his own weapon, but at this distance, in the dark . . .

Apparently, Marlene Bilek figured the same. Because in the next instant, she scooped up a flashlight. Then, as they watched, she took off across the grass.

"She's running away," Tessa exclaimed.

"Or giving chase. Where's Nicky?"

"Shit!"

They both took off into the night.

Leaves slap my face. I twist around one tree only to become briefly entangled in a bush. The woods are thick, heavily overgrown, and I have no light to guide my way. Already I'm thrashing and heaving, whacking my way through the vegetation like an enraged bear.

She will find me. She has a flashlight. She has a gun.

She's already taken out Thomas, and now it's my turn.

I will die in these woods, just like I did twenty-two years before.

Now, with my heart heaving in my chest and tears pouring down my cheeks, it amazes me all the pictures popping into my mind. They are not of the dollhouse. They aren't of Vero. They are of Thomas.

I am running for my life. Approaching the precipice of my third death, and mostly, I'm remembering the man who loved me.

Days and weeks and months in the doll-house. Exchanges of looks but never words. Coconspirators before either of us was ever brave enough to verbalize the crime. But he knew, and I knew that he knew, and it was enough to give both of us hope.

Because what is love, if not an exercise in faith?

The nights he never left me. I cried and cried. I railed at him; I hit him. I blamed him; I begged him. And he took it. He held me and stroked my hair and whispered it would be all right. Because what is love, if not perseverance?

I forgive you, I think, though until this moment, I didn't realize just how much I blamed him for the fire. But he was right; we were just kids. We didn't know what we were doing. And none of us should've been there anyway.

Vero knows that. If I could stop right now, sit and have a cup of tea, Vero would be wearing her finest dress. She'd hug me, and I would hug her back, and we'd hold each other tight.

Because what is love, if not forgiveness?

More crashing. From behind me. Coming closer.

I'm running blind. Maybe even in circles. There's no place to go. Just trees growing steadily larger, bushes filling out thicker and thicker. I come to a small clearing, and that's that. I spin around and around. But I'm trapped.

This is it. What I've spent twenty-two years waiting for.

Deep breath. I stop, turn, prepare for the worst.

Shouts in the distance. The police, I realize. Here and in pursuit. Meaning if I can just find a way to buy time. Two minutes? Three, four, five?

I should climb a tree. But just as I try to figure something out, I hear a fresh snap right behind me. I whirl around, and Marlene Bilek is standing there.

The woods haven't been any kinder to her than to me. Her face is scratched and bleeding, her short Brillo hair now a rat's nest of leaves. Her chest is heaving from her exertions and it's clear the chase has only increased her rage. She fumbles slightly with the gun; then she's got it up.

"Don't move," I hear myself say.

She frowns at me. "What are you talking about?"

"She's here. Can't you feel her? She's here. Right here. With us."

"Girl, you've taken one too many hits to the head."

"She would've gone anywhere with you, you know. A homeless shelter, a women's home. She loved you so much. You were her world. The one person who kept her safe."

"Stop it!"

"She remembered that night. Ronnie beating her so savagely. Felt like it would never end. But then he was gone and there you were, holding her in your arms. You whispered to her all night long. You begged her to live. She heard every word. For you, she came back again."

Marlene's arm is trembling. She thins her lips; I can see her willing her finger to move on the trigger. I wonder if she knows she has tears streaming down her cheeks.

"Five thousand dollars. That kind of love, and you sold it for a measly five grand?"

"Stop!"

But I don't. I can't. "Tell her you love her. Now. Say the words. She's been waiting thirty years! Thirty years for you to return to her. Thirty years for you to remember how much you love her."

"No —"

"You have to!"

"I can't! Don't you understand? I didn't know. I didn't understand. I really did tell myself it was for the best. Then, when she was gone, when I realized what I had done . . . There was no going back. Don't you understand? I ripped my own heart out of my chest, and there was no putting it back again!"

"Did you miss her?"

"Yes! Every day!"

"Do you love her?"

"Yes. Yes, yes, yes!"

"She loves you, too. She loves you and she hates you, and there is nothing I can do to save you from what's going to happen next."

Marlene frowns at me.

"Girl, you're crazy!" She takes a determined step forward, as if to end this once and for all . . .

She doesn't see what I already know. The jumble of objects all these years later, still sticking out of the earth. Because the night had been dark then, too, and time compressed and my vision blurred by the thickness of my tears. As I'd dragged her body through the woods, away from the flames. As I found the half-filled grave dug just hours before. As I sat back on my heels and used my bare hands to further excavate the heavy, wet earth.

Of course, I'd been exhausted and shell-shocked and traumatized. I hadn't dug very deep, before depositing my most precious possession in the earth. Her limbs flopping awkwardly. Her sightless gray eyes staring back at me. Not enough time for perfect. Just good enough.

As I closed her eyes.

572

As I kissed her cheek.

As I whispered, "I'm sorry."

Before dumping a few handfuls of mud, then running off into the night.

Now Marlene comes for me.

She steps forward.

She trips over the first protruding object. Stumbles into a second, then a third. Throws out her left hand as if to catch herself, but it's no use. The objects have won.

She falls back.

Simple really. Stumble, fall, get up again.

But this time there's a crack. Loud enough to echo through the silence as Marlene's head smashes against a particularly round and smooth rock.

Such as the kind a girl might find in the woods and use as a marker for her best friend's grave.

The wind, whispering again. I swear I hear her voice. I feel her tears. The lost princess of the secret realm, finally reunited with the magical queen after all these years . . .

I open my arms. "I'm sorry," I tell her. "I love you, Vero."

Marlene doesn't get up again.

Minutes later Wyatt comes crashing into the clearing, drawing up short as his flashlight finds me. He illuminates me, then the body, then the objects sticking out of the earth.

"Thomas?" I ask quickly.

"Tessa is tending to him. Ambulance is on its way." He takes a step closer to Marlene's body, his flashlight dancing over her cracked skull, sightless eyes. There's no need to check for a pulse. It's as obvious to him as it is to me; what's done is done.

His flashlight returns to the ground near her feet. To the mass of skeletal bones protruding from the earth.

He looks up at me.

"Wyatt, meet Vero. Vero, meet Wyatt."

After that, neither of us says another word.

CHAPTER 42

I died twice before.

I remember the sensation of pain, burning and sharp, followed by fatigue, crushing and deep. I'd wanted to lie down. I'd *needed* to be done with it. But I hadn't. I'd fought the pain, the fatigue, the fucking white light. I'd clawed my way back to the land of the living.

For Vero. I came back from the dead for her.

Now I am finding the ability to move forward for me.

Marlene Bilek shot Thomas in his side. Not a serious injury, as the bullet grazed his ribs without hitting anything important or lodging anywhere permanent. I still spent a sleepless couple of days bedside in his hospital room, holding his hand while fixated on the steady rise and fall of his chest.

How had he done it? I wondered. Accompanying me after three separate accidents, where I got to sleep off the pain, while he was forced to sit, wait, watch, wonder. To love someone so much and feel so powerless.

I marvel at this man I married. Maybe it's taken me twenty-two years, but I'm finally starting to appreciate my own good fortune. To have found love. To have built a life. It's all there, really.

It's simply up to me to grab on with both hands and claim the future as my own.

In the immediate aftermath, the police had many questions. I did my best to answer, while my brand-new lawyer, produced by Tessa, was careful to remind everyone of my young age at the time of the alleged incidents as well as the abusive situation: mitigating circumstances.

From my own perspective . . . what is memory? What do any of us truly know about the past? I described that last night with Vero the best that I recall it to be true. But as I think Sergeant Wyatt can attest from several days in my company, truth can be relative, the mind a fickle beast. What I think I know, and what I actually know . . . All I can say is, ask Vero. Spend an afternoon. Have some tea.

This is her story after all.

Marlene Bilek's body was claimed by her

husband, Hank, and daughter, Hannah. They have not asked to meet with me and I don't think I could meet with them. It is too hard to look at Hannah, Vero 2.0, and not think of what might've been. For their part, I would guess I'm the woman who tried to exploit Marlene by claiming to be her long-lost daughter.

What do they know of the police's suspicions regarding Vero's disappearance thirty years ago, let alone Marlene's actions that final night in the woods? Technically, Marlene died from a fall. She tripped; she cracked open her skull. I saw it with my own eyes. She shot Thomas, definitely. From our perspective, she acted aggressively, to cover up the truth from thirty years ago. But it would be just as easy for her loved ones to believe she acted out of revenge against two people associated with Vero's abduction.

The past is the past. Whatever sins Marlene committed, she paid for. I saw her pain with my own eyes. I watched her die.

Now it's between her and Vero.

This is Vero's story after all.

Of the two of us, Thomas faces the most legal scrutiny. First, there is the suspicious fire that destroyed our home. Second, possible charges of manufacturing evidence, given the presence of Veronica Sellers's fingerprints in my Audi. Finally, the burden of the unsolved burning of the dollhouse, not to mention the death of his mother, twenty-two years ago, plus the recent discovery of skeletal remains on the property.

Our lawyer isn't worried. It would appear we are the only two witnesses from that night so long ago. It's our official statement that Thomas's mother died falling down the stairs. While Vero, trapped in the fire, jumped from a three-story window. That leaves the matter of what started the fire, but apparently the original evidence wasn't preserved. Small towns, limited resources and all that.

As for more recent events . . . Hard to prove Thomas created fake fingerprints, given that the three-D printer in question has been burned to a crisp. Speaking of the house fire, so far the arson investigator has only recovered Thomas's fingerprints on the gas can. Nothing unusual about that, as it was his property.

Tessa told me herself, smiling slightly, that a single fingerprint isn't as good a piece of evidence as you'd think. To truly build a case, prosecutors want multiple pieces of physical evidence, not to mention a witness or two. Otherwise, there's always doubt. And in this day and age of intense media coverage of high-profile cases . . . Prosecutors don't like doubt. Apparently, many choose to shelve the case, fingerprint and all.

She and Wyatt came to visit me this morning. I have found a lovely cabin for Thomas and me to rent while he recuperates. I think in our entire married life, this is the first time I've found a place for us all by myself. It feels good to take the lead.

It also feels good to take a stand.

Thomas, bedridden in the hospital: "You should go. New name, fresh start. Get out while you can. For God's sake, Nicky. I could be arrested on arson charges any day. Not to mention I engineered a car crash with you still inside the vehicle. What kind of a man does such a thing?"

"You love me."

"I betrayed you. I created a fake fingerprint glove, tried to literally turn you into a dead girl."

"Only because you thought it would make me happy. After all, I spent most of my time in her company. And God knows my other aliases hadn't worked out. You'd already tried love and acceptance. Twenty-two years later, I can understand you going with a more radical approach."

"I didn't know Marlene had sold Vero," he

tells me urgently, squeezing my hand. "Your reaction to the quilt, followed by your need to track down Vero's mom . . . I thought you needed her, that maybe, somehow, her love might finally make you whole. Given you knew so much about Vero's life and were so mentally muddled from the first two falls . . . I figured if the police identified you as Vero, confused or not, you'd accept her name. And maybe, just maybe, you'd find some peace."

"Except the police didn't just ID me as Vero; they pursued you as the primary suspect in the car crash, leading to you burning down our house in order to cover your tracks."

"I didn't want to leave you. But in the end, it seemed the only way to keep you safe."

"I can't be Vero," I tell him quietly. "I can only be me. But I understand what you did and why. And I understand why you took me back to the house that night, because if I couldn't be Vero, then I had to find a way to face what had happened once and for all. That's why you brought the shovel, right? You were going to take me to her body. You were going to dig her up, and then together, we'd finally do what we should've done twenty-two years ago. Bring her to the police. Get justice for Vero."

"I remember, too, Nicky. That night . . . I remember it always."

My turn to squeeze his hand.

After another moment, Thomas not looking at me, Thomas speaking quickly: "I still think you should go. I'm sole heir to that stupid house. Family property, meaning all these years later, the land, burned ruins, all belong to me. At least the state already cremated my mother's remains; otherwise, I'd have to deal with that, too."

"I'm not going anywhere."

Thomas: "It's a fucking legal nightmare. Could take me years to sort out. Nicky . . ."

"I like that name. I think I'm going to keep it. Nicky Frank. It's a strong name. Fitting for a woman twice returned from the dead."

"Is that the concussion talking again?"

"Maybe. So will you be Thomas Frank? Will you be my husband?"

Thomas not saying anything at all.

Me: "You're not answering."

Thomas: . . .

Me: "Are you crying?"

Thomas: "For God's sake, lean closer so I can kiss you."

Thomas is going to remain my husband. We will live here, and maybe it won't be happily ever after. I still have nightmares. And headaches and problems focusing and good days and bad days, not to mention years of physical and mental recovery before me.

But we all bear our scars. That's what makes us survivors.

Now Wyatt tells me that using DNA testing, the skeletal remains recovered from the woods have been positively ID'd as Veronica Sellers.

Furthermore, Marlene's family has already claimed the body. They plan to bury Vero next to Marlene. Mother and daughter together again.

Even knowing what I know, I can't argue with that.

Home; that's what Vero wanted. What all of us wanted. To go home again.

Tessa tells me she and Wyatt are getting a puppy. She seems more relaxed than the last time I saw her. I catch her and Wyatt smiling at each other several times. When they leave, he takes her hand and she lets him.

I think they're a cute couple. I'm glad they sit closer, knees touching. I can't wait to meet this puppy.

And now . . .

Thomas is resting in the back bedroom. He won't need me for a bit.

So I get out the quilt. I get comfortable on the sofa.

I close my eyes . . . and Vero and I share a cup of tea.

AUTHOR'S NOTE AND ACKNOWLEDGMENTS

It takes a village to write a novel. Or in this case, a small army of medical specialists. I started *Crash & Burn* with the premise of a female who'd suffered some kind of head trauma, which had turned her into a stranger even to herself. Being a sucker for happy endings, I wanted an injury that would be serious, even life altering, but still hold out the promise of recovery. Enter my favorite pharmacist, Margaret Charpentier, and one of her students, Christine D'Amore, who promptly loaded me up with tons of information on traumatic brain injuries, their treatment and long-term impacts.

Given all the possibilities, I also consulted with one of my good friends and fellow thriller author, Dr. C. J. Lyons, who helped focus my search on post-concussive syndrome, a medical condition broad enough to cover just about anything I needed my heroine to do, while retaining the possibility of a positive future. In real life, Nicky would most likely require years to recover from her multiple concussions. Again, being a sucker for happy endings, I like to imagine her already headache free.

Once I'd selected my heroine's injury, next step was to actually maim her. Enter Eric Holloman, accident reconstruction specialist. I like to feel he enjoyed the experience of creating his very own wreck from the ground up, instead of his usual job of analyzing what someone else had already done. Not many guys into physics get to that level of artistic freedom.

Of course, any mistakes are mine and mine alone. I confess, I wouldn't be very good at medical diagnoses or auto accident reconstruction, as science isn't my strong suit.

Policing, on the other hand, I truly love. And it was once again a joy to work with Lieutenant Michael Santuccio from the Carroll County Sheriff's Office. Let's just say when Wyatt does something truly smart and very clever, that's all Michael.

Speaking of which, one of my former consultants, retired forensic expert Napoleon Brito, called me one day with the idea of using a 3-D printer to make fake fingerprints. Given that I'd already been reading up on the controversy surrounding plastic molded weapons, the chance to delve into the world of 3-D printing was too good to pass up. To that end, my deepest appreciation also goes to Jeff Nicoll from Ambix Manufacturing in Albany, New Hampshire, who allowed me to personally tour his plastics-molding company and watch their 3-D printer in action.

Of course, my very own husband and enginerd also assisted with this project. Normally Anthony's the one saying he's scared of his diabolical spouse. After spending an afternoon listening to him and Jeff excitedly discuss all the ways to use manufacturing for evil, right back at you, love. Our daughter also deserves a round of applause, serving as my go-to fashion consultant for all media events, not to mention my sounding board of choice when working out pesky plot problems. She thinks I drive her to horsing out of obligation. It's really to con her into brainstorming my novels.

Congratulations to the winners of the annual Kill a Friend, Maim a Buddy Sweepstakes at LisaGardner.com. To Sally Schnettler, who nominated Marlene Bilek to die. Additionally, Michelle Brown nominated Brittany Kline for her star-making turn as night clerk. While the international winner, Berrin Vural Celik, from Istanbul, named Nicky's doctor in honor of her young daughter Sare Celik. Also, my deepest appreciation to Jean Huntoon, who won the right to be a character in this novel through her generous donation to the Rozzie May Animal Alliance. Thank you for supporting this worthy organization, not to mention all the cats and dogs in our community.

Finally, in memory of Sierra, our beloved Sheltie and best hugger in the family. We lost her in August. We miss her still.

ABOUT THE AUTHOR

Lisa Gardner is the #1 *New York Times* bestselling author of sixteen previous novels, including her most recent, *Fear Nothing.* Her Detective D. D. Warren novels include *Fear Nothing, Catch Me, Love You More,* and *The Neighbor,* which won the International Thriller of the Year Award. She lives with her family in New England.